PI

CIRCL

Ingrid Black is a journalist. She lives in Dublin. This is her fourth novel, following *The Dead*, *The Dark Eye* and *The Judas Heart*.

Circle of the Dead

INGRID BLACK

PENGUIN BOOKS

PENGUIN BOOKS

Published by the Penguin Group

Penguin Books Ltd, 80 Strand, London WC2R ORL, England

Penguin Group (USA), Inc., 375 Hudson Street, New York, New York 10014, USA

Penguin Group (Canada), 90 Eglinton Avenue East, Suite 700, Toronto, Ontario, Canada M4P 2Y3
(a division of Pearson Penguin Canada Inc.)

Penguin Ireland, 25 St Stephen's Green, Dublin 2, Ireland (a division of Penguin Books Ltd)

Penguin Group (Australia), 250 Camberwell Road, Camberwell, Victoria 3124, Australia
(a division of Pearson Australia Group Pty Ltd)

Penguin Books India Pvt Ltd, 11 Community Centre, Panchsheel Park, New Delhi – 110 017, India

Penguin Group (NZ), 67 Apollo Drive, Rosedale, North Shore 0632, New Zealand
(a division of Pearson New Zealand Ltd)

Penguin Books (South Africa) (Pty) Ltd, 24 Sturdee Avenue,
Rosebank, Johannesburg 2196, South Africa

Penguin Books Ltd, Registered Offices: 80 Strand, London WC2R ORL, England

www.penguin.com

First published 2008

2

Copyright © Ingrid Black, 2008
All rights reserved

The moral right of the author has been asserted

Set in Monotype Garamond
Typeset by Rowland Phototypesetting Ltd, Bury St Edmunds, Suffolk
Printed in England by Clays Ltd, St Ives plc

978–0–141–02531–5

www.greenpenguin.co.uk

Penguin Books is committed to a sustainable future
for our business, our readers and our planet.
The book in your hands is made from paper
certified by the Forest Stewardship Council.

December

I

Back home in New England, they used to have these things called winters. Still do have them, probably. The world doesn't stop just because you're not there to keep an eye on it any more.

You know the kind of thing. Proper winters. The snow falls. The snow settles on the ground. More snow falls and settles on that. Snow on snow. A foot of snow can fall easily overnight. A foot is nothing. Power lines are downed, and trees. Before long, there's a wind chill of forty below, snowploughs are cutting a path through the interior, drifts have made mountains out of fields, and houses are blocked up for weeks on end.

Here in Dublin, I don't know what you'd call what they have that time of year, but I wouldn't call it winter. All it does most of the time is rain. In spring, they have a rain like mist. In summer, it sparkles. Come fall, and it starts to grow hard and hostile as grit.

Snow falls occasionally in Dublin, but it is apologetic, half-hearted stuff which rarely stays longer than it takes for the earth to turn a couple of times, and then it's gone for another year. The car wheels turn the snow to slush in hours. And some years there's

3

not even that, and even if snow does come it's long after Christmas when it's wanted most.

That year, though, was different. That year something miraculous happened. It was like the weather had remembered what a winter was. Snow fell. It settled on the ground. More snow fell and settled on that. Snow on snow. Snowploughs were out from 4 a.m. clearing a path and gritting the road. The wind chill hadn't hit anywhere near forty below but I wasn't going to quibble over details. As I stood on the balcony of my apartment, looking out across St Stephen's Green, I could see white roofs disappearing into the distance and the park below heaped with snow, and I watched people carrying shopping bags, slipping now and then on the icy ground and catching hold of one another with a laugh.

The snow had fallen so heavily in the past week that now, three days before Christmas, the roads were impassable, cars abandoned. People said a winter hadn't been this severe since 1947, when the canals froze and it was so cold the city ran short of fuel and people went out with saws and axes and cut down whatever trees they could find to feed the fire, filling prams and wheeling them home. That was the thing about winter. It made you feel intrepid. Made you feel like strapping on a pair of skis and heading out to do the same, like the hunters in the snow in Brueghel's famous painting, cresting the hill through bare trees and looking down on the frozen village and the skaters on the iced-over lake beneath.

In honour of the season, I was doing my best to be less Scroogelike than usual, which wasn't easy for me. I'm a hard woman to please. Still, I trudged out to look in the windows of the department stores on the other side of the green, and resolved to snarl only at every third caroller. I went to the Christmas market to buy gifts, though I'd not many to buy. Sometimes I even went out just to look at the lights strung in garlands across the roads, bathing the snow and people below with light and good feeling. I hung up holly. I put mistletoe over the door.

I made an effort.

Each time I stepped out into the city, I heard people complaining but I could tell the weather filled them with excitement. They appreciated things more. The hot punch that was passed around between gloved hands in the bars. The fire when they finally got home.

That was how life was. Without darkness, how could you appreciate the light?

'They've shut down the airport now,' Fitzgerald told me when she called.

Detective Chief Superintendent Grace Fitzgerald, that is, of Dublin's Murder Squad. We'd been together since I arrived in Dublin ten years earlier and, if it wasn't for her, I doubt I would have stuck around so long. I never had in any other place.

'You sound happy about it,' I said.

'Don't sound so disapproving, Saxon. I am happy,'

she said. 'If they've closed the airport, that means you can't fly off and leave me here alone.'

'Why would I do that?'

'You're always talking about getting away this time of year.'

I couldn't deny that. I frequently suggested we take a house in Connecticut, say, or New Hampshire – even Vermont, I wasn't fussy – and spend Christmas over there; but when you hitch your wagon, metaphorically speaking, to a Chief Superintendent of police it's not so easy to drop everything and leave the country. 'People don't stop killing each other just because it's the season of goodwill, you know,' she used to say wryly, and she was right.

Christmas could get busy.

'I don't need to go anywhere this year,' I said. 'The snow's falling.'

'It's still not home.'

'I can pretend,' I said. 'Besides, what's the point of all that mistletoe if I've no one to hang it up for?'

'I've got you all to myself then?'

'Least till the snow melts,' I teased.

'I hope it never melts,' she said. 'It should always be like this. The world seems cleaner somehow. Less complicated.'

'Pared back to the bones,' I said. 'Everything that doesn't matter is stripped away. You see things as they are. I hope you haven't forgotten we're going out tonight.'

Though to be honest, I don't know why I was

reminding her. It wasn't like I wanted to go. She insisted on dragging me every year to hear Handel's *Messiah* at the cathedral. In Dublin they love Handel because he once lived here for five minutes, and so every Christmas they make themselves listen to *Messiah* and pretend they like it.

But I wasn't complaining. It was a chance for Fitzgerald and I to be together, and there'd be candles, and walking back to my place through the snow.

'I have it in my diary,' Fitzgerald said. 'Don't worry.'

And I didn't – right up until the moment she called and told me she couldn't make it. Disappointment mingled in me with relief at missing Handel.

'What is it?' I said.

'Missing person,' she sighed. 'Nineteen. Out drinking last night with friends. Left about midnight to make her way home. This morning one calls round to see how she is. Turns out she hadn't come home all night. Her parents assumed she'd stayed with friends.'

'What's it got to do with the Murder Squad?'

'The Assistant Commissioner asked me to take a look at it,' said Fitzgerald. 'She knows the family. They're worried. There's no answer from her cellphone.'

'Do they fear the worst?'

'They're her parents. Parents always fear the worst.'

And maybe they were right to do so.

I'd spent five years in the FBI as a Special Agent before coming to Dublin, and I'd seen too much to believe so easily that someone was ever just plain missing. Not even Christmas could fill me with that much hope. Missing usually meant taken – and after that? Well, you don't snatch strangers off the streets to wish them happy holidays.

I remembered one young woman back home. It was Christmas then too, deep snow, and police initially didn't want to know. When they finally realized the seriousness of the situation and launched a search, any hope of finding her alive had gone. They discovered her six weeks later in the forest, her body perfectly preserved by cold, each wound as fresh on the flesh as the moment it was made. At least there was that. Decomposition might've scuppered any chance of finding out who did this to her; cold preserved the evidence. Once the DNA samples that were lifted from the body were run through the computer, it came back with a match to a local man recently released from jail.

It was the same old story. Mom didn't love him. Dad hadn't been around. Santa hadn't made it most years. The usual bullshit. That was the thing about killers. They did the worst things imaginable and then expected you to feel sorry for them because they'd had a hard time. As if that gave them any right to inflict an even harder time on others.

He said he'd taken the woman because she looked so happy, and her happiness was an affront to his own misery. And why wouldn't she have been happy? She was married a month. This was her first Christmas in a new house. She was expecting a child.

He'd kept her in a basement three days before killing her. Christmas Eve, Christmas Day. St Stephen's Day. Some Christmas. Finally dumped her body New Year's Eve.

She was who I was thinking of after Fitzgerald called. Wondering whether Beth Griffin – that was the missing girl's name; even her name suggested cookies and marzipan and *Little Women*, like her own name was mocking her – might be facing the same kind of Christmas. I couldn't help thinking like that. That's the way my mind works. Always has. It sees the worst first, and the thought of the worst then ruins everything. Now I felt my previous good mood slip away. Christmas was a lie. A con trick. What did gifts and carols matter when it could all be snuffed out so easily, when it could be snatched away?

It was 1 a.m. when I woke with a start, and the moon was huge and bright and spilling ice into my apartment like a spotlight. I never pulled the drapes. I liked to know the city was still there and hadn't crept away and hid when I wasn't watching. I got up, half reluctantly, to check my messages. Fitzgerald had left one about an hour ago to tell me there was still no word on the missing girl, and for a long while I stood at the window, looking down on the empty streets.

It seemed to have got colder again.

Suddenly, I felt impatient with myself. I needed to snap out of this mood, it wasn't doing me or anyone any good; and a thought had settled in my head softly as a snowflake.

How *much* colder had it got?

I got dressed quickly, then found what I needed in a bag at the back of the closet and stepped outside into a snow that was suddenly falling gently again all around, for my eyes only. The city had never been so quiet as I scrunched through drifts down Baggot Street towards the bridge. I could hear nothing. No voices. No cars. No sirens.

Just my own footsteps in the snow.

Then there it was.

The canal.

I was right. It had frozen at last. All week it had been threatening to freeze, gradually getting itself ready. A thin skein of ice would appear overnight and then the next day be gone.

Now I could see it wouldn't be gone this time. I picked up a stone from the side of the path and tossed it hard on to the ice. It skittered away with a noise like an approaching underground train. Was it strong enough to take my weight? There was only one way to find out.

I sat down on the bench, opened the bag and lifted out my skates, brought here all the way from New England and never used till now; and I tugged them on and laced them tight till they hurt, then lowered myself on to the ice, waiting for the telltale crack.

Nothing happened. The ice didn't even notice I was there as I ventured out from the side of the canal, getting used to the sensation of being unsteady again, finding my balance.

And I began to skate.

The scritch and swish of the blades as they cut a path in the ice was the only sound in all the city that night as I skated. Everything was asleep except me. The moon was so bright the glacial water beneath me was almost translucent. The night shone and the only darkness was when I passed under the low bridges that crossed the canal, and I tried to remember each name as I went under, Eustace and Charlemont, La Touche and Clanbrassil, then back again to Baggot Street and on in the other direction this time, saluting Huband, McKenny, Macquay.

Through the skates I felt myself connected to the ice and through the ice to all the great winter that had mantled the city, it was all one now, and I was at one with the city itself.

Mistress of all I surveyed.

As I came back finally towards the bench where I'd changed into my skates, I noticed a figure standing on the bridge, watching me approach. A woman, I saw as I got nearer, dark-haired, wrapped in a great overcoat, her scarf lifted up from her throat to cover her mouth, breath escaping through the fabric like steam – and her voice was escaping too.

'I thought I'd find you here,' she said. 'Do I get a turn?'

'Chief Superintendent,' I said, scraping to a halt, and I smiled up at her.

I didn't mind sharing the night and the city with her.

'I never know what you'll do next,' she said.

'You're welcome to take over. I'm beat.'

'Do you think they'll fit me?'

'Let's find out.'

I turned round to make my way to the side of the canal, but for some reason the blade of the skate didn't turn with my foot, instead it stayed fast, and I found myself losing my balance for the first time that night. For a moment, I felt the air support me and then it gave way and there was nothing to hold on to and I thudded down to the hard surface, my ankle twisting sharply beneath my weight. I gasped in pain and cursed extravagantly.

'Saxon?' came Fitzgerald's voice from on high. 'Are you OK?'

'I'm fine,' I lied, and tried to clamber to my feet again, before collapsing uselessly back on to the ice, looking down at my frozen reflection.

My reflection?

But no, that wasn't my reflection. It wasn't close enough to my face to be mine, it was more like the reflection of Fitzgerald's face as she gazed down from the bridge above – but that couldn't be right either because I could hear her now scrambling down the side of the bank on to the ice to come to my aid. And besides, it wasn't moving. The face was a young woman's, transfixed, staring up at me out of the ice, eyes wide open, lips smiling strangely . . .

It took three hours to dig down through the ice and retrieve Beth Griffin's body. They had to call in a specialist team. Forensics was a nightmare, Fitzgerald told me when she called to update me on her progress. It was dark still and I was back in my apartment, nursing my swollen ankle now strapped with bandages, and drinking hot whiskey to keep out the pain that had seeped into my bones with the chill.

'What does the pathologist reckon?' I said.

'He's not done the autopsy yet, but he says death was most likely caused by cardiac arrest. It often happens, apparently, when someone falls into cold water, especially if they've been drinking. The shock of cold water on the skin makes the body cool down too fast and the heart can't take the strain. I used to see it all the time when I was in uniform.'

'No sign of foul play then?'

'Nothing. Seems like she was just making her way back home, slipped on the snow and fell into the water. Would've made things easier if we'd found her before the canal froze, but at least her parents know what happened now.'

'Terrific Christmas they'll have,' I said grimly.

But I felt happy as I put down the phone. That hopeful mood I'd cherished these last few days of snow, and which Beth's disappearance had threatened to destroy, was creeping back. I welcomed it gladly enough, but couldn't explain why it was here. Ever since Fitzgerald had called last night to explain that she couldn't make it, I'd been feeling depressed, imagining Beth dead; yet now my worst fears had been confirmed and I was feeling almost giddy with a bizarre joy. The whiskey must have gone to my head.

No, I realized eventually, it wasn't that. My worst fears hadn't been confirmed at all. My worst fear was that Beth had been taken against her will, was being held somewhere, was suffering, and now I knew she was safe from all that. Dead, yes, but she'd died quickly, peacefully almost, known nothing about it in all likelihood. She simply spent the evening with friends, enjoying the days before Christmas, and on the way home had slipped and fallen.

That was all.

Sometimes things were uncomplicated, however sad.

Sometimes they were uncontaminated by evil.

I spent too long thinking about death probably. It's an occupational hazard. But I couldn't unknow what I knew, couldn't unremember the terrible things I'd seen. There is evil in the world and the best we can hope is to avoid it somehow and not cross its path.

And Beth Griffin had. It wasn't a huge comfort, but in the worst of all possible worlds it was maybe the best that we had.

All I knew was that I was going to savour every moment of the days to come. Tomorrow I'd drag my protesting ankle to the market and buy myself a tree.

14

I hadn't got around to that yet. I'd haul it back over my shoulder through the snowy streets if I had to. String it with lights. A Christmas should have a tree. Then I'd go shopping once more, though I hated shopping at the best of times, and find something special for Fitzgerald, and fill up the coolbox with champagne, and the cupboards with so much food you'd swear there was a bear planning on coming over to the apartment to hibernate and this was his winter store.

Finally I fell asleep, stretched out on the couch with a quilt pulled over me, the pain in my ankle now numbed to acceptable levels of discomfort, thanks to the whiskey, and with the sight of snow falling through a black sky outside my window, my head filled with a memory of bells and a lingering echo of carols; and I slept like a child until morning, when I woke to find Fitzgerald kneeling down beside me, shaking me awake.

'Grace,' I said, 'what is it?'

'The pathologist just finished the autopsy,' she said quietly. 'Beth was dead before she went into the water. She was murdered.'

'Hell, no.'

'And that's not all. We got a call from her own mobile. From a man.'

'What did he say?'

'*This is only the first.*'

Two Years Later

2

In Dublin at the end of October, it gets dark before five and doesn't grow light again next day till after seven, making fourteen hard-won hours of honesty before the deception begins once more.

Dublin's the same as any other city. Only after nightfall is it truly itself. Before that, it's just putting on an act, like a stripper in a wimple. Come the dark and those who think they own the streets tiptoe away, shamefully, back to the suburbs and satellites, deserting rats abandoning the sinking ship. Some may venture in again later to eat or catch a show or prowl cat-like for mates, but they return as interlopers, only there on sufferance, and they rarely last till dawn.

Another tribe by then has taken their place: the city's true possessors, comfortable with shadows as a shark is with getting wet, body clocks adjusted to the different rhythm of night.

After dark human nature is stripped to its elements, and its most basic needs and desires are laid bare. Food. Sex. Alcohol. Companionship. God. The relationship to all of them is more heightened when the lights go out. Night is when we live most intensely.

Night is when we are most free.

Most of all, there are different rules when the lights go out.

The usual restrictions don't apply.

Right now, it was still early. The dark had only lately started settling in, and was not yet complete, and the city was shifting subtly to accommodate it. It was October 31st. Eve of All Saints Day, better known as Halloween. Day of the dead. What the Celtic tribes in this part of the world in days gone by called Samhain, and the pretentious still did.

It was the time of year when the dark was said to be at its strongest, when the spirits of the dead could make contact with the living, and bonfires would be lit to ward off evil – and that was one commodity which would surely never be in short supply.

In his townhouse close to the heart of the city, Daniel Erskine heard nothing of the outside world as he poured himself a drink, his first of the evening, and settled down to wait, gathering his thoughts as he did so like a shepherd rounding up wandering sheep, taking his time. There was no point in hurrying. He had a long night ahead. And that was fine by him.

He'd always loved the night. They all had, once. They were night owls. Hunters. What happened in the day meant nothing to them. It was only when the sky faded and the stars and a discreet moon took daylight's place that they really felt they belonged.

Tonight that felt more true than ever before. Tonight, he couldn't help feeling, was what it had all been about. What it had all been leading to. Tonight would be like all those nights before fused into one. Tonight was the only thing that mattered, and whatever happened in the morning was immaterial. Perhaps there would *be* no morning. He didn't know. He didn't care.

Nothing could stop him now. He felt that with the force of a religious conviction. Nothing could go wrong. He had planned everything out meticulously. There was no room for error. He was a careful man, after all. He didn't take chances. He didn't take risks.

He couldn't afford to cut corners.

What time was it anyway? He glanced at his watch. Quarter past five.

Was that all? He felt the first shiver of excitement, impatience, joy, but he managed to suppress it. *No.* That's how mistakes were made. He would need all his wits about him if he was to come through. One step wrong and the whole thing could collapse. He remembered what his mother used to say: *Half done is worse than not done at all.* There was still so much to do. He knew everything that would happen, but some of the details remained to be nailed down.

It was like chess. The moves may be different each time, the variations infinite; but as long as you were confident in your own ability, then there could be no nasty surprises. Every trick, every diversion, every counter-attack, merely delayed the inevitable.

The only danger was in meeting a better player, but on that score Daniel Erskine had no worries whatsoever. There *were* no better players. Not at this game.

Tonight he would prove it.

Daniel smiled as the doorbell rang at last. The game had begun.

3

It was a man delivering leaflets door to door who found the body. Or rather, who noticed the disturbance inside the house which led uniformed police to find the body.

He had looked through the letter box and seen a smashed vase in the hallway, overturned chairs, a toppled table, a man's shoe discarded by a doorway, a poker propped incongruously against the wall – and blood. His suspicions were roused sufficiently to call 999. Once inside, the police quickly followed the trail of blood across the hall, through a doorway at the end, down the steps to the basement, to its source, now cold.

Very cold, as it happened.

The call to Fitzgerald was placed immediately, despite the fact that this was her first day off in three months. At the time, we were sitting, Fitzgerald and I, among boxes of books and packing cases and various mysterious objects wrapped in sheets of old newspaper in the front room of our new house, with a view of a darkening sea out the window, checking out the takeaway menu of the local Chinese restaurant, not having eaten all day, since that's what tends to happen when you're moving house, and it took some time to locate the phone.

Time was when phones were plugged into the wall and knew their place. Then came cellphones and cordless phones, and phones became free spirits, destined to be permanently misplaced before reappearing, as the saying goes, anytime, anyplace, anywhere.

Fitzgerald's phone was in a cupboard in the kitchen, and she was breathless by the time she found it. She listened silently, then asked for an address.

She didn't need to say what it was about.

'No Chinese then?' I said.

'No Chinese. You coming?'

'I'll get my jacket.'

I was not a policewoman as such. Not a policewoman at all, if the truth be told. But as a former FBI agent – retired, burned out, deserted, call it what you will – I had become quasi-officially attached to Dublin's overstretched Murder Squad in the last year in the same way that I had become attached before that to Fitzgerald. The two inevitably went together.

The arrangement with her had finally taken concrete form in the shape of the house in which we were now sitting. The other arrangement, the one with the Murder Squad, was imprecise in a way that I didn't fully understand, and wasn't in a hurry to clarify either. The indeterminacy suited me since it meant I never had to explain to myself or others what I was meant to be doing, and hence couldn't be accused of getting it wrong if I screwed up. Call me a special adviser. That's what they did. Just don't ask me to define what one was.

We took Fitzgerald's car, because my own Jeep was still parked in the underground bay beneath my apartment building on St Stephen's Green. The apartment was empty now, but not yet sold, and once more, as I thought about what I had done, I found myself questioning my sanity. An apartment's only an apartment. I didn't care about giving up that. But leave the dark, fractured heart of the city for its comfortable, smoothed out, bourgeois edges? I felt like a traitor every time I thought of what I was doing.

I'd never imagined being anywhere other than the city, my substance stitched inextricably into each of its stones, ears tuned like shortwave radio to its discordant, obscure frequencies, its entwined streets mapped through me like blood vessels.

Today, though, I had switched sides. I'd joined the tribe of suburbanites I'd always secretly despised. *Hell, I'd be buying a people carrier next.*

By the time we pulled up outside the house to which Fitzgerald had been summoned, a crowd had already begun to gather, people on their way home from the Halloween parade perhaps or out trick or treating, wearing *Scream* masks and carrying plastic pumpkins, drawn as if by hypnosis by the flashing blue lights and crackling radios of a half-dozen police cars parked haphazardly outside. The morgue van was already there too. Another flash, not blue this time, but white and sudden, revealed that the press hadn't been slow in arriving either. They must have heard the despatch over the police airwaves. The TV cameras would be behind them presently, together no doubt with the hot-dog sellers and the pickpockets. No point passing up a good economic opportunity, after all.

Fitzgerald parked on the other side of the square, preferring to arrive anonymously, and together we walked round the railings that cordoned off the communal garden and crossed the road to the other cordon, the one the police had made in blue and white tape, sealing off the scene in the house of the victim. The policeman on duty recognized us at once, and lifted the tape to let us through, at which point the nearest reporter realized what was happening and fired out a question to which he surely didn't expect an answer but which he probably felt he had to ask all the same: 'Chief Superintendent, can you—?'

No.

Another flash. As if her back would make a great picture for the front page.

'Nice house,' I said as we climbed the steps to the front door. 'Maybe we should have waited a few more days and bought this one now it's going to be vacant.'

'Saxon,' she chided me gently, 'you're a disgrace, you know that?'

'So I've heard. I saw too many Humphrey Bogart movies when I was a kid, that's the problem. You

4

Erskine was dead then, but Daniel Erskine wasn't the kind of man to be kept waiting around even in death. Least that's what I was told. For myself, I'd never heard of him before that night, having gone through life assuming that the business pages of the newspaper were just there to keep the real news company. Consequently the dead man's millions meant less to me than they did now to him and I still wasn't sure how he got them. All I knew was that he must have amassed quite a bundle of them. The fancy address was testimony to that – as was the excess of squad cars outside. Your average stiff couldn't expect this much attention in a city the size of Dublin.

I'd certainly never seen a better-dressed corpse. Italian suit, Italian shirt, Italian shoes (I was taking the word of Patrick Walsh for that, since the young detective, unlike me, both knew about such things and thought they mattered). And now there Erskine was, laid out in the freezer in his own basement like he'd curled up there for a nap, except that his hands were tied behind his back and his feet bound and then both tethered together and his lips and nose sealed off with tape. His hair stood stiff. His skin looked almost transparent.

remember what he says in *The Big Sleep* when the guy comes into his office and tells him he has a bad attitude? He says: *I know, I've had complaints about it before, but it keeps getting worse.* My hero. What hope did I have of turning out nice?'

'*Farewell My Lovely*,' Fitzgerald said.

'What?'

'It's *Farewell My Lovely*, not *The Big Sleep*. And it's not Bogart either,' she added with pleasure, 'it's Dick Powell.'

'Are you sure?' I felt slightly aggrieved at being wrong. It wasn't a sensation I'd ever gotten used to, and I didn't feel like starting now. I must be getting old. First the memory goes, then what? Which reminded me. 'What did you say the victim's name was again?'

'Erskine,' she said. 'Daniel Erskine. At least that's what it says on the victim's credit cards. He owns this place.'

'Owned, don't you mean?'

'True. Property rights may be the foundation stone of every secure democracy, but they're not much use post mortem. Let's go say hello, shall we?'

His eyes were wide open, staring.

If you could have seen the last image they saw imprinted on them, what would it be?

There was blood on his face, though not much; his nose was clearly broken. There was a wound on the back of his head too; blood and ice intermingled with his hair. There'd have to be tests, but it didn't take a genius to guess that the hairs on the poker in the hallway upstairs would match those of the victim. From there, a likely sequence of events could be deduced, with the victim killed upstairs, dragged down the steps into the basement, and hidden in the freezer.

It was the why which was the real question.

It always was.

I shivered involuntarily. The light down here was brackish as stagnant water, hiding fearfully in corners and refusing to be coaxed out for any price, and there was a definite chill of approaching winter in the air, so that it almost felt like we were standing in some dank cave, running out of candles. No matter how many switches were pressed it didn't make any difference.

For now at least, Daniel Erskine was determined to keep us in the dark.

Besides Walsh and me, the only other people standing round were Fitzgerald; a uniformed patrol cop I'd never seen before who looked distinctly uncomfortable under his peaked cap and waterproof blue jacket – I guessed this must be his first homicide crime scene; and finally Alastair Butler, City

Pathologist. For his part, Butler wasn't saying much because he was leaning beside the dead man, like a priest giving the last rites, or perhaps a more appropriate analogy would be with a pickpocket taking his chance to rifle through a victim's pockets for spare change.

There's no such thing as privacy once a pathologist enters the room.

'I heard you were moving house, Chief Superintendent,' Butler said to Fitzgerald affably as he leaned over Erskine's frozen frame, not raising his head from his work.

And they say it's only women who can do two things at once.

'That was the plan,' said Fitzgerald. 'Seems our late friend here had other ideas.'

'There's no point being cross with *him*,' the pathologist remarked with an implausible trace of amusement. 'Mr Erskine's day hasn't exactly been a bundle of laughs either.'

'Surely you're not discovering a sense of humour in your old age, Butler?' I said.

He paused, as if considering the question. 'I don't think so,' he said placidly. 'I am merely taking small pleasure from the thought of you marooned in the suburbs with the rest of us ordinary mortals, Saxon. How will you ever cope? Are you planning on joining the local bridge club, or church choir, for stimulation?'

'It's not the dark side of the moon,' I said, refusing

to rise to the bait. 'It's only thirty minutes into town if there's no traffic.'

'But there always is, isn't there?'

And though I couldn't see his face, I felt the smile all the same. I regarded the back of his head coldly and wished he'd go back to being the stuffed shirt that I knew and loved.

Knew, anyway.

Things weren't as frosty now as they had been when our paths first crossed, admittedly. I was un-official then. A civilian. Now I had a title to put to my name, he was more accepting. That was Butler. He was a man who liked order and formality, who needed to know everything was in its right place.

'I give it six months,' he added, 'before you go ape, as I understand you Americans say, and start chop-ping up the neighbours in boredom with an axe.'

'Look on the bright side. It'd be more work for you.'

'No need,' Butler said grimly. 'Of that, I have more than enough,'

'Speaking of which,' interjected Fitzgerald.

'Don't worry, I was coming to that,' said Butler, rising to his feet suddenly and taking off his glasses to rub them on the cuff of his jacket, as if cleaning them would make it any easier to see in the basement. 'You know, you should really get some arc lights in here. The architecture may be Victorian, but there's no need for the quality of the light to be faithful to the period too.'

'They're on their way,' said Walsh, who was still young enough to believe such things.

'Along with the Fifth Cavalry, I shouldn't wonder,' the pathologist said cynically, replacing his glasses so that each eye became a mere glint reflecting the meagre light.

'You've worked with worse,' Fitzgerald pointed out.

'True. And there's not much to see as it is. What time did you say he was found?'

'The emergency call was logged about an hour ago,' Fitzgerald said.

'That would be about right,' Butler nodded. 'This man hasn't been dead much longer than an hour – not that you're going to pin me down so soon on a *precise* time of death, Chief Superintendent, so don't bother trying.'

'Like I'd dare.'

'So what do we think?' said Walsh, who, I'd discovered, had only turned up moments before we did and hence hadn't had the chance yet to put the scene together in his head. He hadn't said where he'd been, but this was his day off as well so, knowing Walsh, it most likely involved some randomly selected woman, the nearest bed, and an epic lack of serious emotional commitment. 'Burglary gone wrong? Erskine finds some guy in his house, there's a struggle, and the bastard pops him with the poker to shut him up?'

'Burglars don't usually put their victims in the freezer,' I pointed out.

'And another thing,' said Butler. 'There may be a considerable quantity of blood, but the injury to this man's nose was not severe enough to cause death. Most likely, the blow to the face simply knocked him unconscious long enough to bind his hands and feet.'

'And the wounds on the back of the head?' said Walsh.

'Superficial.'

'He probably got those as the killer dragged him downstairs,' I said softly, remembering the spot trail of blood on the steps and realizing at last what the pathologist was saying.

'Then what killed him?' said Walsh.

'Best guess: suffocation. You try breathing with Sellotape across your mouth and nose. Not that he'd have lasted long in there anyway. There's not much air in the average freezer.'

'You mean ...' Walsh struggled to get his head around it, 'he was alive when he went in the freezer?'

And now I knew what the last image imprinted on Daniel Erskine's eyes had been.

It was the lid closing shut.

5

There was a joke he liked. Goes something like this. Two guys meet at the Pearly Gates and get talking. One says to the other: 'How did you die?'

'I froze to death,' he says.

'What did it feel like?' says the first one.

'Well, it's uncomfortable at first,' says the second. 'You shiver, you get the shakes, there's pain in your fingers and toes, it's cold as hell, but then it becomes relaxing and you just go numb and fall asleep and that's it. What about you? How did you die?'

'I had a heart attack. See, I knew my wife was cheating on me, so I came home early one day, found her in bed, reading. Middle of the afternoon. How suspicious is that? So I ran round the whole house looking for the guy she was fucking. Down to the basement. No one there. Up to the second floor. No one there. Then I ran fast as I could to the attic, I knew he had to be hiding somewhere. Just as I got there – boom. I had a heart attack, and here I am.'

The second man shakes his head.

'That's so ironic,' he says.

'What do you mean?'

'If only you'd stopped to look in the freezer, we'd both be alive . . .'

He remembered telling the dead man that joke once, and how they'd both laughed. But he wasn't laughing now. And all things considered, he had to admit there was something hilarious about being the man who'd murdered Daniel Erskine.

He just wished it had gone the way it was meant to.

He'd investigated the subject so thoroughly beforehand. He was determined there would be no mistakes. He needed to know what he was doing. He also wanted to understand, after he left Erskine in the freezer, what was happening each step of the way.

He wanted to share his journey.

Walk it with him.

There was plenty of research to go on. It's not such an unusual way to go. Across Eastern Europe, they drop like flies every winter, homeless drunks curled up in the snow, shovelled up come morning like garbage.

Even in America, 700 people every year freeze to death.

The old and the sick usually, who can't afford the central heating bills; or idiots who go hiking in the mountains without checking the weather reports.

But they served their purpose. Their deaths were his raw material.

His template.

He knew all the stages that would come. The early sensation of numbness and minor impairment of muscle function. The onset of shivering. Then as the body's temperature dips below 95 degrees, the mind starts to get confused and the skin grows pale and chill to the touch. Retrograde amnesia also sets in. Once the temperature falls under 90 degrees, shivering stops. The body has enough to concern itself with without wasting precious energy on shivering. The brain too descends into total irrationality. Under 86 degrees, you reach the stage of severe muscle rigidity. The pupils dilate. There will be no apparent heartbeat. Below 82 degrees, unconsciousness sets in. Patients found in this stage of hypothermia are often thought, wrongly, to be dead. They could be revived but nobody bothers because why revive what has every sign of being a corpse? After that comes the real thing.

They call it the silent killer, and he supposed the name fitted him too now.

He was not merely silent either, but invisible.

Practically non-existent.

Hypothermia wasn't such a terrible way to go. It's not so painful. It's even the recommended way in Australia to kill off cane toads, which are, apparently, something of a national menace. You're supposed to pick them up and throw them in the freezer.

As it gets colder, they're tricked into going into hibernation.

They sleep.

They die.

They don't notice a thing.

That's not so bad, is it?

He'd even heard that, if you freeze to death, then the last few minutes are the most pleasurable of your entire life, because of the number of endorphins released by the body.

You're not even cold at the end. There's only an overwhelming feeling of warmth, which is why victims are often found out of doors virtually naked as they shed clothes to cope with the unnatural heat that pulses through them, the inner summer at the heart of ice.

He wasn't sure he believed the part about it being pleasurable, but pain had never been the point. Erskine was meant to die that way because that's the way people like him are supposed to end up. It's what's fitting. What's right. The slowness was important too. He wanted Erskine to have time to think about what he'd done. To regret it. After all, the mind's pain can often be greater than any inflicted on the body. Instead he'd had to cut corners.

That damn fool disturbing him just as he'd done the hard part, when he'd knocked Erskine out with the poker, as they sat drinking, and tied him up, and got him down to the basement. It was the merest chance. He saw the stranger watching through the window. It was like a bad dream. He tried chasing him. He thought if he could catch up with him, silence him too, then he could still proceed as planned. But he was gone, the night had swallowed him up, and time was limited. So he went back and did what he had to do.

He remembered the look on Erskine's face when he lifted the lid of the freezer. That glimpse of sudden hope in his eyes. He thought he was going to be saved at the last.

Until the Sellotape was torn from its strip and placed carefully over his nose first, and then his mouth. A final murmur: 'No ... please ...'

Then he closed the lid a second time, and he knew from Erskine's eyes that he understood at last that there would be no rescue. No return this time. It was over.

Still he couldn't help feeling cheated. The symbolism of the act had been diluted. But the knowing, that was always the main point. Erskine had to know he was going to die, and he had to know why. And even if he didn't freeze to death, as he was meant to, the symbolism still held. The traitor immersed in ice. Poetic justice, in every sense of the word.

And now?

Now there was more work to be done.

There's no rest for the wicked.

6

Isolate the witnesses. It's one of the first rules when it comes to working a crime scene. Don't touch anything. Don't move the body. And isolate the witnesses. How hard was that to remember? Here there was just one known witness, so isolation shouldn't have been too difficult to manage. Instead Lester Coyle had been left free to wander about the house where Daniel Erskine died as though it was his own. Walsh had found him looking in the fridge for something to eat and demanding to know when he could get a cup of tea.

I hadn't dared mention the word *contamination* to Fitzgerald yet.

Ten minutes had passed since then. Or perhaps fifteen. A clock ticked somewhere in the room where we now stood, a small book-lined study off the main hall, but I couldn't see it. My eye kept being drawn instead to a painting on the wall of figures writhing in torment, flames licking at their naked flesh. It was like something Hieronymus Bosch might have drawn. The contrast with what we'd just seen in the basement was stark.

Fire and ice, but both bringing death.

Through the closed door came the muffled sounds

of activity and raised voices. The team from the Technical Bureau had arrived to make a fingertip search of the scene and to dust for fingerprints. Periodically there was the flash of a camera through the crack at the side of the door as Daniel Erskine's death was immortalized in overlapping snapshots. Mingled together with the constant blue flash coming through the windows from the squad cars in the street outside, it gave the room we were in the same dark otherworldly aura as the hall.

'Now, Mr Coyle,' said Fitzgerald, 'if I could just begin by asking you—'

He interrupted her immediately.

'Am I going to get some tea or not?' he demanded.

'I'm sorry?'

'I've been here an hour at least and no one's so much as offered to put the kettle on.'

Was this guy for real or what?

'In case you failed to notice, Mr Coyle,' said Fitzgerald icily, 'a man was recently murdered in this house. Right now, making tea is coming pretty low on my list of priorities. And I cannot stress to you in strong enough terms that anything you have seen tonight in this house whilst you were unsupervised should not *leave* this house. Do you understand?'

'I only asked,' he said with a wounded expression, but I could tell that he wasn't really taking it in. He was enjoying himself way too much.

There are some witnesses that every police officer dreads. The first is the one so shocked by what

40

they've seen or found that they clam up and can no more answer simple questions about what happened than you can play eight-ball pool on a bouncy castle. The second is the one who relishes every moment of the drama and wants to prolong the pleasure indefinitely.

It was quickly obvious which one Lester Coyle was. He sat there smiling smugly, like an actor waiting for his big soliloquy. And the analogy suited him because there was something unreal about the man. I'd have said he was fifty, going on sixty, and he wore one of those beards that grow along the jawline but with the upper lip shaved clean. I think they call it a chinstrap, though I've heard it called a Newgate Fringe too. Newgate was the name of a notorious London prison in the eighteenth century and the hair is supposed to look like a rope round a man's neck.

Lester Coyle didn't look the type who'd ever end up hanging from a noose. He was too mild-mannered for that. Too pleased with himself as well. The guy was even wearing sandals, for Christ's sake. In October. And it wasn't as if they were Birkenstocks either. He wore them with diamond-patterned socks, and there were moments as he spoke when I found my eyes being drawn by some gruesome fascination to those socks, like they were the key to his entire personality. (Though when I say personality, I mean it in the loosest possible sense.)

'Tell us what happened,' said Fitzgerald, and Coyle sighed with mock theatricality, leaning back in the armchair where he sat and folding his hands in his lap.

'Do I have to?' he said. 'It feels as if I've told the story a thousand times already.'

But it was just a pretence, and we all knew it. Soon there was no stopping him.

He'd been delivering leaflets, he told us, for a local evangelical Christian group to which he belonged. He showed us one, digging a pile of them out of his pocket where he'd stuffed them like banknotes from a raid. *Halloween: Beware The Occult! Dark Influences Can Ruin Your Life!* He always delivered similar leaflets after work, he said, and always walking the same route: starting at Synge Street, across the Portobello Bridge, down through all the squares and streets of this side of town before heading back across the Grand Canal at Charlemont Bridge.

'You don't live in the square then?'

'Me? Do you think I could afford to live in a place like this?' Coyle looked at us both in turn, like he was waiting for one of us at least to enjoy the huge joke. The idea of just answering a straight question with a straight answer was clearly alien to him. 'I've always wondered, though, what the inside of these places must be like. You can see right in sometimes, in the winter, when they've got the lights on and the curtains haven't been drawn. It's another world.'

And he looked around appreciatively.

'Mr Coyle, if you could just keep to the point . . .'

'I know, I know. *Just the facts, ma'am.* That's what

they always say on the TV shows, isn't it? I love those programmes. *CSI. Law & Order. Without a Trace.* I've got cable so I see them all. You know, by now I reckon I could probably do your job better than you do.'

'If there's ever a vacancy, I'll drop you a line,' said Fitzgerald. 'Meanwhile, how about telling us what you saw when you got to the square earlier this evening?'

'I didn't rightly see anything,' he said. 'Not at first. Apart from stars, that is.'

'Stars?'

'In my eyes,' he said. 'He clobbered into me that hard, I didn't know if I was coming or going. He was running out of the front gate. Never seen anyone move so fast. Knocked me clean to the ground.'

'Did he say anything to you?'

'He did indeed. *Get out of my effing way.* Practically screamed it in my face.'

'He said effing?' I said, bemused.

'No, *I* said effing. He used the full word. I didn't want to repeat it in full, since there are ladies present.' And he held up his hand, as if to say: *No need to thank me, girls, it's the least a gentleman can do for those of a weaker disposition.*

'I assure you, Mr Coyle,' Fitzgerald said, 'I've been in the Dublin Metropolitan Police for a considerable length of time. I've heard near enough every expletive under the sun. In fact, I've probably heard a few that would even be new to you. You don't have to worry about corrupting me. So what do you remember next after he told you to get out of the fucking way?'

Coyle closed his eyes momentarily, as if offended, before continuing. 'He ran across the road and turned left.'

'He ran?'

'Well, he wasn't hanging about. I'm not sure you'd call it running exactly. Next minute, he drove away in a white Transit van.'

'Yes,' said Fitzgerald, 'I noticed that in the statement you gave to the first officer who arrived on the scene. You told *him* you didn't actually see the man get into the van.'

'Not actually with my eyes, no.'

'Is there some other way of seeing that's been invented no one told me about?' I snapped.

He fixed me with a wounded gaze.

'He went round the corner,' he replied with exaggerated dignity, 'and the next minute a van pulled out. I don't know if the man I saw got in and drove away, or if someone else was waiting for him.'

'Or if the van had nothing to do with your man at all?'

'There *is* that possibility, I suppose,' Coyle sniffed.

'Did you get a registration?' asked Fitzgerald.

'No. Though it had Dublin plates, I remember that.'

'You didn't exactly give much of a description of the suspect either,' Fitzgerald said.

'I didn't see his face.'

'But you said he practically screamed into *your* face. Surely you must have seen him at that point if the two of you were that close?'

A look of panic came into his eyes.

'It was dark,' he said, 'I was winded. Maybe he wasn't *that* close.'

'You didn't notice any marks on his face then, distinguishing features, tattoos?'

Coyle shook his head morosely, sensing that the evening was not going like he expected. Maybe he'd anticipated glory, praise, attention. All he got was more questions.

'Why did you go up to the door after the man ran off?' I asked.

'Because I had my leaflets to deliver, didn't I? *And* I wanted to know what he'd been playing at,' he answered. 'I could see he was up to no good. I know a villain when I see one. So I went up the path to see if he'd been trying to break in. I didn't think anyone was in.'

'And then, when you couldn't see anything wrong . . .'

'I looked through the letter box, just to make sure, that's all, no other reason. And that's when I saw the mess. And the blood. There was a light on in the hall and I could see the vase lying there. That's when I called 999.'

'How did you know it was blood?' said Fitzgerald.

'Trust me, I know what blood looks like. I saw

enough of it when I was in the army.' He waited for one of us to ask him more, then provided the information anyway when neither of us did. 'Lebanon. Blue beret. Best days of my life. Have you ever been to Lebanon?'

'I've never had the pleasure.'

I caught her eye, and found there an echo of my own thought.

It was going to be a long night.

7

'What do you think?' she said to me once we'd left the study and were waiting as patiently as either of us could manage for the the body of Daniel Erskine to be taken away.

'I think we should go eat,' I said.

'That's not what I meant.'

'I know,' I said, 'but I still say we should go eat. You can't think on an empty stomach, and what'll you find out from hanging round here hungry for another two hours?'

'Who am I going to leave in charge? Lester Coyle, our friendly neighbourhood God-botherer?'

'Healy,' I said, because there he was.

Sean Healy was Fitzgerald's second in command. Whether the Dublin Metropolitan Police had ever got around to formalizing the arrangement and finding a way to express its gratitude in his monthly pay cheque, I didn't ask. But that's what he did. From the moment she arrived in the Murder Squad as an Inspector, Healy had been there for her, offering advice when it was needed and silent support at other times, covering her back when the heat was on, encouraging her to follow her own instincts on cases when others rolled their eyes and dismissed her insights as 'female intuition', something akin to witchcraft. When a male cop has an instinct about a case, of course, that's a different matter. Then it's his inner radar, honed through years of experience and hard work to pick up on what is unseen and unheard.

As she rose through the ranks, Healy had always been at her side; and just as importantly, he'd never been freaked out by our relationship like some of the other cops, for whom the idea of their female Detective Chief Superintendent getting jiggy after lights out with a vertically challenged former FBI Special Agent turned true crime author was on a scale of weirdness that made *The X Files* look like *The Waltons*.

'No sign of a break-in,' said Healy now, as he came down the stairs.

He was looking trimmer and leaner than he'd done in years — proof of what the love of a good woman could do for you. In the past months, Healy had finally put divorce behind him and gotten close to the DMP's newest Assistant Commissioner, Stella Carson. Both of them were walking advertisements for the health benefits of regular . . . ahem, exercise.

'That figures,' I said.

There never *were* signs of a break-in.

That would make life too simple.

'And obviously nobody heard anything, principally because there's no one here *to* hear anything. Except for those no longer in a position to talk.'

'Erskine lived alone?'

'Solitary as a hermit,' he confirmed. 'Didn't even have a housekeeper.'

'Rich people always have housekeepers,' I said. 'You don't get rich by washing your own underwear and doing the hoovering.'

'This one did. He was the secretive type. Reclusive, you might say. He wasn't one to go out of his way to get his name or picture in the papers. Quite the opposite. Look around. He doesn't even have any pictures of himself on the walls. Most of the rich people I know have so many shots of themselves hanging up that it must be like looking permanently in the mirror. Not that I know many rich people. Apart from you, of course, Saxon.'

He stopped suddenly as he came face to face with Fitzgerald.

'Chief,' he told her, 'you don't look well.'

'I look better than Erskine,' she responded.

'Who doesn't?'

'She hasn't eaten all day,' I explained.

'Then you know what to do, Special Agent,' Healy said to me. 'I'll hold the fort. Erskine isn't going anywhere in a hurry, and besides, what's the point of being in charge if you can't abuse your authority once in a while and make the rest of us do all the work?'

'Healy,' I said, 'you're speaking my language.'

Fitzgerald wavered a moment.

But only a moment.

'No,' she said. 'Not yet. Erskine had an older

brother, apparently. He's on his way down to the mortuary to formally identify the victim. I'm going to head over there and see if he can shed any light on why anyone would want to put his brother in the freezer.'

'Anything else?'

'Get someone to take Coyle down to Dublin Castle and have him sign a statement – if he ever gets his story straight, that is. I don't know about you, but I don't believe he just happened ever so conveniently to look through the letter box and saw the blood on the floor.'

'I'll get O'Neill to do it,' Healy said, naming the uniformed cop who'd been there in the basement when Jesus Christ's very own leaflet-dropper paid a call.

'Where is he, anyway?' I asked.

'He's out the back,' said Healy, 'being sick, I got the impression.'

'Sick?'

He shrugged, as if apologizing on the guy's behalf. 'It's his first proper crime scene. His first victim, you might say. He's only been with us a few weeks. Before that, he was with Operational Support. We've been breaking him in gently till tonight.'

'The squeamish type, huh?'

Fitzgerald must have seen me rolling my eyes, because she said: 'Don't be too hard on him, Saxon. It's not easy sharing a room for the first time with the remains of some psycho's handiwork lying on the floor at your feet.'

'He'll see a lot worse than this before he's done,' I said with feeling.

Then I felt bad for being unsympathetic.

Again.

'You remember the first dead body you ever saw?' I asked.

'My great-grandmother,' she said. 'I was six. They laid her out in a coffin, with rosary beads in her hands, despite the fact that she never crossed the threshold of a church in her life and said the whole lot of them, priests and bishops and Popes alike, were charlatans. She's probably still turning in her grave at the indignity of it all, poor thing.'

'You obviously take after her,' I said, smiling, because Fitzgerald had as great an aversion to organized religion as I do myself – and that's saying something. God and I had a longstanding agreement. If He didn't bother me, I wouldn't bother Him. It had suited the both of us for years. 'But I was actually asking about your first crime scene.'

'My first crime scene? Oh, that was different. It was a break-in at a chemist's shop in town. Someone climbed in through a skylight, and stole all the drugs they could get their hands on. They must've spent the entire weekend trying to get high on contraceptive pills and haemorrhoid cream. I remember thinking at the time how exciting it was, lifting prints, taking statements, looking for clues.' She laughed. 'I felt like Nancy Drew.'

'You know damn well what I mean. Your first *homicide* crime scene.'

'Oh, that was nothing very exciting,' she said. 'A man pushed his wife down the stairs during an argument. She cracked her head open. He told the judge he was drunk, he was sorry, he was blah blah blah. The worms got *her*. He got seven years and was out in four. Sorry to disappoint you, but our murders tend to be rather pedestrian affairs when compared to the Grand Guignol excesses of your home country's native fruitcakes.'

'The grand what?' I said; but she'd already turned away to find out what the house-to-house enquiries had yielded so far, which, life being what it was, was probably nada.

I guessed now I'd never find out what she was on about.

'Don't worry about O'Neill,' Healy said to me. 'He'll get used to it.'

And he was right. In many ways, that was the worst thing about working any Murder Squad. You got used to it. Didn't get desensitized, because then you'd be useless, but you learned how to see the worst that a fallen world could present to you – and then go eat lunch, have a beer, and catch the last quarter of a ball game on TV before turning in for the night.

Normal people shouldn't be able to do that.

What did that say about *us*?

8

The mortuary attendant pulled back the white sheet and Michael Erskine nodded curtly.

Yes, that was his brother.

'I'm sorry you had to go through with that,' said Fitzgerald.

'I understand.'

He showed no emotion. He wasn't the sort. He wouldn't let himself go in front of strangers. There was a grimace. His mouth tightened. That was all.

The only sign of distress came later, outside in the corridor, where he lit a cigarette with shaking hands and then seemingly forgot that he was smoking it, staring straight ahead at the wall instead, and frowning distantly, like there was something bothering him that he couldn't quite define, something other than the body of his brother in the next room.

Fitzgerald didn't point out that smoking was forbidden in the morgue, as it was in all public buildings and workplaces now that Dublin had decided to make a bid to become the world's healthiest city – though with hundreds of thousands of cars pouring into the city each day, coughing tonnes of carbon monoxide into the atmosphere, what difference would one small cigarette make? Most of the people in here were way past worrying about their health.

She simply waited for the right moment to begin.

'I can't believe it,' he kept repeating, as if, by repeating it, he finally would. Shock is rarely a spur to original thought. Bad news generally provokes the same narrow spectrum of responses. Disbelief. Anger. Confusion. 'Why would anyone want to kill Dan? It doesn't make any sense.'

'Your brother was a wealthy man,' I pointed out. 'The rich always have enemies.'

Michael Erskine shook his head.

'This is Dublin in the twenty-first century,' he said scornfully, 'not Chicago in the 1920s.'

'Human nature doesn't change,' I insisted.

In reply, he shook his head again, more forcefully this time.

Fitzgerald took the opportunity to interject. 'I'm afraid I have to ask you some questions, Mr Erskine.'

'Michael,' he said, 'call me Michael.'

You couldn't have known that they were brothers, just by looking at them. Some families are like those Russian dolls, so that each one that comes along is just like a smaller replica of the ones that have gone before. I always thought there was something creepy about families like that. Like they were the cast of some horror movie about the dangers of cloning.

Other families bear about as much resemblance to one another as strangers, and Michael Erskine and his late brother were obviously cut from two different cloths.

Perhaps their mother was playing around, who knows?

All I knew is that I took an instant dislike to him. I couldn't help it. There was such a look of innate superiority to his features – those high cheekbones, and thin, pale lips; that arrogant set to his jaw; his eyes hard like polished stones. I tried to suppress it as we waited, tensely, for him to speak again, but it kept bubbling to the surface.

I don't know what it is about a certain kind of rich person. They have the capacity to irritate me, is all. They can't help it. I'm simply allergic, the way some people are to ant spray or pollen. It's not the money. Plenty of people have money, me included. Since leaving the FBI, I'd written a series of books about my experiences, sold the film rights to most of them, and could have lived an easy life off the proceeds of both if the darkness inside which first drew me to the investigation of murder didn't keep luring me back into its unwelcome embrace. It's more the sense of entitlement that the rich often take on. The fact of not knowing how lucky they are and how easily it could all have been different.

I read once that there's only a three per cent difference between the genes of a monkey and those of a Nobel Prize-winning physicist. It's a statistic that ought to make each one of us humble. And between the rich and the dissolute, there's no difference at all, except chance and circumstance. That should make us humbler still.

Michael Erskine didn't look like humility was a concept he'd ever heard of, let alone understood. All he had, he felt wholly entitled to, as if this was the way God had intended the world to be and he wasn't going to argue fruitlessly with the Almighty.

'Yesterday,' he said, and I realized that I'd been watching him without listening to a word he said. 'We spoke on the telephone.' Presumably Fitzgerald had asked him when was the last time he had contact with his brother.

'How did he sound?'

'Same as always,' Erskine said. 'Neither of us is, was, the kind to sit around chatting, you understand, but he didn't give the impression of being concerned about anything, if that's what you mean. He was,' he rummaged for the right word, 'himself'.

'Who called who?'

'I can't remember. I think he called me. Yes, he called me.'

'What did he want to talk about?'

'Money matters,' he shrugged. 'It usually was with Daniel. He was always devising some new way of making more money. It was his passion.'

'Had it ever got him into trouble?'

'What do you mean?'

'Did he ever cut corners, bend the rules, get involved with the wrong kind of people? You know what I mean. Money rarely keeps its hands clean.'

'I resent the suggestion that my brother was somehow corrupt. He's hardly been dead a couple of hours, and you have the nerve to imply that he was no better than a criminal.'

'I have to ask the question, Mr Erskine.'

He threw down the cigarette and stamped it out. Perhaps he thought that would suffice as an answer, because he didn't offer another one.

'What about women? Men?' Fitzgerald tried again. 'Men?'

'Was he involved with anyone right now? We know he wasn't married.'

'Daniel was not gay,' Erskine said firmly. 'Neither did he have any interest in women. He liked playing chess and making money. He liked his own company. He didn't even have many friends. He always said there was no room in his life for a relationship.'

'He might have been seeing someone you didn't know about,' I said. 'Members of the same family don't always share the details of their love lives with each other.'

'And if I didn't know about it,' said Erksine with a look of triumph, 'how am I possibly supposed to tell you?'

That was me put in my place.

'So you don't think it was anyone he knew attacked your brother?' Fitzgerald said.

'How could it be?'

'You don't think he had an appointment with—?'

'Whoever killed him? No!'

Fitzgerald left that final, short, fierce word hanging in the air.

The corridor vibrated with it.

She was about to say more when the sound of hurrying footsteps replaced it. We turned around to see Inspector Noel Fogarty from Serious Crime advancing down the corridor towards us, like a man on a mission.

'Chief Superintendent,' he said, 'I need to talk to you.'

'Right now?'

'Right now.'

Fitzgerald sighed. 'Mr Erskine, if you could just wait here. This will only take a moment.'

And we stepped aside till we were out of his earshot.

'What is it, Inspector?' she asked.

'It's Leko,' he said. 'He's escaped.'

9

'It happened this evening, about an hour ago,' said Fogarty.

We had retreated to a side room. Out of earshot was one thing, but there was no point taking chances on being overheard now that Leko's name had been introduced.

'He'd been complaining about stomach cramps.' Fogarty pulled a face. 'Oldest trick in the book, I know. He obviously had it all planned out. They were transferring him to hospital at the Mater when the van was rammed and the guards overpowered. Leko even had a knife with him. Christ knows how he managed to get hold of one inside.'

'You can get anything if you want it badly enough,' Fitzgerald said. 'But I still don't see what this has got to do with me. Organizing searches for missing prisoners isn't my job.'

'Leko said he was coming after you,' said Fogarty. 'He's told the other prisoners repeatedly that he was going to kill you. You know he blames you for being inside.'

Finally it made sense.

Leko, who never seemed to possess a Christian name, or a Christian bone in his body for that matter, was a Bosnian national who'd come to Dublin claiming asylum during the conflict in the Balkans in the early nineties, and proceeded to ignite a war of his own in the north inner city. Maybe he was trying to make himself feel at home. Starting out with a lucrative sideline in stolen cars, Leko soon moved into drugs, prostitution, various immigration rackets, quickly making himself one of the city's most successful and feared ganglords.

It was only whilst in prison for drug trafficking that his path crossed that of Fitzgerald. She was investigating the murder of Leko's wife, Allenka, who was gunned down on the doorstep of her home by a lone gunman whilst her three children slept upstairs.

It didn't take long to figure out that Leko had ordered a hit on his wife as revenge after he discovered she'd started an affair with one of his own partners in crime, a man whose own decomposed body turned up six months later in the Dublin mountains. What Leko hadn't expected was for anyone to be able to prove that he was behind both murders.

Unfortunately for him, he hadn't reckoned on Fitzgerald. A five-year stretch on drugs charges turned into a fifteen-year jail term for murder, and he was lucky to get away with that. Even so, Leko was going to be over sixty before he tasted freedom again.

And patience clearly wasn't his strong suit.

'I went over to your place to offer you armed

protection, only I got the wrong house. I didn't know you'd moved,' Fogarty explained. 'By the time I got to your new place, you'd gone, so I followed you here. The Assistant Commissioner said you weren't to be left alone until Leko's back in custody. We've got people out all over the city looking for him.'

'What are you going to do?' I asked her.

'What am I going to do?' she echoed. 'What do you think I'm going to do? I'm going to get on with my job. I'm not letting a scumbag like Leko stand in my way.'

'And if he comes after you?'

'I'll deal with that when it happens. He's had plenty of chances to wipe me out before now,' she said. 'The fact that he was behind bars didn't help his wife, did it?'

'But you saw the last report on him,' I said. 'He said he wanted the satisfaction of killing you all to himself. He wanted it to be pleasure, not business.'

'What are you saying I should do? Run off home, and have armed guards standing at every door and window until he's back in prison? I have a murder to work here.'

'Our only concern,' said Fogarty, 'is to ensure that your own killing isn't the next case that the Murder Squad has to investigate.'

Fitzgerald shook her head firmly.

'I'm not stepping aside from this case, Inspector.'

Fogarty was a big man, with a square body, and shoulders made of stone, and the kind of face that looked like it belonged on a Wanted poster, but he looked helpless as he realized Fitzgerald wasn't going to come quietly.

'Chief Superintendent,' he said, 'if anything should happen—'

'I take full responsibility,' she said. 'And don't worry, I'll make sure the Assistant Commissioner knows this is my decision. But there's a dead man lying on a slab back there. His brother is standing in the corridor. I don't have time to go into hiding because Leko wants to play the outlaw. I won't give him that victory.'

There was no room for compromise in her voice. I knew her well enough to recognize when her mind was made up. But when she saw the frown on Fogarty's face, she softened slightly. He had his job to do as well. He was only trying to do what was right.

'Send someone round after me tonight, if it makes you feel better,' she told him. 'As long as he doesn't get in my way, I won't kick up a stink.'

'I was already going to, whether you agreed to it or not,' Fogarty said wryly, but he was happier now. 'And I know just the right man. He's one of our best.'

'Only *one* of your best?' Fitzgerald replied. 'I must be slipping in importance . . .'

Once Fogarty had left to make the necessary arrangements for providing Fitzgerald with sufficient protection to keep her in circulation for the night, I took the opportunity – the last one I would have that night, I guessed; I knew what Fitzgerald was like when she got caught up in an investigation – to ask if she was sure about this.

'Maybe you *should* go home,' I said. 'They can manage without you for once.'

'Would *you*?'

There was an involuntary hesitation before I answered 'Yes' that gave me away.

'You used to be a better liar than that, Saxon,' she said.

I knew when I was beat. 'Aren't you worried?' I asked her.

'Not enough to distract me from doing my job,' she insisted. 'In fact, you know what? I hope Leko does come after me and it gives Fogarty's guy an excuse to blow him away in reply. After what he did to his wife, it's no more than he deserves.'

'You'll get no quarrel from me on that score,' I said. 'I just hope he's the only one who gets hurt. I'd hate to think of the two of us sharing the same mortuary van with him.'

'Not you,' she said. 'You're indestructible.'

10

Half an hour later, we were in a noodle bar on South Great George's Street, helping ourselves to soup noodles and tempura and rice balls, hijiki and fishcakes. That is, the fishcakes were for me. Fitzgerald was on some kind of vegetarian trip lately. She was determined her body should be a temple. Mine, on the other hand, was more like some ramshackle roadside diner that should have been scheduled for demolition by health and safety officers years ago.

Fitzgerald ordered bean curd, and she was welcome to the hijiki as well, since I'd only asked for it because I liked the name without realizing that it was black seaweed. Watching her use chopsticks was a pleasure in itself. She had such nimble fingers, each movement she made was elegant and economical, no more nor less than it should be, whereas I scooped clumsily.

The light in the noodle bar felt so bright that it almost hurt my eyes; but they were glad to be aching. It was a small price to pay for the sensation of being alive.

I was always grateful for that after spending time in the mortuary. Death charged the air there with

64

negative particles. It made the world seem bad. And maybe it was.

'I always wanted to go to Japan,' I said as we ate. 'It's the one country in the world where I wouldn't feel like some dwarf. Why did we never go to Japan?'

'The same reason we never went to Rio for the Mardi Gras, or climbed the Pyramids.'

'Because you're afraid of flying?'

'That, and also because people in Dublin have the inconsiderate habit of being murdered all the time and spoiling our best-laid plans.'

'I forgot about that. Some people are so selfish.'

'Tell me about it. We can't even move into a new house without someone getting killed.'

'Be thankful you didn't have to break the news to brother Michael anyway,' I said.

'I'm always thankful for that,' she said with feeling. 'I'd rather see a hundred dead victims than break the bad news to a single living relative.'

'I'm with you on that one.'

'Perhaps O'Neill will learn that too eventually.'

'O'Neill? Oh, you mean the cop with the weak stomach. Good job he's not here. Have you seen that guy over there eating the squid? It's almost making me throw up.'

'It's rude to stare.'

'It's also rude to talk with your mouth full,' I pointed out, but then murder and manners rarely make good bedfellows, and we *were* in a hurry.

Between mouthfuls she asked me what I made of Michael Erskine.

'I wouldn't believe Michael Erskine if he told me his own name, or what time it was. He was definitely not up to sharing too many confidences about his brother's life,' I said. 'Did you notice how reluctant he was to answer even the most basic questions? Why keep things to yourself when your brother's just been found lying dead in a freezer?'

'Some people hide things from the police, whether it's good for them or not. It's just a bad habit they've got into. It doesn't mean what they're hiding is significant.'

'Doesn't mean it isn't either,' I pointed out.

'True. Let's just hope Ronan Blunt is more forth-coming.'

'Is that name supposed to mean something to me?'

'Ronan Blunt was the last person Daniel Erskine called before he died,' said Fitzgerald. 'Healy called to let me know while you were in the bathroom. I have an address too.'

'Typical. I miss all the fun.'

We were rising out of our seats to go when I saw him looking at us. He was sitting a couple of tables away, drinking coffee and idly picking at a bowl of rice with a fork.

The slightest nod of the head was all he offered in reply to my glare.

'Do we know him?' I said.

'That's Fogarty's man,' Fitzgerald said. 'His name's Morgan, apparently. He followed us here from the mortuary.'

'So that's the reason for the bulge in his pocket,' I said. 'And I thought he was just pleased to see us. I'm impressed. He doesn't look like a cop.'

'Nor do you.'

'I'm not, remember? I'm only along for the ride.'

'Say that often enough, and you might even start to believe it,' Fitzgerald said, manoeuvring into her coat with the same unthinking elegance with which she wielded her chopsticks. It wouldn't matter how long I studied her method. I'd never have the same ease of movement. I lacked the necessary cells. It was like asking a blind person to describe the view.

Our protector and shadow rose and followed us as we left.

Soon, we were back in Fitzgerald's Rover, making our way the short distance from the city centre to Ringsend. Or was it Irishtown? The precise boundary between these two districts on the south side of the River Liffey, whilst it may have been of incalculable importance to the people who lived there, had never been entirely clear to me.

The whole territory was little more than an ugly waste of docks and warehouses, with narrow streets crowding behind for shelter. It was fifteen minutes walk at most from Leeson Street to here, but was so far removed from it that it might as well have been on another planet. In fact, forget that. It was in a different solar system altogether. The houses were so tightly packed together that they seemed to grow, limpet-like, into each other. No wonder the district had the reputation for being one of the most clannish in the whole city. It was like a black hole.

Nothing that got sucked in here had much hope of ever getting out again.

And for some, charmed by such a remnant of Old Dublin remaining under the slick, wealthy exterior of the new country, that alone may have indicated tradition and community. For me, it tended to signify inbreeding, and it was incredible that the children born in its shadow didn't come as a rule with extra limbs or such an array of exotic congenital defects that they made the Elephant Man look like George Clooney in comparison.

'Ronan Blunt lives here?' I said in incredulity as we searched for the address Fitzgerald had got from Healy. 'This is the last place I'd have expected to find one of Daniel Erskine's social circle kicking back his heels.'

'They're not all throwbacks down here, you know,' said Fitzgerald, who knew my opinions without needing to be reminded, and disapproved accordingly.

'I'll take your word for it,' I said.

'Besides, who says Blunt was one of Erskine's friends? Might be just the opposite.'

Rows of lit windows stretched on either side of the road like the portholes of ships – a fitting analogy since the ground all about was still sodden from recent floods. The tide had come in high without warning a week ago, breaching the banks of the river and dispersing where it could. Knee-deep in places, there'd been pictures on the TV news of locals guiding a boat down the middle of streets transformed overnight into canals, and piling sandbags on to doorsteps, and as we climbed out at our short journey's end the air still smelt bad with the aroma of disturbed mud that always comes when a river doesn't know its rightful place. I half expected to find dead fish lying in the gutter, or a beached whale rotting down one of the back alleyways.

Blunt's house was marooned at the end of one such street, the sky behind dominated by the towers of the nearby gasworks and the greyhound stadium at Shelbourne Park, and separated from the rest by the collapse – deliberate or otherwise, I couldn't say – of its neighbours.

It also struck me, when he answered the door at the third knock, that there was something of the same aloofness about Ronan Blunt. Shorter and stockier than the two brothers, with greying hair that needed cutting, owlish spectacles and corduroy trousers a couple of sizes too large, he conveyed a sense of being both at one remove from his surroundings and perfectly integrated into them. He looked like his day had been and gone and he wasn't sure yet what was going to replace him, and he regarded us with a quizzical, half-amused detachment.

'Ronan Blunt?'

'What is it?'

Fitzgerald showed him her ID. 'Detective Chief Superintendent Grace Fitzgerald,' she said briskly. 'And this is Saxon. She's a special adviser to the Murder Squad.'

Having no ID of my own, I tried at least to look the part.

The effort was wasted on Blunt. Fitzgerald alone had done the trick. If there was any doubt about getting his attention before then, those two small words had dispelled them.

'Murder Squad?' he echoed hollowly.

'Can we come in?'

They were showing *Halloween* at the Irish Film Centre. Special performance, one night only, for the day that was in it. Leko smiled grimly as he passed the doorway and saw the poster.

He remembered seeing the movie once on TV, years ago, it must have been Halloween that night too. He'd watched it with Allenka. He recalled how she'd got terrified at all the tense parts, and hid her face in his shoulder. He'd been her protector in those days, before the bitch betrayed him, before he had to punish her for what she'd done.

Leko frowned. There was an escaped prisoner in *Halloween* too, wasn't there? It was the boy who killed his sister. Years later, he escapes from the mental institution where he's been locked up, and makes his way back to his hometown to start all over again.

It wasn't exactly like that tonight, but even a man with as brutal an imagination as Leko could appreciate irony when he saw it.

Not that Grace Fitzgerald would find it so funny...

Leko stopped a while, and watched the couples going into the film centre, hand in hand, or arms wound round one another's waists, cementing their lust for each other by going to watch some other young couples getting butchered by a psycho on the big screen.

He was filled suddenly with the longing for freedom.

For what they had.

Freedom: it was what every prisoner dreams of constantly, waking or sleeping, it makes no difference. The power to do what you want, when you want to do it. To be subject to no one else's rules. What he had right now was only a feeble shadow of the real thing. Leko had freedom only in the sense that he wasn't locked up behind walls and bars any more; but they were looking for him, he could feel their eyes following him as he walked the city.

That wasn't true freedom. It was just a different kind of incarceration.

Earlier, through the window of a pub, he'd noticed a TV flickering high on a bracket fixed to the wall, showing the evening news. His picture had been on the screen. He couldn't hear what the newsreader was mouthing, but then he didn't have to. He'd heard it all before.

All he knew was that they weren't going to make it easy for him. There was nowhere he could go now where he could be certain of being unrecognized. That meant he had to be quick. He had to get the job done, then he could disappear, just like he'd planned.

Then the real freedom would begin.

Leko turned up the collar of his borrowed tweed

coat, trying to hide his face as best he could without exciting suspicion. He'd found it hanging in the hall-way of a church close to where he got out of the prison van. It smelt musty, like it had been locked up too long as well, but it served its purpose. There'd even been a packet of cigarettes in the inside pocket of the coat, and a woollen hat tucked down one sleeve. Together, hat and coat and the dark were the best camouflage he had. He was lucky it was so late in the year. He wouldn't have fancied trying to be inconspicuous on a summer's evening in a tweed coat and woollen hat.

Even now he was feeling nervous as he made his way to the appointed meeting place. He was trusting to other people now, and that always put him on edge. But he was sure Stanic wouldn't let him down. He knew what would happen to him if he did.

He was surprised Stanic had picked this spot for the drop-off. There were so many people around. So many watching eyes. Stanic was usually much more cautious. He was the one who always saw things as problems rather than opportunities. That was why he was no threat to Leko. People with ideas of their own were the ones who made Leko concerned.

Though maybe choosing Temple Bar was a sign that Stanic was changing, starting to think for him-self? If so, he'd need to be watched in future. For now, Leko was impressed. This was the last place the police would be expecting him to show up. They'd expect him to go to ground. To head for the shadows and wait for the chase to go cold on him. Wandering around Dublin city centre on Halloween night was not what they'd anticipate at all.

That's what made it perfect.

Plus, the more people there were, the more cover they provided. Alone, there's nowhere to hide. And tonight was busier than usual. People found any excuse to celebrate, and Halloween was as good a reason as any other.

By the time he turned off Eustace Street into Essex Street East, he was beginning to feel good about the night ahead. That bitch Fitzgerald was going to get what was coming to her. Everything had been cruising along fine until she turned it into some fucking crusade to nail him. He was behind bars, sure, but that didn't bother him too much. Jail was an occupational hazard. The most he was looking at was five years. Then, because he'd been forced to take action after he learned his wife was cheating on him, five years had turned into fifteen, and he was lucky to get away with that. He knew he was fucked if he had to stay inside for fifteen years. By the time he got out, there'd be nothing left.

He'd be yesterday's man.

Maybe that's what Stanic was banking on?

No. He shook his head. No way was Stanic going to make a move against him. Stanic didn't have it in him. Leko was getting paranoid. He had to stay focused.

He quickened his step through the brooding,

narrow lanes of Temple Bar, past the Czech Inn and the Turk's Head, where he'd spent plenty of evenings with Allenka when they'd first moved to Dublin, down to Fishamble Street. Music drifted out of the doorways of the bars. Lights shone in windows. Twenty years ago, the area he was moving through now had been a wasteland. They were going to bulldoze the whole area and turn it into a bus depot. Now it was the first place new visitors headed.

Things could turn around. That was the moral of the story. And things were going to turn around for Leko too – so long as Stanic didn't sell him out.

And there it was again, that doubt. He couldn't shift it.

The doubt increased when he got to his destination and found that he was the only person there. What time was it? It had to be coming up to eight o'clock.

Nothing to do but wait.

'Mr Flynn?'

Leko spun round at the low sound of a voice behind him.

'I'm Flynn,' he said.

He didn't recognize the guy Stanic had sent. That was good. The police would be watching as many of his associates as they could. Strangers could slip through the net much easier. Stanic had learned something from his master, anyhow.

'I have something for you,' the stranger said.

His eyes were unreadable, his face impassive. He

began reaching into his coat. A knot tightened in Leko's belly. He glanced up the street. There were a few people around. Surely he wouldn't ... not here ... with this many witnesses?

He had a split second to make his decision, and he made it.

'What the fuck—?'

Before the stranger had a chance to say another word, Leko grabbed his arm as it reached inside the jacket, and with the other hand he grasped the stranger by the throat and pushed him back against the wall, knocking his head noisily against the brick. There was fear in the other man's eyes now. Leko liked that sight. Out of the corner of his eye, he also saw two men on the other side of the street pause uncertainly, and waver, torn between duty and self-preservation, before one caught the elbow of the other and steered him out of trouble. Seemed there were no Good Samaritans any more. Whatever was happening on the other side of the street, they didn't want to know. Wise decision, Leko thought grimly.

He put his own hand inside the stranger's jacket.

Felt paper.

The gun was still wrapped up. Stanic hadn't turned on him, after all. He relaxed his grip as he pulled out the package and slipped it in the pocket of his borrowed coat.

'I had to be sure,' he said.

He didn't apologize. Saying sorry was a sign of weakness.

The stranger said nothing. He still looked afraid as he rubbed his neck where Leko's fingers had seized it. He was just a kid, Leko noticed. Fancy thinking he was any kind of hit man. Probably Stanic made a few phone calls, and those phone calls led to other phone calls, and this kid was the end of the chain. Chances were he didn't even know who it was he'd been ordered to meet. He just did as he was told.

'You got the money too?' he asked.

'It's in my other pocket.' His voice was unsteady. 'Can I . . .?'

'Be my guest.'

Leko didn't waste time counting it. The Not So Good Samaritans might've called the cops by now. Temple Bar seemed suddenly smaller. Time to be moving on. He simply pulled two notes from the bundle in the second bag, and pushed them into the kid's hand.

'Here,' he said. 'You did good.'

Leko didn't look back. He headed up the road again towards Christchurch. He had money in one pocket and a gun in the other. For the first time since he'd escaped earlier that evening, he began to feel more comfortable. As far as Leko was concerned, there was nothing else a man needed to be happy.

Nothing, that is, except for revenge.

12

Tina Blunt pretended to watch TV, but her eyes kept straying to the French windows that looked out on to the small backyard, where Ronan was talking to those two policewomen who'd arrived unexpectedly about five minutes earlier. But then wasn't that how the police always arrived? They were standing round the patio heater, framed by the familiar skyline of the gasworks and the criss-crossing arms of high cranes over building sites, testimony to the rampage of development that had overtaken the city in recent years.

She'd shut off the sound – there was nothing worth hearing anyway – but she still couldn't hear them talking outside. Like the pictures on the TV, the figures were reduced to mouths opening and closing noiselessly. Occasionally they glanced over in her direction but each time she looked away quickly with that clumsy obviousness that drunks often have and which they always imagine is perfect skill.

Not that she considered herself to be a drunk. She liked to drink. What else was there to do half the time? If Ronan wasn't working, he was out, God knows where. Tonight he'd promised he'd stay in with her when he got home from work, and now there was this. She wondered what they could want. She couldn't believe that Ronan had actually done something wrong. He didn't have it in him. If he had, she'd have had more respect for him. He was too timid to do anything that the police would be interested in.

Maybe it was something to do with the museum.

Maybe someone had stolen a stuffed giraffe or something.

She smiled as she thought of it, but then stopped. No, their faces were too sombre for that. His ex-wife then. With any luck, the bitch had finally killed herself, like she always used to threaten when they first separated. It'd save them a fortune in alimony payments if she had. *Oh please*, Tina prayed to the nameless god of vodka, *let her be dead*.

She looked again at the taller of the two police-women, and a feeling of antagonism washed suddenly, nauseatingly, over her. She hated it when that happened, but she had no control over it. There must be something in women whose husbands have left other wives, betrayed other mistresses, to be with them. They know it could always happen to them next. Every time she saw Ronan talking to another woman it was the same. This one was particularly attractive too, which only made her feel worse. She had long black hair, tied back, and fine features, beguiling eyes. She'd noticed them at once. She was sure Ronan must have too. Inside her coat her figure was undoubtedly shapely and slim as well. She certainly curved in all the right places. She looked healthy, sexy, young – younger than Tina anyway.

Then again, every woman that Tina saw looked younger than her these days. They glowed with life and hope and sensuality. Whereas when she looked in the mirror now, all she saw was ... well, she tried not to look at herself at all.

Mirror, mirror, on the wall, who is the most middle-aged of all?

The other woman outside – the Yank, she'd sounded like when they first came in – was smaller. Had they done away with the height requirement now for the police? Tina wasn't so worried about her. There was something edgy about her, something sparky, and Ronan had always been intimidated by women like that. Women he feared might get the better of him. His ex-wife and Tina had that much in common at least. They were no threat to anyone. He always picked women who couldn't leave him and no one else would want.

Which was why, however much she needed him, she despised him too.

Sometimes she liked to provoke him, just to see how far she could push him before he snapped. She said dreadful things she didn't mean simply to observe the effect of her words.

And maybe she did it because, when she did finally drive him away, she'd have the satisfaction of knowing she'd been right all along. People often did that. She knew because she'd seen them talking about it on TV in the mornings. You learned a lot from daytime TV about the infinite, ingenious ways men and women found to hurt one another . . .

Tina realized, with a start, that she'd been staring at the three of them for a long time, forgetting to pretend to be disinterested, and now she saw that the American was gazing back at her intently, sizing her up. Tina looked away again hurriedly.

She jabbed at the remote control, switching back the sound.

She didn't care what they were talking about, couldn't they see that?

Images of destruction flashed on to the screen. Car bombs. A pool of blood. A man lay weeping over the body of his dead son. Where was it? Iraq? Afghanistan? Africa? It could be anywhere. She didn't want to see it, wherever it was. There was too much misery in the world. Too much violence. But then wasn't it her who'd just wished her husband's ex-wife dead? And there were others she could think of who would be equally unmourned.

It was always the wrong people who died.

Always the innocent.

Damn, her glass was empty. So she got to her feet and walked on small, careful steps to the kitchen to fix another one, squeezing ice cubes from a tray and drowning them in vodka, adding a little tonic water to the top to make it look sparkly, because she liked the way the bubbles clung to the ice and the crackling music it made like fire in the glass.

She could hear them more clearly from in here. The window was slightly ajar. She remembered now. She'd opened it a crack to clear away the steam when she was making dinner.

'*The Dead Zoo*,' she heard.

'The what?'

That was the American's voice.

'The National History Museum,' Ronan explained. 'On Merrion Street.'

'It's known as the Dead Zoo because of all the stuffed animals, right?' added the taller one with the dark hair. 'What is it that you do there?'

'I'm a curator,' the murmur of Ronan said. 'There's a small group of us whose job it is to look after the collection.'

'What's to look after? It's not like they need rounding up.' (The American again.)

Tina heard the wounded pride in her husband's voice as he answered. He was very proud of his job. Bored her to distraction sometimes, talking about it. Though she felt envious too. Wished that she had something she felt a similar passion about.

It was a long time since she'd cared much about anything.

'There are over two million zoological and geological specimens in store at the museum, gathered together over two centuries, with ten thousand of them on display at any given time. I assure you,' Ronan said, 'there's no shortage of things to do.'

'Did Erskine share your interest in stuffed animals?'

Erskine: now there was a name to seize Tina's attention.

'What's that supposed to mean?'

Ronan's voice was sharp suddenly.

'Who says it has to mean anything?'

'I know what you're getting at. You want to know how a low-paid public servant in a crappy part of the city gets to be friends with a rich bigshot like Daniel Erskine.'

'I never said that either.'

'That's what you were thinking, though, wasn't it?'

'No.'

'Well, it's no big mystery,' he said, unconvinced. 'I've known Dan since university and money was never a barrier between us. As for this place, I live in Irishtown because I like it, because it suits me. I grew up around here. My roots are very important to me.'

'Your roots. Fuck me, not that one again.'

'Tina.'

She hadn't been able to resist it any longer. The voices through the unlatched window had been too tempting. Now she'd opened the French windows and stood – swayed would be a better way to describe it – on the step, tumbler in hand, ice clinking, glasses too large for her face so that her eyes would have looked unfocused even without the help of the alcohol.

'We both know why you're still here,' she said, staring straight at her husband, and smiling faintly with pleasure at his obvious discomfort. 'Shall I tell them?

He's still here for the same reason he's still tied to the apron strings of that crook Daniel Erskine. Because he doesn't have the balls to cut them and be free. It's pathetic. You don't even like him. A real man would've got out years ago.' There, she'd said it now. Said it again.

'Tina.' Another quiet warning. 'I told you to stay inside.'

She snorted. 'And the day I do what you tell me to do, dearest darling husband, is the day I cut my own throat with a kitchen knife,' she said bitterly. 'You're just afraid they'll see what kind of man you really are, and what a hold Mr Wonderful, Danny E, has over you.'

'Don't talk about Daniel that way,' he said softly.

'What's he going to do? Have me beaten up? I've told you before. The only way we'll ever be free of that bastard is when he's six feet under.'

'Then you're going to be very happy,' the American said.

'What do you mean?'

'Daniel's dead. He's dead, all right?' said Ronan. 'That's what they came to tell me. So why don't you, for once in your life, shut your mouth and mind your own business?'

No chance of that. Tina opened her mouth wide, at first in surprise, and then to laugh, loudly, with unmistakable glee. She didn't even bother trying to hide it. Why should she?

'Erskine's dead?' she said. 'Well, if that isn't the

best news I've heard all year, I don't know what is. It's about time. I'm only surprised he lasted this long. I always hoped someone would bump him off. What happened to the poisonous stuck-up bastard?'

'He was murdered,' the policewoman with the dark hair replied softly.

That sobered Tina up a little.

'You don't think Ronan did it, do you?' she said.

'What makes you think he didn't?'

Now it was Ronan's turn to be surprised.

'You're not saying you think *I* killed him?' he demanded.

'Why not?' said the American, more as if she was curious at that moment to know how he'd respond rather than because she believed it.

'Why not? Because … because it's ridiculous, that's why not,' he said. 'I've known Daniel Erskine for twenty years. More. Why should I suddenly decide to kill him?'

'That doesn't mean a damn thing,' the woman continued. 'If people were logical, nobody would ever get killed. You can always ask, why now? I knew a man once who killed his wife on the day of their silver wedding anniversary. He beat her to death with the silver candlestick he'd been saving six months to buy for her. You might as well say he couldn't have killed her either because he'd known her for more than twenty-five years. People kill each other all the time for all manner of reasons.'

'But I didn't touch him,' Ronan said, and there was

an edge of panic starting to creep into his voice. Tina felt herself despise him again at the sound of it. Why could he never stand up for himself? 'You've got to believe me. I haven't even seen him since last week.'

'But he called you earlier today, didn't he?'

He looked like he was about to deny it, but thought better of it.

'It was only a brief call,' he said sulkily. 'He wanted to tell me not to come round tonight and to tell the others.'

'Would you normally have been round there tonight?'

'Oh yes. There's a group of us. We've been friends since university. We always got together on Halloween. It was a bit of a tradition with us. Every Halloween and every Friday: those were our regular nights. Daniel said he'd have to cancel.'

'Had he ever pulled the plug on one of your sessions before?'

'Now and then,' Ronan replied. 'There was always the risk of something coming up. Business, you know. Or if he wasn't in the city. Otherwise it always went ahead.'

'Did he say why he was cancelling?' the one with the long dark hair said.

'He didn't say, no.'

'You didn't ask?'

Ronan hesitated a moment before answering.

'He just said something had come up,' he answered vaguely.

'Well, I'll need you to make me a list of the people who were supposed to be at Daniel Erskine's house tonight, along with phone numbers and addresses. Maybe one of them knows more than you about why he cancelled tonight's get-together.'

'I'll get a pencil,' he said.

'You do that.'

'Poor Michael,' said Tina unexpectedly, then she paused as she realized that she'd spoken her thought aloud and that the others were looking at her curiously. She'd always had a soft spot for him. 'Michael isn't like his brother,' she tried to explain, but the words came out slurred and imprecise, stranger than she intended. 'Michael is . . . human.'

13

'Did that story about the candlestick really happen?' Fitzgerald asked me as we walked back to the Rover, hoping that miracles could sometimes happen in these streets and that the car would not only be where we left it but that all four wheels would still be attached to it.

'Are you calling me a liar?' I said.

'Might be.'

'In that case,' I said, 'all I'll tell you is that it contained a kernel of truth.'

'A kernel, or a fragment?'

'He *did* kill his wife, and it *was* on their silver wedding anniversary. I may possibly have made up the part about the candlestick.'

'I knew it,' said Fitzgerald. 'Your anecdotes are always too good to be true. I think you have a database of them somewhere that you can draw on in an emergency. Shit.'

There was the sound of footsteps running as we turned the corner. A group of teenagers was scattering like rats when a light's switched on.

The Rover was still there.

So were the wheels.

It was only the side window that was gone. Or not

gone so much as transferred in little pieces on to the driver's seat. Seems like we'd got here just in time.

'Try to think of it as added ventilation,' I said, picking out the remains of a firework which the little bastards had stuck to the window to make it blow.

'That,' she pointed out frostily, 'is the last thing we need in October. And where the hell is Morgan? Fogarty's best guy, my eye. There's not much point having him traipsing round after us if he can't even make himself useful when he's needed.'

'That's the trouble with this city,' I said. 'There's never a police officer around when you need one.'

'Smartass.'

To make matters worse, it was beginning to rain.

'You think Erskine cancelled their regular little party because he had someone else coming round tonight instead?' I asked as we climbed inside the car.

'That's what I'm thinking.'

She took the list that Blunt had written for us out of her pocket and looked at it.

If you could call three names a list.

Michael Erskine
Nat Tannar
Oliver Niland

'And how come Michael didn't mention any of this, that's what I want to know.'

'You want to take him first?'

'No. Michael can wait. Niland's place is nearest.'

'Niland it is then.'

The right-hand side of Fitzgerald was soon wet as she drove, and the left-hand side of her was no happier either. There had been something missing from the interview with Blunt, something neither of us could put a finger on. Everyone we'd met so far had been the same way. Cagey. Suspicious. Like they had something to hide. Then again, who didn't?

I'd even asked if he'd minded that his regular party with Erskine was off. Having seen his wife and received a brief glimpse into his marriage, I imagined he might welcome any opportunity to get away. It hadn't been a pretty sight, after all.

But he'd said it was a relief not to have to go round to Daniel Erskine's house for once . . . it had become something of an obligation . . . a chore he couldn't get out of . . . until now. And then he had looked clumsily guilty, like he'd said too much already.

'My wife's always telling me I should spend more time with her,' he'd explained hurriedly. *'Tina never liked Daniel.'* And we'd seen that for ourselves soon enough . . .

'Maybe we'll have more luck at Niland's place,' I said.

But we were set to be disappointed a second time. When we got to the address that Ronan Blunt had written down, it turned out to be the wrong one.

Or not wrong so much as out of date. The young strawberry blonde in the cocktail dress who answered the door said that Niland had moved out a year ago. She'd bought the place off him. And no, she didn't have a forwarding address or telephone number. From behind her where she stood in the doorway, a languid cloud of tasteful jazz-lite oozed from the CD player: music for people who didn't really like music.

Blondie didn't exactly hide the fact that we were interrupting her evening.

'We keeping you from something?' I said sarcastically.

'I'm in the middle of a dinner party,' she said.

Of course she was. I should've guessed.

'Then just help us out here and you can get back to your hors d'oeuvres,' said Fitzgerald. 'You're not seriously telling me you didn't get some of Mr Niland's mail after he left? Even if he did get it redirected, some always slips through. What did you do with it?'

'Oh that?' she said. 'I had instructions to give it all to the woman downstairs.'

Now we were getting somewhere. It was just a shame she hadn't shared her meagre scraps of information with us straight away and spared us the preliminaries. And so one fruitless interview held on someone's doorstep led to another one equally frustrating, because the old woman didn't know where Niland had got to either, and she was half deaf, so even discovering that much was a struggle. It was a relief when we managed to get away.

'Sod's law,' Fitzgerald pointed out. 'Anything that can go wrong will go wrong.'

'I thought that was Murphy's law.'

'Different name, same crap. There any point trying the third one on the list, you think?'

'Probably not, but let's try it anyway.'

'You're right. Who said life was supposed to be fun?'

Fun was certainly the last word to come to mind when Nat Tannar's wife answered the front door of their cramped semi-detached 1930s house on Harold's Cross Road. Her name was Sally and she looked frazzled and exhausted. Her hair was a bird's nest that the bird had just flown home to after a long absence to find trashed. Behind her rose the smell of cooking, and a cacophony of children: the sound of ungovernable, primeval chaos. From this was formed the stuff of the universe. Children were the parts that were left over when the useful work was done, the bits that God didn't know what to do with and so dumped on parents, probably as punishment for Adam and Eve getting acquainted with one another's nakedness in the Garden of Eden when they were supposed to be hoeing the hollyhocks.

Still, it *was* Halloween. They had an excuse for being up.

'We're looking for Nat Tannar,' Fitzgerald said.

'Join the club.'

Sarcasm was rarely a good start.

'Do you know where we could find him?'

'No,' she said directly, 'but if past experience is anything to go by, which in Nat's case it usually is, then he's probably with one of his whores.'

Talk about awkward.

'I'm sorry, Mrs Tannar, this really isn't any of—'

'Or if his whores don't know where he is, try his sluts. One or the other is your best bet. Between them, they should be able to tell you where he is.'

Fitzgerald left a card for Nat, with her cellphone number on it. He was to ring immediately when he arrived home. *If* he did. She didn't tell his wife what the call to her door had been about, but the official nature of those neatly printed words *Detective Chief Superintendent* did the trick of quietening the anger she had misplaced towards us.

The men in the late Daniel Erskine's social circle, we reflected sombrely as we returned to the car, were not the world's best advertisement for marriage.

Maybe that's why Daniel had never married. Examples like this were hardly a breeding ground for optimism about matrimony.

'There's one good thing about everyone being unavailable for interview,' Fitzgerald observed as she climbed once more behind the wheel.

'There is?'

'At least this business won't take all night.'

If only she'd known how wrong she was.

14

As we returned to town, I saw that the earlier migration out as the stores and offices emptied had been replaced with an incoming tribe of nightwalkers and nightworkers: foreign women with sad, defeated eyes cleaning for the minimum wage; students who would spend a few hours flipping burgers before heading to the late-night bars to vanish the money they'd just made; waitresses and security guards and nurses. Hookers were starting to appear on the corners near the Grand Canal too, and the pushers, who during the day worked the boardwalk along the Liffey River, were now moving deeper into the city, looking for richer pickings.

The night had its own economy, its own winners and losers.

It was ironic really. For centuries, in the long years before street lighting spoiled the fun, the poor had used the dark to indulge in some unofficial wealth redistribution. Through crime mainly, but the shadows were certainly their domain. Now night work was a way of keeping the poor down at the bottom of the heap, whilst screwing up their bodies and their social lives alike, and messing up their minds into the bargain. Body clocks askew, half of them didn't know whether they were coming or going, living or dead.

It never got as crowded as during the day, though. That was one thing I liked about the night. There was enough room for everyone after dark. They could all find their own place. And the later it got, the more room there was, so you felt capable of possessing more of the city with each passing hour, though right now it was still early, only a little after nine.

Hardly the night at all.

Fitzgerald, her sleeve now soaked with rain and her spirits equally dampened, turned with relief into the car park beneath my apartment so that we could switch rides, my Jeep for her Rover, now that the driver's seat of hers was scattered prettily with fragments of glass.

'Besides,' I said, 'my car's much cooler than yours.'

'And this is a primary consideration in law enforcement, is it, Special Agent?'

'Always was for me.'

Briefly, we went upstairs to my apartment so that Fitzgerald could use the bathroom, because the next stop for us after here was Daniel Erskine's place again and she could hardly make herself at home there with its owner lying cold on a mortuary table.

With the furniture gone, my apartment looked huger even than usual. Rain-broken moonlight cascaded in through the large windows that led out on to the balcony, and stretched out on the bare floorboards, making them glisten almost wetly. I'd slept here the night before for the last time, alone, just me and a roll-up mattress, like some cowgirl out under the stars. I'd wanted to be alone once more. Wanted to savour every last bit of it.

'I'll miss this place,' I said, as Fitzgerald rejoined me.

'You're not regretting it already, are you?' she asked.

'It's not that.'

She was unconvinced. 'You're sure you're doing the right thing?'

'Really, that's not what I meant,' I said; but maybe I did a little.

I didn't want to hurt her feelings. She might take it as an indication that I wanted away from her, whereas I simply liked having my own space. This had been my home for ten years. More than my home. It had been my sanctuary. Now I was abandoning it. Already I felt that it had ceased to be mine in some way, that it had withdrawn from me. I didn't know if we were doing the right thing, but the trick was to keep moving and not think about it too much. It would be someone else's space soon, anyway, and then I'd have to let go, whether I wanted to or not.

'You don't have to sell it,' she said. 'We don't need the money, not really. You could keep it to work in.'

'It's too big for an office,' I said. 'I'm going to get a room somewhere in town, with enough floor space for a desk, and a filing cabinet, and maybe a fold-down bed in case you're working over and I don't feel like making my way back to Smugsville in the suburbs. I already looked at a couple of places. The rent wasn't too bad. It's only somewhere to work.'

'You're *supposed* to be working with the Murder Squad,' she pointed out.

I smiled. 'I am, but you know me. I'll need to do another book soon. Besides, it's too late. I already found a buyer for this place.' A young man in a pinstriped suit, with a camera cellphone and a laptop and an over-abundance of self-satisfaction who said it was exactly the 'pad' he'd been looking forward to and did I think it'd impress the ladies. He was moving in in a few weeks and then he'd wipe all traces of me from it and it'd be just another apartment.

It was no big deal. There were millions of them in every city. People came and went. Nothing stays the same for very long any more, let alone for ever.

We stood at the window and looked out at the city.

I'd miss that view too.

From up here, I could see right down into the heart of St Stephen's Green. I knew it in all its seasons, all its moods: the slow awakening in spring, to summer, when it was crowded and the light from the water sparkled; and then in autumn when all the trees changed colour; and winter when it went into hibernation and looked stark and forbidding.

I'd miss opening the windows when the weather was fair and hearing the horses' hooves clattering round the streets, taking tourists for an over-priced jaunt. I'd miss the buses, and the trams on the Harcourt Street line terminating on the western side of the park.

I'd miss it most at night, when the city came into its own, and voices and music drifted on the air from nearby bars and restaurants, and it was only when the sound was unexpectedly switched off that you really noticed it was there. Otherwise it was as much a part of the night's soundtrack as the whirr of bats' wings or the screech of a hunting owl would be in the vicinity of an old ruined castle in some more remote part of the country.

These were my landmarks: the Shelbourne Hotel, and the glass cathedral of the shopping mall on the far side; Newman House, and the Royal College of Surgeons.

'Not to mention the charming sight of the winos relieving themselves up against the wall of the Anglo-Irish Bank,' teased Fitzgerald, who grew up in the country and had never shared my enthusiasm for the rough pleasures of the urban life, 'and the knife fights at closing time, and the periodic outbreaks of road rage beneath your window.'

'It's what the city is all about.'

'Violence and squalor.'

'What else does a girl need?'

'Look!'

On cue, the rain had suddenly ceased and the black clouds were parting. A big moon was sailing into view from behind them, filling the sky, one corner bit off by darkness.

'Now *that's* what I call a view,' she said. 'You forget sometimes what it's like to see natural things. I wonder if it's waxing or waning? I can't remember, is the moon waxing when the corner that you can't see is at the bottom or when it's at the top?'

'Who do you think I am – Copernicus? I'd have thought that was more your thing.'

'It was, once. I knew all the phases of the moon when I was a kid. Crescents and quarters. The constellations too. I used to lie in bed and watch them through the skylight. Cassiopeia. The Great Bear. Orion the Hunter.'

'And now you're the hunter in the dark,' I said.

'Don't remind me.'

But I had, and it was time to leave the stars behind. Out there somewhere was the man who killed Daniel Erskine. He was our night's prey. Where was he now? Was he afraid of what he'd done? Was he waiting nervously for the knock on the door? Or was he still enfolded in the warm embrace of the greatest pleasure of them all: that of a long-held desire finally fulfilled, and the confident expectation of getting away with it?

15

Improvisation is fatal. If there's one thing he had learned, it was that. Do. Not. Deviate. The key was always to have a plan and stick to it. A non-stick plan is no use to anyone.

He laughed at his own joke, then suppressed it. He remembered what a teacher had told him once in school: *Only a fool laughs at their own jokes.* That never really made sense to him. How can you expect other people to find them funny if you don't laugh at them yourself? Thankfully, he had always found himself infinitely amusing.

But now was not the time or place for laughter. What he was doing was dangerous enough already without drawing further attention to himself.

He was standing among the crowd of onlookers opposite the house.

The victim's house, as the press would call it now.

There must have been about thirty people there, together with reporters and cameramen. He made sure to stay well away from *them*. It was a cold night. No one questioned why he had his hat pulled low or his collar turned up high. No one thought it odd.

All of them were playing at being horrified, whilst secretly loving every moment. They wanted to be a part of it so badly that their bodies must ache from the effort of concealing the pleasure. And so they gathered, as near as they could get to the action, diverted from their normal routines by something that made their own little lives look tedious and insubstantial in comparison. And they knew it. *They knew it.* He didn't know what they expected to see, but he couldn't blame them. They were experiencing a fraction of what he was feeling, an offshoot of it, a fragment broken free of its true being and floating untethered in the night air. He couldn't blame them for finding it addictive, for all that they shook their heads and tutted and disapproved and wondered what the world was coming to.

He'd seen it in them the last time.

He'd seen it in them the first time too.

He'd see it again soon.

So he shouldn't have come, fair enough, but he couldn't help himself. There was something deliciously transgressive about being here, harbouring his secret, like being at a party where you're screwing the host's wife and the both of you are the only ones of the night's guests who know it. You've made love only moments before and now here you are, pretending all's well, and wondering why the others can't tell just by looking at you. Are they blind? Can't they see how flushed your skin looks, and how you can't stop grinning?

He wondered if *his* skin was giving the game away right now. Could they see it on his face? What he'd done? Of course not. He only had to look around to know that they had no idea. He'd got away with it. For now.

He knew it couldn't last, but it didn't have to last, that was the beauty of the plan. All he needed was tonight. That's why he wanted to savour every moment, and why he was here, dangerous as it was, watching the comings and goings his work had prompted into being.

All this fuss so easily caused! It almost gave him a hard-on, knowing that all these people were here solely because of him. Because of the things he'd done, they had cast aside whatever they were doing and come to pay homage to him instead.

At least that's how he saw it.

But he couldn't stay long. He might be noticed. He might be recognized. Once he stopped being another face in the crowd, all was lost. That's how mistakes were made.

By being careless. And the only people who failed were those who allowed themselves to entertain the possibility of failure. He wasn't one of them.

The prospect of not finishing what he'd started was enough to make him so angry he wanted to scream, to hurt someone, to strike the person standing nearest to him, to kill them. He could bear anything except not completing the circle.

Then he stopped himself, ruthlessly. Control was everything. He mustn't get angry. He mustn't seem disturbed in any way. He had to be normal. Another curious bystander, no more. He had to be invisible. So he took a deep breath, put back on the mental mask he'd constructed for tonight, and prepared to leave, pausing as he did so only to observe the arrival again of Detective Chief Superintendent Grace Fitzgerald and her absurd American shadow.

Saxon, wasn't that it? What kind of name was that?

They pulled up to the kerb in a different car from the one he'd seen them getting into earlier, then climbed out, and, without looking round, went inside.

A shiver of pleasure ran through him again at the sight of the Chief Superintendent. That woman was hot, no doubt about it, and he knew exactly what he'd like to do to her. He wondered what she'd be like in bed. What it'd be like to see that icy self-control melt into obedience and abandonment. To be honest, he was amazed that their paths had never crossed before. It wasn't the first time he'd done this, after all. He'd always expected her to come after him. And oddly, he realized that he felt no hostility towards her whatsoever.

She had her job to do, and he had his.

You could say that they balanced one another out.

Yin and yang.

Order and chaos.

Life and death.

He doubted that she'd see it the same way, but then what was it Jesus Christ said? A prophet is not without honour, except in his own country.

He knew what he was talking about, that guy.

16

Back at Daniel Erskine's house, all was quiet efficiency. There was no rush. No raised voices. The atmosphere was almost polite. There were jokes intermittently (black humour and death were traditional companions), but mostly the mood was of determined concentration, cops and technical staff both like monks almost, heads bent to the work, though meditating not on God's glory and wisdom but man's wickedness – and, the hope was, man's mistakes.

To anyone who had never been part of that world, it might seem strange, callous even, to see so many people treating the worst things that a human being could do to another with such apparent matter-of-factness, or to be so unaffected by it, as if murder was merely another day at the office. But it couldn't be any other way. Psychologically, the police needed to create a barrier between what had been done and themselves in order to survive.

Keeping the right distance was also the only way to make sure the job was done properly. Too much emotion could make you miss things. Important things.

Nothing would bring back the dead. What's done

is done. All they could do was catch the perpetrators, and make sure they couldn't do it again – or, more precisely, at least ensure there was enough evidence to bring the matter to a succesful conclusion in court, and not have the case torn to shreds by some smooth-talking defence attorney with as much concern for the truth as the lowlife scum they represented had shown for their victims. That's what was so troubling about Lester Coyle's intrusion into the crime scene earlier.

That's what the scene in front of us now was all about.

Of course, at that point we were all still killing time, as it were, before the real action began. Door-to-door enquiries were ongoing. Potential witnesses were still being sought. This then was a time for collecting, gathering, collating, analysing. Later, the threads could be drawn together, and a satisfying unity found from all the diverse elements. But until the patient, backbreaking, often soul-wearying work of gathering evidence had been completed, there could be no resolution. So that's what they were doing. Lifting fingerprints. Picking out fibres and hairs from furniture, chairs, curtains and rugs with tweezers and putting it all in bags for subsequent testing. Nothing was to be removed from the scene without being examined first, and, once it left the scene, it was essential that the legal chain of custody remain unbroken, otherwise all that work would be for nothing. Most of what the Technical Team found might turn out to be entirely innocent, but they had to treat each piece of physical material as if it was the key to the whole case. Anything that could subsequently place a suspect at the scene could be crucial to wrapping up a case.

Seamus Dalton was as far removed from anyone's idea of monkishness as it was possible to get. Square-headed, red-faced, and almost as wide these days as he was tall, the detective was a man without any discernable hidden depths – or if he did have them, they were so well hidden that even he couldn't find them. In many ways, he was the Murder Squad's yin to Sean Healy's yang. Where Healy had been supportive to Fitzgerald from the start, he had been obstructive. Where Healy had helped, he had hindered. If Fitzgerald had walked in on crutches, he'd have kicked them away. At least he would have wanted to. Only self-preservation would have stopped his foot from fulfilling his longings.

It offended him to the core that a woman should have authority over him, and, if it wasn't for the fact that he was such a good detective, he'd have been on suspension, or more likely fired, years ago for insubordination, disobeying orders, you name it.

Right now, he seemed to have taken charge of things – I didn't know where Sean Healy was – and he took it upon himself to appraise Fitzgerald of the current state of play, pointedly ignoring my existence as he did so. This was a traditional pastime for him.

It turned out that O'Neill, the cop with the weak

stomach, had recently returned from Dublin Castle, where he'd taken Coyle, the only witness so far to have seen anyone in the vicinity of the crime. He hadn't, however, brought back news of a break-through. No one had expected that he would, but the disappointment was acute all the same.

'O'Neill showed him a few mugshots. You know, villains we have on file with white Transit vans who'd be capable of a job like this. Coyle got excited about a few of them. Trouble was, two of them are in jail and one's dead. The other one's being checked out right now, but if you want my opinion your boy's eyewitness testimony is a pile of shite.'

'Just like Saxon and I figured from the start,' Fitzgerald said to me, and I appreciated the way that she kept a straight face as she neatly ruined his attempted putdown. 'Have any of the door-to-doors come up with anything more solid?'

'Nothing ... Chief.' He had to force the word out. The pain showed in his brow. 'There are a few descriptions of people seen coming and going, but none of the times match up. Besides,' and here he smiled his own secret smile, secure in the satisfaction that he could now impart some new information, 'it doesn't look as if the killer left the front way at all.'

'It doesn't?'

'It doesn't.'

In the last half-hour, the hall had been sprayed with luminol. Luminol is a chemical that reacts to the presence of blood, glowing when it comes into contact with the tiniest trace of it. Microscopic flecks had been found here leading from the hallway, where it seemed Daniel Erskine had been struck first with the poker, down to the basement, where he was lifted into the freezer, and then back up the stairs and towards the back of the house.

Dalton led the way, showing the route that Erskine's killer had taken into the bright kitchen ('There was some blood on the door handle, the boys managed to lift a partial print'), and across the black and white chessboard-patterned tiles to the back door. The key was still in the door. Either it was in the lock when he got here, or the killer knew where to find it.

'And out he went,' Dalton said.

'Are you sure it's human blood?' I said. Luminol also glows in the presence of other substances: copper, fecal matter, certain bleaches, even horse-radish.

Dalton gave me that special look he always reserved for me. The one he might give a worm that had dared to crawl out from under a stone in his presence.

'Unless the killer was crapping himself as he went along,' he snarled at me, 'I think we can safely assume that it's blood. You got any better ideas?'

I didn't bother answering. There was never any point with Dalton. Not that I'd let that stop me in the past, but at that moment I was more interested in keeping on course.

Literally, in this case.

I pulled on gloves, opened the door, and stepped out. The garden was lit up like a football stadium, showing a path, and an overgrown lawn, flanked by tangled beds of weeds.

Whatever else he was, Erskine had been no gardener.

'Was it in darkness before?' I asked.

'Before the light went on? Yeah, Einstein.'

'I meant before the police arrived.'

He nodded curtly, unhappy at having to tell me anything.

So the killer made his escape in darkness. All the better to avoid the potential prying eyes in the high windows all around. Had the garden light been on, they could hardly have missed the sight of a man running – and it was obvious from the pattern of the footprints in the wet grass that he *had* been running, not walking; it was the first sign at the crime scene of anything other than total calm and control – away from the house and down towards the far wall. Why the grass? Perhaps it had been too black out here to stay on the path.

Our man had strayed from the straight and narrow in more ways than one. That had its benefits. I could see that the police had already taken moulds of the prints.

'Size elevens,' Dalton murmured somewhere behind me.

'And shoes, not trainers.'

No ordinary burglar then – but no one had really thought it was.

At the bottom of the garden, there was a garage, where Erskine's car lay untouched, and next to that a gate. Rusty bolts had been pulled back, and then – a narrow alleyway, just wide enough for a car, running between the two blocks of houses to a street at either end. The gaps were sealed off with crime-scene tape, and a pair of matching police stood guard.

'He probably went thataway,' said Dalton sarcastically, pointing left.

'What makes you say that?'

'Because the other way leads to a busier road. He wouldn't want to risk bumping into anyone.'

'You're assuming he's familiar enough with the area to know the parts to avoid.'

'He knew what he was doing all right,' Dalton said, and for once I could find nothing in what he said to disagree with, only the fact that it was Dalton saying it. 'We'll know once we get the dogs in. We were going to bring them down to see if they can pick up the trail from the end of the entry. Depends how far he went on foot, or if he had a ride waiting.'

Fitzgerald allowed herself the slightest whisper of a sigh. She didn't need to put it into words, I knew what was bothering her. The crime scene had just got bigger.

That was one of the first things that you tried to do when you reached the site of a murder. Define the crime scene. Was it the immediate vicinity in which the victim died? The whole house? Or larger even than that? In this case, the crime scene kept getting bigger. We'd thought it was the hall. Then that expanded to include the basement. Then it was the kitchen, and the garden. Now the alleyway. And who knows how far it might stretch beyond that? We couldn't seal off the whole city, and yet how did we know valuable evidence was not being destroyed even as we stood here? Meanwhile, the alleyway was piled high with trash, and that would have to be checked in case the killer dropped something in passing, which he almost certainly hadn't, meaning more hours would be wasted. Rather them than me.

Where we were standing was almost like a metaphor for the business we were in. The foreground was expensive houses and bookshelves and wine cellars; civilized lives; a shining surface of order, stillness, stability. *Normality.* In the background lay the festering, trashy secrets that were best left hidden, the evidence of far less savoury existences, and all so close to this other world that they shared the same air. That was a variety of normality too, however distorted, but you only ever noticed it when the first facade was torn away and exposed for the hollow lie that it was. And afterwards, it was impossible to see anything else.

Was any knowledge worth that price?

17

Upstairs was Healy's domain, as it had apparently been Erskine's till a few hours earlier.

Here was the dead man's bedroom, a paperback copy of Dante's *Inferno* on the table next to the bed, bearing the same picture on the cover as he had hanging on the wall downstairs. The walls up here, however, were lined with tasteful erotic prints of a bland conformity that managed to be wholly un-erotic. Here also was a home gym, complete with exercise bike, rowing machine, weights and a tread-mill. Erskine had clearly been a man who liked to keep in shape, for all the good it did him in the end. There was also his office, taking pride of place amongst a brace of mostly empty rooms that were not even kitted out for guests, though they all displayed the same range of vaguely Greek-looking prints of semi-naked goddesses draped in silken scarves being ravished by men with muscles like Arnold Schwarzenegger. Whatever turns you on, I guess.

'Do you think they're originals?' I asked Healy.

He made a show of being offended.

'Since when was I the designated authority on dirty pictures?' he said.

'Dirty?' I echoed scornfully. 'The Pope probably has racier paintings than this hanging on his walls in the Vatican.'

'I'll take your word for it,' said Healy. 'But since you ask, Erskine wasn't exactly hard up, so I'd say they could well be worth something. Everything else in the house is.'

The dead man's office was, at that point, the hub of the investigation.

'There's no sign that the killer came up here,' he went on to explain, leading Fitzgerald and me back down the corridor as he spoke. 'Nothing has been disturbed. No drawers opened. No cupboards turned out. But if his death did have anything to do with his business life, then here's where the ripples of it are going to be found.'

Healy opened the door on a spacious room with nothing in it except a desk on which sat a computer screen, sprouting wires at its back like air pipes from a diver's helmet, and a large leather office chair on which sat O'Neill, with his chin cupped in one hand and the mouse in the other, eyes fixed straight ahead, a frown of concentration on his face as he searched methodically through Erskine's files.

Healy had clearly found a suitable channel for O'Neill's talents.

Hard drive, soft drive, floppy disk, control panel, cookies: it all meant about as much to me as goat-herding in Patagonia. And if I had to choose between the two, then it was the goats who'd win out.

'What exactly did Erskine do?' I said, because I still wasn't clear about that point. All I knew was that he was rich, but there are infinite ways of amassing money.

'He inherited most of it,' said Healy. 'Erskine Senior was a property developer who made a fortune from buying land up cheap and then bribing politicians to get it rezoned for residential and commercial development. He put up huge housing estates and shopping centres all round the city. You've heard of the Gallagher Group?'

'No. Should I have?'

'Well, Erskine was second only to them in terms of size. If Gallagher didn't own it, then Erskine did. Between them, they practically had the city sewn up. Gallagher eventually went down the pan, but Erskine had the good business sense to die at the height of the property boom in the 1990s, leaving his money equally to the two brothers, Daniel and Michael. The mother died when they were very young and there was no other family. They'd never joined their father in the business, but it was expected that they'd take over where he left off. Instead they sold up, cashed in their chips, and effectively vanished from the scene.'

'So Daniel didn't actually *do* anything for a living?'

'He dabbled,' said Healy. 'Mainly on the stock exchange. Stocks and shares, you know. He had a large portfolio of interests from Hong Kong to New York, London, Tokyo . . .'

'You sound like you know what you're talking about.'

'I'm a fast learner.'

'Was he any good?' said Fitzgerald.

'He was richer when he died than he was when he inherited his money, so he couldn't have been a total washout. And it was all above board. I've been on to the Criminal Assets people and the Bureau of Fraud Investigation, and there's no evidence that Erskine was involved in insider trading or anything else untoward.'

'Untoward? I like that word.' I rolled it round my tongue. 'Untoward.'

'Nor was he being pursued by any pissed-off clients or partners, because he didn't have any clients or partners to piss off in the first place. He was a one-man money-making operation. There may have been people who felt aggrieved with him, but he hadn't ripped anyone off. Sorry if that's the angle you were going on, Chief.'

'It wasn't,' Fitzgerald said. 'Disgruntled business associates don't generally put you in the freezer, any more than burglars do. Except in the movies perhaps. I just had to ask.'

'So that leaves . . .'

'Either someone who had another reason to want Erskine to suffer, a personal reason, or someone who did it for their own reasons and the identity of the victim was neither here nor there. Whatever it is, it has a meaning. There's a message behind it.'

'The only message I can see,' I said, 'is always remember to defrost the freezer. You never know what you'll find in there.'

O'Neill laughed, and then looked embarrassed for doing so. My tastelessness and lack of tact was tolerated. No one expected any better of me. Others were required to show more sensitivity.

'Saxon, I'd be grateful if you didn't go around corrupting the entire Murder Squad with your cynicism.'

'Sorry.'

'As for you, O'Neill,' she went on, 'you find anything in his inbox to indicate that he was expecting a visitor tonight?'

'No, Chief. It's mainly business-related. That and a bunch of people he was playing chess with online. This guy played a lot of chess.'

'Perhaps he permanently deletes the personal ones,' suggested Healy.

'Can you recover deleted emails?' I asked.

'Afraid not.'

'I thought computers kept an imprint of everything in their memory?'

'Websites, yes. They can't be permanently erased. The echo of them's always left in the system somewhere. Not emails, though. The servers keep a central database of sent messages for a certain period, but they wouldn't simply offer it up without a good reason.'

'What about the websites?' I said. 'Was he in

contact with any escort agencies who might've sent round women to try out a few of the positions in these pictures?'

O'Neill coughed to cover his discomfort.

'I haven't found anything so far. Like I say, it's mainly chess.'

'Oh well, that was a long shot too.'

Prostitutes didn't make a habit of murdering their customers, after all. It would be bad for trade. It usually happened the other way round.

But someone had a grudge against Daniel Erskine. It could be someone buried deep in his past, whose reason for hating him was so well camouflaged that all visible trace of it had disappeared. The other possibility, that he was a random victim of a killer with a motive so crazy that it could only be uncovered by chance, was too remote.

Not to mention too scary.

Was it worth calling in Lawrence Fisher at this stage? Fisher didn't believe there was any such word in the dictionary as random. To him, everything meant something, and it was his calling to discover what it was. His job description was forensic psychologist, but unofficially, as far as I was concerned, magician was closer to the mark.

A former academic whose work studying the thought processes of convicted killers had made him invaluable to police both in London, where he started out his career, and now in Dublin, where he'd moved for tax purposes, Fisher was best known to the public for his numerous appearances on screen and radio and in the opinion pages of the leading newspapers. Vain as a coot, to me he was friend, mentor and verbal sparring partner. What he didn't know about reading a crime scene wasn't worth knowing. From photographs alone, he could frequently ascertain what had been in the mind of a killer, what had triggered his rage. He could pick up discrepancies. Isolate inconsistencies.

'We'll call him in the morning,' said Fitzgerald when I suggested it to her. 'It'll wait. Even Fisher deserves a night off once in a while.'

'Then we'll just have to concentrate on the people closest to Erskine,' I said. 'Either as suspects or sources of information, they're the ones who hold the key.'

'I wonder ...' she said, and she reached down to open the drawer in Daniel's desk.

Quickly, she rifled through the pile of papers inside – financial reports, bills, newspaper cuttings – until she found what her instinct had told her to look for.

'An address book,' she said with satisfaction, holding it up like a referee in a soccer game showing a red card. 'Maybe Daniel had a better idea than Blunt where Oliver Niland was living. Let's see. McGarry ... Mulligan ... Nevin ... here we are, Niland.'

She laid the page flat with her hand so that we could all look.

The space where Niland's address should have

been written looked like a child had scribbled all over it. There must have been a dozen different addresses, each one crossed out, including the one that Fitzgerald and I had tried earlier. Oliver Niland clearly never stayed in one place for very long. Was there a reason for that, or was he simply the restless sort?

The only address that wasn't crossed out was one in Geraldine Street.

'You know it?' I said.

'It's on the northside, near the City Basin.'

'Then what are we waiting for?'

18

In all truth, it was a blessing to be out of Erskine's house, and it felt good to be on the move again. Crime-scene work was critical; where a murder happened was always the focal point of any investigation. But it could be stifling too. Some people are suited to it, but patience had never been my strong point. I was always restless to get going on to the next thing.

I'm like a shark in that respect. If I stay still too long, I die.

We drove north across O'Connell Bridge, the very heart of the city of Dublin, where the brown river surged in a high October flood under the pillars, and up O'Connell Street, past the Spire that pointed a warning finger at the threatening clouds overhead.

I took my hand off the wheel as we went, to fiddle with the dial and find the right radio station, till Fitzgerald admonished me. 'I'll give you a ticket,' she said.

'You do it then.'

She knew what I wanted to hear. The main news stations were so far only reporting that a man's body had been found in a townhouse in a square close to the city centre. They didn't even name the victim, though they must have known who he was by now.

I wondered what was holding them back. The media wasn't normally so accommodating. I wasn't complaining. The fewer details that people knew at this stage, the easier it would be to keep the situation watertight. Once too many details leaked into the open, it immediately threatened the integrity of eyewitness testimony. They started to believe they'd seen what they'd heard about on the news, not what they actually had seen. Facts become mythology. Mythology becomes fact. Soon as it became known how Erskine had died, the crank calls would undoubtedly start too. People who wanted to claim the credit for finding an imaginative method of murder.

'Where now?' I said as we came to the crossroads on Dorset Street, because I wasn't familiar with the particular address where we were headed, only its approximate vicinity, but once again I was struck by the fact that another of Daniel Erskine's friends lived in what was generally considered a less desirable part of town. There was nothing wrong with this part of the city, the houses were solid and attractive and there was no shortage of people wanting to live here; but some of Erskine's neighbours probably considered the northside to be practically a Third World township, only to be visited under armed guard and never after nightfall. Did it prove that money meant nothing to Erskine, and that loyalty to his friends took precedence? Or did he stay friends with them precisely because the comparative modesty of their means meant they were no threat? Whichever it was, I didn't have the chance to ask.

'Straight across into Blessington,' Fitzgerald said. 'But it's traditional to wait until the lights turn green in Dublin. I don't know what the custom is back where you come from.'

'I'm laughing so hard my sides're going to split.'

We followed the curve of the road round into Berkeley Street, and maybe it was what Fitzgerald had just said but the name of the street made me think momentarily of Boston, and another Berkeley Street. Strange how words can set off these associations.

An image came into my mind suddenly of the Berkeley Building, also known as Old John Hancock Building, taller even than Dublin's Spire (not that size is everything, so they say), a prominent landmark in the city that anyone who's been there must know. It has a weather beacon on top that flashes red or blue, using a code to tell people the weather forecast for the next few hours, easy to remember because of the rhyme that goes with it: *Steady blue, clear view. Flashing blue, clouds due. Steady red, rain ahead. Flashing red, snow instead.*

The rhyme went round in my head: Flashing blue, clouds due.

Flashing blue.

And so there was, filling the rear-view mirror, as a fire engine, bright with the flash of metal, came into view behind us, its siren screaming. I pulled over to let it pass, and we watched with curious fascination as it took the second left into Geraldine Street.

'Something always goes up in flames on Halloween,' I said.

'Let's leave the car here then,' agreed Fitzgerald. 'It'd only be in the way.'

So we finished the last couple of hundred yards on foot, turning into Geraldine Street to find that an earlier fire engine was already here, and a hose was discharging a sparkling angle of water towards a broken first-floor window, from which flames could be seen crackling.

I knew without looking whose house it would be.

I don't know how I knew, I just did.

'Is that—?' began Fitzgerald, but she didn't need to go any farther.

She knew too.

A terrible feeling took hold of my chest as I joined the small crowd of onlookers, who were laughing and treating the fire like part of the Halloween celebrations. I stared up at the flame-enfolded front of Niland's house, and I felt like I was going to throw up. Or was it simply the effect of the smoke? The fire, thankfully, had not yet spread beyond the house in which it started, but the air was thick with smoke all the same, billowing up and making the sky blacker than it was already, night being added to night. And also there was the noise, a rattle of machinery and a roar of water filling the narrow street and assaulting our ears, as a second hose was pulled from the newly arrived engine and its stream added to the attack on the fire's source. Then another window blew out, showering glass into the road.

A further huge bang followed, lower down this time, as the front door was forced in, and a pair of firemen wearing breathing apparatus stepped into Hell. Two figures – the house took them – they were gone. The wait was anxious until they emerged again.

They hadn't stayed inside long.

'Come on,' said Fitzgerald. 'I want to know what they found.'

'Stand back!' said a voice as we approached, betraying an understandable edge of panic, because there was always the possibility that a member of the public would decide to join in the fire-quenching and put everybody's life in danger as a result. I knew what that was like from my days in the FBI. It was incredible how often the presence of a maniac with a weapon brings people out to watch, when they should be inside with the doors locked.

And fire is even less predictable than maniacs.

He was noticeably relieved when Fitzgerald showed him her ID.

'I'm sorry, Chief Superintendent, I didn't—'

'It doesn't matter. Where's the Sub Officer?'

She meant the commander of the station from which the engines had come.

The fireman pointed to a man standing about ten feet away, talking to one of the two officers who'd just come out of the fire, their faces smudged with the effects of smoke like they'd recently been auditioning for the part in a minstrel show. They were sitting on the wall at the front of the house, taking deep breaths of air now that the masks had come off, and shaking their heads in apparent disbelief. That only increased my sense of foreboding, because they must have attended the scenes of plenty of fires before without the same effect.

What had they seen?

'For fuck's sake, what do *you* want?'

The Sub Officer stopped in mid flow as he recognized Fitzgerald's face, and he was so surprised that he didn't even apologize.

'What happened?' she said.

'There's someone inside,' the Sub Officer said.

'Dead?'

The fireman who'd been into the building nodded stiffly.

'The fire killed him?' I said.

'I don't know,' he said, his voice rough with emotion. 'He's tied to a chair in the kitchen. He's got tape over his mouth. I don't know how he died. His eyes . . .'

He broke off.

'I think he saw it,' he said.

19

It was late by the time Nat Tannar got home. It usually was. He made sure of it.

He'd told his wife he had to stay behind and finish some paperwork. That old excuse. The truth was that he simply couldn't be bothered going home. He didn't want to play with the kids, or bath them, or read them their bedtime story. He'd go mad if he had to hear another word about Postman Pat and his black and white fucking cat. He didn't want to hear their voices or see their faces at all, and he knew, if he stayed out long enough, then they'd be in bed by the time he got home. He didn't feel guilty about it. He had things on his mind. And besides, his colleagues did it all the time to their wives and saw nothing wrong with it.

Why shouldn't they? Men needed their space, that was all.

Thankfully, he only had one more night of this torture to endure and then he'd be free. Free to be himself. Life was going to get so much better. He was going to start losing weight – properly this time, he was going to get a personal trainer, work out a strict diet, everything. He was going to stop smoking too. If he was feeling really virtuous, he might even cut down on his drinking. But he'd have to feel very virtuous to do that.

Most of all, he was going to move out.

Get his own place.

He just needed to get through this evening first. He held his mobile phone tightly in his hand like it was the answer to all his prayers. He didn't want to miss the crucial call. Once that call came, his old life would be over. The waiting was killing him.

The clock was striking the hour as he stepped through the front door. Downstairs was in darkness and for a moment he wondered if anybody was in. Then he heard his wife shouting. She was bathing the children upstairs. Why were they up so late? Then he remembered. It was Halloween. They'd have been out in the garden, lighting sparklers, playing games, ducking for apples. Did they go out trick or treating? Nat didn't know. For a moment, he was seized with a sense of what he was missing. He should be with his kids. They had a right to expect him to be part of their lives. To be interested.

But the sensation passed as quickly as it came.

Who was he kidding? He wasn't made for family life.

He decided to sit silently downstairs until they were asleep, checking his phone again first to make sure he hadn't accidently put it on silent. He did that sometimes so that his wife wouldn't hear any incoming calls from Penny. Then he breathed in deeply to try and calm himself, like Penny had been teaching him. She was a yoga teacher. It was she who was urging him to get fit. 'You're not getting any younger, you know,' she always remarked brightly. Sometimes he thought she enjoyed saying it. He knew what she said about looking after himself made sense, but there were limits, and he'd never get to grips with this breathing correctly crap, not in a million years. He was still alive, wasn't he? He can't have been that bad at breathing. A drink, he decided, yes, that would calm his nerves better than oxygen.

Nat tiptoed quietly down the hall to the kitchen and, without turning on any lights, took a bottle of beer from the fridge, hoping that his wife wouldn't hear him creeping about because then she'd know he was back and he'd have to talk to her and she would see that he was tense and agitated and she'd ask what was wrong and he'd say nothing was wrong and she'd say 'Yeah, right' in that irritating way of hers. He couldn't face it.

The kitchen was littered with the remains of the children's party, half-eaten slices of fruit bread and buttered barmbrack, traditional fare of a happy Dublin family Halloween. Not even his kids could make this much mess on their own. They must have had friends round. He added it to the list of parts of their lives in which he wasn't involved.

The list got longer every day.

He walked back to the sitting room, wishing his wife would see how difficult things were for him right now, instead of bitching at him all the time, instead of making him feel bad, making him feel small. Then he jumped as his phone suddenly went off.

Now he wished he *had* put it on silent.

'Nat, is that you back?' his wife called from the bathroom.

Where was that phone? He couldn't recall now where he'd put it.

'Yeah, it's me,' he shouted.

The kitchen. That's where it was. He'd put it down on the worktop whilst he opened his beer. He walked down the hall again as quickly as he could without running. His heart was beating so fast that he thought it might explode with the pressure. He picked up the phone and felt mildly irritated when he realized it wasn't the call he was expecting.

Instead it was Penny.

He slipped out into the back garden so he wouldn't be overheard.

'You want to come round later? I miss you.'

Fuck, they were all the same. All so needy, wanting reassurance all the time that you still loved them, that you still desired them, that you still thought the world revolved around them. Nat couldn't help wondering what he was getting himself into. With his luck, it would be a case of out of the frying pan into the fire. He just wanted to get off the phone.

'I can't talk,' he said.

'Is everything OK?'

What was wrong with the woman? Which bit of

the phrase 'I can't talk' did she not understand? Struggling to keep his voice steady, he assured her he was fine, and yes, of course he loved her, and he'd see her later, he'd come round, bye, yes, bye, I have to go, bye.

He pressed the button to end the call, and closed his hand tightly round the phone. He'd keep it with him the rest of the evening. What was he thinking, leaving it in the kitchen like that? His wife might have answered it. Might have looked at his text messages.

Then he smiled. He had to admit he loved keeping secrets from his wife. He loved having affairs. He was going to miss that. Though why stop just because he was with Penny?

The world is full of available women . . .

Next thing Nat knew, his wife was standing in the doorway, glaring at him.

She was good at that. She'd had plenty of practice.

He wondered if she'd heard him talking to Penny.

'You're acting like you've done something you shouldn't,' she said, staring pointedly at his phone.

'Don't be ridiculous,' he snapped, slipping it into his pocket. 'I'm just getting a beer here, if that's OK with you. If I'd known I was going to be interrogated about it—'

'There's no need to raise your voice, dear. I can hear you perfectly well. I just thought you might want to know there was a woman here earlier, looking for you.'

'A woman?'

He tensed, awaiting the explosion.

But it didn't come.

'She left you her number. Said she *wanted* you.'

'Look, I don't know what she said, but—'

'Oh, stop looking so guilty,' his wife said, a bitter smile coming to her lips as she knew she'd got him flustered. 'Sorry to disappoint you, Casanova, but this one wasn't after your body. She was from the police. She had another woman with her too.'

Nat frowned.

'What would the police want with me?'

'How should I know? Maybe they picked you up on CCTV kerb-crawling for a new girlfriend. You should call them and find out. And if it's not too much trouble, maybe once you've finished talking to Cagney and Lacey, you can come up and say goodnight to the kids before they go to bed. Remind them what you look like, you know.'

'Very funny. I'll be up in a minute.' In his pocket, he felt the phone vibrating as a text message came through. God, what was wrong with women? They couldn't leave you alone for a second. 'And don't look at me like that,' he added. 'I had a tough day.'

'You had a tough day? What do you think mine was like?' But she was gone before Nat could point out that he couldn't actually care less about her day.

He took out his phone and went to his inbox.

Nat frowned.

It wasn't Penny, after all. But what was *he* doing sending Nat a message? They'd agreed on a call. His hands were shaking as he opened it and read the words: *Change of plan. Nothing to worry about. Meet me in half an hour at the usual place. Repeat, don't worry.*

In Nat's experience, there was nothing more guaranteed to make you worry than someone telling you not to. What did it mean by 'Change of plan'? Something had gone wrong, he knew it. Could it have anything to do with why the police wanted him?

Hands shaking, he left his beer unfinished, took his coat down off the peg in the hall, and went outside. He heard his wife calling after him, but ignored her.

He'd be able to walk there in twenty minutes if he hurried. He didn't want to drive. He couldn't risk losing his licence if he was stopped and breathalysed.

Though maybe that was the least of his problems?

Change of plan. The words haunted him. He couldn't breathe. He didn't think his legs were capable of bearing his weight. His knees felt weak.

'Be rational,' he told himself. Nothing was so bad that it couldn't be put right ...

As the message said, there was someone waiting for him at the usual place. But it wasn't who he'd expected. He felt a knot of fear tighten in his stomach. He wanted to be sick. He knew now that there were some things so bad they could never be put right again.

20

'We must stop meeting like this,' quipped the City Pathologist.

Even by Alastair Butler's low standards of humour, it was a feeble effort. But the cool reception to his banter did not dim his uncharacteristic cheerfulness.

Nor the sight of what he'd lately seen inside the house.

The fire had been doused, and its source located to the kitchen. As far as the fire brigade could tell from an initial check, a pile of papers had been left to smoulder and burn on top of the lit stove, and had spread from there up the wall to the ceiling, and then out, from the kitchen to the adjacent rooms and the ones above, until the whole interior of the house was an inferno from which the victim would surely have been unable to escape, even if he had not been tied to a chair and forced, helplessly, to watch it happening.

'You're sure he was alive when the fire was lit then?' Fitzgerald asked Butler after the pathologist had conducted a preliminary examination of the body and crossed the road on light feet to join us on the other side. It was like a new version of the old joke.

Why did the pathologist cross the road?

Because that's where the victim was.

'Can't say for sure until I get him down to the mortuary,' he said. 'If he was, then there should be carbon particles in the layrnx and trachea. And even if there's no sign of carbon, that doesn't mean he wasn't. But your fire fighter chap had it right. There *was* something haunted about his eyes. There was knowledge in them. Too much knowledge.'

'Haunted?' I said. 'It's not like you, Butler, to ascribe a property to the dead that you can't classify or quantify or measure.'

'True,' he conceded. 'But in this case, I'll make an exception. *You* didn't see him.'

I hadn't. Fitzgerald wanted to keep the scene as undisturbed as possible. The Sub Officer who'd overseen the operation to bring the fire under control could not say for certain that the house was structurally secure. Further checks were needed. Until then, he wanted to keep the number of people going in and out of the building to a minimum.

I hadn't decided yet whether to be irked at being kept out of what was now a crime scene, or glad that I didn't have to look at another corpse. Especially one in such a gruesome state. I'd seen worse in my time, but sometimes one more can be one too many.

'If it's science you want,' Butler continued, 'then there did seem to be soot in the nostrils, usually a reliable indicator that the victim was still breathing at least, if not strictly conscious. Some of the burns and blisters on his skin also appeared to have the traditional characteristics of ante- rather than post-mortem injuries. As for consciousness, there were signs that he tried to struggle to free himself. Hence my admittedly sketchy and unscientific first conclusions. Thankfully, the fire was caught fairly quickly, so the burning on the body was not too severe. Identification should be straightforward enough. Otherwise ... well, suffice to say that it might have proved a much more problematic case.'

'It still might,' I said.

'It still might,' he echoed. 'Let's not get our hopes up too high.'

'I abandoned hope long ago,' said Fitzgerald.

'Like Dante,' he replied.

'Like what?'

I was taken aback because he'd reminded me of the book by the late Daniel Erskine's bed, but he mistook the reaction and fixed me with a pitying gaze.

'The poet, Dante Alighieri, author of the *Divine Comedy*. Don't you read Italian?'

'I never had need to,' I said, playing along because I couldn't be bothered explaining. 'All the Italians I ever met could speak English better than I can.'

'That wouldn't be hard. You are an American, after all. But if you had read it, then you'd know how, in *The Inferno*, Dante wrote that, above the gates of Hell, were written the words: *Lasciate ogni speranza voi ch'entrate.*'

'Come again?'

'*All hope abandon, ye who enter here.*'

'That should be the motto of the DMP,' remarked Fitzgerald drily. 'There's certainly little enough to work with here. The flames saw to that.' There was nothing better than fire for messing up a crime scene. Eventually, the evidence could be sifted, sorted, analysed, recovered, but it all took time. It gave the hunted a head start on the hunter.

'None of the neighbours saw anyone enter the house then?' I said.

'It's Halloween,' she pointed out, lifting her eyes to encompass the length of the street, where pumpkin lanterns glowed sinisterly in almost every window, a mocking echo in their eyes of the fire which had just burned so fiercely outside. 'People are accustomed to seeing strangers wandering about on a night like this. Walking up and down pathways. There were some kids seen messing around with fireworks in the street, but in answer to your question, no, they didn't see anyone enter the house, not so far, but that doesn't mean no one did. He can't be invisible. But you know how it is. By the time we get anything . . .'

It might be too late.

The dead man's neighbours certainly hadn't seen a white Transit van parked outside the house. But the killer must have had transport. He was able to move about the city with ease and it was unlikely he was using public transport for that. Which meant he had to park somewhere, and wherever that somewhere was, he might've been spotted.

House-to-house enquiries might eventually turn up something, but it was a slow and frequently thankless business. The occupants of every house up to a five- or six- or seven-street radius would have to be interviewed and then cross-checked against the lists to make sure that no one was missed. And if our boy parked nine streets away, or eleven, then he'd be missed entirely, unless a witness voluntarily came forward to say that they'd seen such and such a vehicle in such and such a location at such and such a time. If the killer knew what he was doing, he could cover his tracks comparatively easily – at least for the time being.

And he did know what he was doing. That much was obvious from the two crime scenes so far. He used nothing that he couldn't find in the victim's own house. He carried no apparent weapons. To all intents and purposes, he appeared unthreatening to them. They let him into their homes. (There was no sign of a break-in at this scene either.)

Chances were that they knew him.

Trusted him.

That was something at least. Nothing can be more impervious to the normal tools of police work than a motiveless stranger killer. A killer known to the victim is much more likely to be caught. Still, I could appreciate Fitzgerald's frustration as she glanced at her watch, and cursed at the time.

'I'll have to call the Assistant Commissioner,' she said. 'Bring her up to speed on what's happening.

Like I have the faintest idea. You know, it's strange. *This*,' she waved at the house, 'is the last thing I expected when I was driving over here and yet I don't feel at all surprised. It feels almost . . . inevitable. Like it couldn't have been any other way.'

'You are assuming the body *is* that of Oliver Niland then?' said the pathologist.

'Until the facts say otherwise, I'm going to have to. And that means two of Daniel Erskine's circle of friends and comrades are now dead, and both by the same MO.'

'Completely opposite MOs, surely?' Butler said. 'What could be more different than ice and fire?'

'But both of them were left alive long enough to know what was happening to them,' pointed out Fitzgerald. 'At least that's what the intention was in Daniel Erskine's case, and he managed it this time. That's the link. That's what they have in common.'

'And the others?' I said.

'They'll need to be warned. Offered temporary protection, maybe. Someone certainly seems to have their worst interests at heart. They can't all be entirely ignorant of *why*.'

'I told you Michael Erskine knew more than he was saying,' I said.

'That only proves you have a suspicious mind, not that he has anything to hide.'

'Everyone has something to hide,' I insisted, but she was already punching numbers into the phone and didn't hear me.

'Including you?' Butler answered for her.

'Including me. But if you think I'm going to share my secrets with you . . .'

I left the sentence unfinished as Fitzgerald waved a hand for silence. She had her cellphone pressed to her ear. The Assistant Commissioner of the Murder Squad, Stella Carson, was on the end of the line. I seemed to remember Fitzgerald telling me earlier that day that Carson was at some conference in London on international policing cooperation and wouldn't be back in town for a few days, but I might've been wrong. Earlier that day we'd been moving house. My only thought had been for what went where and ensuring nothing got broken. Earlier that day had been part of another world. It didn't seem real in retrospect.

Fitzgerald walked up and down the centre of the road, wearing a virtual groove in the tarmac. How she could hear a word that was being said on the other end was anyone's guess. There were so many people milling about, police now added to the ranks of the fire crews, not to mention the obligatory quota of bystanders. I only caught a few words: '. . . Oliver Niland . . . yes . . . the second, possibly . . . yes . . . no . . . before morning . . . I don't know . . . there's no need, we can handle it . . . no, you stay . . . I can handle it . . . don't worry . . . he sent someone to watch over me . . . I'll think about it . . . I'll think about it . . . I'll call back later when I hear more.'

'I can't imagine a worse way to go than burning to

death,' I said to Butler as we stood in the cold, waiting for her to finish and rejoin us.

'It's certainly nasty,' Butler agreed. 'That's why they burned witches. Because what they'd done was so awful, only fire could cleanse their souls. But if it's any consolation, very few victims of house fires actually die of burns. The smoke and noxious gases get them first.'

'Pathologists obviously have a different definition of the word *consolation* to the rest of us,' I said grimly. 'You'd be useless in the Samaritans, that's for sure.'

'That's the problem with working only with the dead,' he admitted. 'You never have to develop a sympathetic bedside manner. They don't care.'

'You just need a good deadside manner instead,' I said.

'Exactly.'

'You found *what*?'

Fitzgerald's risen voice cut unceremoniously across our conversation. It didn't take a genius to guess she wasn't talking to the Assistant Commissioner any more . . .

'We'll be right over.'

She snapped shut her cellphone and returned to join us.

'Healy has something he wants to show us,' she said.

'Bet he says that to all the girls.'

It was a door. More precisely, a secret door. Now it was my turn to feel like Nancy Drew.

Where were the Hardy Boys when you needed them?

One of the crime-scene officers had found it by accident in Daniel Erskine's room when searching routinely through the wardrobe. His hand had slipped, a wooden panel had slipped in turn under his hand, and, hey presto, there it was, revealed in all its glory.

And behind it? *That* was the problem. The door was locked, and secured with an electronic combination lock that showed little inclination to be cooperative.

'All we know is that it's a seven-letter word,' said O'Neill. 'The system's straightforward enough, but without a keyword, there's not much to go on. It could be anything. FUSILLI. SAUSAGE. PANCAKE. POTROAST.'

'POTROAST has eight letters,' I said. 'You hungry by any chance, O'Neill?'

'A little,' he confessed. 'I haven't eaten. I didn't feel so good earlier.'

'Yeah, we noticed. And now?'

'Now? Fine ... I think. And I'd feel a whole lot better if we could get in here.'

'We tried everything we could think of. ERSKINE first,' Healy explained. 'Then DANIEL with an E for Erskine on the end, and MICHAEL. Tried them all backwards, forwards, anagrams. Street names, and family names, names we could see on the pictures here, or the spines of books. After that, we were just guessing.'

'Try INFERNO,' I suggested, catching the tail end of a thought that hadn't gone away and which I wasn't in the least part sure what to make of either.

'Inferno?'

'Bear with me' – and they did. But that wasn't the right word either. The door gave a smug chirrup of rejection. 'It was worth a shout,' I said with a shrug.

'I wonder what Erskine kept in there?' said Fitzgerald.

'There's no room to keep anything much, Chief,' said O'Neill. 'We measured the room next door compared to this one, and there can't be much more than two or three feet worth of space inside. It's little more than a broom cupboard.'

'Though who keeps their broomsticks under lock and key?' I said.

'A paranoid witch?' offered O'Neill with a smile.

He really had recovered.

'Whatever he has in there, I want to know,' said Fitzgerald. 'It could be crucial. Two men are dead – two men who knew each other – who, under different circumstances, should be spending the evening together right here in this house. This is where the answer will be. Either in there, or right in front of our noses out here. This is where the answer lies.'

She was right.

That is, I sensed she was right.

All crime scenes are equal, but some are more equal than others. As of the last hour, there were two in the city, each intimately connected to the other, but it was this one which was the crux. Here's where the feeling of significance was stronger. The other one was secondary. It was simply an offshoot of the first. A symptom.

'What about the other men?' I asked her.

'I've put Walsh on it. He's heading over to Blunt's place to bring him in as we speak, and then on to Mr Tannar's, if he's home yet. If we can get them down to Dublin Castle for the next few hours, answering questions, there may be a chance of finding out what this is all about.'

'Then the faster we get this baby opened,' Healy said, 'the sooner we can get home.'

Though the prospect of home anytime soon was looking extremely remote, and Healy knew it. He was simply playing the preacher, murmuring comforting words to make the righteous feel less weary. No one believed it, but they pretended that they did.

'And Michael?' I said.

'He's ours,' Fitzgerald answered.

'Lucky us.'

There was a peculiar sensation of emptiness in the streets as we walked round to his house. (There was no point taking the car, he lived so close to his brother.) It was like the city had been evacuated without our knowing, leaving only those who had nowhere else to go or who had not been considered important enough to inform of the impending disaster. Even the crowd outside Daniel Erskine's place had thinned down to the last few stragglers.

By now it was after ten o'clock, and raining again. Maybe that's what was keeping everyone indoors. That's another difference between night people and day people. Night people accept the city as it is. They don't fight the weather. They understand that the rain has as much right to be there as they do. The street lights were hazy glowing balls in the slanting streaks of rain: damp stars forming curious constellations in the surrounding dark.

'What did Stella Carson say?' I asked her as we walked.

'She seemed more concerned about our friend Leko,' she answered with a grimace. 'Said the last thing she needed was a dead Chief Superintendent on her hands. She wanted to know if I was sure about what I was doing.'

'She didn't order you to stand down tonight, though?'

'She left it up to me. For the moment. I told her I was under protection.'

'If you can call it that,' I pointed out, because we

certainly seemed to be alone in the city right now. Or were we? All of a sudden, I stopped and held Fitzgerald's arm.

'Look,' I told her.

At the far end of the street along which we were walking, a shape had appeared, something small and quick and furtive. It crossed the road to a group of municipal trash cans from which black refuse bags protruded, and lifted its legs to rest against them.

'What is it?' she said.

'Must be a fox,' I said, and it was almost like the animal had heard itself being spoken about because its ears pricked tight suddenly, and it looked around briefly, before continuing to tear at the edge of one bag, attracted by the scent of discarded food.

I'd never seen a fox before, but I'd heard them occasionally in the dead of night through the open window of my apartment. The sound of their screeching is one of the eeriest noises imaginable. There's something unearthly about it. It's a cliché, but it really does make the blood run cold. This is what banshees would sound like, if banshees were real – and, if you heard a fox cry whilst walking alone across some moor at midnight, you'd be half-tempted to believe that there *were* banshees, or worse, watching your every move.

It's too easy to forget that there are inhabitants other than ourselves sharing the city. Creatures who come out when shadow and silence make life easier for them. These snatched moments were all we had of them, and Fitzgerald and I stood watching briefly before a sudden burst of dazzling light from a car turning the corner disturbed the scene.

Its headlights picked out the fox's red blur as it sped out of sight.

A moment later, the street had returned to normal, and we continued on our way, similarly fox-like, feeling like nocturnal scavengers too, alert in our own clumsy way to what those safe behind closed doors could choose to ignore. Sometimes I envied the ignorant that ability to close their eyes to the hunters in the shadows around them. More often I pitied them. If you don't know what's out there, how can you ever hope to protect yourself against it?

22

Michael Erskine's house was in darkness by the time we got there. Not a light was showing from any of the windows except those reflecting back weakly from the street lamps.

'Maybe he's gone to bed,' she said.

'After what happened to his brother?' I said with disgust, because when someone you cared about dies in such a way, sleep ought to be as unattainable as salvation.

'There's always sleeping pills,' Fitzgerald pointed out. 'Sometimes oblivion's the only thing that works at a time like this.'

'Or he might be sleeping like a baby because he doesn't really give a damn.'

'There's that too.'

'Maybe he never even came back from the mortuary,' I added.

'That's another possibility I'm considering.'

Not that there was necessarily anything untoward, to borrow a word, if he had. When my sister died, I hit the bar in Boston, and I don't remember much of the next few days. I might not've been able to sleep, but oblivion comes in many forms. Michael Erskine couldn't be blamed if he'd done the same thing. Equally, there are always people to tell, plans to make, decisions to take, when someone dies. Michael might be telling, making and taking them as we spoke.

We looked up at the house, like the answer was there, if only we could read the signs hidden in the brickwork. There was something about that house that fascinated me, if for no other reason than that it was the exact replica of the one Daniel had lived in too, down to the same fanlight above the door, the same letter box, the same railings out front.

If we could see inside, would the decor be a match as well?

I wondered who'd been copying who.

Fitzgerald rang the bell.

Three short, three long, three short.

SOS.

'If he knows Morse code, he'll know it's important at least.'

But no one came to answer the distress call.

Chivalry sure was dead.

She was about to ring it again when I caught hold of her arm for the second time that evening, and stopped her.

'Don't say you've seen another fox,' she said.

'Not a fox, no, but there was . . .'

I couldn't finish because it was hard to say. I had the strongest intimation of being watched. That there was someone back there, in the garden square, looking across at the house and at us. I even thought

I could pinpoint the exact spot. Strangely, the thought of Leko didn't even cross my mind. What I'd sensed I'd seen was nothing like him.

I felt foolish, but that didn't stop me looking for signs of movement. Some people say the feeling of being watched is an evolutionary trait from the days when humans were prey to larger animals. You needed to know where the enemy was, or risk becoming lunch.

Spiders know when they're being watched, so why not human beings?

'It's nothing,' I said eventually, turning away and ignoring the natural nervousness you get from having your back to a room or road.

Call it a natural defensiveness.

This time, Fitzgerald didn't ring, but knocked instead – at least that was the plan. However, when her knuckles made contact with the door, it shifted slightly, and she realized it was open. Why would he leave his door open, inviting intruders?

Fitzgerald pushed it till it swung back. Dark hallway. Dark stairs. Dark corridor down to another open door leading into a dark kitchen. Again, the same layout as his brother's place, except that here there was no overturned table or smashed vase.

'Mr Erskine?' she called. 'Mr Erskine, are you there?'

'There's no one here,' I said.

You can always tell. An empty house just feels different from an occupied one.

Nonetheless, she tried again.

That was her job.

'Michael?'

The name returned only as an echo.

'Shall I turn on the light?'

'I don't know,' she said, 'it doesn't feel right being here.'

I reached over anyway and switched on the lamp on the hall table, and immediately saw a scrap of paper, roughly screwed into a ball, that had been left there next to the phone.

'Hey.'

I handed it to her. She was the Chief Superintendent, after all. If anyone had an excuse to go snooping, it was her. Wasn't that why detectives wanted the job in the first place? She took the ball of paper in her hands gingerly, and unfolded it.

The message that was revealed was made out of letters and words cut from a magazine and glued to the paper. They were of different colours, different sizes, different typefaces, but together they spelled out a simple message: *Don't try to run and don't hide I know about Erin I know about everything I'll be in touch.*

Punctuation didn't seem to be the correspondent's strong point.

It was a classic anonymous threatening note, so crude in its simplicity that it might have been made by someone using an *Idiot's Guide To Blackmail.*

But there was worse.

'Don't move,' said Fitzgerald, grabbing my arm,

and then she pointed and I saw why I wasn't to move. A couple of yards further down the hall, there was blood, and there were clumps of hair in the blood, torn out at the roots. On the wall, there was a red handprint too, smeared where the fingers had dragged against the wallpaper, and still wet.

And a little further still . . . a single tooth, pink with blood.

Something had happened in this house in the last . . . well, what? Thirty minutes?

And it hadn't been pleasant.

Before we had a chance to figure out what to make of it, however, we both jumped, startled by the sound of the telephone on the table suddenly ringing, filling the empty house.

'Shall I?'

Fitzgerald nodded curtly, and I snatched up the receiver, using my sleeve so as not to leave finger-prints.

'Hello?'

'Saxon, is that you?'

I recognized the voice at once.

'Healy? What are you doing calling this number?'

'The Chief left her phone here in Erskine's place. I sent O'Neill out after you both with it. He wanted time out to go see his girlfriend anyway. Apparently she lives in a flat in the same square as Daniel Erskine. Did he not catch up with you?'

'No.'

'For fuck's sake. Someone should tell O'Neill that

there's a time and a place for romance, and this isn't it.'

'When you're young and in love, anytime is the right time.'

'My memory isn't good enough to recall being young,' he said wistfully.

'What was it, anyway?'

'It doesn't matter. It can wait till the Chief gets back. I just thought if you were with Erskine's brother . . .' He trailed off. 'Is he there?'

'The house is empty,' I said as Fitzgerald moved from room to room, switching on lights and looking to see if there was anything to indicate where Michael Erskine had gone. 'The door was open when we got here. What's the hurry anyway? You crack the code?'

'Nothing so hopeful. Walsh just called,' Healy said. 'Blunt and Tannar aren't home. Tannar's wife says she told him when he came in from work that the police were looking for him, and then the next thing she knew he wasn't there. As for Blunt's wife, she says her husband got a call less than an hour after you were at their place, picked up his coat, and buggered off without a word as well. I thought the Chief should know.'

'I'll tell her,' I said, 'though I doubt she's going to like it. Michael isn't here either, and there are signs of a struggle.' That was putting it mildly. 'You'd better send the Technical Team over here soon as possible. The scene will have to be secured until we know what happened. By the way, you come across the name Erin in anything so far tonight?'

'Doesn't ring any bells. Should I have?'

'Ask around, it might be important. *Oh.*'

'What's the matter?'

'Nothing,' I said, 'it's just O'Neill with the cellphone.'

He was standing in the doorway, out of breath from running to catch us up, and with the smile on his face crumbling as he saw the look on my own.

'Did I miss something?' he said.

23

'Is there anything else I can do for you, sir?'

Nick Elliott – lying face down on a white table in the massage parlour where he'd spent the last ten minutes being clumsily pummelled by a Latvian girl who couldn't have been more than eighteen but looked like she'd seen it all, and more besides – sighed deeply.

He knew the sign outside the door said *Friendly And Discreet Service* (actually it said *Fredly An Dicret Svice,* because so many of the letters had fallen off since the place opened, and the owners hadn't bothered replacing them; the customers knew what they were getting for their money, they didn't need it spelled out). But why all the corny euphemisms? Elliott had heard them all in his time, from hookers on street corners who asked if you were 'looking for business' to the leaflets by the bed in foreign hotels telling male visitors where they could find 'company' for the night – or, more likely, half an hour whilst the wife went shopping.

Why didn't they just say 'Do you want a blow job, sir?' and be done with it. (The 'sir' part he liked, he'd definitely tell the girls to keep that in if he was the boss. It made you feel good. Made you feel like you were in charge, the way it should be.) They both knew that's what he'd come here for. If a massage was what he really wanted, he'd have gone somewhere they knew how to give one properly, instead of a grotty backstreet fleapit that stank like sour milk and unwashed laundry and where your shoes stuck to the linoleum.

But they went through the motions: haggling over the price, him handing it over, her counting the notes twice to make sure it was all there. Christ, some people were so untrusting. It's not like the woman was some choirgirl herself.

Then he lay back and let her get on with it, not even sure if he was relishing the sensation, or whether it was the self-loathing which he enjoyed at such moments.

Never let it be said that Nick Elliott ever passed up an opportunity for making a melodrama out of the series of small crises that constituted his existence. He could meditate for hours on what he considered his tragic misfortune. Here was a woman reduced to selling her very body to stay alive, but he was sure he was the true victim in the situation.

It was all to do with the level of expectation. That's how he saw it. She probably expected nothing better from her life. This for her was as good as it was going to get. He, on the other hand, shouldn't be where he was today. Time was he'd been somebody. People knew his name. His face and voice were familiar fixtures on TV and radio. His opinion was valued by people whose own opinions mattered. His future had been a silver path unfurling at his feet, like the Yellow Brick Road to Oz. And then it had all gone tits up, the road had veered off suddenly into disaster – and why? Because some bitch had pulled the path out from under his feet as if it was a roll of carpet and sent him sprawling.

He'd been seeing a woman, a prostitute, who'd gone and got herself murdered. That was all. It wasn't his fault. He'd even loved her in his own way. At least that's what he liked to think. It was all the more tragic that way. But no one wanted to know him after it happened. He was persona non grata. The whole untidy affair could have been kept quiet, they didn't need to drag his name into it, but the police hadn't been willing to play ball.

Instead of the successful future he envisaged, he'd had to go away. He'd gone to South Africa for a few years. Laid low. He had friends there, some family connections that he could call upon to start afresh. Slowly he'd begun to glue his life back together. He'd even had offers of work down there, good offers, but he always knew he'd come back to Dublin in the end. This was his town. He knew it inside out, back to front, every which way.

And right now, he was on the brink of the breakthrough he'd been looking for since his return. A story that would make his name again. Put him back on the map. Back on top, where he should have been all along. His rightful place. He'd been working on it for months, and now all the pieces were assembled neatly. He only had to say the word.

And that was when his worst nightmare came true. A nightmare so awful and unlikely that he hadn't even realized it was his worst one until it happened.

The massage girls had TVs in their cramped rooms, to pass the time between clients. Sometimes they turned the sound down when a customer came in. Other times they didn't even bother doing that, simply carried on watching it whilst they worked. This girl had her sound switched off, which is why he saw her. *Her.* The bitch who made it all go wrong for him. She was on the screen. Saxon. Fucking Saxon. It was dark and bulbs were flashing, but he could see her clearly, together with that other bitch from hell, Grace Fitzgerald – Detective fucking Chief Super-fucking-intendent Fitzgerald. The pair of them had ruined his life, and now there they were. Those bitches haunted him. Why the hell were they on TV?

Slowly the camera pulled back and showed the house at which they were arriving, and that's when the nightmare became horribly true.

He recognized the place at once. He'd been there often enough – not that Daniel Erskine ever let him into the actual house. By the end, he wasn't even opening the door, he'd perfected the art of telling Elliott to fuck off through the letter box. And yet there was still something in Nick Elliott that wanted to deny what he was seeing, until the rolling news scrolling across the bottom of the screen confirmed it: *The body is believed to be that of Daniel Erskine, joint heir to the Erskine property fortune. Police have not confirmed how the victim died, but have appealed tonight for information. The number to call is—*

'Shit!' barked Elliott, and he was so shocked that he sat bolt upright without warning, so suddenly and violently that he knocked his knee into the face of the young Latvian girl whose existence he'd almost forgotten in his distress at what he was seeing.

She fell heavily to the ground, and started yelling at him in what he presumed was Latvian. How was he supposed to understand? All he knew was that there was blood on her lip, and blood always looks bad even when the wound is superficial. He started apologizing lamely, trying to explain, but she wasn't exactly in the mood for listening.

Instead she screamed some more.

Before he knew it, footsteps had come running down the corridor and there was hammering at the door, loud voices asking the girl what was going on in there.

There was no point hanging around. Elliott dressed as quickly as he could, gave the girl a couple more notes to stop her moaning, then got out of the building as fast as he could, scattering apologies as he went. He could tell they didn't believe him. Why should they?

He almost ran before telling himself that running made him look guilty, and he was sweating enough already. The night air was chill but his face was hot as a sauna.

With the gratitude of a man dying of thirst in a desert, he found a bar (never a difficult thing to do in Dublin), went inside and ordered a large whiskey, drained it in one, then asked for another. He took the second one to a private booth in the corner and sat down with it. His hands were shaking so much the ice clinking in the glass sounded like music.

The world had ceased to make sense. Erskine was *his* story. Now it was going to be everybody's. He recalled how his editor had wanted to go to press last week and he'd said no, there were still some holes, some details, he wanted to confirm. He'd needed this to be perfect. It was his comeback into the big time. He didn't want to mess up.

And now who was going to care about his story any more? Erskine being dead – as of tonight, that was the real story.

Well, he knew one person who'd be interested.

That phrase on the TV about the police appealing for information came back to him. Elliott had information all right. It was the one thing he did have. And yet if he went to the police with it, he was robbing himself. He could still use what he had on Erskine, after all. Only he knew what he knew. There could still be a market for it. And there was another consideration. If he did take the information he had to the police, he'd be helping Saxon and Fitzgerald, the two women he despised more than any others in the whole city. And yet how could he say nothing when he might be the only one who knew why Erskine was killed?

Elliott ordered a third drink to help him think things through, figure out the angles. 'Shit,' he muttered again, because he remembered that he'd never even got the satisfaction of finishing what he started with the cute little Latvian, and he doubted he'd be very welcome if he went back and suggested they take up where they left off.

It just wasn't his night.

24

Irishtown didn't look any better with the passing of the last hours. The same sullen youths, probably the ones who'd put in Fitzgerald's car window earlier, were hanging around the same street corners, hoping trouble would kick off so that they could join in, not having the imagination to think of any of their own to start.

Blunt's wife didn't look any better either. Her eyes were more unfocused than ever, and her glass was full again. She'd been crying. Her eyes were laced with red cracks, and looking at them made me feel like it was my own which were stinging. There was a vacant expression behind the eyes too, as if only her body was present and her mind was somewhere else. Tina Blunt was way gone.

As she led us into the sitting room and slumped down heavily in front of a TV with the sound turned down, showing perfect happy people laughing mutely on screen, I guessed that getting any sense out of her was going to be a lengthy and trying business.

Eventually she managed to relate how her husband had received a call about a half-hour after we left. He didn't tell her who it was, only that he had to go out immediately.

'I begged him to stay but he just ignored me. He got his coat and out he went.'

She made a puffing sound with her lips and waved a hand towards the door to demonstrate the desultory nature of his departure. It wasn't hard to picture the scene: a demanding, weepy, drunken woman, the man taking no notice as she pleaded.

'Does he drive?' said Fitzgerald.

Tina shook her head.

'Did he call a taxi?'

'There wasn't time for calling anything,' she said, sounding bitter now. 'He just ... left. We were supposed to be spending the evening together. He promised. We never have any time with each other. Tonight was meant to be different.'

Tonight was certainly that, I thought grimly.

'Why different?' Fitzgerald asked. 'Because his regular Halloween night with his friends was off?'

'Friends.'

She snorted derisively, but said no more.

'You didn't like them then?'

'I wasn't allowed to know them well enough to like or dislike them,' Tina said.

'You obviously had your own opinions about them, though,' I said. 'You said earlier, for example, that Michael was different from his brother. What did you mean?'

'What?'

'You said Michael wasn't like Daniel. You said he was *human*.'

'Did I? I suppose I meant that Michael was the only one of them who didn't treat me like dirt. He talked to me.' She smiled a little flirtatiously, though in her intoxicated state it merely made her mouth look slutty. Seems she had a little crush on the older brother. 'But he was just totally under Daniel's thumb. He idolized him. He practically wanted to be him. That's why he did whatever Daniel told him to do. They all did. If he said jump, they jumped.' She snapped her fingers. '*How high, Daniel?* Wankers. It's pathetic.'

'Daniel must have had a pretty strong personality,' I said. 'Normally it's the older brother who's dominant, isn't it?'

'Is that what you call it? Strong?' She laughed blackly. 'I can think of a few other words to describe a bastard like Daniel Erskine.'

'Such as?'

'Evil, how about that one?' she said.

'Evil's a big word.'

'He didn't care about anyone apart from himself,' Tina insisted. 'People to him were just …' – she searched for a way to describe it, 'pieces on a chessboard, that's it.'

'Did that include your husband?' asked Fitzgerald.

'He was the worst of the lot,' she spat. 'Ronan never said boo to him. And if *I* ever said a bad word about him, he just told me I should be grateful for all the things he'd done for us. *Us.* That was a joke if ever there was one.'

'What did Ronan mean when he said that?'

'My husband's not the brightest,' Tina said, getting to her feet and walking carefully to the kitchen to refill her empty glass. Her voice drifted through the open door. 'Oh, he knew everything there is to know about animals. He's like David bleeding Attenborough sometimes. Bores the tits off me, the way he goes on about his work, like the things the rest of us have to say are just background noise.' She tottered back, cursing softly as the glass, which had been filled to the brim, spilled over, splashing her hand. She placed it next to her chair and sat down again, sucking her fingers shamelessly, not wanting to waste a drop. 'But when it comes to real life,' she finished dismissively, 'he hasn't a clue.'

'In what way?'

'A couple of years ago, he got into debt. Serious debt. He was gambling. Daniel Erskine used to take him and a few of the others to the casinos in Leeson Street and a couple of other illegal places too. Poker, roulette, blackjack, you name it, they were playing it. I got the impression Daniel encouraged Ronan to do it. Even when he knew he was getting in over his head, he kept calling round to the house, like a kid asking his friend if he wanted to go out and play football. He knew Ronan couldn't afford it, but I think Daniel just enjoyed seeing him getting deeper and deeper into trouble.'

'How deep did the trouble get?'

'We nearly lost the house. Ronan missed so many

mortgage payments, and he was taking out other loans against the house so that he could carry on gambling. Things got so bad they threatened to take the house away. I thought we were going to go bankrupt.'

'So what happened?'

'Daniel happened,' she said fiercely, like his name was an obscenity, like she needed to wash out her mouth with soap after uttering it. 'He bailed us out. He paid off the arrears on the mortgage, cleared Ronan's loans. Put us back,' she added sarcastically, 'on the straight and narrow. He also fixed Ronan up with a psychiatrist to treat him for his addiction.'

'Isn't that what friends are for?'

'You don't understand. Daniel loved it. I could see it in his eyes. He'd planned the whole thing so he could have Ronan right where he wanted him. His little puppet.'

'Your husband's a big boy. He had choices.'

'But he's not up to these people,' she said, 'to the games they play. They mess about with your mind, your life, they know how to manipulate everyone around them.'

It was a familiar story. Daniel saved Ronan's ass and then he was heavier in his debt than ever. More under his control. Gratitude could trap people. By saving someone, you could enslave them as effectively as if you put manacles round their wrists and ankles and threw away the key. I wondered if that might give Blunt a reason to want to get his own back on Erskine. Gratitude could easily turn to resentment, and resentment to hate.

But it didn't explain why he would want to kill Oliver Niland as well.

Or where the others were.

Or the note in Michael Erskine's house.

Come to think of it, it didn't explain anything.

Fitzgerald was obviously thinking about the note as well, because she suddenly asked, 'Did Ronan seem troubled by anything lately? Was anything preying on his mind?'

'There was always something preying on Ronan's mind,' she said, 'but how would I know what it was? He never told me a damn thing. I don't know why he married me in the first place. He hates me. He never wants to sleep with me any more. Whenever I try to touch him ...' She trailed off. She was beginning to slip off into self-pity now. She'd be no use to us there. Fitzgerald took control hastily before we lost her for ever.

'Where was Ronan when he took the call?' she said.

Tina glanced up with a start, like she was emerging from a dream and had forgotten we were there.

'In his office,' she said.

'We need to take a look,' said Fitzgerald, making it a statement rather than a question so that there was less chance of her objecting. Tina Blunt was a woman who needed firm direction. Ambiguity simply confused her.

She got to her feet immediately and led the way back into the narrow hallway through which we'd come and then opened the door into a cramped closet-sized office, with barely enough room for the table, chair and filing cabinet it contained. It was devoid of decoration, save for a calendar on the wall showing his appointments for the month.

Without another word, Fitzgerald began to sift through the papers on his desk, whilst I opened the top drawer of the filing cabinet and commenced my own search.

Most of the stuff in here was of little relevance to tonight's business (at least, I couldn't see how it could be): academic quarterlies from the exciting world of zoology and museum studies, photocopied articles, pictures, correspondence from colleagues at various other institutions. There was certainly no sign of a threatening note. Though what did I expect – that Blunt would have it filed meticulously under B for Blackmail?

The only thing of interest was a framed photograph in the bottom drawer, showing a smiling group of men in black tie and dress suits lined up at some party. It must have been taken twenty years earlier, but some of the characters were unmistakable.

First there was Michael Erskine, then Blunt, and Daniel, with his arm draped protectively or proprietorially, however you wanted to interpret the gesture, around Ronan's shoulder. Next to Daniel stood Nat Tannar and Oliver Niland – Blunt's wife identified them; it was the first time I'd seen Niland's face, and I wasn't looking forward to seeing it a second time, if that was indeed who'd died tonight in the fire at his house. Finally, there were another two men standing on the end of the line that I didn't recognize either.

'That's Toby Fraser,' Tina Blunt said, pointing to the man second from the end. 'He was one of the group too.'

'Was?'

'He died about five years after that picture was taken,' she said. 'I'm not really sure of the details, but he died just as he was about to move to America.'

'You know how?'

'No. He was killed or something.'

'And the guy next to him?' I said.

'That's Sean Riordan,' she said, as though we ought to have known who it was without being told. 'He's a composer, and a musician. Plays the violin. He has his own string quartet. They do concerts.'

'He's one of Daniel Erskine's group too then?'

'Yes.'

'He goes to their gatherings, Halloween and Friday nights?'

'Yes.'

Then why hadn't Blunt mentioned him in his list?

'Do you know where we can find him?'

'I think Ronan said he was playing a concert tonight. I really couldn't say.'

Tina looked again at the photograph. It seemed

to make her melancholy in the way that old photographs do. It's seeing people as they were when they were young and full of promise, not washed-up and middle-aged and disappointed. There they stood, young guns thinking they could take on the world. Now three of them were dead.

Three at least, that is.

'We're going to need this,' said Fitzgerald briskly, taking back the photograph. Then, when Tina looked alarmed, she added in a gentler voice: 'Is that OK?'

Tina nodded thickly. 'Of course . . . if you . . .'

Fitzgerald prised open the fasteners at the back of the frame and slipped out the picture. That's when she noticed the handwritten words on the back.

The Second Circle (c) DR M NOTT.

'Who's that?' I said.

Suddenly Blunt's wife looked hostile again.

'Don't say you've never heard of the great Dr Nott?' she said. 'That's practically all I do hear about sometimes. I've never met him, but I think he works at the Dead Zoo. My loving husband never introduces me to any of his colleagues. He's ashamed of me. I'm not good enough for him. Ronan's always talking about him. How he has to work late because Dr Nott asked him, or stay up late writing some report instead of coming to bed with me because Dr Nott needs it for the morning. I didn't know they knew him back then, though . . .'

She frowned, seemingly bewildered by how little she knew of her own life.

'You will find Ronan, won't you?' she said. 'You'll bring him back to me? I don't think I could cope without him.'

I don't know which was more pitiable: that she needed so badly a man who seemingly had such contempt for her, or that she wanted one she so clearly despised in return.

25

Names, names, names. And now there were three
more to add to the puzzle. Toby Fraser. Sean
Riordan. Dr M Nott. Or was it D. R. M. Nott? The
punctuation didn't make it clear.

Fraser wasn't so important because he was long-
since dead. But what about the other two? Ronan
Blunt had said nothing about this other member
of the group. Was that because he only mentioned the
people who were supposed to be there tonight? Had
he taken Fitzgerald's request for a list of Daniel's
friends too literally?

And who was Dr M Nott?

It didn't take long to establish that there was no
Dr Nott working at the Natural History Museum,
or in any other of the national museums which were
clustered round the same area of the city. Nor had
there been any academics with that name working at
Trinity at the time the men in the Second Circle went
to college. The telephone directory only showed a
handful of Notts in the city, from Sallynoggin to
Ballybrack. There was also a haulage firm with the
same name. But none of them were listed as Dr, and
none of their first names began with M. Of course,

Nott may have lived outside the city, or be listed under a different name for some reason; or the M mentioned may have been the spouse of one of the listed Notts.

Whatever the answer, there seemed little profit in pursuing that avenue. It was Riordan who was the crucial part of the triumvirate. He might know what was going on, and for once we knew where he was. A quick call had confirmed that he was playing a late recital at the National Concert Hall. It hadn't finished yet so there was still time to find him.

I drove us round there in the rain, whilst Fitzgerald spoke to Patrick Walsh on her cellphone to find out how he'd got on at Tannar's house. She put it on to the speaker so that I could hear what he had to tell. It turned out he had another new name to throw in the mix: Penny Nightingale. Apparently, she was Tannar's girlfriend, mistress, other woman, casual screw, whatever the linguistically correct name was for her role in his life.

Tannar's wife had eventually provided the girl's name, though it took plenty of coaxing to wrestle it from her. She knew Penny Nightingale's address and phone number too. She confessed she'd been round there a number of times when she suspected her husband was inside. She used to bring her kids with her and let them eat ice cream in the car whilst she looked up at the closed curtain in Penny's bedroom. Love makes fools of everyone indeed.

These women had a lot in common, it occurred

to me, Blunt's wife and Tannar's. Both seemed to define themselves entirely in relation to the men who shared their beds. They had no inner resources at all to protect them against the damage caused by their husbands' errant ways. They should dump the pair of them and move on, though I doubted that they would.

Walsh was round at Penny Nightingale's now. She'd confirmed that Tannar was meant to come round to her place that evening, but he'd never arrived. She was furious with him. And no, she didn't have any idea where he was. Tannar had certainly never mentioned anything to her about being blackmailed, any more than he had to his wife.

But that was the point about blackmail.

You kept it secret.

Walsh said he was nearly done and he'd meet us back shortly at the National Concert Hall. There were just a couple of things he wanted to go over with her. And if the guy's past record was anything to go by, he was probably offering to fill in for the missing man . . .

I pulled up to the kerb in Earlsfort Terrace, directly in front of the National Concert Hall, and we got out, looking up with undoubted pleasure, despite what else was on our minds, at the grand old building which was lit up like a palace in a fairy tale.

Indeed a palace is what it once was — or what it was once called, at any rate. The Exhibition Palace, to be precise, setting for the Great Exhibition of

1865, though for many years in the last century the building was used by University College Dublin before the scholars headed for the suburbs, leaving free the perfect venue for a concert hall.

We climbed the steps and walked in between the huge grey stone pillars of the front entrance, where Fitzgerald promptly introduced herself to the manager in charge. Like the prospect of being executed in the morning, the arrival of a Detective Chief Superintendent of the Murder Squad has the wonderful effect of concentrating the mind. The manager assured us he would get word to Riordan as soon as the concert was finished.

It wouldn't, he assured us, last longer than another ten minutes.

'He's still here then?' I said.

I'd half-expected to find that he too was no longer in the building. Everyone else had gone AWOL that night – Erskine, Blunt, Tannar. None were answering their cellphones. Under different circumstances, I might have suspected they were in this together, that they were together right now, planning their next move. But tonight I wasn't so sure. I had a bad feeling about the whole matter, made more intense by the signs of violence in Michael Erskine's hallway. A feeling of dread that something awful was underway and that these men were potentially as much the victims of it as Daniel Erskine and Oliver Niland.

Maybe finding Riordan where he was supposed to be would be our first break?

In the meantime, the manager ordered coffee for us, and we sat in the bar, waiting.

To pass time, I picked up the programme for the evening's show which had been left on the seat. No, not show. Recital. I stood corrected. The Riordan Quartet were performing three works. Two by young Dublin composers whose names were unfamiliar to me, one of which came saddled with the irritating title *The Eclecticity Generator*, and a third by another composer whose name was equally obscure: Alban Berg's *Lyric Suite*, featuring soprano Aisling O'Hare. I don't know much about music – Cole Porter is as classical as my tastes ever get – but I figured Alban wouldn't exactly be thrilled to find himself on the same bill as a man who thought coining a pun on the word electricity made him a major artist.

Idly I began to check out the programme notes.

'People were sure screwed up in those days,' I said as I read.

'What days?'

'The nineteen twenties,' I told her. 'That's when Berg wrote his *Lyric Suite*. You know the story behind it?'

'Not off the top of my head.'

'The composer was married, see? But then he met this woman called Hanna and fell madly in love with her.'

'Don't tell me. She was married too?'

'Her husband was an industrialist, so you can hardly blame her for falling for the romantic charms of an Austrian composer instead. But they couldn't get divorced, and the only way they could communicate was by secret notes. In the end, they had to resign themselves to being apart. He was so miserable he used to wander the streets at night, drunk.'

'He should've waited for Tina. Sounds like they were made for each other.'

'I thought I was supposed to be the cynical one?' I said.

'Your bad habits must be rubbing off on me,' she said. 'Don't mind me, I'm not really knocking your new interest in high culture. Makes a pleasant change. I just wish Riordan would get a move on in there.' She glanced over her shoulder impatiently, but the door into the recital room remained firmly shut, mocking her.

'You know what the Supremes always said: *You Can't Hurry Love.*'

Alban Berg certainly hadn't. It took him over a year to write his *Lyric Suite*, and it only lasts a half-hour. What fascinated me was how he had, according to the programme notes I was reading, encoded the unspoken story of his passion in the music, taking the initials of both their names and repeatedly using the notes they represented in the piece. He was telling the world of their love without letting slip a word of the hidden truth. Secrets and mysteries: the inner language behind all human behaviour. Nothing had changed much.

By now, however, I was growing anxious too.

Stand still too long and you just become a part of the scenery. It wasn't only the closed door that was mocking us, but the clock as well. Our surroundings were so startlingly at odds with the way the evening had been so far. On one side there was this outward civility and peace. Only a short way across town, there was fire and ice, and murder. How could two such extremes exist side by side?

How did the first world not get hopelessly corrupted by the second?

And yet I couldn't deny that it was the second world in which I felt most at home – or at least as much at home as I felt anywhere. Fitzgerald belonged to the first, and her only desire was always to restore it. As for me, I couldn't help thinking something was missing when I was in the midst of normality and order. That it was nothing but a pretence.

That's why she fitted in here, and I didn't.

I took a deep breath, suppressing my negative thoughts. Riordan would be out shortly, and then ... Well, and then? A feeling of weariness overcame me. That was another reason for not stopping. Inactivity bred doubt. The night stretched out before us, and nothing now made sense. It was always the same. Everything could be cured by one person simply telling the truth. That's all it took. That's all it ever took. But it so rarely happened that way.

Instead there were lies and evasions and obfuscations, and the truth had to be chipped away at methodically like a sculptor cutting with a chisel at a stubborn block of stone, trying to release the shape within. It's just that the shapes we released were more often hideous than harmonious, and you couldn't help wishing they'd stayed trapped in the rock.

'They're done,' said Fitzgerald quietly.

And so they were. The door had opened, and gradually people started to trickle out of the recital room and make their way respectively to the bar or the exits.

Fitzgerald rose to her feet as the manager appeared again, leading Sean Riordan across the lobby towards us. I recognized him at once from the photograph in Ronan Blunt's office. He was older, greyer, his face more worn, and he'd filled out round the middle more than a little in the intervening years, but the eyes betrayed the same keen intelligence.

'Mr Riordan,' said Fitzgerald. 'Thank you for seeing us.'

Like she'd have given him any choice.

She waited till the manager had left us alone before continuing, keeping her voice low so that we wouldn't be overheard. Curiosity didn't only kill the cat, it had also ruined many a promising interview with suspects and witnesses alike.

'There's something we have to tell you,' she said to him. 'I don't know if you're aware of it, but Daniel Erskine was killed earlier this evening.'

Riordan didn't flinch.

Not a muscle.

He simply said absently: 'Are you sure?'

His response was so unexpected that for a moment Fitzgerald was lost for words. So much for reactions to the news of premature death usually being predictable.

'I assure you we wouldn't be here if we weren't,' she replied at last. 'His brother, Michael, identified the body.'

'Fair enough,' said Riordan. 'If Michael says Dan's dead, that's good enough for me. But I still don't see why you came here to tell me that. Who did you say you were again?'

'We're from the Murder Squad,' said Fitzgerald.

'The Murder Squad,' he repeated, as if the information was only now seeping into a brain that had spent the last hour and more wrapped in Alban Berg and eclecticity and was reluctant to let go. 'You mean it wasn't an accident? You mean Dan was . . .?'

'Murdered, yes.'

This time there was no confusion in his response.

'Good,' said Sean Riordan.

26

To catch a man that cool off guard, you have to be quick. Fitzgerald didn't hesitate. 'Does that go for Oliver Niland too?' she said, her voice hardening in reaction to Riordan.

'Sorry?'

'Oliver Niland was killed earlier tonight as well,' she said. She left a pause to let the information sink in. 'He burned to death at his house in Geraldine Street.'

Riordan didn't look so satisfied any more. He was either a very good actor, or the news of Niland's death had caught him totally unawares. He slumped down into a chair and stared at us, massaging his forehead roughly with his fingers like it was sore.

'Why – why would anyone—?'

'We were rather hoping you could throw some light on it.'

'Me? How should I know?'

'They were your friends—'

'Oliver was my friend,' he interrupted firmly. 'Daniel was not my friend.'

First Tina Blunt, now Riordan. It didn't seem like Daniel Erskine was the most popular guy in Dublin.

Drawing up a list of likely suspects wasn't going to be a problem.

It was narrowing it down which could prove tricky.

'Then let me put it another way,' said Fitzgerald. 'Can you think of a reason why anyone would want to kill them?'

'I can think of a million reasons why people would want to kill Daniel Erskine,' he said. 'He was not a good person. He was smart, he was shrewd, he could be amusing company when he was in the right mood. You could even say he was charismatic in his own warped way. But he didn't have a decent bone in his body. But Oliver?' He shook his head vigorously. 'No one had any reason to want Oliver dead.'

'Someone did,' I said.

He still seemed unwilling to accept it.

'It couldn't have been an accident?' he suggested.

'It was no accident,' said Fitzgerald starkly. 'He was deliberately left to die. Besides, wouldn't it be a bit much of a coincidence for him to be *accidentally* killed in a fire in his own home on the same night that Daniel Erskine was deliberately killed in *his* home as well?'

His silence acknowledged the truth of what she was telling him.

'Can I ask how Erskine died?' was all he said in answer.

'That doesn't matter at the moment,' she said. 'The cause of his death is being kept quiet for operational purposes. The details will be released in due course.'

'Can you at least tell me what time?'

'He was killed, you mean? Until the autopsy's completed, it won't be possible to state a time of death with any accuracy. But not long after five.'

'Five o'clock,' he echoed softly, and he seemed to be making a sort of calculation in his head. You could almost hear the whirr of clockwork behind his eyes.

'Naturally we need to ask what you were doing at that time.'

'Five o'clock ... I was here probably.'

'Probably?'

'Probably,' he repeated, but his mind was far away, and the answers had become formulaic. 'I'm usually rehearsing around that time. The rest of them ...'

'The rest?'

'The quartet,' he explained. 'They'll be able to confirm where I was.'

'We'll be asking them,' she confirmed.

'Do you really have to bring them into it?'

'When someone is murdered, the police need to know the whereabouts of everyone who was familiar with the victim. It's purely routine.'

Fitzgerald even managed to say it like she meant it.

'That's what you people always say,' Riordan answered testily.

'You sound like you have experience of being questioned about murder,' I said.

'If you've done your homework properly, then you'll know that I have. When Toby disappeared, it was the same. The questions went on for weeks.'

I exchanged furtive glances with Fitzgerald. Disappeared? Tina Blunt only said he died. I wondered if she knew the details of what happened either. I couldn't believe that, in the drunken state we left her, she was up to the finer points of deception.

'Your little group doesn't seem to have much luck, does it?' said Fitzgerald, betraying nothing of her surprise.

'What little group?' he said scornfully.

'The Second Circle,' she said. 'Surely you haven't forgotten them already?'

And she pulled out the photograph she'd taken from its frame in Blunt's house, and laid it flat on the table in front of him.

'Oh, *that* little group,' he said when he saw it. 'Well, when you put it like that, I suppose it doesn't look good.' He picked up the photograph and stared at it a long while. 'We all look so young. How time flies when you're having fun,' he said sardonically.

'Why did you call yourselves the Second Circle?' I asked him.

He looked faintly embarrassed as he answered.

'It was Daniel's idea. Most things we got up to in those days *were*. It came from Dante. You know, *The Divine Comedy*? The Second Circle was the place in Hell where they put all the people who were dedicated to pleasure, to satisfying their own appetites.

The wanton and the lustful. The carnal malefactors, I think Dante calls them.'

The Italian's name was certainly coming up regularly that night.

'Charming view you had of yourselves,' I said caustically.

'It was youthful bravado, nothing more. We'd go out drinking all night, come home with the dawn. We thought we were the most decadent people on the planet.' He shrugged self-deprecatingly. 'It was all a long time ago.'

'And yet you still all meet up again every Friday, and Halloweens to boot, to relive the old days.'

'They do. Not me.'

'Why not you?'

'I told you before. Erskine was no friend of mine. I had no desire to spend my free time with him. We both learned long ago to keep a healthy distance between us. If only the others had done the same.' He looked again at the photograph. 'Poor Niles,' he murmured.

'Niles?'

'That's what we called Oliver,' he explained. 'He hated being an Oliver. He preferred Niles, from his surname Niland. That's how we first met. I overheard him at university telling some girl he was chatting up how he hated being called Oliver, and I jumped in and told him how I never used my own name too.'

'You hated being called Sean?' said Fitzgerald.

'Sean's my middle name,' he said. 'My real name is Tybalt, if you can believe that. My parents must have had a peculiar sense of humour. I think they thought it sounded grand, whereas of course everyone at school just thought it was hilarious. I never heard the end of it. So as soon as I could, I made sure everyone who knew me called me Sean instead.'

'What about the girl?' I said.

'I'm not following you.'

'The one that Oliver Niland was chatting up. Did he get lucky?'

'Not exactly. I ended up marrying her. Simone. My first wife. She's dead now too. Poor Niles,' he repeated, and he reminded me of Tina Blunt, expressing sympathy for Michael when she first heard the news about his brother. Seemed like we'd be kept waiting a long time for anyone to show any sorrow for the younger Erskine brother's passing. 'He never did have very much luck. He always seemed to come out second best.'

'Aren't you worried?' asked Fitzgerald. 'Half the people in that picture are dead. Two of them died tonight alone. Someone certainly seems to have something against you.'

'What can happen to me with you sitting here?' he replied. 'There's safety in numbers, isn't that what they say? I can look after myself anyway. You've no call to be concerned about *me* coming to any harm.' But he was silent for a while, as if calculating the odds. It was like he was considering how much he could say. Or should say. 'It just doesn't make any sense,' was all he managed to produce in the end. 'None of it.'

'Then you ought to know that there may be worse to come,' said Fitzgerald. 'Three of the other men in this picture have gone out of contact since the two victims died.' She pointed them out on the photograph, one by one. 'Michael Erskine, Ronan Blunt, Nat Tannar. We don't know where they are. You are the only one left.'

'Who did you say had gone missing?' he said with interest.

Fitzgerald pointed them out one by one again.

'Michael Erskine, Blunt, Tannar.' She prodded a finger on to the image of each one. 'And if you have any idea where they might be ... what might have made them vanish ...'

Riordan didn't answer. His face was set in deep concentration. I watched him intently. Something had made things clearer to him than before, but what was it? There was almost a smile on his lips. Like he knew why they'd all upped and walked out into the night.

Like he knew where they were.

But before I could ask him any further questions, Patrick Walsh walked through the door of the concert hall and stood in the lobby, looking around a little awkwardly.

I guess, like me, he'd never been here before.

'Walsh.'

Fitzgerald summoned him over, and he looked relieved. He'd found his reason for being here once more. He bent down when he reached her chair and whispered something in her ear, and she nodded in return, taking in what he had to say but giving nothing away.

'Who's Dr Nott?' she said when Walsh was done.

'I beg your pardon?' said Riordan.

'Nott,' she said, and this time she turned over the picture so that he could see the writing on the back. 'His name's right here. He took this photograph. And Detective Walsh here tells me Nat Tannar's girlfriend received a text message from him whilst he was there tonight, saying he couldn't make it because he had to go meet the good doctor.'

I took it all back about Walsh. He might keep his brain in his pants half the time, but for the other half he was no slouch at his job. Despite my prejudice, he *had* managed to get more out of Penny Nightingale than her phone number and a date for the weekend.

'I'm tired of answering questions,' said Riordan in reply. 'If you want to know anything from me, you can go through my solicitor. I've had enough for one night.'

He rose to his feet.

'Where do you think you're going?' said Fitzgerald.

'Home sounds good.'

'We're not through asking you questions yet.'

'Are you arresting me?' he said.

'Why are you being so difficult? No one mentioned arrest except you.'

'Then I'm free to go?'

'If that's how you want to play it,' she confirmed. 'You know where the door is. I only hope you'll feel as satisfied with your decision tomorrow morning when your sponsors are reading on the front page of the national newspapers that you're wanted for questioning in relation to the murder of two men in the city tonight. Running a string quartet can't be cheap these days. It'd be a shame if people got cold feet about putting money behind the Riordan Quartet because of a bit of bad publicity, especially when it could be so easily avoided . . .'

'Are you threatening me?'

'Sir, I am shocked that you could even make such an allegation.'

He stared at her hard for a long time but her gaze back was equally unyielding.

'What do you want?' he said.

'Just come down to Dublin Castle with us to answer a few more questions. Tell us what you know. Tell us who Dr Nott is. It's for your own good. We don't know why two members of your circle have been killed, but I'd rather not take any chances. Would you?'

He conceded defeat. He clearly wasn't happy about it, but the prospect of being thrust from the quiet world of the National Concert Hall into the harsher and less forgiving arena of the national media was more of a risk than he was willing to take.

'Very well,' he said a touch sulkily. 'Have it your own way, if you think it'll do any good. But I'm telling you now that you're wasting your time.'

'That's a chance I'm willing to take.'

'Then I'll get my coat. And can I go to the loo first, at least?'

'Of course you can, sir. We're not the KGB.'

'I'll be right back,' said Riordan, and we watched in silence as he crossed the lobby and turned down a corridor towards the men's room, leaving his violin behind, propped in its case against the chair, better than a hostage at ensuring his return.

'You'd better go after him,' Fitzgerald said to Walsh.

'Right.'

He followed Riordan.

'There's another one who knows more than he's giving away,' I remarked. 'And don't bother calling me paranoid this time. You thought so too.'

'He's holding out on us,' she agreed. 'But that doesn't mean you're not paranoid.'

'They're the paranoid ones. Why are they all being so coy? That's what I don't get,' I said. 'Is whatever they have to hide really worth dying for?'

'Until we know what it is they've got under wraps, we can't possibly say. Some things are worth dying for, aren't they? What they're hiding might be too.' She checked her watch. 'What's keeping him so long in there? And they say women take too long.'

'Maybe he can't go with Walsh looking over his shoulder,' I joked.

Fitzgerald took out her cellphone and jabbed in Patrick Walsh's number.

Listened.

Frowned.

'No answer,' she said. 'Why is there no answer? There shouldn't be no answer.'

She got to her feet and followed the path down to the men's room, steps quickening as she neared it. I caught up with her as she started knocking on the door.

'Walsh, what's going on? Walsh?'

When there was no answer, she didn't waste time shouting a second time, she simply pushed the door to open it, but it wouldn't open, it was locked tight. She put her shoulder to the door and shoved hard against it. There was a small give but it held firm.

'Together,' I said.

On the third attempt, the door crashed open with a sound of splintering.

Inside the men's room, Walsh was lying on the floor, eyes shut, blood trickling from a wound on his forehead. The room was cold, mainly because of the wind coming in through the open window above one of the toilet cubicles. So much for leaving the violin as surety.

Tybalt Sean Riordan had made a run for it.

27

The sea was wild tonight. Or was it always this fierce? Spumes of black water, flecked with white that might have been foam or might have been reflections of shattered light, crashed with irregular monotony over the wall that divided the Strand Road from the stretch of low strand itself, now buried in water. A few brave souls were walking, some with dogs, some with others, but Leko was the only one walking there with a gun.

He caressed it with his fingers, where his hands dug into his pocket. There was something almost blasphemous about the feel of the metal, cold as a crucifix next to his skin. From the age of thirteen, this had been his answer to the long-bearded, murmuring priests of his childhood whose prayers and confessions had done nothing but keep those among whom Leko grew up in poverty: weak, exploitable, despairing. He'd determined then that he wasn't going to be one of them. He'd escape. He'd survive. Whoever said power comes from the barrel of a gun had not been far wrong. There was happiness there too, Leko might've added.

Earlier that evening, after he'd taken the package away from the drop-off guy and hurried to some quiet place where he could unwrap it without interruption, he'd felt again the shiver and thrill of his first gun, all those years ago. The memory was always there.

Soon as he had it in his hands, he felt better. He was in control of his own destiny now. After years behind bars, at the whim of authority, of barked commands and arbitrary restrictions, he began to feel anew the sensation of being his own master.

He wasn't going back. That much he knew without contradiction.

He paused a while at a bus shelter nestled up against the sea wall, seeking an excuse to stop and take his bearings without attracting attention. Leko wasn't so familiar with this side of town, but he knew where she lived. He could see the turning off the main road that led into the small housing development. Half a dozen identical houses, semicircled around a small cul de sac like card players around a table. Well-kept gardens. Paintwork kept up to date and spotless. Curtains opened and closed at all the correct times.

It was the kind of place Allenka would have liked them both to settle down, with him driving off each morning in suit and tie, home at seven, dinner on the table,

Fuck that. Leko wasn't made for that kind of life, and, if she'd been honest, she'd have admitted that neither was she. She'd just let her brain get ahead of itself, dreaming up fantasies whilst he got his hands dirty to give her the things she wanted.

And look how she'd repaid him.

Leko felt his fingers tightening on the gun, and controlled himself. Gritted his teeth till it hurt. Why was he thinking of Allenka at a time like this?

But secretly, Leko knew why. It was because he'd been denied the satisfaction of being there when she died. He'd had to leave that job to someone else. It wouldn't wait for him to get out of jail, and it never crossed his mind at that time to risk breaking out to do it himself. It was only now that he had nothing to lose that he'd taken such a chance.

So now he was going to relish what was to come. It had to count twice. Fitzgerald would give him the sense of fulfilment that he'd been denied with Allenka.

He left the bus shelter and walked round the block a couple of times before he was sure there was no one watching the estate. He hadn't expected it to be so easy, but he wasn't complaining. He was certain Fitzgerald would be there. He'd done his research; he'd had men staking out the place for weeks, checking out her comings and goings. Unless something had happened at the last minute to call her away, she'd be home right now, a sitting target.

He made his way round the back, and hopped the fence of the house next door. Through French windows, he could see a family gathered round the TV screen, the remains of an earlier Halloween party scattered across a kitchen table: bottles, cakes, an extinguished pumpkin, black and orange balloons.

The detritus of domesticity. It made him feel sick.

He crossed the garden quickly, no one saw him, and scaled a second fence into the policewoman's darkened driveway. As he did so, a light, activated by his movement, clicked into life. *Shit*. Why hadn't his own people told him about this? He tensed, waited.

No one came. Maybe she hadn't noticed the light switching on. Or maybe she just presumed it was a stray cat which had activated the mechanism. Either way Leko realized he'd had a lucky escape. But still he didn't continue. *Something was not right.*

There was a car in the driveway ahead of him, but it was an SUV. Looked brand new too. Grace Fitzgerald drove a ten-year-old Rover. Had she traded it in for a new ride?

Or was someone else here as well?

Leko grinned in the dark, his humour as malicious as his thoughts. Downstairs was in shadow. Upstairs he saw a light shining on the landing. He was imagining the scene now if he broke in on her whilst she was in bed, getting it on with her girlfriend. He knew all about her. He'd done his research. He hadn't figured on getting to shoot the bitch whilst she was buck naked, but how funny would that be? Of course, he'd have to shoot the girlfriend too.

Buy himself some more time to get away.

Sorry, girl, but business is business.

He tried the back door quickly. Locked. Well, he'd anticipated that. The French windows then. They were never up to much, security-wise, in these new houses; and you didn't get to Leko's position without picking up a few tricks along the way.

It took only seconds, and he was in. He left the door slightly ajar, then turned to look at the room – and once again he got the same feeling that something was wrong.

There were packing cases all around the room – and children's toys in clear plastic bags. Fitzgerald didn't have any children, far as he knew. Or was this something else they'd forgotten to mention? Stanic was going to be in deep shit if this whole thing went wrong at the last moment because he hadn't done his homework properly.

Struggling to stop his building frustration from seeping out and ruining everything, Leko stepped silently to the fireplace. There was a row of greetings cards lined up along the shelf. He lifted one and read the message inside: *To Bob, Pat & kids, best of luck in your new house.* Fuck, Stanic was going to be so dead for this. What the hell was going on?

Was he in the wrong house?

Had Fitzgerald *left*?

Leko was just wondering what to do next when the decision was taken out of his hands. The door swung open, he'd been so lost in his own thoughts that he didn't hear anyone approaching, and now the light came on too, and there, framed in the doorway, was a woman fresh from the shower, bathrobe loosely tied, white towel wrapped around her wet hair.

The smile of contentment froze on her scrubbed pink face when she saw him.

She didn't even have time to scream. Leko lifted the gun and fired. Instinct had taken over. Stanic hadn't even thought of arranging a silencer. No fucking initiative, that was his problem. The air exploded with the sound, startling even him and stopping him from firing a second shot. He saw the woman drop heavily, and he was running before she hit the floor.

He didn't recall the fences, but he must have scaled them, because now he was back on the Strand Road, and then he was off the Strand Road, because that was the last place he wanted to be found right now. The police would be here at any moment. They were probably already on their way, together with the ambulance crews, fire brigade, coastguard, Samaritans, boy scouts, and who knows what other fuckers. The place would be swarming.

He thought briefly of the woman back there in the house; wondered if she was alive or dead, before realizing that he didn't care. She shouldn't have got in his way. He was only angry with himself that he'd been taken by surprise and had to rush things.

When the real moment came, he didn't want it to be so hurried.

He wanted to take his time.

But what if he didn't get another opportunity? That's what was eating at him. If Fitzgerald didn't live here any more, then Leko didn't know what information he could trust. He was lost. The only thing he could rely on was that she'd have to make her way to Dublin Castle at some point. That was her fixed point in the city. All he had to do was wait for her there. He was a patient man, when he had to be. A few more hours wouldn't kill him.

What they'd do to *her* was another matter altogether.

28

'Why?' I said. 'Why did he do it? He couldn't have killed Erskine if he was here rehearsing, or Oliver Niland either. Yet by running, what else are we supposed to think?'

'Who says he was here rehearsing?' Fitzgerald replied. 'We only have his word for that. And in this instance, actions definitely speak louder than words.'

Walsh had regained consciousness a few minutes after we found him. An ambulance had come to take him to hospital for a check-up. He didn't want to go but Fitzgerald insisted. He seemed more alarmed by the fact that he'd been lying on the floor of the men's room than that his lights had been temporarily put out by a fleeing violinist.

'Do you have any idea how much this coat cost me?' he groaned.

'You can have it dry-cleaned.'

'It'll never be the same. It's Gaultier.'

Once he got over the shock of falling, he was able to explain what had happened when he followed Riordan. He was waiting for Walsh when he came through the door of the men's room. Expecting him. Walsh didn't see what the guy used as a weapon – his cellphone, most likely. All he knew is that he was struck hard on the side of the temple with something, and his next memory was of waking up to find us bending over him, practising my usual technique of resuscitation, which consists of shaking the patient and shouting his name.

'There *was* one strange thing,' Walsh said. 'He said sorry before he hit me.'

'If he was that sorry,' said Fitzgerald, 'he wouldn't have done it.'

Riordan, meanwhile, was nowhere to be seen. Fitzgerald was having the building searched as a precaution, but the locked door made it unlikely that he was still anywhere in the vicinity. Chances were that he'd quickly locked the door to delay discovery and then shimmied out of the window. From there, he could have cut across the grounds at the rear of the National Concert Hall and made his way out into Harcourt Street or Hatch Street Upper.

Beyond that, the city lay open before him.

What he intended to do with that freedom was another matter, another mystery.

He couldn't seriously expect to get far if he was guilty. The days of stowing away on a slow boat to Havana were long gone. And if he wasn't guilty, then he was going to have to come forward to the police sooner rather than later to clear his name anyway.

'It's like he had something to do,' I said. 'Something that couldn't wait. It had to be done right now and he didn't know another way to get away without arousing suspicion.'

'He has a peculiar way of trying not to arouse suspicion,' Fitzgerald observed wryly, and then she stopped as, on the other side of the lobby, she spotted the manager she'd spoken to earlier. 'Did you find it yet?' she called over to him.

She'd asked him to get her an address for Riordan. Not that she expected him to return to his own house, but you never knew. He looked too smart to go straight to the one place police would be looking for him, but he wouldn't be the first person to do something stupid when the police were chasing him. He already *had* done something stupid.

'I really can't emphasize enough how out of character this is for Sean,' the manager said as he joined us, wringing his hands together in a near-parody of anxiety. 'He's such a gentleman normally. The balance of his mind must be disturbed for some reason—'

Fitzgerald cut him off in mid flow.

'His mind wasn't so disturbed that he couldn't plan how to abscond from the police,' she pointed out, and then she cut him off a second time as he opened his mouth to respond. It hadn't been a question. 'Are the other members of Riordan's quartet still here?'

'I put them in the recital room to wait,' he confirmed. 'Do you want to talk to them?'

'No, I want them to play me a small selection of pieces from Bach whilst I mop my colleague's blood off the floor. Of course I want to talk to them.'

'I'll tell them you—'

'All in good time.'

'I'm sure they had nothing to do with all this,' he digressed again.

That much seemed to be confirmed by the time we got around to seeing the two women and one man who made up the other three-quarters of the ensemble. Once again it was the incongruity of the situation which struck me. The women in evening gowns. The rich red carpet. The huge crystal chandelier sparkling above our heads. And Riordan climbing out the window of the men's room, after assaulting a detective ... There was something almost comic about it, though the three musicians didn't look as if they were in the mood for laughing.

Chances were they'd never had any dealings with the police before.

Certainly not the Murder Squad.

Fitzgerald tried to keep it as brief and businesslike as possible. All she wanted to know was Riordan's movements earlier that evening. She quickly established that he hadn't turned up for rehearsals at five o'clock. He hadn't come in until nearly eight.

I felt cold suddenly.

He could have killed Daniel and Oliver easily enough.

'What was his mood like when he came in?' asked Fitzgerald.

'Distracted?' suggested the woman with the cello, like she wanted reassurance that this was the right answer. 'He didn't say very much. But he'd been drinking, I could smell the alcohol on his breath. Not that I said anything to him about it, mind you.'

'Because he's the boss?'

'You got it,' she shrugged. 'I have rent to pay. And after tonight, I suppose I'll have to find a new way to pay it. Great. I sure do pick 'em.'

Fitzgerald considered the woman's answer for a moment before continuing with another question: 'How much would you say Riordan had drunk before he got here tonight?'

'Don't get the wrong idea,' the man replied quickly. 'He wouldn't have been able to play if he'd been plastered. But it was enough so that we knew he had been.'

'Has his drinking been a problem before?' I cut in.

The three of them exchanged uneasy glances.

'I wouldn't say it was a problem,' the first woman eventually offered.

'But it could be ... noticeable,' the other woman added awkwardly. 'You know?'

'I get the picture,' said Fitzgerald. 'He didn't actually tell you, though, where he'd been tonight when he should have been here rehearsing?'

'He *never* explained where he'd been to us,' the man said pointedly.

Seemed that the light-footed Riordan didn't exactly confide in his fellow musicians. They'd never heard him mention the name of Daniel Erskine, or

Oliver Niland, or any of the other members of the so-called Second Circle. His private life was a mystery to them, and they hadn't judged him for it before tonight. Music was what they shared, not confidences. Now they had been left with that edge of doubt which the police always created in the minds of those they encountered, the sense that the world beforehand had been hidden from them, and they didn't really understand yet, if they ever would, the new one ahead of them.

Fitzgerald finally left them to sign formal statements. There was no need to detain the three of them any longer than necessary, especially since one of the women hadn't stopped sobbing the whole time we were there. Besides, the night was getting on. All there was left to do here was confirm that Riordan was not still in the Concert Hall, and the inspector from Harcourt Street police station who'd been assigned to organize the search of the building did just that.

'Do you want to go over to Riordan's house?' I said as we walked back to the car.

'What's the point?' she answered. 'He won't be there, and we both know it. Nothing will be there. It's Daniel we should be concentrating on. It's always been Daniel. That's where the answer lies. We have to know *why* Daniel Erskine was murdered.'

'Riordan didn't seem to think that was such a surprise,' I said. 'To listen to him, the only wonder is that someone didn't do it years ago.'

'But why *now*? Why this particular moment in time?'

'You've got something in mind,' I said. 'I can tell. Come on, out with it.'

'I think it's time we paid a call on Fisher.'

I couldn't help smiling.

'He's going to be so pleased to see us.'

29

Nat Tannar concentrated on his pain. It was the one thing he had left that he could rely on. The one thing that made sense any more. Everything else had gone wrong. Everything else had gone *crazy*. The pain he could feel was the only thing he now knew to be true.

But where was it? He couldn't find it. It was as if the pain was diffused through his whole body, diluted, and he had to swim through it in search of the source. But he kept drifting, drifting, that was the problem ... and here we went again ... he was lost ... and there was shadow. . and finally sleep, blessed sleep. *Then he screamed silently.*

The cry was silent because there was a gag round his mouth. Tannar didn't know what it was, but it tasted bad. It tasted sour. Or was that the taste of his own blood?

Panic welled up in him once more. Why had he screamed? Because of his wrists, that was it. He could feel the agony in them, and Tannar couldn't understand why he hadn't noticed it before. Someone had tied his wrists with rope, and his ankles too, and pulled them so tight that the cords had sliced into the skin. And then he found another source of pain, right behind his eyes. His skull felt like it had been smashed and broken like an egg, and inside it was as if someone had scraped out his tissue and nerves with a scalpel. His face was numb.

He remembered now. How the blow had made him reel and everything lurched and the night sky had tilted sideways and upside down. Or he had, at any rate.

He wished the darkness that followed that moment had lasted.

Tannar wished it had lasted for ever.

He tried to raise his head, but he couldn't, and when he attempted the movement again there was a roaring inside him like some beast rampaging with hunger, and he couldn't make sense of it, couldn't find a name for it, and he closed his eyes tight until it stopped.

Where was he? Where was he?

Then he remembered. The wasteground where they were building the new football stadium. He was in the narrow space between the houses and the rising wall of it. He'd come here to meet him. He'd sent Tannar a message. But when he got here, it wasn't him at all.

It was someone else.

Someone terrifying.

And now he was lying with his face pressed to the dirt, and his skin felt wet with blood or mud, he'd forgotten what the difference was. The pain was bad now, as if someone had finished scraping out the tissue and had started pouring car battery acid into the hollow. But was he alone? Had *he* left Tannar here, thinking him dead?

That was when the roaring came again, filling his head, and he realized what it was. Not a beast, but a train passing on the tracks nearby as it picked up speed coming out of Landsdowne Road station. With effort, he managed to raise his head to see the lighted carriages flickering by behind the wire fence that separated the track from the houses.

Silhouetted by the rushing train, *he* was standing.

'You didn't think I'd leave you here alone, did you?' he said when the roar had subsided enough to allow him to be heard and the noise of the train was reduced to a diminishing rattle. 'Who knows what could happen to you in a place like this?'

Desperately, Tannar tried to struggle, to wriggle free, but it only made the pain worse, and he could tell at once that the effort was wasted. He was tied too securely. Even if he could loosen the bonds around his wrists, he wouldn't have time to untie the cords around his ankles before the other man made up the distance between them.

Already he was walking towards Tannar.

'Why bother struggling?' he said as he got closer. 'Why do people always insist on struggling when there's no hope of escape? You *can* see that, can't you?'

Bastard.

'Don't glare at me like that. Are you trying to make

me feel bad? Am I supposed to feel sorry for you?' He crouched down in the dark beside Tannar, putting his lips close to his ear so that his whispered words were as much a breath of air as sound. 'I didn't feel bad about the others, so why should I feel guilty about you?'

Tannar could practically smell his own fear now. For the first time he realized how alone he was. No one was coming to his rescue. No one even knew where he was.

It was down to the two of them.

And he was talking again, and Tannar was straining to hear what he said, because he felt that as long as the other man went on talking there was a chink of light in all the blackness. Silence was what he feared now more than anything. More than *him*.

'Did you really think I'd stand by and let you get away with it? That I was so stupid I wouldn't see through what you were planning? You betrayed me. You all did.'

Tannar tried to shake his head, but it only looked like more struggling.

'You only have yourselves to blame.'

His eyes pleaded, but the eyes that returned the gaze were stone.

'It's time.'

No.

And then Tannar felt himself lifted slightly and dragged across the rough ground to the wire fence. It was then that he understood at last what was going to happen to him, and this time he genuinely did struggle, frantically, savagely, a drowning man fighting against the sea even as it swallowed him. But it made no difference. There was a hole cut crudely in the fence, and Tannar was hauled through it like a roll of carpet on to sharper stones with jagged edges that scratched and scraped his skin, though he no longer cared about the pain, only what was to come. And then there was a coldness against his cheek, and he was laid almost gently down on to the railway track, so that his eyes were level with the lines of parallel steel that curved a hundred yards or more into the distance before turning a corner out of sight.

'Night, night, Tannar, sleep tight.'

As the shivering took hold of him, he knew it was over. He still couldn't believe it had come to this. They'd had it all worked out perfectly. They were going to be *free*.

Instead they were dead. Erskine already, then Niland. *He* had told Tannar what he'd done to them. The rest would follow. He wasn't going to stop until he was through.

Gradually the shivering got worse – if that's what it was. For it was more of a vibration deep within him now, a murmuration in his flesh, a humming of the bones.

It seemed to have a pattern to it too.

A regularity.

And then it turned the corner up ahead and Tannar knew what the sensation had been. It was a warning: the gentle shaking of the tracks as the train drew nearer. And it was getting faster, faster, and its headlights were the eyes of a hunting wolf, and the animal had seen its prey, and the roaring was so loud now it drowned out all Tannar's thoughts, except one.

Oh God, let it be quick, let it be quick, let it—

30

Lawrence Fisher, oddly enough, was not thrilled to see us. He did his best to hide it because he had manners, and because he was our friend and a professional to boot.

But he knew what we wanted from him.

'Half an hour,' were the first words out of his mouth.

'What kind of a greeting is that?' I said. 'Not even a "Good evening, ladies" or an offer of a drink?'

'Half an hour,' he repeated with mock severity, before leading us across the hall and into the book-lined library where we could talk undisturbed. Through the doors of the dining room came the small discreet noises of a dinner party: the chink of wine glasses, interweaving voices, ripples of laughter. The sounds of normality.

And right now, normality sounded pretty good.

'I'd better tell them I'll be otherwise engaged for the next while,' Fisher said. 'Do you want to come in and say hello?'

'Interrupt a roomful of psychologists?' I said. 'I wouldn't dream of it. They'll analyse us for the rest of the night.'

'They're not psychologists,' he said. 'Well, apart

from Miranda and me. It's actually my producer. He wants to make a new TV series with me.'

'Haven't you made enough of them already?'

'You know what Gore Vidal once said,' he replied. 'Never pass up the opportunity to have sex or appear on TV. It's a philosophy that's stood me in good stead.'

'All the same,' said Fitzgerald, 'we'd better not.'

'It's serious then?'

'You could say that.'

'In that case, I'll be right back. In the meantime, make yourselves at home.'

He put down the brandy glass he'd been carrying when he answered the doorbell and went out of the room, returning a couple of minutes later with a decanter to refill it.

I couldn't help smiling at the sight of him. I'd always thought there was something impossibly grown-up about decanters. Me, I just let the stuff sit in the bottle it was sold in. Booze generally wasn't around me long enough to justify going to all the trouble of pouring it from one vessel to another. Besides, I liked the labels on the bottles.

'Now I know it's serious,' he said as he topped up his glass. 'You haven't helped yourself to any-thing from the drinks cabinet, and Miranda reminds me that this was your day for moving house. Congratulations. Why aren't you spending the night unpacking?'

'Who needs cutlery and crockery when there's corpses for company instead?'

'That's corpses in the plural, I notice.'

'Two, so far,' said Fitzgerald. 'But I'm not hopeful of getting through the night without more – not until I know better what's going on, at any rate.'

'In that case, let's not beat around the bush. What have you got?'

'The primary scene,' she said, and she took out a folder from her bag. 'It's preliminary so far. The murder's only a few hours old. These are the best photographs.'

Fisher took his spectacles from his jacket pocket and slipped them on, then sat in a chair at his desk, working through the pictures one by one, not hurrying, whatever he might've said about a time limit on his involvement. When he came to the picture of Daniel Erskine in the freezer, he murmured: 'Sweet Jesus.' But that was the only emotion he betrayed. He examined the image for a long time before closing over the flap of the folder.

'He was alive when he went in there?' he said.

'Yes.'

'Was the second victim killed in the same way?'

'No,' said Fitzgerald. 'Except in so far as he was also conscious of what was happening.'

She handed him the second folder. This one made the first killing look virtually compassionate. She apologized for the incomplete state of the file.

'The Technical Team did their best, and the photographer can't get right inside the house until morning. It's not safe. Think of them as rough sketches.'

Fisher worked through the second file much more quickly, but in the short time it took him to read the reports from the scene all the last remaining traces of bonhomie in his face had been entirely erased, to be replaced by a melancholy look of resignation.

'Why do we do this job?' he said.

'Because someone has to,' I reminded him, 'and because if we want to stop these bastards doing what they do, then only the best is good enough. And that means you.'

'You shameless old flatterer,' he said, but I could see that the compliment had had the desired impact. Men were such pushovers – albeit that in Fisher's case, I meant every word I said. 'Even I sometimes need a little more material to play with, however.'

'The photographs no good?'

'Slow down, I didn't say that. I'm simply presuming that you must have more to go on if you came so quickly to the conclusion this was the handiwork of the same offender.'

'Both victims knew one another,' confirmed Fitzgerald reluctantly, and I could tell she didn't want to say too much in case what she revealed influenced his initial impressions.

'And both were similarly restrained, yes?'

'They were.'

'Indicating a high degree of control. There's no

sexual component here either. So what are we looking at? According to the usual definitions, it should either be some sort of thrill-oriented hedonist who gets a kick from the excitement of a victim's final agony, or a control freak who gets pleasure from manipulation and domination of a contrastingly powerless victim. But you say both these happened in a short space of time tonight?'

'That's right.'

'And what relation did the scenes have to one another geographically?'

'They're a couple of miles apart, no more. Both on the edge of the city centre, one southside, one northside. It wouldn't present a problem if he has his own transport.'

'Oh, your man has his own transport all right. And we're definitely looking at a single offender. Arsonists rarely work in pairs, for one thing. Setting fires is a secretive business. Having said that, arson is also largely a crime of the young. The majority of criminal fire-setting is done by the under eighteens, but there's no way *these* scenes bear the imprint of an adolescent. He's older, mature, intelligent, socially adept, and very highly organized. He attacked his victims in their own homes. That means he's one cool customer. And I don't need to tell you, I trust, that both these victims were familiar with their killer?'

'That's what we figured.'

'Nor that he hasn't finished yet?' he added soberly.

'Seems to me,' I said, 'that he's barely even started.'
Fisher didn't contradict me.

'But what does he want?' demanded Fitzgerald. 'Why is he doing it?'

'Revenge,' said Fisher firmly. 'Of course, all murder is a form of revenge. It's revenge against a loved one for screwing your best friend, or against society for not making your life easier, with the anonymous victims acting as representatives of everything you hate about the world. But when I say this killer wants revenge, I mean it literally. This is personal. These men have done something to him. They've wronged him. So he's punishing them.'

'And he wants them to know it?' I said.

'That's why he wants them to be conscious when they die,' he confirmed. 'Not for any innate satisfaction he'd derive from their final suffering. He doesn't even hang around long enough to get any potential thrill from it, after all. He simply wants them to be aware of what's happening so that they grasp his purpose. That's why he's initially willing to take the risk of leaving them alive at the scene. They might be rescued, they might escape, but he has to take that chance because without them knowing why they've been targeted, their deaths are irrelevant. But they have to die, otherwise the pattern would be incomplete. That's why he went back to number one to finish the job when he was disturbed.'

'You spotted that?'

'That he was interrupted? Of course. It's obvious.'

A slight trace there of the expert's sin of pride. 'This wasn't how it was meant to be. You can see how carelessly the Sellotape on the face was applied, compared to the careful staging of the rest of the scene.'

'Can you also tell by looking at the pictures what triggered his rage tonight?'

'On the face of it, it could be anything. Any life crisis could suffice to set off a rampage like this. The breakdown of a marriage, the loss of a job, being thrown out of college, some slight to an offender's self-esteem, a random stranger insulting them in the street . . . When you're building to such an explosion, anything could set it off. The question now isn't so much what provoked it, but rather what's going to bring it to an end.'

'If it's personal,' I said, 'then he has goals, surely. Targets. Once he's reached them, won't he stop?'

'In theory, yes. In practice, it's rarely so straight-forward. What you've got on your hands tonight is a form of spree killing. The US Bureau of Justice defines that as a number of murders at two or more locations with almost no time break between them. The spree killer's a vastly different beast from the average serial killer. They frequently defy easy categorization. They may begin by taking out their revenge on friends and family, but it's easier to start than to stop. The more time passes, the more gener-alized the rage becomes. Eventually anyone who crosses their path will suffice as the next victim.'

'You mean if we don't stop him soon, the situation could get even worse?'

'That's what I mean. The normal constraints don't apply to a spree killer. Even serial murderers try to avoid detection. They have the same impulse to self-preservation as the rest of us. At least, they do to begin with. The spree killer, by contrast, doesn't care what happens to him. He's given up on hope. He doesn't care about his own welfare. That makes his actions unpredictable, his next move all but impossible to second-guess.'

'Is there no way to get through to him?'

'You want the hard truth? The man you're seeking has no interest in you whatsoever. He doesn't want to play cat and mouse with the police. He doesn't want to mock you with his cleverness, or tease you with hints as to his identity. You don't exist to him at all. You're not a fixture in his universe. His entire focus is on finishing the job and he'll let nothing distract him from it. The only way he'll stop is if you catch him or someone else kills him first.'

'That's what I like about you, Fisher,' I said. 'You always fill us with such hope.'

'Don't mention it.'

He'd certainly paid us back for gatecrashing his party, that was for sure.

31

We were making our way to the door again when the idea struck me.

'Fisher,' I said, 'do you have any books by Dante?'

'Dante the poet?'

'No, Dante the world middleweight boxing champion. Of course the poet. And don't look at me like I've just suggested becoming a rocket scientist. Even Americans can read poetry, you know.'

'I wouldn't dare to suggest otherwise,' Fisher said. 'You want it in the original Italian?'

'A translation would be just peachy,' I said sarcastically.

He returned briefly to the library, and came back with a small leather-bound book.

'One copy of Dante's *Inferno*,' he said, presenting it to me with a bow. 'Try not to turn down the pages at the corner, you know I hate that. And I'll expect it back in a week or I may have to start charging you overdue fees.'

He paused when we reached the door. Wisps of laughter from the dining room still floated out, winding round us like mist. Fisher looked as if he was unsure of how to rejoin his own party. After seeing what was in the police reports, it would be unnatural if the appetite for celebration was not dulled.

'If you need anything else,' said Fisher, 'and I mean *anything*, don't hesitate to call me again. Doesn't matter about the time. I know you've never let that stop you calling before, but I wanted to say it all the same.'

'Thanks, Fisher,' said Fitzgerald, 'you're one of the good guys.'

'Considering the competition,' he growled, 'that's not saying much.' Then he stopped suddenly, looking out into the dark street, where a man in a car was watching the house. 'Looks like you've got company,' he remarked.

'So you noticed him too? Not exactly Mr Invisible, is he?' I said.

'I think that's the point,' said Fitzgerald, and she quickly explained to Fisher what had happened tonight – Leko's escape, and his threat to kill the woman who turned his stay in prison from a temporary inconvenience into a long-term pain in the Bosnian ass. 'Our knight in shining armour out there is supposed to deter Leko from making an attempt on my life, or to make sure he doesn't succeed if he tries it all the same. It makes the powers that be feel better. They can always say afterwards they did the best they could to protect me.'

'Be careful,' Fisher warned, not mistaking her joking tone for real flippancy for a moment. He knew she understood the seriousness of the situation.

'I know Leko. I was called in to provide a psycho-logical assessment when he was up for parole first time round. The man's cold as a polar bear's dangly bits. There's nothing he wouldn't do. Can't you take the night off until he's caught? Forget it,' he added hurriedly. 'Your expression says it all. I think you secretly like dangerous cases. One killer on the loose who doesn't care about being caught isn't enough for you, you have to throw in another one to spice things up some more.'

'What is life without a little complication?'

With hugs and goodbyes, we made our way back to the car. It felt unwelcoming after the warmth of Fisher's house. The fall air was unforgiving once the clock crept beyond midnight. I climbed into the driver's seat and switched on the heater, waiting for the windows to clear of condensation.

'On second thoughts,' I said, 'you can drive, and I'll read. Unless you have something more important to do?'

'The very thought,' said Fitzgerald. 'Why would I have anything important to do? I'm only a humble servant of the law. I'll gladly be your designated driver.'

So we switched sides.

'These old poets sure had a twisted imagination,' I said once we were underway and I'd begun reading – or flicking the pages in search of the juicy bits, at least.

'Look who's talking.'

'I'm serious. It must have been all that sexual frustration. And then there was the guilt if they managed to relieve the frustration in any way that wasn't approved of by the Church. No wonder they were so screwed-up inside.'

'According to you, they weren't *screwed* enough.'

'I'll do the jokes, Chief Superintendent. You concentrate on the road.'

There was a sense of winding down in the night air. Everything was slowing, stopping, sleeping – or soon would be. It ought to help the investigation. Clarify it. As the night emptied, there were fewer hiding places for those who wanted to move around, as the killer of Erskine and Niland seemed to be doing. The others would be exposed too. Whatever they were doing by cutting themselves adrift in the city, they might now be easier to find.

But what was this? As we turned into Herbert Road, the way ahead was suddenly snarled with traffic, and we came to a standstill. It was like morning rush hour without light.

'There must be an accident up ahead,' said Fitzgerald. Then she sighed, the irritation of being stuck in a line of cars escaping her lips. She hated being inert as much as I did. Seems I'd made a good decision letting her drive. At least I had something to do.

'What are you reading that for, anyway?'

'I want to know more about the Second Circle,' I said.

'Which one?'

'Both. They must have chosen the name for a reason.'

'*They* didn't,' she pointed out. 'Daniel did. He seemed to do everything for them.'

'Then *he* must have chosen it for a reason,' I said.

'Riordan already told you why. They were devoted to pleasure. The sins of the flesh.'

'That's his story. Who knows what he's leaving out? Maybe I'm wasting my time, but it's better than plotting homicide against every other driver on the road, like you're doing right now.'

'Am I that transparent? OK, I'll chill out. What've you found so far?'

'Check this out: *Unto such a torment the carnal malefactors were condemned, who reason subjugate to appetite ... No hope doth comfort them for evermore. Not of repose, but even of lesser pain.* You can't even hope for the pain to reduce, never mind go away.'

'Charming stuff.'

'Told you they were messed up in those days. And it's not just the carnal malefactors either. He's got the gluttons in the Third Circle, the avaricious in the Fourth, the irascible and sullen in the Fifth, the violent against their neighbours in the Seventh ...'

'And where do they put you if you're guilty of all of them, like a certain FBI agent I know?'

'*Former* FBI agent. And since when was I avaricious?'

'You're admitting to the rest then?'

'I might as well. There isn't a sin that doesn't get you damned for all eternity, as far as I can see. It's a wonder anyone made it to Paradise.'

'Maybe the boys in the Second Circle thought the same way,' she said.

'What do you mean?'

'In for a penny, in for a pound. If eternal torment was all you had to look forward to, you might as well have a blast before you go.'

'Not having much of a party now, are they?'

'That's true. For them, punishment has come a lot sooner than expected. Damn it.' She suddenly slapped the steering wheel with the flat of her hand. 'I'm not sitting here for the rest of the night waiting for whatever the hell problem it is to sort itself out. Let's go.'

And she turned the wheel as far right as it would go and began to ease forward and out, forcing the car in front to edge forward a little further to avoid being shunted out of the way, and the car ahead of that one in turn. Horns sounded in protest, provoking others to press their horns in response, so that soon it was as if we were in the middle of a colony of angry seabirds honking at one another. Fitzgerald laughed out loud as she executed a 180-degree turn in the road and headed back the way we'd come to a yelling chorus of protest.

'That,' she said, 'was better than sex.'

I was about to take offence when I noticed

someone walking down the sidewalk in the opposite direction, meaning I could see his face.

'Hey, isn't that our friend O'Neill?' I said.

'So it is.'

Fitzgerald pulled in to the kerb and sounded the horn. By now, O'Neill had passed by without noticing us, and turned round with a curious look on his face, not even sure if he was the one being summoned. Then he brightened as I wound down the window on the passenger side and he saw who it was. He came trotting over to the car.

'Chief,' he said, bending down to look through the window.

'You want a lift?' I said.

'Sure. Thanks.' He climbed into the back seat and fixed his belt.

'What are you doing out this way, anyhow?' asked Fitzgerald.

'I was interviewing a witness, Chief,' he said.

'I thought you were working on Erskine's computer?'

'I got as much out of it as I could. Then they brought in an expert to see if he could get anything more out of it. And since Walsh was attacked, I got the job of coming round here. Resources are getting a bit stretched. The only problem is, I can't drive.'

'Then aren't you glad we happened along?' I said.

'Resources,' muttered Fitzgerald. 'That's my least favourite word. If anyone wants to get away with the perfect murder, tonight's the night to do it. We probably wouldn't even notice, what with the rest that's going on.'

'Any idea what the problem was back there with the traffic?'

'Apparently, some guy threw himself in front of a train near the football stadium. They've had to shut down the line temporarily whilst they scrape him up. They closed the traffic barriers too so they can search the scene. So everyone who was trying to get home, can't. Not for a while, at any rate.'

I felt my heart tighten at his words. That was how my sister died too, escaping a dead-end marriage and a husband who was too free with his fists. The bastard.

Reminders were everywhere.

I switched my brain off that line of thought. Shutting it down like they'd shut down the other line back there. I didn't have time for it. I needed to stay focused.

I thought again about the Second Circle. Where were they? What were they doing? Were they together? Were they dead? Why did someone have them in his sights in the first place? What had they done to make themselves the targets of such a calculating rage?

I zoned back in and found that Fitzgerald and O'Neill were talking about the witness he'd been to interview. She was a cleaner, working at lots of the houses round the square where Erskine lived. She said she'd noticed someone hanging round for months, looking in people's houses and windows. He was there earlier tonight, staring in at Erskine's. It was only later, when she heard the news, that she realized she might have seen a killer.

'Did she get a good look at him?' Fitzgerald asked.

'Not really. She didn't get much of a look at him. The only thing she remembered is that he had this weird beard round his chin but no moustache. Oh, and he wore sandals.'

In the rear-view mirror, I saw him smile as he watched the recognition dawn on us.

'Lester Coyle,' I said.

'The very same.'

'We'd better see what we have on him in the files,' said Fitzgerald, shaking her head with frustration. 'I'm telling you, I am going to be so pissed off if it turns out that the guy we were looking for was sitting right under our noses the whole time.'

32

This time he was able to watch as Tannar died. Not that he saw much of what occurred. Everything happened so fast. Tannar was lucky in that regard, even if he was unlikely to have felt so fortunate as he waited for the wheels to reach him, or felt the first –

Well, the first what? What exactly would he have felt? That's the great disappointment about death. There is no coming back afterwards to describe what it was like, unless you're the kind of gullible fool who believes in the possibility of communicating with departed spirits. Thankfully, he had never been prone to that kind of irrationality.

He knew what the autopsy would say. He'd read the available literature on railway injuries as well. Cause of death would be listed as a complete transection of the neck. The head would most likely be crushed too. Where the train went over him, Tannar's skin would also be soiled by axle grease and other filth from the wheels and track.

It was an ending to life as near instantaneous as it was possible to get.

Tannar's body – and it was curious to note how quickly Tannar went, in his mind, as he would in others' minds too once his absence was noticed, from being Tannar the architect, Tannar the lover, Tannar the friend, to just another corpse, Tannar the nothing – had been flung aside when the train went over him, like a dog flinging aside the torn flesh of a rat whose throat it had torn out seconds before. He'd wondered beforehand if it would be dragged under the wheels by the speed of the train, but no. The mutilation would be less severe than it might have been, though it was unlikely his wife would request an open coffin.

He had to confess to a certain disappointment in the quickness of it all. Revisiting it in his mind, he found he was able to slow the memory down, the way a video clip can be replayed frame by frame; but there was still an inevitable distortion to the picture.

What he wanted to see with telescopic clarity was instead blurred and indistinct. And it wasn't as though he had time once the deed was done to relish the aftermath. He had to, as they say, make his excuses and leave before the police arrived.

He returned to the road then turned up towards the level crossing. The barrier was down, the light was red, the cars backed up.

'What's the problem?' he asked another pedestrian waiting to cross.

'The train's stopped. Dunno why.'

'Probably another suicide,' he remarked lightly. 'It's worse than the Golden Gate Bridge down here some nights.' And then he clambered over the barrier, enjoying the intake of breath from the small crowd of onlookers as he crossed the line, vaulted the second barrier, and continued on his way towards the crossroads at the end of the darkened street.

Something in him felt empty, though. Killing Tannar – and, more importantly, watching it happen – hadn't been as satisfying as he thought it would be.

There was something missing.

Maybe the haste of the procedures was why tonight hadn't been like the other times. Why it hadn't been as satisfying. Why it hadn't touched him the way the other ones had.

He only hoped the next one would be more gratifying.

There was a law of diminishing returns when it came to murder. The pleasure from the first killing led directly to the second, but the second offered less gratification than the first, and thus there was need of a third, and a fourth, and so on – and soon what had, at one time, felt thrilling and exciting, became merely a dulled echo of the original stimulus.

Call it the exquisite ennui of the serial murderer.

The one good thing about tonight was that there was no need for restraint or discipline any more. No need to avoid mistakes. He could do whatever he wanted, and to hell with the consequences. He was beyond worrying about consequences.

About tomorrow.

What did tomorrow matter? Now was everything.

Speaking of which, what time was it?

Late and getting later, that's all he knew.

He quickened his step. He had more work to do, but still he couldn't resist taking a peek, when he got back to the car, looking round first to make sure no one was watching.

Reassured it was safe, he lifted the lid of the boot, and there he was, sleeping, curled up like a baby, not a sign of stirring yet. He was another one who'd wish soon that he'd never woken again. Well, they should have thought of that first. Never start something you don't know if you can finish. Once you were in, you had to be in all the way, right to the endgame.

Sometimes it's way too late to change your mind.

33

The lights were never turned off in Dublin Castle. Murder did not keep office hours. Normally there was something almost surgical about the light there. Harsh and uncompromising, the strip lights that lined the corridors were normally a depressing sight, Tonight, with the yellow light flooding from the windows into the Halloween night, it was almost inviting, a refuge in a storm. Upstairs, the incident room was already being set up. It was strange. It felt as if the investigation was well underway, and yet Fitzgerald hadn't even chaired her first 9 a.m. meeting with the assembled team. I wondered if there would be anything left to *do* come morning, except count the bodies and clear up the mess.

We made our way up to Fitzgerald's office, and I opened a window and leaned out so that I could smoke a cigar in peace, keeping within the letter of Dublin's smoking ban, if not its spirit. This way I may have been in the building but I was smoking outside.

Dame Street was still. Only occasional walkers passed by, and crawling taxis. It was almost 1 a.m. now, the time when the body clock slows and human beings need sleep. Most of them, that is. I have always found the dead hours of night are when I'm at my most productive, my most alert, my most alive. There is something about darkness which invigorates me.

From far off came the sound of the odd firework being let off, the last of the night's festivities by those who still had some left. Now and then the scream of a rocket whistled into the sky, or there was the bang of firecrackers being set off, the sound magnified by the narrow streets. Rain was still in the air, but it was thin stuff, the kind that gets you wet through without you even realizing that you've got wet at all. The reflection of street lamps gleamed in puddles. A wet October had given way to a wet November.

'Hey,' said Fitzgerald, 'you want to take a look at this or not?'

The file on Lester Coyle had arrived up from Records. She'd sent one of the night staff down to unlock the office and search out what she needed.

Reluctantly, I let the cigar fall from the window, its glowing end like the last pathetic squib of the night, and everything so quiet I could hear the soft sizzle as it hit the damp ground. Then I shut the window and sat down at the desk to join the fun.

The file made for interesting reading, even if its relevance to the matter in hand wasn't immediately apparent. Our civic-minded, Christianity-spouting friend, it seemed, had spent six months in Arbour Hill prison on various charges of being a peeping Tom, stealing underwear from women's washing lines, making nuisance phone calls. He'd received the skeleton of some therapy there to help him cope with his urges, but, if what the cleaner said was anything to go by, it hadn't done him much good. He'd slipped back into his old ways.

'But that's still a long way from murder,' I said. 'Why would a man who likes stealing women's knickers and watching them undress through a crack in the curtain graduate to murdering a man, especially when we have no evidence that Coyle and Erskine even knew of each other's existence?'

'Beats me,' she confessed. 'But he was hiding something; and until we know what it was he was hiding, then he remains on the suspicious list. You have any luck tracing him?'

The last remark was addressed to O'Neill, whose knuckles had been hovering in the vicinity of her half-open office door, waiting to knock.

'The address on file is the right one,' he said, entering. 'One of the uniforms went round to bring him in for questioning, but there was no answer.'

'So either he hasn't come home yet, or he's not in the mood to talk.'

'Can you get a warrant to go in?' I said.

'Shouldn't be a problem. O'Neill, follow it up.'

O'Neill turned to go, before spinning on his heels and returning. He laid another file down on the desk in front of Fitzgerald. 'I almost forgot,' he said sheepishly. 'I was asked to give you this, Chief. Is it the one you asked for?'

Fitzgerald picked it up and nodded.

'Missing Persons,' she explained to me.

Not that there was anything much in it to go on. Toby Fraser, fellow member of the troubled Second Circle, had been an archaeology student at Trinity, who'd moved smoothly into academia on completion of his doctorate. At the age of twenty-seven, he'd been offered a seat in Harvard. The week before he was due to fly to America and begin his new life, he'd disappeared whilst on a night out. There was some CCTV footage of him in the city centre, and then he'd walked off, it was presumed in the direction of the taxi rank, only he'd never got there. His bank account had remained untouched ever since, his cellphone unanswered. There'd been no letters, no phone calls, no nothing from him since.

'So he's dead,' I said.

'Looks that way,' agreed Fitzgerald, 'but you never know. You write someone off, all the evidence points that way, then, years later, they just turn up.'

'There's nothing here to indicate that's what happened here,' I said. I was looking at the evidence from family and friends. 'He wasn't troubled, or depressed, or in any kind of mess he needed to escape from. There's none of the usual indicators to suggest why he would want to run away, or what he was running from or running towards.'

'Not everyone needs a reason,' she said. 'They just want to get away from their lives, begin again, make a fresh start.'

'But that's exactly what he *was* doing,' I pointed out. 'The following week, he was off to the States. He was leaving his life behind anyway.'

'Maybe he realized it wasn't what he wanted,' she suggested. 'Anything is possible.'

'Anything is possible,' I conceded, 'but he *is* dead.'

She didn't argue with me. She knew. You could always tell the ones who were likely to run from the ones who'd disappeared against their own free will.

The ones who weren't coming back.

'Is this really all your resident sleuths got?' I said wryly, indicating the case notes.

'Missing Persons do their best,' she said defensively. 'We didn't have the resources in those days. We still don't. You have any idea how many people go missing each year?'

I did. The newspapers carried regular reports of people who'd vanished from their own lives. Most turned up after a few days or weeks of their own accord and unharmed, but each one had to be investigated the same way. It was difficult to tell those who had vanished for a benign reason and those whose disappearance was more sinister. What could the police do? They took reports, they sent round an officer to take down details and a description of the missing person. If the officer decided it was a genuine cause for concern, then they could search the missing person's property to ascertain possible whereabouts. Then a report was forwarded to the missing persons bureau; hospital and mortuary records would be checked to see if anyone matching that description had been admitted. It was a time-consuming business.

Toby Fraser's disappearance had been given the full works – no one admits it officially, but there's a hierarchy when it comes to the missing, same as there is when it comes to the dead; and in the pecking order, putative Harvard professors come out well ahead of teenage drug addicts from the wrong estates – but even that had come up blank. His details were eventually entered on the missing persons website, but, despite a couple of new appeals, they'd had no new information about him in years. Not a single one. These days it was taken out and dusted off occasionally for the sake of appearances, but that was the extent of it. There was the name of an officer assigned to keeping the file up to date, but he'd since retired. Even academics with the right background get forgotten eventually.

Toby Fraser was simply immortalized in the record, together with a careful description of what he'd been wearing the night he disappeared. Navy hooded top. Blue jeans. Sneakers. Like he'd still be wearing the same clothes now.

'Do you really think this has anything to do with what's happened tonight?' I said.

'I have absolutely no idea, but I do know I have to examine every possible angle. You never know what might turn out to be important. Besides, what else do we have?'

'I need another cigar,' I said grimly, but I never got the chance to light it, because as soon as I got over to the window I saw him, standing on the other side of the street, trying to look nonchalant, but staring unmistakably up at the window.

'It's Leko,' I said.

34

Morgan, the armed officer that Serious Crime had assigned to protect Fitzgerald, was in the lobby downstairs, standing before the vending machine, coins in hand, brow knitted impressively with concentration, trying to make that important decision perhaps between the latte and the hot chocolate. Under different circumstances, I'd have taken the time to stop and point out that it didn't make any difference since they both tasted exactly the same. Tonight I simply dashed past, yelling back at him before I reached the door: 'He's here!'

The next moment, I was outside, leaving a wake of startled confusion.

Dame Street's emptiness mocked me. He must have seen me looking down at him, I thought. And there was me thinking I'd been so inconspicuous, backing away casually from the window in Fitzgerald's office as if nothing was wrong, and only breaking into a run when I was sure I was out of the eyeline of anyone watching in the street below.

I could see the doorway where I was sure I'd seen Leko, and almost thought I could see the outline of him still in the rain, the last trace of his presence lingering like an echo in shadow. Where would he have gone? By now, I'd been joined by Fitzgerald's knight in shining armour, who had his gun drawn and was glancing up and down the road for some telltale sign of Leko's presence, some unconscious flicker that would betray his whereabouts.

'Morgan, tell me what you're thinking.'

'What I'm thinking is, he won't stay on the main road. He'll have taken the first way back into cover.'

'Crane Lane then.'

Soon as we turned into it, the hunch became reality. Someone was down there. Someone who ran at the first sight of us. He'd been pressed against the wall, out of sight, but he wasn't going to rely on shadows if anyone started approaching. The lane filled with the clamour of his footsteps, the narrow walls magnifying and multiplying the sound till it seemed that we were chasing a football team rather than a single man.

'Stop, police!' shouted Morgan pricelessly, but the words were wasted on Leko.

I stumbled on the cobblestones which ran down the centre of Crane Lane, and fell heavily to my knee. Pain shot up my leg into my spine and for a moment I almost thought I'd been shot. Looking up, I saw I was outside the Red Door Centre, a place I'd read about in the newspapers where they ran courses in astrology and other crap like that. The cosmic vibes obviously weren't on my side tonight. I got to my feet again and continued. I'd have to run off the pain. Leko was out of sight now, he'd reached the end of the street and turned right, and Morgan wasn't far behind. Thankfully, he hadn't stopped to help me.

By the time I reached the end of Crane Lane, the two of them had vanished, and there was no one around to ask which way they'd gone. The lights were still on in the late-night Asian café but the tables in the window were empty.

I listened for footsteps, but that sound had faded too.

I went down towards Rory Gallagher Corner, a place renamed recently after some late rock singer from the past, and into Meeting House Square, slick and grey with rain. On the other side of the square, the huge windows of the Gallery of Photography gaped back at me. I saw my reflection in the glass, but that was the only other figure anywhere in view.

I ran across the square and up the steps through the tunnel into Eustace Street, where I emerged, panting and dishevelled with dripping hair, into a small group of late-night stragglers who fell into silence at my arrival. I guess I wasn't looking my best.

'Have you seen—?'

But then I fell into silence as I saw Morgan approaching from the bottom of the street.

'Did you get him?' I said, as the stragglers hurried on their way, no doubt wondering what bizarre scene they'd stumbled upon, with me hyper-alert and out of breath, and Morgan with his gun drawn.

Morgan shook his head stiffly.

'I lost him,' he said. 'He could be anywhere now.'

I cursed softly. There was no point blaming him for what had happened. Maybe if Serious Crime had assigned more men to protecting Fitzgerald ... but then it was she who'd ordered them to stay out of her way. What a Halloween night it was turning out to be.

We made our way back up towards Dame Street, passing the Irish Film Centre along the way. I couldn't help smiling grimly as I did so. They'd been showing *Halloween*, I saw from the poster outside. That was a film I knew well. I remembered seeing it when it came out as a kid in Boston and scaring myself silly, little knowing then that the monsters on the screen would one day be part of my life too, and that I'd be close enough to them to breathe the same air. That was the thing about evil. It could be found anywhere, and you'd never be aware of its presence unless it chose to manifest itself.

That it was *Halloween* they'd been showing made me pause for a different reason. That was about an escaped prisoner too. The only difference was that Michael Myers was mad, and Leko was as sane as I was – for what that qualification is worth. Evil hadn't entered Leko through a disturbance of the mind. He had invited it in. He liked its company.

They didn't catch Myers at the end of that film, did they? They let him escape so that they could bring him back for the sequel. There was another difference too. I was determined that Leko wasn't coming back after tonight. One way or another, he had to be taken out of circulation. Fitzgerald could never be truly free whilst he remained at large. Either dead or alive, he had to be dealt with. I'd prefer it Morgan's way, but that was out of my control.

Fitzgerald herself wouldn't look at me when I got back to her office. She kept her head bent down to the file, making notes in the margin as she went along.

'We didn't get him,' I said eventually.

'Is that right?' she said.

Her lips were tight and pale.

'You're angry,' I said.

'Why would I be angry just because you rushed off and nearly got yourself killed? Why would I be angry about a little thing like that?'

'I just wanted to help . . . I thought—'

'No,' said Fitzgerald. 'You didn't think. That's the problem. You never do.' She stared hard at me, and I saw the fierce emotion in her eyes. 'I just took a call from Fogarty over at Serious Crime. About an hour ago, Leko shot Patricia Quinn.'

'The woman who bought your house?'

'Obviously his information was a little out of date and he didn't know I'd moved.'

'How is she?'

'She'll live. She's in surgery now. Stella Carson wants me off the case. She wants me to take up the offer of a safe house. I've been avoiding her calls like the plague. What she doesn't say to me directly, I can always pretend not to have known. But the last thing I need is you rushing off into danger without a second thought. If something had happened to you . . .'

I opened my mouth to speak, without knowing what words would come out, because I knew she was right, running off like that had been crazy, selfish; but no words came into life at all. What could I say? *I'm sorry*? I'd said it before, and meant it, and it still meant nothing. There was still something in me which exulted in danger and the proximity of darkness.

Something that made me charge towards it, heedless of my own self.

Heedless of her.

A knock at the door saved me from the awkwardness of the moment.

Fitzgerald sighed, and called out: 'Come in.'

'Walsh,' I said.

The detective was standing in the doorway. He'd changed his coat.

'What are you doing here?' said Fitzgerald. 'I sent you to the hospital. Or is this a night for putting your life in danger for no reason?'

A slight movement of the eyes in my direction was the only hint she gave of the true target of her sarcasm; it was so insignificant a glance that Walsh missed it entirely.

'The hospital has enough to do, Chief,' he said simply. 'You should see Casualty down there. Filled with people who've been injured by fireworks. I saw one guy with a missing finger, another one who'd gone blind. I figured I wasn't doing so badly. In the end, I decided I could do more good down here. So I just upped and left, went home, got changed, and came back here.'

'You didn't drive, I hope? There's still a danger of concussion.'

'The doc warned me about that. I took a cab instead. But the main thing is, Chief, what I found waiting in the lobby when I got back. Something I think you'll be very interested in. I thought I'd bring it up for you to take a look at. Well, someone, to be precise. A man.'

'I'm intrigued,' said Fitzgerald. 'Show him in.'

Walsh put his head out of the door again, and called: 'Elliott. They'll see you now.'

Elliott?

35

Nick Elliott and I had never been the best of buddies. In fact, we'd never been any kind of buddies at all. We didn't have mutual respect for one another so much as mutual loathing. At least that's the way it had been when our paths first crossed. It had been many years since I'd seen him, however. Maybe the intervening years had improved his personality – or given him one to improve in the first place. But I doubted it on an initial glance. Some of the old arrogance had been knocked off him; disgrace and exile tended to make a man less sure of himself. But there was still the same sulkiness about him, that aura of a man who couldn't understand why the world wasn't exactly as he demanded it should be.

This, though, was no time for indulging my personal distaste for the fallen reporter. Last time we met, we'd both been free to snipe at one another without restraint. Now I was here in a quasi-official capacity, and I had to bite my tongue. Even my natural antagonism towards much of the human race had to take a back seat when murder was on the menu.

He didn't look surprised to see me as he stepped into Fitzgerald's office and sat himself down in the chair that Walsh pulled over for him to the front of the desk. I guessed he'd heard that I was now attached loosely to the Murder Squad. I'll say that for him. He may not have been up to much as a human being, but as a reporter there wasn't much that he missed. He knew the city like a car mechanic knows the workings of the internal combustion engine. He knew what made it tick. That must have made being forced to leave it, even if temporarily, a painful experience. Where was it he'd gone? South Africa?

I didn't ask. I may not have been in a position to give free rein to my feelings, but that didn't mean I had to make pleasant small talk. Still, I was interested to find out why he'd come. It can't have been easy for him to walk through the door of Dublin Castle. We were the last people he'd want to help out, considering that he blamed us for what had gone wrong in his life. His courage on that score earned him some credit, at any rate.

Fitzgerald had better manners than me. Then again, most people did. She asked if he wanted coffee, if he was warm enough, how he was getting on these days.

I bit my tongue harder.

'I was doing very well – until tonight,' said Elliott, declining coffee with a wave of his hand. 'This whole thing with Daniel Erskine has just thrown a total spanner into the works. It's going to ruin everything I've been working on for the last few months.'

'Your cooperation is all the more appreciated then,' said Fitzgerald smoothly, without letting a trace of sarcasm into her voice. 'And I assure you that any information you have to provide will be held in the strictest confidence. Only if it's relevant to the investigation will it be released. No one else need know a thing about it.'

'Oh, it's relevant to the investigation all right,' he said. 'I mean, it has to be. It couldn't be anything but relevant, given what happened tonight . . .' He trailed off uncertainly.

'Did you know the victim? Daniel Erskine?' said Fitzgerald, adding the name because it didn't seem that Elliott was aware that there had been more than one murder tonight and there was nothing to be gained from complicating things by mentioning the others.

'I'd spoken to him a couple of times,' he answered. 'We weren't exactly friends, and not likely to become friends either after he knew what I was going to write.'

'You'd found out something incriminating about him?'

'Yes,' he said, then added hurriedly: 'No. That is, yes I had, but it wasn't really him I was interested in. I was working on a story about' – and he took a deep breath as if he had to steel himself to reveal the name – 'Fergus Costigan. You know Costigan?'

'The politician?' said Walsh, who'd taken up position against the wall behind Elliott. The reporter looked round with a start at the sound of his voice, like he hadn't realized the other man was still here. He was obviously uneasy about sharing what he knew with too many sets of ears just yet. He looked as if he was about to object, even ask Walsh to leave, then decided against it. Whether it was the obvious injury on Walsh's forehead that made him feel bad about not wanting the detective there, or whether he simply decided there was no point being discreet any more, I couldn't say.

Whatever it was, he eventually continued with what he was saying.

'The politician, yes,' he said, but even I, who rarely looked beyond the crime and sports sections of the city's newspapers, knew that Fergus Costigan was much more than an ordinary time-serving politician. He was only in his thirties, but was already a prominent government junior minister, and had been making quite a name for himself in recent months with a series of controversial speeches stirring up trouble about immigration. The past ten years had transformed Dublin beyond recognition. Once the traffic in people went in only one direction: outwards. East to England, or west to the United States, it didn't matter. The important thing was to get out. There was nothing to stay for in Dublin. Now the city was booming and people were flocking in, from Eastern Europe, Africa, elsewhere. Some of the natives were finding it hard to adjust to being a net importer of people rather than an exporter, and these were the ones who tended to blame immigrants when anything went wrong.

Coming from Boston, a city into which a sea of Irish blood had flowed for a century and more, not to mention the Italians, Haitians, and more latterly Vietnamese, I found the attitude of many people in this city incomprehensible, not to mention hypocritical in the extreme, but it certainly meant there was a ready audience willing to have their prejudices confirmed and exploited by populist politicians on the make. That was Fergus Costigan to a T. His smug, self-satisfied face was rarely off the TV screens as he called for tighter controls on incomers, and more restrictions on those who had already managed to enter the country. There was even talk that he could be the next Minister for Justice. After that, who knows?

The sky was the limit.

From the look on Nick Elliott's face right now, he had something on Costigan that would make him feel a lot less confident about his political future.

'The thing you have to understand about Costigan,' he explained, 'is that he's broke. I don't mean simply short of cash. I mean bankrupt. He hasn't a cent to his name. And that might be embarassing for your average Joe Soap, but for a politician it's career death. Any politician who is declared bankrupt has to resign his seat. It'd be the end of Costigan's career if it got out. He could kiss goodbye to the office of Minister for Justice. Goodbye to any other ambitions he might have as well. At least for the foreseeable future. He'd be yesterday's man, another of the next big things that were never heard from again.' Elliott spoke the words with some bitterness like they might be referring to his own downward trajectory as well.

'Why's he broke?' I asked, still not sure what this had to do with Daniel Erskine.

'Where do you want to start?' said Elliott. 'He's made some bad investments, got involved in deals that he should have kept well away from. Basically, he took his eye off the ball. It happens when you're ambitious. Other parts of your life you let slip. Plus he's always lived way beyond his means. Politicians don't earn as much as they think they should, but they don't want to trim their lifestyle to suit their shallow pockets.'

'I thought Costigan was loaded,' said Walsh.

'That's the point,' Elliott said. 'He had to keep up a facade. That's why, when his money started running out, he turned to Daniel Erskine for help.'

'Why Erskine?' said Fitzgerald.

'Erskine's father and Costigan's father were close friends for over thirty years. They both came up to Dublin from the country at the same time, started working the building sites together, made their first forays into business together. You know how these things work. It's the old boys' network. Even though they went their separate ways – Erskine into construction and Costigan Senior into politics – it was a bond that was never broken. They always made sure to help each other out. It was the accepted way things were done in those days. So when Costigan Junior was in a hole, it was Erskine Junior that he turned to. For the past year and a half now, he's been going round to Erskine's house every couple of months and coming away with bundles of cash to keep himself in the manner to which he has become accustomed.'

'How did you get to know about it?' said Fitzgerald.

'I have my sources.'

'Do these sources have names?'

Elliott looked almost pained by the question. 'Journalists never reveal their sources, you know that,' he replied piously. 'It's a sacred rule of the profession. You wouldn't expect a priest to reveal the secrets of the confessional box, would you?'

'If murder was involved, I would,' Fitzgerald said without hesitation.

He shook his head. 'I couldn't,' he said.

She let it go for the moment.

'I don't get it,' I said. 'So Erskine helped out an old friend of the family who'd gotten into a mess. What's wrong with that?'

'Nothing in itself,' said Elliott. 'If it came out, it'd be embarrassing for Costigan, but probably survivable. It's what happened afterwards that was the nail in the coffin.'

'The Docklands contracts,' said Walsh unexpectedly.

Elliott looked startled. 'You know about that?' he said.

'Just putting two and two together,' said Walsh, and he looked almost as surprised at getting the right answer as Elliott had been. 'I have a cousin who works down there, he told me Erskine Properties had recently been awarded a large contract for re-developing land down there. He was pissed off about it because the company he works for had expected to get it.'

'And who do you think had the final say in where the contract went?' said Elliott.

'Costigan?'

'The land was owned by the government. They put the redevelopment contract out to tender. It was all supposed to be above board. You can't get away with the same things these days as you could before. But Costigan managed to pull a few strings to make sure that Erskine's company got the job. It's going to be worth tens of millions once it's finished.'

'Did nobody make a connection between the two of them?' asked Fitzgerald.

'Not directly. Erskine isn't involved in the day-to-day running of the company any more – in fact, the board probably don't even know that the deal was fixed – and Costigan and Erskine don't move in the same circles either. Just because their fathers were both friends doesn't mean their sons are connected at the hip too. No one knows there's a link between them. The only way they could be caught out is if one of them talked.'

'And one of them isn't in a position to do much talking any more,' I said.

'Exactly.'

'You certainly have a good story there,' said Fitzgerald appreciatively, and I could see her praise was the last thing Elliott had expected. 'Bankruptcy is one thing, but this is major league corruption. Soon as you publish, Costigan's dead meat politically. And who says it ends with him? A scandal like this could bring down the government. I'm surprised you haven't printed yet. Weren't you worried someone else would get to it in the meantime?'

'I've hardly slept or eaten properly for weeks, I've been so scared,' admitted Elliott. 'But you can't just go around accusing people in this town without making sure first that you have all the facts at your fingertips. Do you know what the laws of libel are like? We'd pencilled in the weekend for publication. But after what happened tonight . . .'

'You still have your story,' I pointed out. 'A cynic might say that Daniel Erskine's death had simply made it bigger and better than it would have been otherwise.'

'But if we publish now, we'll have to be doubly sure we've got it right. Costigan's bound to deny getting any money from Erskine, and Erskine's not around to contradict him, so all I have is my source, and if Costigan gets to him too, pays him off or threatens him or worse, then the whole thing could still fall apart in my hands.'

'Or worse?' echoed Walsh. 'You're not saying you think Costigan had Erskine killed?'

'Why not? These people will stop at nothing to get what they want.'

'But what about the others . . .?' Walsh began to say, but Fitzgerald silenced him before he could give anything away.

Thankfully, Elliott didn't seem to have picked up on the slip.

'This is why it's so important you tell us your source,' Fitzgerald went on instead. 'We can offer him protection. That way, he's safe, and so is your story.'

He thought about it for a while, though probably not as long as someone would who truly believed in the quasi-priestly sanctity of his duty to his source.

'It's Costigan's ministerial driver,' he said. 'He despises the guy. He's been keeping records of his boss's visits to Erskine's house. One time, Costigan even sent him round to pick up a package when he couldn't make it personally. The driver took the chance to look inside before resealing the pack. It was stuffed full with money. Ten thousand at least, he reckoned. And that was only one payment. He came to me with the story soon after.'

A wistful look came into his eyes. It wasn't hard to interpret. He could publish his story now, there was nothing stopping him, but an essential element of surprise had been lost. Daniel Erskine's murder would undoubtedly prompt a media free-for-all, in which Elliott's revelations might be lost, or quickly overtaken by events. Who was going to care about accusations of a populist government minister's corrupt land deals when murder was in the frame as well? Elliott had wanted to bring down Costigan personally. Now he feared that Costigan may have brought himself down first, and he'd simply be kicking a dead dog.

I almost felt sorry for him.

But only almost. I hadn't changed that much.

36

'What now?' I said once Nick Elliott had signed his statement and gone miserably into the night, still lamenting his bad timing and griping about his lost story.

'I'll have to call Stella,' Fitzgerald said, meaning the Assistant Commissioner. 'She'll need to know about this. And there was me trying to avoid her ...' She gave me a sharp glance to show she hadn't forgotten how I'd complicated matters earlier by running off after Leko. 'Can you give me five minutes?'

Walsh and I left her alone to make the call, and walked down to the empty incident room, getting coffee from the machine, though it still tasted as bad as it had before. It was so quiet. Hard to imagine that by the morning the place would be filled with noise, and people milling round like it was a railway station during rush hour.

I asked him how he was, how he'd gotten on at the hospital. Even in the brief time he was there, it turned out he'd been able to get a phone number from one of the nurses.

'She's Lithuanian,' he said. 'I never dated a Lithuanian before.'

'Is that what they call it – dating? In my day, we called it screwing around.'

'Forgive me my sins, Sister Saxon. What can I do? I'm a prisoner of my male urges.'

'I don't think Riordan hit you hard enough,' I said wryly.

It was hard to know how to get a handle on where this was going. Elliott's information had put an entirely different slant on the night's events. It was hard to see how it could all fit together but there was no denying this was where the investigation was bound to head now. However you looked at it, what Elliott had said was an important development.

Walsh thought so too.

'Fergus Costigan,' he whistled. Walsh had always been a sucker for a famous name. 'Who'd have believed he could be involved in something like this?'

'What's so hard to believe?' I said. 'He's a politician. Those guys would sell their grandmothers into slavery if they thought there was something in it for them.'

'There's a big difference between corruption and murder,' Walsh said.

'Is there?' I said. 'All I know is that there are three main motives for murder: sex, money and revenge. We know there's nothing sexual in what's been happening tonight, so that leaves money and revenge, both of which potentially put Costigan right in the frame.'

'But why would he kill the very guy who's been

bailing him out financially? It doesn't make any sense.'

'So that he couldn't talk? Couldn't reveal the state of Costigan's finances and the extent of his corruption? Who knows?'

'And the others?'

'The others . . . well, they need to be taken one at a time. You know how simple this stuff is. It's how plus why equals who. We already know how, more or less. Maybe now we've come a step closer to figuring out the why. From there, it's a matter of following the thread and pulling in whatever's tied to the end of it, fish or shark or old tin can.'

Though that wasn't going to happen tonight. I might have felt that a corner had been turned, a new avenue opened up in front of us, but it lasted only as long as it took Fitzgerald to call Assistant Commissioner Carson to update her on the case. By the time she walked down the corridor to join us, her face showing the strain of the hard persuading in which she'd had to engage to convince Carson that she should be left in charge of the case, despite Leko's attempts on her life, the road ahead had been blocked off by barriers.

'She thinks we should go easy on this one,' Fitzgerald said.

'You're not serious? Only a short while into the job and she's been sucked into the old boys' network already? You scratch my back and I'll scratch yours? Don't say she's afraid of stepping on a few toes.

What does she want to protect a creep like Costigan for?'

'It's not about protecting him,' Fitzgerald said. 'It's about being careful. She's right. Costigan's a big fish. You don't go trying to reel him in without the proper preparation.'

'So you're doing what she says?'

'I have complete operational independence here to make my own decisions about the investigation, but this time I happen to think she's right. I can't just go blundering in without all the facts at my fingertips. I don't want to be left looking like an idiot.'

'Dammit,' I said, and my frustration was all the greater because I knew that she was right. Costigan would have insulated himself well against this sort of unwelcome intrusion into his affairs. Go in too fast and too hard and the shutters would come down. He'd surround himself with lawyers and press agents. His people would circle the wagons and make him harder to reach than Saturn on the Number 84 bus. Not without stirring up even more problems for ourselves, at any rate. Christ, how I hated politics.

'Piece by piece is how it has to be then?' I said. 'So be it. So what now?'

I wasn't built for sitting around waiting, kicking my heels.

'I've already spoken to Devine at the Criminal Assets Bureau. Got him out of bed. I asked him to look out for anything he has on Erskine and Costigan. Also Fogarty again. He's so busy tonight trying to save my life, he might as well do some work for me too. I couldn't give him too many details, but he has enough to go on. In the meantime, we have to concentrate on finding the others. Tannar's still out there somewhere, and Blunt. Michael Erskine too. Not to mention Walsh's friend Riordan.'

Though how we could make a difference, when half the cops in the city were already on full alert for the missing men and had seen nothing of them so far, she didn't specify.

'I'd certainly love to catch up with Riordan,' Walsh said with feeling. 'Do you want me to go round to his house and see if I can rake up anything there, Chief?'

'How are you going to get over there at this time? By night bus? I told you, I don't want you driving anywhere. You shouldn't even be here. You had concussion.'

'I'm fine . . .'

'Since when did you get a medical degree? The graveyard's full of people who went in for self-diagnosis. I don't want you doing anything until you've been seen by a doctor.'

It was one of those moments when a little chink opens in your head, and a shaft of light peeps through. Whether anything worth finding was revealed was another matter.

'A doctor,' I echoed, trying to figure out why that word had made me pause. Then I realized what it was. 'Has Healy got that hidden door in Erskine's house opened yet?'

'Presumably not, or he'd have let me know,' Fitzgerald said. 'I told him to contact me immediately if he did. Why? You got an idea?'

'Maybe.'

I reached for the phone and dialled Healy's cell-phone number, waited impatiently for it to ring, and then even more impatiently for him to answer.

'What are you thinking?' said Walsh, but I raised my hand to shush him.

'Healy, that you?' I said instead.

His familiar voice echoed down the line from across the city.

'Saxon,' he said, 'what can I do for you?'

'That password you're looking for. It has seven letters, right?'

'Yeah.'

'Try Dr M Nott. D – R – M – N – O – T – T. You got that?'

'Wait a moment,' Healy said, and I heard him calling through to another room. In the background, there was a small whoop of triumph. 'Well, what do you know?'

'Are we in?'

'We're in.'

'We'll be right over,' I said.

37

He was almost home when the text came through on his mobile. HOW WOULD YOU LIKE THE BEST STORY OF YOUR CAREER? He didn't recognize the number and there was no way of identifying the caller, so he simply texted back: *That depends. Who is this?* The reply was almost instantaneous, as if the caller had known what he would ask: THE MAN WHO KILLED DANIEL ERSKINE. ARE YOU INTERESTED NOW OR SHALL I TAKE THE STORY TO SOMEONE ELSE? BILL MCMAHON, FOR INSTANCE?

Nick Elliott was sure it must be an elaborate joke, but he couldn't take the risk of it not being. He had to play along. *What do you want me to do?*

Elliott wasn't a brave man. He never willingly put his neck on the line when it could be avoided. Other reporters flew to war zones, courted danger, sought out those parts of the world where evil shone through a thin gauze of normality. But not him. He liked his comforts. He hated pain and discomfort. The thought had occurred to him, when his career went 'tits up', as he described it, to find a nice little war somewhere and use it to claw back his soiled reputation, like a missionary making amends for touching up the choirboys by heading to deepest darkest Africa and converting the natives away from cannibalism or headshrinking or whatever else it was they did out there. He could have made a name for himself all over again. But when it came to it, he just couldn't face the risks involved.

His heart was a timid beast. It needed to be treated gently.

The thought of meeting the man who had killed Daniel Erskine – even of talking to him – petrified him. The police hadn't told him how Erskine died, but his imagination filled in the gaps. Even so, this was an opportunity he couldn't pass up. A while ago, his world had collapsed. Suddenly a new opportunity was opening up in front of him. The networks would pay a fortune for his story if he managed to meet Erskine's killer. He could even do a book. He thought about Anne Rule, the woman who made a fortune with a book about how her friend and colleague Ted Bundy had turned out to be a serial killer. He even thought of that Grade A bitch Saxon. The woman had written books about her experiences in the FBI. Made a fortune, by all accounts. Why couldn't he get a piece of the action too?

There might even be a movie. Elliott wondered who could play him. Someone edgy. Someone a bit unconventional, but still handsome. Rakish. Nicholas Cage, maybe. The more he thought of the possibilities, the more excitement overcame his misgivings.

It wasn't moral disquiet he felt about meeting Daniel Erskine's killer. He'd told the police all he knew. There was nothing more he could do. The man warned him not to go to the police. He said he'd watch him and make sure he didn't bring anyone else along with him when they met. If he got any hint that Elliott had contacted the police, he'd be out of there. He didn't threaten Elliott with what he'd do if the reporter tried to get smart with him. He didn't need to. He just said he'd be gone. He knew for an ambitious man like Elliott, that was the worst threat of all. No, Elliott's uneasiness was entirely about his own personal safety. But the fact that he hadn't actually been physically threatened reassured him slightly.

At home, he gathered together what he needed, what his anonymous caller had told him to bring along. He stuffed them all into a sports bag, then checked his watch. He was shaking so much that he could hardly see the dial. Cold as it was, he was sweating. He wished he had time for a shower. He didn't want to seem so desperate, so scared. He wanted to look . . . nonchalant, that was it. So he simply sprayed under his arms with deodorant and checked his appearance in the mirror. It was almost like he was heading out on a date, except that he looked terrified. He had to be cool. He had to act like he knew what he was doing.

Nicholas Cage wouldn't be terrified. He'd be nonchalant . . . yes, that was the effect he should go for, like he met killers every day.

He'd never forgive himself if he missed an

opportunity like this, after all. More to the point, neither would his bank manager. He had an overdraft bigger than that of the average Third World country. He'd been relying on his story to turn around his fortunes.

And if he didn't do it, someone else would. If there was one thing Elliott had learned from journalism, it was this. Someone else was always waiting to take your place.

He thought again of Bill McMahon. That arrogant little shit had been nothing when Elliott was last in Dublin. He'd taken the scraps that fell from Elliott's table and been grateful for them. He couldn't write for toffee either. He'd no more a nose for a story than Elliott's grandmother. And now he was Chief Crime Reporter for the very paper Elliott had once worked for. He'd even published his first book. What if the killer did go to him instead? McMahon wouldn't have any doubts about doing it. He'd get round there so fast he'd leave scorch marks in the road. Elliott couldn't bear the thought. He had to go through with it.

He'd bring a knife, that's what he'd do.

To protect himself.

Elliott went into the kitchen, took one from the drawer and tucked it into his coat pocket. Then he set out, feeling shifty, and sure that everyone who saw him would know that he was acting suspiciously. Not that there were many people around to see him.

He saw a policeman on the corner of Fitzwilliam Square, trying to sort out trouble which had started among a bunch of youths, and he almost cried out, he was so tense.

What if he was searched and they found the knife? He hurried, trying to look inconspicuous at the same time, back along Baggot Street and left into Pembroke Street and down Mackie's Lane. Back here, at the bottom of a short hill, was a collection of small offices housing trendy media companies, TV production companies, ad agencies, all shut up now for the night. Past them and then he saw it. There was a cramped terrace of houses that might have looked good when they were put up a few decades back but which now looked a little seedy. On the ground floor of each there was a garage, either belonging to the people who lived in the houses or rented out, he didn't know. Was this where the killer lived?

Elliott looked along the row of garages to find the number he'd been told to wait at. Even at the last minute, his nerve almost failed him. The only thing that stopped him was the feeling he'd had since he turned off the main streets that he was being watched.

As he'd been told, there was a key in the door. No turning back. This was it. He turned the key and lifted up the garage door with a loud metallic clang that made him jump.

Inside, a bare light bulb in the ceiling showed a concrete space empty except for two plastic chairs with the words Dublin City Council on them, and a small fold-up table on which sat a white envelope. He crept forward nervously to look at it.

On the front was written: *FAO Nick Elliott, Ace Reporter.*

He tore it open with shaking hands, not even noticing the insult. Inside, there was one of Daniel Erskine's calling cards. On the edge was a spot of dried blood. He shouldn't have been touching this, he told himself. It was evidence. But he turned it over all the same, and saw the four small words written on it.

Look Behind You, Nick.

Fear gripped him. He wanted to run, but he couldn't move. He almost couldn't turn round, his body was so reluctant to obey his commands, but he managed it in the end.

Behind him in the doorway, framed by shadow, stood a man.

The man who said he'd killed Daniel Erskine.

'You,' Elliott managed to gasp.

'Are you sure you weren't followed?' the man said.

'I think so . . .'

'And you told no one you were coming?'

'No!' His voice almost cracked as he spoke, he wanted this man to believe him so much.

The man looked at him a long time. Then – 'OK,' he said. 'No need to be so jumpy. I won't bite. Did you bring the tape recorder, like I asked?'

Nick Elliott reached into his sports bag and took it out. He placed it on the table with shaking hands.

'Then let's get to work, shall we?'

38

I don't know what I expected to find when we got to Erskine's house, but not this.

'This case just keeps getting bigger,' I said.

'It's the only thing that does in this cold,' replied Healy ruefully, and he was right about the weather at least. It was so cold you could see your own breath in the air of Daniel Erskine's room – and in the hidden vault which now lay open before us, it was colder still, like a church; an airless, private, sacred space.

There were no windows in here. The room was lined instead from floor to ceiling with shelves, and each shelf was burdened with the weight of countless red box files, all numbered and titled and arranged chronologically, two years to a file, with some dating back twenty years. They were packed so tightly together that you could barely have slid a razor blade between them. Each file was devoted to a particular person, and inside there were what could only be described as surveillance reports on them, chronicling their movements and secrets, mistresses and mistakes, an entire record in some cases of the lives of the people Daniel Erskine had been watching. Erskine's friends in the Second Circle took pride of place, Blunt and Riordan and Tannar, but there were others. Business partners; politicians – not just Fergus Costigan, but others almost equally as well known; neighbours; distant family members. Everything that might be useful was laid down against them in black and white.

'I wonder if they had any idea they were being watched so closely?' I said.

Or if there was ever a moment when they were beyond his scrutiny.

In some of the files there were transcripts of telephone calls, tapes of private conversations, photographs. Daniel Erskine had been like a multiple stalker, whose obsessive interest in the minutiae of his subjects' lives had got way out of control.

What he did with this avalanche of information was anyone's guess. Flicking through the reports briefly revealed most of it to be of such banality that getting hold of the knowledge seemed to be considerably more trouble than it was worth. In fact, the only beneficiaries of the process seemed to be the private investigation firms that Erskine had hired to carry out the surveillance. I recognized the names of at least six such outfits listed among the invoices and receipts which Erskine had also filed away alongside the reports, perhaps in the hope he could claim his snooping back against income tax.

'*June 12th,*' I read out loud. '*Ronan Blunt left his house at 7.30 a.m. and made his way to the Natural History Museum, stopping only briefly to pick up coffee at the pancake café at the bottom of Kildare Street. He remained at the museum until 12 noon, when he lunched at Bewley's with a female colleague from work and one unidentified male (photograph included). He returned to his office at approximately 1.30 p.m.* . . . Is there no end to this crap?'

'It's like the Stasi in East Germany,' agreed Fitzgerald. 'They amassed huge amounts of data on targeted individuals without ever stopping to ask what use any of it was. Gathering the information became an end in itself.'

'Daniel Erskine must have had his reasons,' I said.

'Must he?' she replied. 'You heard what Blunt's wife said. Erskine liked to control people, he liked to have power over them. Maybe this was how he did it.'

'By knowing where they drank coffee on the way to work?'

'For a man like that, it would all be part of the picture. To control people, you need all the information you can get. Only then can you sort the wheat from the chaff, what's useful from what's irrelevant . . .'

'Useful in what way?'

'I don't know, but you're not forgetting the note in Michael Erskine's house.'

'*Don't try to run, and don't hide, I know about Erin,*' I recalled. 'You're saying Daniel Erskine was blackmailing his own brother about some woman?'

'Who knows? I wouldn't rule out the possibility. Not now. Not after this.' Fitzgerald extended her arm to include all the box files. 'And if he was involved in blackmail of some kind, then that's more than enough motive for someone to want him dead.'

'You mean Erskine may have been murdered for something in this very room?'

'Until we've been through every scrap of paper,' she said, 'it's an angle we can't discount. Meanwhile, I'm looking forward to seeing how the agencies Erskine hired are going to explain how they managed to get hold of the verbatim records of so many private conversations. Last time I checked, phone tapping was still illegal in this country.'

I said nothing, though I was unconvinced. This didn't feel like the hideaway of a blackmailer, not in the strictest sense, more the lair of a spider who needed to know, for his own satisfaction, the source of every quiver and disturbance in the web around him. He didn't necessarily intend to do anything with the evidence he collected, except relish its possession, enjoy having an advantage over those who crossed his path, even if they didn't know he had it. Omnipotence was his desire rather than any short-term sordid gain, though that wasn't to say he mightn't have stumbled inadvertently on something which led him into danger.

My hunch about Erskine's motives for gathering information were bolstered in part by the discovery alongside the files of a number of sophisticated portable scanning devices of a sort that could be used to pick up amateur and CB radio transmissions but were more commonly used by enthusiasts to listen in on police radio broadcasts.

That Erskine had used them to listen in on the emergency services was confirmed when Healy switched on the first one we found and the sound of voices from the squad cars parked outside drifted into the small room where we stood, transporting me back in my own mind to my adolescence, when I would lie awake long into the night in South Boston, listening in to the despatches from police patrolling the area. Drugstore robberies, domestic disturbances, homicide: it was my first contact with the murky night world that infected the neighbourhood in which I grew up, even if I couldn't see it during daylight. There was something glamorous about the world I heard across the crackling airwaves in those days, like it was the CBS Radio *Mystery Theater*, only better because it was real.

Now I felt I knew where Daniel Erskine was coming from. How the dark pulse of the police radio broadcasts connected him to a part of the life of the city that was all too often hidden but, without which, the city didn't make any sense at all.

It wasn't illegal to listen to police radio, Healy explained, but it was against the law to own the equipment which allowed you to do so. That's the kind of precise distinction only a lawyer could have framed. In the States, I told him, anyone can listen to police radio.

'Unless you're in a car,' chipped in Walsh, who fancied himself as an expert on all things American. Indeed, I sometimes think not being born American was his one great regret in life and that he'd give up all the women if only he could make that wish come true.

Well, maybe half the women.

'With that one proviso, yes,' I agreed. 'Personally, I don't see the problem. The public pays for the cops, why shouldn't they know what they're up to?'

'Because criminals might be listening too,' Healy pointed out.

'That's the price of democracy,' I said.

My argument failed to sway him, but he didn't labour the point. 'It's all academic, anyway,' as he pointed out. 'Soon as we switch over to digital, no one will be able to listen to the transmissions any more except those who are supposed to. They've already done it over in England. Here it's only a matter of time before we have the systems in place to do the same.'

'Healy, I never realized you were such a killjoy,' I said, thinking again of my younger self and the fragmented nocturnal education I'd received across the airwaves all those years back. I wasn't sure I'd ever have got to where I was now if it hadn't been for those nights listening in on the Boston Police Department. Whether where I was now had been worth getting to, or whether I'd have been better off following a different path altogether, was another matter. I'd certainly have slept better in an alternative career.

Thankfully, I was jolted out of introspection by a shout from Fitzgerald.

Thankfully? That depended how you looked at it. Self-analysis of my life had never served me well. It was action not thought that kept me together. In that respect, I welcomed the interruption. I was less relieved when Fitzgerald showed me what she'd found.

It was another box file, only this one was not tagged or dated, nor was it filled with the same surveillance reports as the others. All it contained was a silver necklace with a tiny jewel-encrusted mask dangling from the chain, a phone card, a passport-sized photograph of a well-dressed man and woman in their fifties, and a few miscellaneous notes and coins.

It was no wonder Fitzgerald had exclaimed when she opened the file. I didn't need to remind her of the significance of what she'd found. But I said the words anyway, because I felt they should be said; that not to say them would be another betrayal of the young woman who had once owned these possessions and had them taken away one night in the snow.

'Beth Griffin,' I whispered.

Perhaps it was only then that I realized how peculiar this night had become.

39

He told Nick Elliott everything. He left nothing out. Kept nothing back. Most important of all, he told him why. He explained to him about the body in the freezer and how everything flowed from that. He told him how he'd knocked on Oliver's door less than an hour later and invited himself in. How Niland had been so scared when he realized what was going to be done with him, and how his life would end. He supposed everyone must wonder how they'll die. Lying in bed, surrounded by their loved ones? Falling asleep and never waking up?

He doubted if Niles ever imagined it would be strapped to a chair with a bloodstained gag over his mouth, waiting for the flames to reach him.

He saw Elliott flinch slightly when he told him what he'd done, imagining the scene, trying not to let it show that he was disgusted; but how could he possibly understand? He had to harden his heart against them, to do what had to be done. Justice demanded it.

He told him about Nat Tannar too, and the late train, the rattle of the carriages and the last shudder his body gave before death. He told him how Blunt was going to be next. He'd turned up as instructed on the telephone, on the dot, obedient to the last. He was lying now in the boot of the car down by the docks. He was tied up. Soon as he was finished here, he was going to go straight over there and push the car in the water and wait and watch whilst he drowned. He wouldn't be able to see it happening, sadly, only imagine the car filling with water and Blunt struggling. But he wanted to be there all the same.

Proximity aids the imagination.

He'd have done it already but Blunt was still unconscious when he left; he'd had to hit him to get him into the boot in the first place and must have hit him harder than intended. A blow to the head is never an exact science. If he'd pushed him in then, Blunt wouldn't have known a thing about it and he didn't want it to be that easy. As with the others, it was important that he got the chance to explain first why he was doing what he was doing.

That, however, was taking longer than expected. The reporter's hands were shaking so much as he made notes, for one thing, that he could scarcely form words on the page at all. His handwriting was like some abstract squiggle; Picasso doodling hiero-glyphics. Poor bastard. He'd only picked Elliott because he'd been sniffing around for months now making a nuisance of himself asking about things he didn't really comprehend. He wanted Elliott to know that he'd been barking up the wrong tree the whole time.

That he'd missed the real story under his nose.

There was a certain relief in confessing, he had to admit. Not that he was a religious person in any way. But this must be what it feels like in the confessional box, offloading your sins into another's hands and watching them vanish like smoke. Besides, who can resist the opportunity to talk about themselves at such length and without interruption?

To justify their choices?

It wasn't a full confession. Some things would remain private for now. Some things were too private to share. But there was always the possibility that he wouldn't be alive after tonight and he wanted people to know what he'd done and why, and why none of them could be allowed to live. He didn't want to be misunderstood. That was his greatest fear.

'But if you dump the car,' asked Elliott, the consummate reporter, when he'd been told of the plans for Blunt, 'how will you get around the city?'

'I have another car. How do you think I got here? On the bus? And if that gets found, I have another one again. That's why I got this place, and I have other places too that no one knows about,' he told Elliott. 'It's important to have secrets. That's what you reporters don't grasp. You think secrets are there to be exposed. All secrets except your own.'

'I . . . don't have any secrets,' he stammered.

'No? Then you're too good for this world. And you're certainly the first reporter I ever met I could say that about.'

Throughout the interview, with the tape recorder whirring between them on the table, he watched revulsion wrestle inside Elliott with ambition. He didn't need to tell the newsman how much this story might mean to his career tomorrow. All he had to do was get through tonight. He hated to see that look in another's eyes, though. That *disapproval*. It was as if he was some kind of monster. Something twisted and inhuman. Elliott's look of horror was even more pronounced when his summoner had come to the end of his testimony, and rose from his seat, walked to the wall and lifted down a coil of rope he'd stored here for the purpose.

'What are you going to do?' he said, his voice trembling.

'I'm going to tie you up. No need to look so petrified. You're no good to me dead. I need you to tell my story. You're my witness. My conduit to the world. I just need to make sure that you don't spoil things by talking too quickly.'

'I won't, I promise, I—'

'Sorry, Elliott. I appreciate your promise, but a rope doesn't change its mind.'

'But what if something happens to you? How will anyone know where I am?'

'They won't,' he said brightly. 'So you'd better start hoping that nothing does happen to me in the meantime. Though if that happens, there's always the tape. You'll still have your story. Your big scoop. It's just that you won't be around to reap the benefits.'

He laughed again, he couldn't help it, Elliott looked so helpless and stricken. They were all so desperate to cling on to their pathetic lives, however worthless. They were barely alive at all. Death for these people was merely an official confirmation of their non-existence. He didn't even struggle as the rope went round him and the tape was placed over his mouth.

Was no one going to fight back?

He checked that the bonds were secure just on the off chance that Elliott made an attempt at escape once alone. Then he switched off the light, pulled down the metal door, and locked it. He checked his watch. He should hurry. Quickening his steps, he walked round to the old hospital where he'd parked the other car and climbed inside, switching on the radio as soon as the key was in the ignition, hoping they were talking about him. Three bodies in one night so far, and still he wasn't done. What else could they possibly be talking about?

40

The snow had melted within a week and the chances of catching the man who murdered Beth Griffin and left her body in the canal to freeze seemed to vanish with it. It was one of those investigations that went nowhere from the start. It was as if the police got off on the wrong foot and never recovered their balance. Every angle flattened out into a straight line. Every lead turned into a blind alley. Sometimes a case needs an early breakthrough, a stroke of luck, lightning-bright, from the sky, or it runs into the sand. This was one of them.

But Beth wasn't a mere case, she was a young woman who had been snatched from life just when it was beginning to open up and show promise, and she deserved better from those charged with eking some kind of justice from the horror of her death.

It's wrong to differentiate between victims. The dead are the dead and they have a right to demand justice from the living. Still, there are usually reasons why things happen the way they do. There are wrong paths taken, bad decisions made. Beth, though, had done everything in her life right. The only poor choice she ever made was believing she could walk home in the snow one night in her own town, days from Christmas.

That she'd been killed by a stranger, there was little doubt. Her life was raked over, a picture drawn. There were no obsessive ex-boyfriends lurking in the background. She'd had no fears for her safety. The Murder Squad commissioned a profile of the killer from Lawrence Fisher, which stressed again the random nature of her fate. The motive remained unclear. There was no sign of sexual assault. There were a couple of missing items – a necklace, some money – but this wasn't a robbery which went wrong.

Thieves don't usually steal photographs of their victims' parents as trophies, or taunt the police with the threat of more to come.

Everyone on the various routes Beth Griffin could have taken on the night she died from the last place she was seen alive to the canal where her body was found was interviewed, sometimes several times over. Occasional fragments of information looked promising, a sighting here, an overheard quarrel there, but they all came to nothing.

The tape of the call which the killer made to the police on Beth's cellphone was also analysed as much as possible, but he'd been concealing his true voice, he wasn't stupid enough to give that much information away, and electronic manipulation of the tape yielded little except a bizarre mutliplicity of potential accents and identities. All we knew was that the killer had to be sufficiently non-threatening for Beth to trust him to get close enough to kill her. There was no sign of a struggle. What happened came out of the blue.

I hadn't been much help to the investigation. So much for the expertise of this Special Adviser. I wasn't alone in my failure to make headway, and no one blamed me directly, though there were inevitable sarcastic comments from some of the team, but I felt my inadequacy acutely. I was there to add something extra to the mix, to offer insights that might be overlooked by the local cops, but I was as baffled as they were. I couldn't help wondering if my touch had deserted me, or if I'd ever had it to begin with. I doubted my own ability, that sixth sense I'd thought I had in the past, and on which my whole sense of self had been based.

Eventually, Beth's body was returned to her parents, and she was buried in the family plot on a graveyard north of the city. Shortly afterwards, the family home in Dublin was locked up and abandoned and they moved away. To a huge place on the Californian side of Lake Taho, I heard. Her father came from San Franscisco. They'd only moved to Dublin because of his work. It made it all the more poignant. It meant that out there somewhere there was a shadow Beth, the Beth who might have been if they'd stayed in the States.

It wasn't that Beth was forgotten, but other matters were bound to distract the attention of the

Murder Squad. Other murders, all demanding the same attention, the same resources. I'd seen it a hundred times. Without a breakthrough, it looked like it would take a mistake on the part of the killer, or, God help us, another victim, before the case could be closed, and another young woman dead was the last thing anyone wanted.

Beth Griffin was effectively buried a second time.

And then came the second killing.

Shirley Heuston's body was found almost six months to the day that Beth Griffin died. A waitress who worked at the Hard Rock Café in Temple Bar, Shirley was an aspiring rock singer who sang with a band weekends and holidays. They'd made their first demo; they were picking up some radio play and gigging around town; there were plans for an up-coming appearance at an open-air festival in Spain during the summer. The band had high hopes.

Shirley's death put an end to all that.

She was found dumped on wasteground near the airport in the north of the city, wrapped in an old rug. Analysed, it yielded traces of motor oil and petrol, suggesting she had been kept in a garage during the three days since she went missing. Unlike Beth Griffin, she had not been killed immediately. There were signs of sexual torture. Given the lack of forensic evidence, police might not even have linked her death to that of Beth at all, had it not been for the subsequent call made on her cellphone: '*This is the second.*'

It was a year before the third victim died. Jocelyn Finch, known to her friends as Joss, was held a whole week before being killed. Like Shirley Heuston, she was strangled.

'*This is the third.*'

The torture had been much more pronounced this time. Our perpetrator was intensifying. He was at the stage where each killing had to be more sadistic to satisfy the impulse inside him. What had worked for him when he took the first victim was no longer sufficient to deliver the same charge. What he would do to the next didn't bear thinking about, but, with each week that passed, the chances of saving a fourth victim looked more and more remote. Every potential suspect in the city was hauled in and questioned. Lock-ups and garages were searched. Additional forensics experts were called in from London. The FBI provided a profiler on request, but he came up with no more than Fisher had already done.

He was smart: that was the sum total that the experts had to offer.

And we didn't need a profile to tell us that.

Was he *too* clever for us? I was reluctant to say so; despair had always been the demon I needed to fight against, despite the fact that I had seen many cases which were closed just when the odds looked insurmountable. But it was looking that way.

The killer was effortlessly evading every net into which the Murder Squad tried to entrap him. He also resisted the temptation to make further contact beyond the original claim. He was strategic. He knew that too much communication with the police would only provide them with extra information. The thrill of taunting them was not worth the risk to him.

And now, out of nowhere, here were Beth Griffin's necklace and money, and the picture of her parents, hidden away in a box file in Daniel Erskine's house, and only the chance of his murder had brought them to light at all. That's the way it goes sometimes. The answer doesn't always lie where you expect. Sometimes it just jumps out when you're not even looking for it. But what to make of what we'd found tonight? That was the problem.

'*Could* Daniel Erskine have killed Beth?' I said.

'He certainly fits the profiles,' said Fitzgerald. 'A man in his forties, above average intelligence, controlled, living an apparently normal life to everyone around him. Fisher said the killer would be well used to concealing his true nature behind a facade.'

'He lived along one of the possible routes she took that night too,' I pointed out. 'He must have been interviewed, though obviously his answers didn't give rise to suspicion.'

'Who'd suspect a man like Daniel Erskine of being a killer?' said Walsh.

'We need to find the officer who questioned him at the time.'

Fitzgerald frowned. I could tell she didn't like the turn tonight's events had taken.

'Daniel dies, then Niland, the other members of

his precious Second Circle disappear, Riordan runs when we ask him a few questions about his friends, then Elliott comes in and says Erskine was up to his neck in political corruption, and now there's Beth Griffin too? Where's the connection? How can they all be part of the same puzzle?'

'Maybe there isn't a connection,' I said. 'Maybe what's happened to Daniel and his friends has nothing to do with Beth Griffin's death, they're just two separate roads which happened to intersect tonight. Daniel killed Beth, someone else killed Daniel.'

'You're forgetting how Erskine died,' she said.

He was left to freeze.

'Is that a coincidence too?'

Now I understood why she was having such a difficulty making the disparate elements of tonight's events fit together. The symbolic nature of putting Daniel Erskine in the freezer suggested that his killer knew what he had done, if indeed he was Beth's murderer. Perhaps it was intended then as a kind of poetic justice. Revenge in the form of ice.

But then why kill Oliver Niland too?

Could it be that Erskine hadn't acted alone? That the revenge, if that's what it was, had to be shared out between the guilty?

'This is crazy,' I conceded. 'We don't even know that Erskine *did* kill Beth Griffin. If he did, then where are the trophies of the other two victims? Their cellphones, money, personal effects. The killer took those from all three women. And they're not here.'

'You mean, they haven't been found yet.'

'There's nowhere left to look,' I said. 'All the boxes have been opened. And look at his creepy little hideaway back there. Isn't it just as likely that his obsession with watching what was going on in the city led him, by accident or design, to finding out who really murdered her, and that he was killed tonight by someone wanting to protect his secret?'

'Then he was disturbed before he could get his hands on the incriminating evidence upstairs?' Fitzgerald added. 'It's possible. But why go on to kill Niland?'

'The others might have known the identity of Beth Griffin's killer too.'

'That's an awful lot of people to include in the conspiracy.'

'Conspiracies are, by their nature, collective. And the Second Circle is unbroken after all these years. They must have a pretty strong bond between them.'

'I fear the only bond they'll have by the end of tonight is that they'll all be dead,' Fitzgerald remarked bitterly, 'and that the secret of Beth's murder will die with them.'

'One of them's still alive,' said Patrick Walsh unexpectedly.

'What do you mean?'

'Didn't you hear?' he said. He pointed to the scanner which had been switched on the whole time, picking up the police radio broadcasts. I hadn't been paying attention to them. They'd become background sound. It wasn't so long since Walsh had been in uniform, however, and he obviously still paid more attention to what he heard crackling out of the speakers. 'Someone you've been wanting to talk to for the last few hours has just been spotted walking along Fenian Street. Someone answering his description, at any rate.'

'And I think,' I said when he told us who it was, 'that I know exactly where he's going.'

41

The sign outside on the railing said the museum closed at 5 p.m., but the gate was ajar. Either they were expecting some after-hours visitors, or someone had recently unlocked it and gone inside – and there were no prizes for guessing who. The only other candidate was Thomas Heazle Parke, Victorian surgeon, explorer and naturalist, whose bronze statue guarded the grounds of the museum, and he was giving nothing away. A plaque on the granite pedestal below commemorated the moment in 1887 when he sucked the poison from an arrow wound in the chest of a fellow explorer. Whether the Africans who had been sold into slavery as a result of earlier explorers' heroic exploits felt it all worthy of honour, no one bothered to ask.

Our footsteps sounded unnaturally loud as we walked down the curving path to the front door through a rain of exhausted leaves from the trees on either side. Silence accentuated them. There was no chance of arriving unannounced, that was for sure. The grey windowless ghost of the building rose above our heads, framed by the night sky.

'Look,' said Fitzgerald quietly, and pointed to the door.

That was open too.

I reached out a hand and pushed at the door. The creak as it gave way beneath my hand sounded louder even than our footsteps.

'After you,' she said.

'You're too kind,' I said.

I slipped through the gap into shadow, pausing a moment to let my eyes adjust to the dimness within. There is something creepy about public buildings after dark, when they've emptied, and there's nothing but the exhibits and the mice to keep a soul company, and this one was creepier than most. I'd expected to come into a lobby but instead a huge room opened up before and above me, with only a small area up front for buying booklets and gifts. The only light there was came from a couple of strip lights which had been left on at the far end of the room. Otherwise the sole illumination was the glint of the bulbs on glass.

The room was filled with glass cases, in which the obscure outlines of stuffed animals could be seen. That is, I knew they were stuffed because that was the point of the museum, but you could almost have sworn the creatures were still alive, watching, biding their time.

They didn't call it the Dead Zoo for nothing.

'Hello,' called out Fitzgerald, and I jumped. I hadn't realized she was standing so close. 'Is anyone there? Blunt, we need to talk to you. Can you hear us?'

Her voice echoed to the end of the giant room and back, but it went unanswered.

'I hope they're friendlier during the day,' she commented.

I took out the flashlight we'd brought along with us, in case it was needed, and directed the beam down the length of the hall, the light glancing off the red and black tiled floor like the last flickerings of a dying fire. Glazed taxidermic eyes blinked back.

'What the hell—?'

'It's a shark,' said Fitzgerald, 'suspended from the ceiling.'

'Terrific way with interior design they have in this place,' I said.

'Don't worry, it won't bite,' she replied. 'It's only a basking shark. They only eat plankton, not Americans. Besides, all its teeth have been taken out.'

'Why?'

'Better safe than sorry, I guess. Come on, let's try upstairs.'

'You mean there's more?'

'Another three floors,' Fitzgerald said.

'And everything dead in them except us.'

'And Blunt.'

'If he's really here,' I pointed out. 'He must have heard you calling.'

'Ever thought we might be the last people he wants to see right now?'

'I do tend to have that effect on people . . .'

Stone steps led upstairs from either side of the

room. We took the stairs on the left, Fitzgerald calling out to Blunt a couple more times as we went on up, though she might have been announcing her presence to the stuffed animals for all the response she got.

I began to wonder if we were wrong about Blunt coming here. Just because he was in the vicinity of Fenian Street didn't mean he was making his way to the museum, and that was even assuming it was him in the first place. One sighting proved nothing.

The gate being open? That could have been a coincidence.

The light was dimmer still on the next floor up, the shadows crowding among the display cases like spilled water, though the space itself was much more expansive. This time the room rose a further two floors through empty air with railed balconies around the sides until it came to a glass roof, now black with night and a hint of stars, the rising view broken only by lines of metal poles like prison bars connecting the balconies on either side.

In fact, I thought, that's what the whole place reminded me of; it was a prison rather than a zoo. The closer I looked, the more bars I saw. The ranks of square pillars; the line of the floorboards; the strips of wood on the glass cases – they all suggested the same theme.

Here what hung from the ceiling was not a shark but the whole skeleton of a humpback whale, and even along the length of this creature's tail the sharp, picked-clean bones protruded straight outwards in the same rigid, regular pattern of lines.

'So this is where Seamus Dalton lives,' said Fitzgerald absently, interrupting my thoughts, and I turned to see that she was looking at the display case nearest the stairs rather than the view up to the top of the building. 'I've often wondered.'

'Dalton?' I frowned, because I wasn't following her train of thought.

Then I saw what she was looking at. The first case contained a family of mean-looking primates, apes and monkeys and orang-utans doing what apes and monkeys and orang-utans do best, and looking vaguely pissed that someone had disturbed them from scratching themselves and slouching and eating and knocking one another about the head – or any of the various other civilized activities in which your average primate passes another productive day.

'It does look rather like the canteen in Dublin Castle on a bad day,' I conceded.

'Only this lot are marginally more civilized,' she added.

'Can I help you, ladies?'

The sound of an unfamilair voice made Fitzgerald and I both jump. We hadn't heard anyone approaching on the tiled floor and it wasn't like noises kept themselves to themselves in a big open space like this.

Turning, we found an unfamiliar man standing behind us. I just had time to clock a pair of blue pants, white shirt and yellow tie – not the best sartorial statement, it had to be said – before he flicked the switch of his own flashlight and blinded us with a direct blast of the beam. The sudden illumination felt like flecks of fire burning in my eyes.

'Hey, switch that off!' I demanded.

'Tell me how you got in here first,' he said, and his voice had a crowing quality that made no attempt to hide the fact he was enjoying our discomfort.

'We got in through the door,' Fitzgerald answered coolly. She hadn't even raised her hands to shield her eyes from the light. She wasn't going to give him the satisfaction. 'Isn't that how visitors normally get in?'

'Most of them wait until opening hours.'

'If you're so concerned about keeping people out during the night,' she pointed out, 'you should make sure they can't just walk in off the street. That is your job, I presume?'

'I'm the security attendant, if that's what you mean,' he said, and he lowered the beam fractionally, almost reluctantly. I resisted the urge to blind him with a return blast of the flashlight. I didn't want this turning into some surreal re-enactment of the scene in *Star Wars* where Obi-Wan Kenobi and Darth Vader battle it out with lightsabres on the Death Star.

He was no one's idea of Darth Vader, that's for sure. He was a small balding man with blotchy skin and a moustache that made him look like a Burt Reynolds impersonator.

His name tag said he was called Norman.

That figured.

'Who are you, anyway, and what do you want?' he said now, a little resentfully.

'We're from the police,' said Fitzgerald, and she showed him her badge, though it might have been her credentials for the Girl Guides for all the attention he paid it.

'I suppose this is about the robbery,' he said.

'You had a robbery?'

'Last weekend. Our busiest day. I wasn't on duty, but some young fella apparently came in with a knife and a pair of tights on his head and demanded all the day's takings from the till. He obviously hadn't done his homework or he'd have known we don't charge for entry. He just took the money from the shop and ran off. It was all captured on CCTV.'

It was almost touching, the way the security attendant seemed to believe that the Dublin Metropolitan Police would send someone out at 3 a.m. to investigate a week-old robbery. Oh well, as long as it made him feel he was paying his taxes for something . . .

'It's not about the robbery,' Fitzgerald said apologetically. 'We're actually here to talk to someone. A member of staff. We have reason to believe he might be in here.'

'Then I'm afraid you've had a wasted journey. There's no one here but me,' Norman said. 'Unless it's one of these lads you want,' he added with a sudden laugh, sweeping the beam of the flashlight round to where the dead animals in their glass cases waited out eternity and mounted heads on the wall stared down on the proceedings below like a bizarre jury, 'and I don't think they'll be able to tell you much.' Awkwardly, he turned the laugh into an impromptu cough when he realized it wasn't being reciprocated.

'Ronan Blunt,' Fitzgerald continued.

'I told you, there's no one—'

'I wasn't talking to you,' she said, and that quietened him. 'Hello, Mr Blunt.'

The passing beam had picked up a figure lurking by one of the cases, and standing so still that he might have been one of the exhibits. He still made no effort to move now that his presence had been noticed. He was staring through the glass at a polar bear. White teeth bared in a fixed snarl, it might have been menacing as it readied itself to strike, if it wasn't for the mangy fur and the fact that there was a bullet hole visible in its skull.

'Mr Blunt,' the security attendant said in surprise, 'I had no idea you were—'

'It's OK, Norman, I'll take over from here.'

'Can I get you—?'

'No, really, I'm fine. If you could just go down and close the outer door. I think I may have left it open.' Blunt's voice was mechanical, like the words were issuing from his mouth without any knowledge or effort on his part at all. 'I don't remember . . .'

'I'll do it right away,' Norman said without

enthusiasm. He was intrigued, he wanted to stay and hear what this was all about, but such was the fate of security guards, always to be left on the sidelines. Fitzgerald waited till his footsteps had faded on the stairs.

'You see this bear?' said Blunt when there was silence again. 'It was shot in 1852 by Captain Francis Leopold McClintock. Have you heard of him?' He didn't wait for an answer. 'He was an Irish explorer in Victorian times. He mapped scores of islands in the Canadian Arctic archipelago. Found the remains of the infamous Franklin Expedition too. The whole crew of 130 men starved to death after becoming trapped in ice when they tried to chart the Northwest Passage. No one knew what had happened to them. Boats were sent, rescue missions mounted … You know more men died trying to find the missing men than died on the original voyage? It's ironic, when you think of it. But it was McClintock who did it. He brought back the skin of this chap here as a souvenir.' He sighed. 'I wish I'd lived in those times. You could make a difference then. Really do something that mattered. Make a mark. What have I ever done apart from waste my life in this dump? It's been more like a mausoleum than a museum. Nine to five. Nine to five. I've been as dead as this stupid bear the whole time and I didn't even realize it. And now it's all too late.'

'You know why we're here, don't you?' said Fitzgerald.

'It's about *her*, isn't it?' said Blunt. For the first time he raised his terrified eyes and returned Fitzgerald's gaze, and a chill colder than the polar bear's former home fell on the museum as he spoke the next words. 'We shouldn't have done it. I told them it was wrong, but they wouldn't listen. We killed her and now we're all going to pay for it.'

A thousand eyes glared back at him in silence. Rarely can there have been so many witnesses to a confession. That's one thing you can say about the dead.

They make good listeners.

42

'Do you want coffee?' said Blunt with the air of a man who was trying to remember what normality felt like but could find no template for it in his head any more. 'Or maybe you drink tea? There's a kettle somewhere. At least there should be. Or I could ask Norman?'

Somewhere in the building, Norman was whistling loudly and tunelessly. It was one of those whistles designed solely to remind the listener that the whistler was still there and that they didn't care about the fact they were being excluded from what was going on. The *Guinness Book of World Records* could have listed this one as the most passive-aggressive whistle ever heard in the confines of a small museum after dark.

We were in Blunt's office, if an area the size of a broom closet could be called an office. The living in the Natural History Museum took second place to the dead, and since there were plenty of dead animals needing a place of their own here, space was at a premium. Offices were afterthoughts squeezed into the edges of the building like murder holes.

This one reminded me uncomfortably of Daniel Erskine's hidden room. Box files were piled high here too, teetering in piles on the tiny desk, and stacked on the floor. The bones of some unidentified creature were scattered on a shelf like some macabre jigsaw puzzle. The only difference was that, instead of a transmitter to pick up police radio broadcasts, there was a portable transistor radio. Blunt had switched it on as soon as we were all inside, and the low hum of an orchestra playing something half familiar hung in the air.

Next to the radio there was a framed photograph – the same line-up of the Second Circle that he'd had on display in his office at home. What was it? Some kind of cult?

Since his unexpected confession in the room below, Ronan Blunt had slipped into a weird state of composure; or maybe it was more a kind of pathological detachment, a protective distancing of his inner self to cope with the shock of what he'd just admitted.

Maybe he was regretting having said too much and needed to gather his thoughts for a moment by pretending it hadn't happened. There was nothing to be gained by rushing him, so we waited patiently, and let him ramble on about coffee and the broken central heating.

He'd talk eventually. Men like Blunt always did. They couldn't help themselves.

It was the ones who nursed silence like it was a vocation who were the problem.

I was still trying to reconcile my image of Blunt with that I'd pieced together in my mind of Beth

Griffin's killer. He was very far from being the icy, controlled, manipulative type. If Blunt killed anyone, I figured it would be more hurried, unplanned. He'd screw up. He'd give himself away. Beth's killer had made no mistake. Or was that down to the fact there were others involved, like he'd said downstairs? *We killed her.*

And yet that didn't make much sense either. Lawrence Fisher had drawn up the profile of her killer last winter, and he wasn't some wet-behind-the-ears forensic psychology graduate bungling his first reading of a crime scene. If there'd been more than one person involved in the death of Beth Griffin, he'd have seen it. That he'd seen nothing of the kind made me wonder if Blunt had cracked and lost all sense of reality. His eyes screamed of a barely concealed panic. They didn't stay still for a second, but darted here and there about the room like a lizard scanning the air for flies – but he never looked at either of us once.

'If you want a lawyer . . .' Fitzgerald began eventually.

Blunt stopped searching obsessively for the kettle, and his face was a study in bewilderment. It was almost as if he was offended by her suggestion.

'What would I want with a lawyer?' he said.

'So that you can tell us about Beth Griffin,' she said. 'Isn't that why we're here?'

Beth? His mouth framed the name, but he didn't speak it.

'I don't know who ... I've never ... I've never heard of ... what did you say?'

'Beth Griffin,' Fitzgerald repeated. 'Isn't that who you were talking about downstairs? She was murdered two years ago. Her body was found in the canal.'

I saw recognition strike him like a fist.

'That girl a couple of Christmases ago? You think I ... killed her?'

'You weren't talking about Beth Griffin?'

'Of course not! I couldn't do a thing like that. What kind of man do you think I am?'

'Right now,' I said, 'I don't know what kind of man you are. I'd say the jury's still out, wouldn't you? Who *were* you talking about if it wasn't Beth?'

'I was talking about Erin,' he said, but it still seemed that he was sore about being suspected of another woman's killing rather than the one to which he'd wanted to confess. I exchanged glances with Fitzgerald and could tell that she was as confused now as I was. She shook her head with exasperation. Nothing was destined to be straightforward tonight.

'Who was Erin?' she said slowly.

'Erin was a stripper. No, I shouldn't call her that,' Blunt said thickly, sitting down on the edge of the desk like he wasn't sure he had the energy to both stand and talk. 'It was Daniel who found out about her. He saw her card in a telephone box near the university. He said we should hire her for the night so she could put on a show for us, you know?'

'How old were you?'

'We were second-year students at the time. What would that make us? Nineteen? Twenty? I'm not sure. It was all so long ago. More than twenty years.'

Was that supposed to make a difference?

'Was Erin her real name?'

'Yes, though she didn't tell us that's what she was called at the time. We only found out later, when we read about her in the paper. Erin Gilroy, they said her name was. The card in the phone box only said she was called Honey. She did home visits, birthday parties, stag parties, that sort of thing. Daniel called her up, booked her for our usual Friday-night get-together. We thought it'd be a laugh. Like I say, she was going to put on a show.'

'Who exactly was there that night?' said Fitzgerald.

'Me, Oliver Niland, Michael, Nat, Sean Riordan, Toby Fraser. The usual crowd.'

'Not Daniel?'

'He was supposed to be there, he was always head of the Second Circle; first among equals, you might say. But he called at the last minute, said he couldn't make it, something had come up, so we went ahead without him. Worst mistake we ever made.'

'What happened?'

'She turned up around nine at Toby's flat. It was Toby's turn to play host. We'd already been drinking at this point. We usually started pretty early. That was the point of the club. To lose yourself to pleasure. To cast off the shackles of convention.' He said the words lightly, making it sound as though he recognized in retrospect how pathetic the philosophy that bound them together really was; but there was something wistful in his voice too that made me think he hadn't entirely let go of his former self's childish illusions. 'We just let her get on with what she'd come to do, but we could see that there was something wrong.'

'Go on.'

'She wasn't all there, if you know what I mean. Her eyes were unfocused. She was woozy. She kept slurring her words. We thought maybe she was drunk, like we were, but there was more to it than that. She kept disappearing into the bathroom. Toby was freaking out. He thought she was going to pull a knife on us and steal his stuff. The third or fourth time it happened, he said he'd had enough, he wanted her out of the place, but then she said there was more on offer if we wanted it, if we had the money to pay. We let her stay.'

'So you each took turns with her?'

'Everyone apart from Niles. He said he was too drunk to get it up. We didn't care, it just meant there was more of her for us. We were having a good time.'

'And Erin?'

'She was acting more strangely the longer the night went on. Eventually, we realized why she kept sneaking off into the bathroom.'

'She was doing drugs,' I said.

He nodded.

'One time, she didn't come out, and she didn't answer either when we called through the lock. In the end, we had to break down the door to get inside. She was lying on the floor by the toilet, a needle still sticking out of her arm. Her whole body was shaking.'

'An overdose,' said Fitzgerald.

'That's what it looked like. We just panicked. We didn't know what to do.'

'How about calling an ambulance and getting her some medical help?' I said.

'That's what I said, I begged them to get her to a doctor, but they said they couldn't risk it getting out that they'd been paying for sex with some cheap stripper who advertised in phone boxes. You have to remember who they were. Michael was heir to a fortune. Toby's father was one of the top barristers in the city. Niles's family was loaded too.'

I wondered where that money had all gone. Niland had obviously not had much of it when he died or he wouldn't have been living in that hole on the northside.

'They said the publicity would ruin them. Besides, it wasn't our fault that she'd overdosed. We hadn't known she was a drug addict when we hired her.'

'You thought she just took her clothes off for drunken strangers for the fun of it?'

Blunt flinched, and Fitzgerald cast me a reproachful stare. There was nothing to be gained by antagonizing him now. We needed him to talk. We needed everything we could get.

Blunt, thankfully, didn't climb on his high horse and clam up. It seemed like he wanted to tell someone what happened that night, however badly it reflected on him.

That the time for silence had ended.

'Sean Riordan had a car,' he told us softly. 'He said he'd bring it round to the back of the building, we were to get her downstairs, lift her into the back seat, then we'd drive her anonymously to hospital and they could treat her there. It seemed like the only choice we had. So what's what we did. The only problem was she started moaning the minute we moved her, and then she threw up on the stairs, and there was blood in it, and she was shaking so badly by this point that we could hardly get her into the back seat of the car at all.'

'Even then, you still didn't call an ambulance?'

'I don't think it would have made any difference. It was too late. It already looked like she'd stopped breathing by the time we got her to the hospital. We left her in the car park and then called to say where she was. It said on the news next day that she never regained consciousness and died later that night. Another dead junkie. They probably didn't even bother to count them in those days, there were so many. Times were different.'

'And her death was never connected to you or your friends?'

'We worried for a while that Erin might have told someone where she was going that night and that the police would come asking questions,' said Blunt, 'but she must have kept quiet, because we never heard another word about it. We just got on with our lives. We felt bad about it, but we couldn't change what had happened. What was done was done.'

And so the years passed, and they prospered, or survived at any rate, and Erin joined the ranks of the forgotten. I felt weary all of a sudden of this night, this city, this world we lived in. Life seemed to be a worthless commodity, and happiness an illusion. Nothing lasted. Death was everywhere around. The air reeked of it. Past and present alike were infected with it, and the future only offered more of the same.

Blunt and his rich friends in the Second Circle hadn't killed Erin Gilroy; not in the way Beth Griffin had been killed. Not calculatedly. Not with malice aforethought, as the saying goes. She would have died without their help eventually, and probably sooner rather than later. A woman like that is only ever one needle away from disaster. As Blunt said, it was a common occurrence in the city at that time when drugs were still an underclass problem not merely a way for the middle classes to pass time between dinner parties.

But Erin had died when she died and how she died and where she died because of their indifference to her humanity. By putting their own superficial needs first when her very life was in the balance, they had hastened her end and made themselves complicit in it.

Such a stain on the soul was not so easily removed. Or maybe I was wrong about that too. Some people seemed to live with the darkest of secrets and remain untouched.

'But I still don't see what it has to do with all this,' Fitzgerald said frustratedly, interrupting my thoughts, and I was glad of the interruption. They were getting me nowhere. 'You said you were all paying tonight for what you'd done. What did you mean?'

'Someone found out,' I said suddenly, remembering the note in Michael Erskine's house, and some cell deep inside me delighted in knowing that Erin Gilroy had not been forgotten for ever.

Whatever the consequences, the fallen have a right to be remembered.

43

'I got a letter,' said Blunt. 'A blackmail note, I suppose you'd call it.'

'*I know about Erin I know about everything I'll be in touch.*'

'That was the one. You know about that?' he asked in astonishment.

'We found one exactly like it in Michael Erskine's house,' explained Fitzgerald. 'No punctuation. Letters clipped and glued from a magazine. *Don't try to run and don't hide.*'

'When did it come?' I said to Blunt.

'A couple of months ago? It just dropped through the letter box one morning at breakfast, along with the bills and a copy of a journal I'd been waiting for.' He shook his head, the incongruity of the letter's arrival seemingly bewildering him anew in retrospect.

'What did you do?' I said to Blunt.

'Do? I didn't *do* anything. Not at first. I couldn't think straight. Tina knew something was wrong when I opened it, but I told her it was bad news about the museum's funding. She didn't believe me, but it was the first thing that came into my head.'

'Did the others get the same note?'

'I called Nat on my way to the museum. He'd got

one too, and so had Niles, he'd already spoken to him. Everyone who was there that night had received the same note. We decided we should meet up that evening after work and figure out how to respond.'

'The writer didn't make any demands?' I said.

'Not inititally. I think the first note was just a shot across the bows. A warning. He wanted to put the fear of God into us and then leave us to stew for a while.'

'You must have been scared.'

'We all were. We thought what happened that night with Erin Gilroy was way in the past. Now here it was coming back to haunt us.'

'That's what the dead do,' I pointed out.

'But after all that time ...' Blunt trailed off helplessly, unable to express the shock he'd felt. 'It was the last thing any of us expected, that's all. We had families, careers, responsibilities. It was almost worse for it to happen now than back then.'

'How did you decide between yourselves to respond?' said Fitzgerald.

'There was little we could do,' Blunt said. 'Like I say, there were no demands, nothing we were being told to do – and there obviously wasn't a return address. He wasn't that stupid. It looked as if we'd simply have to wait and see. But he started to get bolder. He sent one letter to me at work. Niles found one pasted to his door for everyone to see.'

'There was no direct approach, though?'

'No, but he was getting closer every day. It was

only a matter of time before he made his move. That's when Niles suggested we should go to Daniel and ask for help. He'd always relied on Dan to get him out of trouble. We all had, I suppose.'

'He seems to have had quite a hold on you all,' I commented.

'He did. He always had. He was younger than the rest of us. Michael's little brother.' He gave an ironic laugh. 'But Daniel wasn't one to play second fiddle to anyone. He dominated us, it's the only word for it, from the moment Michael brought him into our group. It was he who came up with the whole idea of the Second Circle.'

'Did Daniel know what had happened to Erin Gilroy?'

'Daniel knew *everything*,' insisted Blunt, and he didn't notice as Fitzgerald and I exchanged meaningful glances, remembering Erskine's hidden treasury of surveillance files back at his townhouse. 'It was probably Niles who told him about that too.'

'You sound like you'd rather he hadn't known about it at all,' I said.

'No, no,' Blunt answered hurriedly. 'Don't get me wrong. Daniel *helped* us. Anything he could do to protect someone in the Second Circle, he'd do it without question.'

'So what did he do in this instance?'

'He said to leave it with him and he'd find out who sent the letters.'

'And did he?'

'It took him a few weeks, and there were more letters in the meantime, but yes.'

'More letters?' asked Fitzgerald. 'Saying what exactly?'

'They were all variations on a theme,' Blunt explained. '*I know why she really died . . . you're going to regret you ever heard her name . . . Don't think you'll get away with this forever . . .*' He made a gesture indicating how the threats kept on coming relentlessly.

'Did the writer progress to specific demands?'

'He mentioned money in some of them. He said he knew we were all loaded and that money meant nothing to people like us. Well, that was a joke for a start. Daniel and Michael may have had money, but the rest of us weren't exactly rolling in it, to say the least.'

'That's what happens when you amass large gambling debts,' I remarked idly.

Blunt looked momentarily startled, but quickly recovered.

'I see you've been talking to Tina,' he said dismissively. 'Give you her life story, did she? Tell you what a bad husband I am – useless in bed, useless with money?'

'She didn't mention the part about being useless in bed.'

'I suppose I should be grateful for small mercies. In fact, I'm surprised you got away before morning. Once she starts listing my deficiences, she's a hard woman to stop. She must have given you the edited version rather than the five-hour Director's Cut.'

'She was worried about you. When you went out without a word –'

'The only thing Tina ever worried about,' said Blunt, 'is where her next bottle of vodka is coming from. As long as I left her a blank cheque at the off-licence, she wouldn't care where I was. After the first few glasses, she doesn't even notice if I'm not there.'

There was a look in his eyes when he spoke about his wife that twisted his features. It was strange how often relationships can turn into battles of hate like this. They must have loved one another once. Now there was only mutual dependency and ill-concealed resentment left. Why didn't he just leave her if it was so bad? Because whatever it was she did to him, he still needed it. We're meant to be grown-ups, but few of us rarely progress beyond childhood. We just want attention. Positive or negative, it makes no odds. It made me sick.

But it wasn't getting us anywhere right now to dwell on it, and I cut him off abruptly before he could start on another rant. 'Tell us about Daniel instead,' I said. 'How did he find out who was behind the letters?'

Blunt shrugged, accepting it as one of the things Daniel could do. Daniel seemed to be accepted as the one in the group who got things done, who always knew what to do.

'He mentioned something about a firm of private detectives he used occasionally.' It was a little more than occasionally, not that Blunt was to know it. It was probably even the same people he used to spy on his own friends. There's irony. 'We didn't ask questions. If he said he'd do something, Daniel did it. He was reliable. That was enough. One night he called us round to his place and told us he'd tracked down the writer.'

'Who was it?'

'It was a man by the name of Conn Gilroy,' he said.

'Gilroy,' I said.

'The very same.'

44

Erin, it seemed, was not only a junkie, stripper and part-time prostitute, but a mother as well.

'He was only a baby when she died,' said Blunt. 'Daniel told us that the child had been brought up by his aunt, that she died when he was only four, and he'd been taken into care. Apparently, he had a rough time of it.'

'And now little Conn was back looking for a pay-off for his silence. How did he find out about you? About his mother? You said there was never anything to link you, or anyone else for that matter, to her death. Wasn't she supposed to be another anonymous junkie?'

'I genuinely haven't got a notion how he tracked us down, or even how he found out his mother had died the way she did, or that anyone but herself was to blame.'

'Maybe being in care had made him resourceful,' I suggested sarcastically.

'Or maybe one of your circle had let the cat out of the bag inadvertently,' Fitzgerald butted in. 'Talked too freely whilst they were drunk, or confided to a lover, a stranger?'

'No.'

'It happens,' she said. 'People will talk. The urge to confess is as old as Adam.'

'You don't understand. We took a ... well, you could almost call it a vow of silence. It was what bound us together. Whatever happened, the knowledge of what we'd done was always with us. It made us dependent on one another. None of us would have broken the pledge we made to protect one another. It would have been the ultimate betrayal.'

'Your sense of the vow you'd taken might have been what made it all the harder for one of you to admit letting the secret slip,' Fitzgerald pressed on. 'No one wants to be accused of betrayal. No one wants to feel they've let down their friends.'

'I hear what you're saying,' Blunt answered, 'and maybe you're right. It's not ... impossible. It's just that after all this time ... you know ... why now?'

'All I know is that someone must have alerted Conn Gilroy to the fact of your existence and the effect you'd unknowingly had on his life. It didn't just come to him in a dream. And once he knew, finding you wouldn't have presented much of a problem. You'd all kept the same names. You'd stayed in the same city. You made it easy for him.'

'What did you decide to do?' said Fitzgerald.

'Daniel said we should leave it with him. He'd sort it out, he said. He told us we weren't to worry about it any more. It was in his hands now.'

'Just like that?' I said.

'Just like that.'

'Did he say what he was going to do?'

'No.'

'Pay off your tormentor? Send in the heavies?'

'I told you, he didn't share the details—'

'What you mean is, you didn't ask.'

'I didn't need to ask. Haven't you been listening? When Daniel said something would be done, he got it done. We were under pressure. He gave us a way out.'

'But it didn't work, did it?' I said. 'Otherwise, we wouldn't be sitting here now.'

'We thought it had. For the last week, there's been silence. We thought Daniel had ... sorted it out.' He stumbled over the pause, clumsily avoiding eye contact, guilt written on every pore of his skin. I guess they weren't so dumb about what they thought Daniel would do. 'But after tonight,' he said, wrestling back his composure, 'with Daniel being killed, and what happened to me, I know he's back.'

'What did happen to you? You didn't say.'

He took a deep breath.

'I got a call shortly after you left the house. You know when someone sends a text to your landline instead of your mobile and you get a spoken message instead? Some disembodied, robotic woman's voice reading out the words? That's how it was. It was almost creepy. It said it was from Michael. He said he thought he knew who had killed Daniel and that we were all in danger and he needed my help and could I meet him in ten minutes at a building site near where I lived. So I went. The whole place was deserted when I got there and I couldn't see where I was going. Next thing I knew I felt a pain like I'd never felt before. Someone had given me a crack on the back of my head. Everything went black.'

He showed the wound to us. Blood had dried around a deep gash, entangling his hair. It looked nasty. It was a wonder he was able to stay lucid. Nervous energy must have been keeping him going. That, and fear. He was a man on the run, not knowing where to go.

'How long were you out?'

'It felt like hours,' said Blunt. 'I didn't have a watch, so I couldn't say for certain, but I knew as soon as I woke that a long time had passed. You can tell somehow.'

'Where were you?'

'I was tied up, and there was no light, I didn't know where I was. My first thought was that I'd been buried alive. Then gradually my eyes adjusted to the darkness and I realized I was in the boot of a car. I could feel the metal against my skin, and these sharp ridges digging into my ribs, and there was a sour smell of petrol. It made me feel sick.'

'That could have been the concussion too,' I said.

'I don't know what it was, but he'd put tape over my mouth and I was terrified I was going to vomit, that I'd choke, but I knew I couldn't panic or the air would run out.'

Grimly, I remembered an old joke. How long can

a man survive in the locked trunk of a car? *Don't worry, there's enough air to last for the rest of his life* ... Not panicking at that moment must have been the hardest thing Ronan Blunt had ever done.

Getting out of the locked trunk of a car isn't easy either. Blunt explained how he'd first had to cut the cords around his wrists. That the car in which he was held was clearly a junkyard candidate helped him there at least, as there were plenty of rusty edges to get him started on the job. Not to mention the fact that whoever had abducted him had tied his captive's hands together at the front of his body rather than round the back. Blunt had managed to find a jagged edge of metal on the inside of the trunk, lift up his wrists and slowly saw through the rope. After that, he was able to take the tape from over his mouth, untie his ankles and use his feet to kick out the brake lights, giving him some precious extra air and a space through which to call for help.

'I'm impressed,' I said. 'Not many people would know what to do in the circumstances.'

'I have Tina to thank for that,' he said, his voice thick with sarcasm. 'She's always watching television, she never switches it off. Night after night, she sits there watching these crappy American detective series and drinking herself silly. I hate them. But there was a programme running one night that I found myself watching. There was a man locked in the boot of a car, the air running out. It showed how he got out. I just copied what he did.'

'Someone heard you shouting then?' said Fitz-gerald.

'No. I called and called but it was a waste of time. So I started looking for something with which I could prise open the lock from the inside. In the end I found a screwdriver. He probably didn't even know it was there. I used that to force the lock, and climbed out.'

'Where were you?'

'A place down by the docks. There were factories, warehouses, a huge ship docked nearby. Here, I'll give you the address.' He tore off an edge from a sheet of paper on his desk, scribbled down a name, and handed it to Fitzgerald.

'I'll get someone down there straightaway,' she said with a glance at it.

'Do you think he might be there?' said Blunt eagerly.

'I doubt he'll hang around long once he discovers you've escaped,' said Fitzgerald, 'but there's always the possibility that he might not have returned yet. We might still pick him up. There's just one thing I'm not quite clear about.'

'Who exactly is this *he* you keep talking about?' I ventured.

'Exactly.'

Blunt looked blank for a moment, staring from one to the other of us as if we had just sprouted an extra head.

'Conn Gilroy,' he said deliberately. 'Erin Gilroy's son. I told you. He's come back.'

'You saw Conn Gilroy tonight?'

'No.' Blunt stretched out the word doubtfully. 'I didn't see him.'

'Then how do you know it was him who hit you on the back of the head and dumped you in the boot of a car?' asked Fitzgerald.

'Because ... well, who else could it have been?' Blunt said, but even he seemed to realize that his argument was weak. 'Who else could hate us that much?'

Fitzgerald didn't bother arguing with him. 'We'll follow it up,' was all she said. 'You know where he lives?'

'Daniel knew,' Blunt said. 'He didn't tell us, though. We left the details to him. He did say Gilroy was recently out of jail, if that helps.'

'Information always helps,' Fitzgerald answered patiently, and was about to say more but there was a sudden confused clamour of voices rising from inside the museum.

Someone was shouting Blunt's name.

'Ronan!'

Almost simultaneously, Blunt's phone rang and he snatched it up.

'Yes, Norman, what is it?' A sigh. 'Very well, I'll be right down.'

He replaced the receiver and turned to us with a

look of exhaustion, like this latest disturbance of the peace was the last thing he needed, tonight of all nights.

'It's Tina,' he said. 'She's with Norman. I don't know how she knew I was here. I'll have to go and talk to her. Calm her down. Do you mind waiting?'

'Be my guest,' said Fitzgerald. 'I have to make some calls anyway, follow up on the details you've given me. But Blunt,' she raised her voice as he headed to the door, 'don't leave the building. We've not finished with you yet.'

'I understand.'

They were the last words Ronan Blunt ever spoke, and perhaps he did understand at the end. A moment after he stepped out of his office on to the balcony, he gave a loud cry, there was the sound of scuffling and struggling, and then a long-drawn-out scream from him which grew more distant and then ended in what sounded like an enormous explosion.

It all happened so quickly that we didn't have time to react. By the time we ran out of the office on to the balcony, there was no one there, only the sound of Tina screaming somewhere down below. I looked over the railing of the balcony. Blunt had fallen over the edge and into the middle of one of the glass cases on the floor beneath us.

That was the sound we'd heard. Glass lay scattered across the black and red tiles, radiating out geometrically from the epicentre where Blunt's body was sprawled unnaturally, limbs twisted, blood pooling under his head like a pillow. A tiger stood by his side and roared silently as if in triumph at a kill. The museum had a new and macabre exhibit.

45

'Get that bloody woman out of my sight,' snarled Fitzgerald through gritted teeth, 'or I swear I won't be responsible for my actions.'

Tina Blunt certainly wasn't helping. Since seeing her husband fall to his death, she hadn't stopped shouting and crying. Every so often she let out a loud scream, like she was reliving the moment. She'd had to be restrained on a number of occasions from rushing forwards to where he lay. Her grief might have been understandble, but it was making life difficult for everyone. The museum was a crime scene now. Her late husband was no longer hers alone – if he ever had been. His body was public property.

'There's a doctor on the way to give her a shot,' said Patrick Walsh, who'd arrived shortly after the news had got out about Blunt's death and was now helping to secure the scene and make sure the physical evidence was not compromised. He'd already spotted that Blunt seemed to have traces of something dark under his fingernails, fragments of blood and skin perhaps, even hair, suggesting he'd struggled with his assailant before his death. Whatever it was, it might be all we had to go on.

'Terrific,' said Fitzgerald sarcastically. 'Then she'll be even less use to us than she is now. If that's possible.'

Right on cue, another scream erupted from somewhere in the building.

From the few words she'd managed to force out, it seemed that Tina had seen her husband grappling with his killer on the upstairs balcony, though he was too far away for her to recognize a face, and everything had been in shadow as it was. The hope was that, with patience and a lot of coaxing, she might furnish further details of what she'd seen, but hope was in short supply tonight, and of patience there was even less.

The killer had vanished, as Sean Riordan had vanished from the Concert Hall. Bedlam was always the best cover for making an escape. There had been the sound of footsteps clanging on the metal walkways, the sound of stairs being descended, other doors opened and slammed; but in the echoing hall of the museum, sounds were impossible to place. Fitzgerald and I had chased one way, separated, following this hint of footsteps and that clatter in the darkness, shouting instructions and questions at one another across the void – *'Where are you? Can you see? Where is he?'* – before eventually our paths joined again and we realized that he had slipped out of our grasp. Though the same question we'd asked Blunt still lingered in the air, tantalizingly unanswered. Who *was* he? Erin Gilroy's son?

'I can't believe I lost him,' she said now as she stood by the museum curator's body in the calm after the storm. 'I had him in my grasp and I let him go.'

'It's not your fault,' I said. 'There were only two of us here. If we'd had more officers here, it would have been a different story.'

'There are no more people,' Fitzgerald snapped. 'We're already stretched to breaking point, and now there's this to make things worse. Three crime scenes in one night . . .'

'Make that four,' said a familiar voice.

'What the hell are you talking about?' said Fitzgerald, as the City Pathologist strode into view, accompanied by Seamus Dalton looking strangely pleased with himself despite the chaos which the night had unleashed on us. I guess anything which made his Chief Superintendent's life more difficult made him feel much more content with his own.

'You tell her, detective,' Butler said to Dalton, 'my services appear to be required over there by the tiger. Let's just hope he doesn't bite.'

'Dalton?' said Fitzgerald.

'There was a body on the railway line . . . Chief,' Dalton responded, the final *Chief* as strained and begrudging as ever. He'd perfected the art of leaving a pause so fractional that you'd almost swear it wasn't there unless you knew him better. It was a pause that had deniability written all over it, and which he obviously never tired of practising.

328

'I heard about it. A suicide. What's it got to do with us?'

'It wasn't a suicide. It was Nat Tannar.'

'I've just come from there,' chipped in Butler, obviously forgetting that he'd passed on the task of relating the story to Dalton. 'That's why I was delayed in getting over here. Lovely scene. He was tied up and left on the tracks by the football stadium.'

'There wasn't much left of him,' said Dalton with relish.

'Transection of the neck,' Butler explained. 'It could have been worse. The body usually gets dragged under the wheels, though the victim's usually dead by then anyway, so I suppose it's all academic.'

'So Tannar's gone too,' I whispered. 'That only leaves two of the infamous Second Circle, Michael Erskine and Sean Riordan, and who knows if they're still alive?'

'Since when did Riordan become a potential victim?' said Dalton scornfully. 'Last time I heard, he was Suspect Number One. Or did Pretty Boy over there,' he threw a dismissive glance at Walsh, 'get that bump on his head banging it against your headboard?'

'That's enough, Dalton,' said Fitzgerald sharply. 'We have enough on our plates tonight without you bitching away like an old woman. Go and see if Walsh needs any help.'

For a brief moment, Dalton looked like he was going to refuse.

'I said go,' she repeated.

'Whatever you say, Chief.'

'He has a point,' I said when Dalton was out of earshot. 'Where does Riordan fit into all this? He was being blackmailed too, according to Blunt. Why did he run?'

'Perhaps he was afraid of what we'd find out about him,' said Fitzgerald. 'If only half of what Blunt told us is true, then these people have more secrets to hide than the Vatican. Who knows how much else he might've been keeping back?'

'You mean Beth Griffin?' I said. 'I'm not so sure. Blunt looked pretty stunned when we mentioned her name. Either he was a damn good actor or he knew nothing about it.'

'I wasn't just thinking about Beth and the others,' said Fitzgerald. 'I was wondering if Daniel Erskine's file on Riordan might be worth taking a look at.'

'You want me to head over and see what I can find?'

'I'll call Healy,' she said. 'I have another job in mind for you.'

'Why do I get the feeling you're about to break some bad news?'

'It's not bad news. Not as such. I want you to go down to Islandbridge. There's a probation hostel there. Conn Gilroy's been staying there since his release from custody.'

Fitzgerald had not been idle. She'd already managed to confirm both Gilroy's existence, for which we'd only had Blunt's word until then, and we still didn't know how much store we could set by that, and his criminal record. The latter mainly consisted of a dizzying number of minor charges – drunk and disorderly; petty theft; driving under the influence – leading up to a two-year conviction for assault on his partner. Gilroy had been released early from that sentence a couple of months ago, since when he'd been living at a bail hostel on the edge of the city centre awaiting more permanent accommodation.

'If he's involved in any way with what's been happening tonight,' she said, 'he'll not be hanging idly around the hostel afterwards waiting to be picked up, but we'll have to follow it up all the same. And even if he's not involved, we'll still have to interview him.'

'No problem. What are you going to do?'

'I'll have to wait here till Butler's finished up. Then I suppose I'd better head over to the railway line and see the scene for myself. For all the good it will do,' she added resignedly. 'One corpse looks much like another after dark. I'll leave Walsh in charge here. He's already been overseeing the search of the surrounding area in case Blunt's killer is stupid enough to wait around the corner to be arrested.'

'That'll please Dalton,' I said, 'having to take orders from Walsh.'

'Oh, Dalton's not staying here.'

'He isn't?'

'No, he's going with you. Did I not mention that part?'

'It must have slipped your mind,' I said, and prepared myself to object.

She cut me off before I could begin.

'Do it for me,' she said. 'Think of it as recompense for running off after Leko and giving me a heart attack earlier.' My intended resistance started to fade, as she'd known it would. There was nothing better than a pinch of guilt for getting people to do what you want. 'You can't go alone, and I don't trust Dalton on his own. You know what he's like sometimes. He's a bull in the proverbial china shop.'

'Not to mention a pain in the not so proverbial ass,' I replied.

'That's precisely why I need you to be there for me, keeping an eye on him.'

'From FBI agent to Dalton's babysitter in one giant leap,' I sighed. 'Or a series of smaller leaps, to be more accurate. That's what I call a downhill career path.'

'I'm guessing that means yes?'

In answer, I called out Dalton's name. He pretended not to hear me straightaway, presumably for fear that his manhood would shrivel up and drop off if he was seen to respond too rapidly to the greeting of a mere woman. When he eventually did deign to glance in my direction, it was with the same practised disdain that Hannibal probably used for the man who cleared up the elephant dung on the journey across the Alps.

'Yeah?'

'Your luck's in, Dalton,' I told him. 'I'm all yours.'

46

There was an exhilaration in being alone. He always had been alone. He never had anyone he could honestly call a soulmate. But now he had cut every last tie he had to his former life and he was floating free. There was no going back. He only wished the sensation could last for ever. That the morning would never come and darkness become his element.

He felt like Jack O'Lantern in the old Irish tale. That one was always wheeled out at Halloween, who knows why, for tradition's sake maybe, or as a warning against wickedness. Whatever the reasoning, it was wasted on him. If anything, the story had the opposite effect.

This was the way he remembered hearing it. Jack was a lazy farmer, or some say a blacksmith; a liar, drunkard and cheat, who delighted in playing tricks on friends and neighbours alike and who managed somehow to trap the Devil up a tree. He'd forgotten the details. It was something to do with carving a cross in the trunk so that the Devil couldn't climb down again, though how Jack got Old Nick up there in the first place has been erased from his memory. Did he play him at cards? That might have been it. Or was that a different version altogether? There was something about apples, he was sure of that.

Either way, Jack had the Devil where he wanted him and told him he wouldn't set him free again until His Infernal Majesty promised Jack that, when the old scoundrel's time came to die, he wouldn't let him into Hell. And the Devil kept his promise. (Say what you like about the Devil, but at least he keeps his word. At least he knows the meaning of loyalty.)

The problem for Jack was that God wouldn't let him into Heaven either, so he was homeless and friendless, forced to wander the earth eternally, with nowhere to call his own.

For light as he walked, Jack carved out one of his own pumpkins from the field and put a candle inside. Some tales say that the Devil mocked him by tossing him a coal from the fires of Hell, and that he lit the pumpkin lantern with that. After that, people would see the light glowing on lonely roads, and travellers were warned not to approach him.

'Now sleep,' the adults would say when the story was done, but sleep was usually the last thing on his mind. Instead he'd pull back the curtains and lie awake, watching the stars through the window, and envying the wandering pumpkin man his solitude, the lonely road he owned. And here he was now, following in Jack's footsteps, cast out and feared, and rootless, except that he was still flesh and blood, and Halloween would soon be over.

And what then?

Last night, it had seemed that he had all the time

in the world. That the night was his to command. Suddenly he was aware of a ticking clock. The approach of morning. Soon they would know him and the chance would not come again, but to leave things unfinished now would be agony. To let even one of them live to see tomorrow would make everything else meaningless, not least after all the trouble he'd gone to with Blunt.

The risks he'd taken for him! He couldn't believe it when he returned to his car in the docks after leaving Elliott tied up in the lock-up and found the boot prised open and Blunt gone. Part of him was impressed at Blunt's ingenuity. Of all the things he'd expected, the last was that the weak-minded curator would turn into Harry fucking Houdini.

Then he began to compute the dangers. Would Blunt go to the police? Unlikely. He had too much to hide. Home then? No, he wouldn't feel safe there.

Then it came to him. The museum. That's where Blunt would flee.

Even so, he hadn't anticipated it would be so easy. He'd been close enough to hear them talking to Blunt inside his office. He'd even looked through the keyhole and watched them inside, stealing glances as Blunt talked on and on, wrapping himself in words as a cloak for his ignorance. He hadn't had a clue at the end.

The world had ceased to make sense for him, if it ever had. That was often the way with clever men – that is to say, men deemed thus by their peers. Their superficial intelligence only masked their stupidity. What was the point of a head filled with facts and figures and theories if, at the end, you couldn't even tell from what direction death was tiptoeing near?

In his fall, Blunt had understood more than in all his previous decades.

The truth blazed in his eyes.

He'd returned to his car straightaway, after getting out of the building – and with the front door standing open so invitingly, that hadn't exactly presented much of a difficulty. What idiots were they employing to guard the museum anyway? They might as well hang signs outside inviting burglars to help themselves. For the last half-hour or so since then, he'd been driving, with no particular destination in mind, just winding through backstreets and suburbs, the city's residential deserts, because he still wasn't sure how the endgame would play out and he needed the space to think, to devise the right strategy for action.

He kept one eye on the speedometer too, because the last thing he needed at this point was to be pulled over for speeding. They might sense some tension in him that would make them suspicious. He didn't want to be breathalysed either. He'd been drinking tonight. He needed it. Did his breath smell of alcohol? He didn't want to give the police the chance to find out. Too many people had been caught making junior-grade mistakes like that.

For a moment, he imagined driving like this for

ever, Jack O'Lantern behind the wheel, his headlights transformed to flares of coal borrowed from Hell, never needing to stop.

Free.

If only his choices were that simple.

Besides, who would notice another lost soul in a city like Dublin? The night around him teemed with latter-day Jacks and the flicker of lonely lanterns, and every end of day heralded a kind of Halloween, in which the dead never truly left you alone.

He'd come full circle. The bedtime story of childhood was now his reality, and sleep would be no escape. He had no option remaining but to see the tale out to the end.

And even if there was an alternative, he wouldn't have taken it.

47

The conversation wasn't exactly sparkling en route to the probation hostel. Not that Seamus Dalton would have been capable of witty repartee even if his immortal soul depended on it, but in this instance the silence was deliberate. At some point in our relationship, if mutual hostility could be called by such a grand name, Dalton had realized that his attempts to knock me off my stride were futile, and had largely given up the attempt, restricting himself to insults on meeting which had long since taken on a ritualistic character.

The only sign of his inner tension at being forced into close proximity with me for the immediate future was a little vein that pulsed in the side of his neck in time to the terrible country music that was oozing out of the radio and to which he was humming with deliberate tunelessness, his fingers going up and down on the steering wheel like a marching band.

I could see the vein out of the corner of my eye and it had a strangely hypnotic effect, but I wouldn't look at it directly for fear he might start to think his existence interested me.

I guess we could both be petty when we wanted to be.

Fitzgerald always said it was because we were both alike that we clashed so regularly. Stubborn, pig-headed, reluctant to change our ways, both Dalton and I had serious issues with how the world was ordered and both let our frustration at it get the better of us. The only reason I resisted the comparison is because being compared to Dalton didn't do much for my already battered ego, and besides, it was such a cliché. Then again, assertions only become clichés because they happen to be true a high percentage of the time.

All we could do was get this thing over with as quickly as possible.

The hostel was situated on the northern side of the Phoenix Park, which meant we drove through trees and falling leaves to get there, our headlights picking out glimmers from the eyes of lurking creatures hiding in the shadows. That's the thing about night. Far from being the time when life shuts down, it's when much of it wakes up. Believing that nothing of any importance is happening just because you are asleep is the worst sort of solipsism.

I wondered what Dalton's response would be if I shared my observations with him.

'What are you laughing at?'

'Nothing,' I said.

He tutted and reached to turn up the radio.

The news on the hour was just beginning when we pulled to a halt outside the hostel. Dark windows, terraced house, a light shining by the door. I only knew we'd come to the right place because of the number next to the bell. Maybe they didn't want to frighten the neighbours by admitting too loudly who they had staying inside as temporary guests.

It could have been worse. The authorities still had a habit of putting the hostels for sex offenders around the corner from the local school and then throwing up their hands in astonishment when the discovery of their presence didn't go down too well with parents.

A large crack across the main downstairs window was the only indication that this hostel's true purpose was not the city's best-kept secret.

'Honey, you're home,' I said in my best Jack Nicholson voice, but the joke was lost on Dalton.

'Let me do the talking,' he grunted in reply.

'Do you want me to walk ten paces behind you as well, wearing a burka?'

'Finally you have a good idea,' he said. 'Anything that covers your face has to be progress.'

How the man had stayed single so long when he was such a sweet talker really was a total mystery.

Dalton rang the doorbell long enough to dispel any doubts in the minds of the people inside that the caller would go away if his summons went un-answered. The appearance of a light in the hallway was enough to show that the message had gotten through.

Into the light a woman's face loomed, framed with pale rat's-tail hair, tiny eyes narrowed with suspicion, thin lips set already with resistance.

'What do you want?' she mouthed through the glass.

Dalton flashed his badge and jabbed a finger to indicate that he wanted inside. With a deep soundless sigh, the woman pulled back the bolts on the door, then stepped aside to let us through. She was the probation hostel's night warden, presumably. Or one of the residents.

It was hard to tell the difference sometimes.

Another face, unshaven and hostile, appeared over the banister one storey up as she made the entrance secure again, then ducked back as I caught his eye.

Our arrival had not gone unnoticed.

'Do you know what time it is?' the warden said resentfully.

'Haven't a clue,' said Dalton. 'Sorry, did you have plans?'

'I just wondered why it couldn't wait until morning,' she said. 'It's hard enough for the men here to get any sleep with the *respectable* citizens of the neighbourhood throwing bricks at the windows or putting dog shit through the letter box.'

'I really feel for them,' Dalton said, and I smiled despite myself. Sometimes his attitude was almost as bad as mine. 'You want me to pop upstairs and tuck them in?'

'There's no need to be sarcastic,' the woman said. 'I was only saying I—'

'Don't know why it couldn't wait until morning. Yeah, you said already. Trust me, it couldn't. We're here to talk to one of your residents, if that's OK with you, Miss . . .?'

'Madden,' she answered, and was about to object to being called miss, which was fair enough, when she too saw the same face as before peering over the edge of the banister. 'It's all right, Billy,' she called up to him. 'They're here to see me. You go back to bed now. Some of the men,' she explained in a lower voice as Billy reluctantly moved back from the edge, 'are very protective towards me. We'd better go into my office.'

There was a card pinned above her desk: *How many social workers does it take to change a light bulb? None, it's the system that needs changing.*

At least she had a sense of humour.

'Who is it you wanted to see?' she asked as we took our seats, and then she stiffened visibly as Dalton told her. It was like someone had put ice cubes down the back of her sweater. Her shoulders froze. 'Gilroy? What's he supposed to have done?'

'What are you?' said Dalton. 'His lawyer?'

'I feel responsible, that's all it is,' she said slowly, picking her words with care. 'The men who come here have served their time. They've got a second chance. It can upset their rehabilitation if they're constantly being questioned and pursued and harassed.'

'Hey!' said Dalton. 'No one's harassing anyone, all right? I said I wanted to question him. I didn't say I was going to hook up his testicles to the power supply.'

I noted how, even at his most abrasive, Dalton didn't forget to use the singular *I* rather than the collective *we*. A mere woman like me clearly wasn't going to be invited to contribute to the interview with Conn Gilroy, if it ever came. And there was the rub. *If* it ever came.

Ms Madden was being coy to the point of obstructiveness.

'I told you, I'm simply trying to do what's in Conn's best interests . . .'

So it was first-name terms now. This was starting to look less like a probation hostel and more like a free hotel, with tea and sympathy thrown in as standard.

'Look, miss, I don't want to spend the rest of what's left of the night debating the rights and wrongs of the probation system with some kid who's still wet behind the ears and probably thinks those scumbags upstairs are the victims of society rather than the other way round.' I had to admit, I couldn't have put it better myself. 'But since we're pushed for time, I'll just remind you that you're paid out of public money to keep a watch on these men not to be Florence fucking Nightingale. So for the last time, why don't you just give me his room number and I can get on with doing my job, something you seem to find impossible?'

'He's gone, hasn't he?' I said when she still hesitated.

I felt the sting of Dalton's glance. He was furious that I'd spoken at all, and even more so that I'd figured out what he should have grasped already for himself.

'What?' said Dalton thickly.

'He's not here,' she said, and her hands were shaking almost as much as her voice.

Dalton got to his feet as fast as his heavy frame would allow it, and reached for his cellphone so fiercely that the woman flinched, like she thought he was going to hit her.

'When was the last time you saw him?' he demanded.

'Six days ago,' she said. 'He left to sign in at the police station. He has to sign in each week. He said he'd be late back. He called a while later to say he had to go away for a few days.'

'And you didn't report him missing?'

'If they knew Conn had broken the terms of his probation, he'd have been sent back to jail. I thought if I could just cover for him until he had to sign again, it'd give him a chance to finish whatever he had to do and then no one would be any the wiser.'

'And what,' said Dalton, 'if what he wanted to get finished was murder?'

Now it was like he really had struck her. She slumped into her chair, and dropped her head into her hands. 'You're joking,' she said. 'Conn's not like that.' But there was no conviction in her words. They were merely noises her mouth made to buy time.

Dalton retreated to the hall to call Fitzgerald, and I gave the warden a moment to compose her thoughts. Things were going to get nasty for her soon enough without me joining in the attack. She couldn't be blamed for Gilroy jumping ship. These hostels were leakier than the *Titanic*. But not reporting it went beyond stupidity into a new dimension.

I'd seen it before, though. She'd gone native. Spend too long listening to ex-cons whine and you started to adopt their view of the world as unfair, weighted against them, not giving them a chance, and then, when one of them stepped out of line, you colluded with them in making excuses and covering their tracks. By the time you realized the mistake, it was too late. Dublin was full of idealistic young people like her, suckers for a sob story and ready to swallow any poisonous political bullshit about the essential goodness of mankind.

She'd learned the hard way how wrong that was. Part of me even felt sorry for her. I should check my temperature first chance I got. Being sympathetic wasn't like me.

'Did Gilroy give any hint of where he was going?' I said when I judged she'd gathered her thoughts sufficiently to process the question.

'I'd have remembered,' she said. 'He never said a word.'

'He didn't mention family, friends?'

'He didn't have a family, I don't think. He said his mother had died when he was young and he'd never known his father. He never mentioned any brothers or sisters.'

'Was he friendly with anyone else in the hostel?'

'Not really. He was a loner, I suppose you'd say.'

Aren't they always?

'Weren't you worried what would happen if he hadn't turned up by the time it came for him to sign in at the police station?'

'I trusted him. I knew he wouldn't let me down . . .'

'Maybe he already has.'

Dalton returned shortly and barked at her: 'Show us his room.' She rose obediently and led the way upstairs in silence to the second floor. At the end of a narrow corridor, a plywood door showed a number ten. A *Do Not Disturb* sign, probably stolen from a cheap hotel somewhere, hung from the doorknob. Unless they supplied them here along with the sheets and blankets and towels. Nothing would've surprised me any more.

Dalton snatched the pass key from the warden and unlocked the door, stepped inside and switched on the light in what looked like one angry movement. Pale yellow light illuminated an untidy room with an unmade bed and clothes littering the floor.

A mug of cold tea sat on a bedside table, encrusted with mould.

'What are we looking for?' I asked him.

Dalton didn't bother answering. His hand reached instead for the nearest drawer and yanked it open unceremoniously. It tumbled out of his clumsy fingers and broke on the floor, spilling its contents, which were mainly bits of newspaper, magazines and other scraps.

He flicked through one magazine until he found the place he was looking for. He held it up so that the hostel warden could see the gaps cut out of the page.

'Guess who's been gluing himself together some nice little blackmail notes?' said Dalton with a cruel relish as the realization dawned on her that Conn Gilroy might not have been what he seemed. 'And guess how many of the men who received those nice little blackmail notes have been murdered tonight?'

'Oh shit,' she said.

In the circumstances, 'Oh shit' covered most of the bases.

48

I hitched a lift back into town with one of the squad cars that had been sent out to the probation hostel in response to Dalton's announcement that Conn Gilroy had split. I wasn't needed back there. It was just procedure from now on, statements and evidence. I left Dalton to it.

But where to go? Fitzgerald was out by the railway. Walsh was taking care of business at the museum. Healy was still at Daniel Erskine's house processing the scene.

'Can I be of any use?' I asked Healy from my cellphone as we drove southwards, this time along the North Circular Road. Either the driver was avoiding the road through the Phoenix Park because he was afraid of the deer or it was quicker, plain and simple, and Dalton had simply chosen the long way round first time because he liked my company.

'You're always of use, Saxon, you know that.'

'Sweet talker,' I said, touched that he'd made the effort to make me feel wanted. It was no wonder the Assistant Commissioner had fallen for him big time. He was a good catch. 'Dig up anything else in Erskine's files, or are they still holding out on you?'

'Where do I start? Turns out Niland was gay.

Erskine had been keeping tabs on him for years. There are names, dates, pictures, you name it.'

So that was why he hadn't taken his turn with Erin Gilroy on the night she died. It wasn't moral scruples on his part about boning a stoned stripper. She just wasn't his type.

'Perfect material for Erskine to embark on a spot of blackmail of his own,' I said. 'He almost makes Gilroy look like an amateur.'

'But no evidence that he ever used it against Niland. It's like we said. It's knowledge for knowledge's sake. He was a scholar of human behaviour. Unless what he got from them in return is something we can't see or quantify.'

'Such as?'

'Their subservience,' Healy suggested. 'Power over them.'

'That's what Blunt's wife said all along.'

'She should know.'

'She should?'

'Erskine had her on the payroll, in a manner of speaking. He wrote her a cheque every couple of months in return for spying on her own husband. Not that she delivered much in the way of information in exchange for the money, but again maybe that wasn't the point.'

'It was having her under his thumb that Erskine was after too?'

'I'm beginning to think there wasn't anyone that he hasn't watched at some point,' said Healy. 'Give me another couple of hours, and I fully expect to find my own file stashed away with the rest. *The Secret Life Of A Dublin Policeman, Part 26.*'

'I'll wait for the movie, if it's all the same to you. Nothing more about Beth Griffin?'

'Not a speck. Erskine had a file on her father, though. He was a board member of the Erskine company. He had files on them all.'

'No shit? That blows apart the theory that Beth was a random victim anyway.'

'I wonder what Beth's father would have done if he knew Daniel Erskine had his daughter's belongings under lock and key in his house?' Healy mused.

'Might be worth checking if he happens to be in town.'

'We're on to it.'

'What about the others?'

'There's definitely nothing here on Shirley Heuston or Joss Finch. The one lucky break was that we managed to find the cop who did the door-to-doors round here after Beth Griffin went missing. He was doing guard duty outside the house tonight.'

'What did he remember?'

'Only that Erskine couldn't have been more helpful. He offered to put up a hundred grand as a reward to help track down her killer. But he didn't actually have any information of his own that he felt like sharing with the police.'

'So either he was lying, or he didn't have her things at the time?'

'Those would indeed appear to be the two options.'

O'Connell Street flashed by, eerie in its emptiness. The clock outside Clerys showed four and it felt later. Suddenly I was suffocated with weariness. Could it really have been yesterday that Fitzgerald and I were moving in to our new house, ignorant of the existence of these people whose names now dominated our night: Erskine, Gilroy, Riordan?

It sounded like a firm of small-town solicitors. *Have you had an accident? Let Erskine, Gilroy and Riordan make a claim on your behalf.*

'Saxon?'

'Sorry, my mind was drifting. I'll be there soon as I can, Healy, OK?' Then, to the driver: 'Drop me in Baggot Street. I'll walk the rest of the way. I have to do something first.'

The air smelt sweet when I climbed out of the squad car, which is to say that it was as stale and musty as any city street at 4 a.m., but it smelt sweet to me. I felt like I'd been cooped up too long, starved of air in museums and hostels and the houses of the dead.

I took a moment to breathe it in, finding my feet again in the peculiar simulacrum of normality that was Dublin in the hours between night and morning and becoming aware as I did so of a dull throbbing in my temple, which I now realized had been there since ... when? Since Dublin Castle, I decided, yes, since then at least, only I'd been trying to ignore it.

Now it was demanding attention with a vengeance.

Tablets were what I needed, and I knew where to get them. There was an all-night store open on Baggot Street for all the people overtaken with a fierce desire for Pot Noodles and chocolate bars. The dopeheads, in other words, though, as I stepped through the automatic doors and heard them swish shut behind me, there didn't seem to be many of them about tonight. Most likely they were all in bed now, blissfully sleeping off the night's excesses. What remained were the people with nowhere else to go.

A young girl, not old enough yet to take offence at being mistaken for anything other than a grown woman, lingered in an aisle, pretending to look at cosmetics. She was so conspicuous, they could have filmed her as the perfect illustration of How Not To Shoplift. She'd already torn open a shrinkwrapped chicken sandwich and was devouring it messily.

A prostitute marking the end of the late shift, was my guess.

At the end of the aisle, a businessman in a sharp suit, tie loosened, heading home reluctantly after a night on the town, was feeding coins into a cigarette machine, and an old man wheeled a mini trolley, half-filled with tins of cured ham and baked beans. Someone else was inspecting jars of pesto with a seriousness of purpose which made it seem like they were picking out a suspect from an identity parade. Who needs pesto at 4 a.m.? An Italian insomniac, perhaps. Or maybe it was one of those occasions when being at home is too depressing a prospect and you just need to get out for a while, however flimsy the excuse.

Nearby, two store workers conversed quietly in Polish. Curious how other people's languages always sound more fascinating than your own. They could have been discussing the football scores for all I knew, but their voices threw up visions of far-off streetscapes.

Escape.

I felt inadequate momentarily for never having learned to speak another language, but then I had no need to. The whole world speaks American these days.

They shouldn't make it so easy for us to be lazy.

I couldn't find what I wanted, so headed to the counter, where a young man with tousled hair and eyes deep-set with tiredness was asking for mouse-traps.

'You're the fourth person I've had in here tonight,' the woman behind the counter told him. 'It's the time of year for them. They come in to get out of the cold, poor things.'

'Fuck the little bastards,' the young man said. 'I can't sleep. I can hear them scratching in the walls. I have to feel I can do something . . .'

I asked for headache tablets once my turn came to be served, but, unbelievably, they were all out. What's the point of a 24-hour store that doesn't keep well stocked with medicines? Drugs are part of the staple nocturnal diet of the city. It wasn't my night.

Only when I got outside did I remember about the boxes that still remained in my apartment. It was around the corner. It would only take me a few minutes to get them.

The building was silent when I got there, no sign even of the doorman. Did that mean he really did have a home of his own to go to, after all? Knowing him as I did, it seemed improbable. I stepped into the lift and it took me, shaking, clattering, to the seventh floor.

I let myself in, turned on the light.

Of course, the tablets had to be at the bottom of the packing case rather than sitting conveniently on top, but it only made finding them at last all the more satisfying. I pushed two out of the tinfoil packet and leaned across the sink to drink water from the tap to help them down. And that's when I felt the barrel of a gun pressed into the small of my back.

'Don't move,' ordered a voice, rough and heavily accented, and at once all my illusions about the exotic allure of other lands and languages vanished. There were evil bastards everywhere, and right now one of the worst of them was in my apartment.

'Dr Livingstone, I presume?' I said, but that's the problem with fugitive Bosnian gangsters. Humour is just wasted on them.

49

'I thought I'd never get through to you. What took you so long to answer the phone?'

'I've been busy.'

'So I've heard.'

'Busy indeed.'

'You'll never get away with it, you know.'

'I practically have.'

'You'll be caught.'

'You still don't get it, do you? Do you think I care about that now? I'm not a fool. I knew what this would mean. I didn't think that there was some easy route back into normality after a night like this.'

'Why did you do it?'

'You know why. After what they did, it was as much as they deserved. Throughout history, the punishment for treachery has always been the same. The death sentence.'

'You're very self-righteous for a man who's just spent the night murdering innocent people.'

'They weren't innocent, haven't you been paying attention?'

'Compared to you, they were.'

'I did what I had to do.'

'And what about me?'

'You're next on the list.'

'I wouldn't give you the satisfaction.'

'You won't have a choice.'

'You're insane.'

'What's that old saying about sticks and stones?'

'You haven't got me yet.'

'I'm a patient man. I'm used to waiting for what I want.'

'You'll have to find me first.'

'That won't be a problem.'

'You're very confident.'

'I won't even need to track you down.'

'I could disappear.'

'You won't.'

'You'd never find me.'

'I won't have to.'

'Are you listening to yourself? You've lost it. Whatever thin veneer of sanity you had left has peeled away. You don't even realize how ridiculous you sound.'

'Can I offer you a word of advice?'

'Can I stop you?'

'You should never underestimate your opponents. It can be a fatal mistake.'

'You underestimated me.'

'On the contrary, I always knew you'd be the tricky one.'

'Is that right?'

'That's why you were meant to be first. I was following you.'

'What are you talking about?'

'This afternoon. I followed you. You had no idea. I intended to kill you there and then. But there were too many people around. The right opportunity never presented itself. Consider that your one lucky escape for the day. You won't get another.'

'Forewarned is forearmed, isn't that what they say? And even if what you're telling me is true, which I don't believe for one moment, there's a crucial difference between then and now. This time you don't know where I am.'

'I told you, that's something I don't need to know, because *you'll* come to *me*.'

'Why would I do that?'

'Because why else are you still out there, calling my number, looking for me? You could have gone to the police at any time. You didn't. That means you know we still have unfinished business. We both know it. We've been tiptoeing around each other all night. It has to stop. This thing must come to a conclusion, one way or another.'

'You sound like you have a place in mind.'

'It has to be somewhere quiet.'

'That goes without saying.'

'Somewhere empty. I don't want to be disturbed.'

'Where then?'

'There's a place I know in the Phoenix Park.'

'In case you failed to notice, it's getting difficult to get around this city. I suppose we have you to thank for that. There are police everywhere.'

'I've managed.'

'You've had more practice.'

'True.'

'It has to be somewhere nearer.'

'Nearer to what? As you pointed out, I don't know where you are right now.'

'I'm . . . I'm by the river.'

'I'm guessing that's a lie.'

'Shall I hold up the phone so that you can hear the water?'

'No need. I'll take your word for it. What about King's Inn?'

'No.'

'Kilmainham?'

'No.'

'Are you going to say no to every suggestion I make?'

'That depends.'

'I'm making you nervous.'

'Call it cautious. Why should I make this easy for you?'

'Hard or easy, the end result will be the same.'

'I'm not walking blindly into a trap.'

'If that's what scares you, then I'll leave it up to you. Name the place and I'll be there. This is too important to allow mere details to get in the way.'

'Let me think.'

'Take your time.'

'Very well. Yes. I know a place. There'll be no one there at this hour.'

'Sounds perfect.'

'That's what you think. You're not the only one who can make plans.'

'Plans, is it?'

'I'm going to stop you.'

'Careful. You're starting to sound like me.'

'Do we have a deal or not?'

'Consider it done. On your territory it is. After all, it's only fair that you should get to choose the place where you're going to die.'

50

With one hand he held the gun pointed into my back, and with the other Leko emptied my pockets. Keys, wallet, a few coins, cellphone, my last cigar, a half-finished packet of mints.

Finally, in the inside pocket of my jacket –

'What the hell's this?'

'It's a book,' I said. I'd forgotten it was there. There hadn't exactly been much time for reading in the past hours. 'Surely you must have seen one before?'

'*Dante's Inferno*,' Leko read on the cover.

'It's a poem about Hell,' I told him. 'You should read it. It might give you a few pointers about what's in store for you when your turn comes to move in.'

Once again, the joke fell on deaf ears.

Or perhaps just stupid ones.

Leko opened the book at random and awkwardly read a passage out loud: '*I turned me round, and saw before me and underfoot a lake that from the frost the semblance had of glass, and not of water.*' He tossed the book aside with contempt. 'You read this shit?'

'It passes the time when I'm not being held at gunpoint.'

He let me sit down, but kept the gun pointed at me the whole time.

'You try to get away, I shoot you. You shout for help, I shoot you. You don't do something when I tell you to do it, I shoot you. Do you understand?'

'What's not to understand?'

'I said, do you understand?' he repeated.

'I understand.'

And I did.

Leko had the same look I'd seen on the face of countless career criminals. Taking another person's life was nothing to them. It caused them not the slightest psychological discomposure. They weren't like serial killers; yes, pleasure came into it – there would always be satisfaction for men like Leko in exerting the ultimate power over other human beings – but they didn't *need* to hurt and destroy the innocent in order to get their kicks. But if they had to kill to get what they wanted, or if killing made their job easier, there was never a chance that moral considerations would stop them from doing it, and doing it repeatedly.

That was why, right now, I needed to keep my wits about me. One false move and he wouldn't hesitate to eliminate me. So why was he here? Finding that out was my priority.

'I need your car,' was the answer to that question.

'My car?'

He held the keys up and jingled them.

'Your car. Remember it?'

'Oh, *that* car? It's not here,' I said.

'Not here?'

'That's what I said.'

'If you're lying to me—'

'Why would I lie to a man with a gun?' I asked reasonably.

For a second, there was irritation in his eyes. Then he shrugged.

'Doesn't matter,' he said. 'If it's not here, it's not here. I can get another one.' I noticed that he didn't say *we*. Seems that I wasn't included in his immediate plans. He obviously didn't want it so that we could elope to the continent together, that was for sure. Before I could dig further, though, he continued: 'Where is yours, anyway?'

'I left it at Dublin Castle.'

Leko frowned at the mention of the Murder Squad's HQ, troubled by some thought or memory that the words stirred up, before smiling faintly.

'It was you,' he said at last. 'It was you who chased me, wasn't it? I didn't recognize you until now. I was hiding. I saw you run past, thinking you could still get me ...'

'Is that what this is about?' I said. 'You're annoyed because I spoiled your plans?'

'No,' said Leko. 'You win some, you lose some. It's all business to me. Do you think I'd come all this way just to get my revenge on some interfering little bitch who got in my way? I have better things to do. No, I came here because I know you can help me get to your little fuckpuppet Grace Fitzgerald. You're probably the only one who can.'

'And how do you figure I'll do that?'

'Simple. You're going to bring her to me.'

'And then?'

'And then,' said Leko, 'I'm going to kill her.'

Ask a silly question.

'What about me?'

'When I'm done, I'll let you go.'

He was a good liar – he'd stood up to hours of police interrogation about the murder of his wife without giving an inch – but he was a liar all the same. I was on his To Die list too, and I could see in his eyes that he knew I knew it. But there was a pattern to these things, and neither of us was going to admit it directly.

'I'll have to think about it,' was all I said.

'Of course.'

'Then what say you come back in a week or two and I'll give you my decision? No? Oh well, you can't blame a girl for trying . . .' I was talking to buy myself time to think, and that was part of the pattern too. He wasn't letting it bother him unduly.

But something *was* still bothering me.

'How did you *find* me?' I asked.

'Luck,' said Leko. 'I knew all about you. I did my research on Detective Chief Superintendent St Grace Fitzgerald when I was inside. I read everything there was to read, and your name kept cropping up. When I realized I couldn't get to Miss Wonderful my way,

I knew I had to find another way to finish what I'd started. I hit on you.'

'You followed me then?'

'Follow you, no. I came here looking for a new address for your girlfriend. The information I had was out of date. You probably heard what happened. This seemed a good place to start, only when I got here the apartment was empty . . .'

'Sorry about that. I have this conscientious objection to furniture.'

'. . . and I realized you weren't here. Dead-end time. Very fucking annoying. Then who walks through the door but you? I guess you could say I got lucky.'

'You can say that again. Remind me never to play you at poker.'

So now here I was, all because of a sore head, facing the prospect of being killed now for *not* taking him to Fitzgerald, or killed later if I did, with her joining me at the mortuary. Neither outcome being especially appealing, I needed to find a third alternative.

And fast.

'You know,' I said, 'if you were really that pissed about being locked up for life for ordering your wife to be murdered, you should have just left her alone. That way, none of this would have happened.'

The mention of his wife's name darkened Leko's mood visibly.

'Allenka knew the rules,' he said. 'She chose to break them, she paid the price. Back home, that's the way it works. You don't humiliate your husband without consequences.'

'But you're not back home any more.'

'Does that mean I should have let her make a fool of me?'

'Better a fool than a murderer.'

'You only say that because you don't understand. Let me tell you a story . . .'

'It's not the one about growing up poor and hungry in Bosnia, is it?' I said.

'You people,' his teeth tightened around his words like a finger around a trigger, anger rising in him like electricity in a circuit, looking for an outlet, 'you people have no idea. You sit here with your money and your cars and your nice little lives and you don't have one idea about what life is like for other people. How hard it is to get by.'

'So it *is* the one about growing up poor and hungry in Bosnia?'

'You want to know about my village?' he demanded.

'No. If Allenka had wanted to tell me,' I said, 'I would have listened. But you just want to use your village as an excuse for having killed her. You didn't have shoes? Your father died when you were small? Get over it. Plenty of other people have gotten over worse without becoming monsters in the process.'

'You'd better shut up, lady.'

'Or what? You'll shoot me too? That's your answer to everything, isn't it?'

'I'm warning you—'

'Yeah, I heard you the first time. It was right after the part where you started telling me about what a hard life you'd had. Change the record, Leko, it's getting boring.'

I knew I wasn't doing myself any favours, but I couldn't help it. I'd heard the speech he wanted to deliver a thousand times before. God spare us from criminals who want to romanticize what they do as some great rebellion against an unfair world. I'll take the ones who admit they're selfish, greedy bastards with no sense of right and wrong anyday.

At least they keep the soliloquies to a minimum.

'Right,' he said, 'that's it. Time's up. You're coming with me.'

There was venom in the gun as it jabbed into the small of my back again and Leko used it to push me towards the door. It was like all the wickedness in him was flowing down his arm and into the barrel of his weapon and I could sense it aching to do me harm.

The next five minutes were going to be crucial. I was willing to die, if I had to, to keep Leko away from Fitzgerald, but whilst he still needed me alive then there were alternatives to dying, and I intended to pursue each one to the limit.

Leko wasn't good enough for me to give him the satisfaction of killing either one of us.

He didn't want to take the elevator. Maybe he didn't fancy his chances with me in a confined space; wife killers are invariably cowards when it comes to women who know how to fight back. So we were going downwards slowly on the stairs – thankfully deserted at this time, because I didn't know what he'd do if anyone got in his way at that moment – when he held my phone out to me, and said: 'Call her. Tell her to come over. Tell her to come here right now.'

Think, girl, think.

'Why don't you just announce what you're going to do on the radio?' I said.

'What are you talking about?'

'I'm talking about the fact that she'll be suspicious if I ask her to come over here. She'll know something's wrong. She's a Chief Superintendent, Leko, not some rookie.'

Luckily, Leko didn't ask himself why I was suddenly being so helpful by pointing out the flaws in his plan. It was the flaws in the plan themselves which were preoccupying him.

He came to a swift decision.

'Then we'll have to go to her. Find out where she

is,' he said. 'Tell her you want to meet her.' He dropped the cellphone into my hand, adding a final warning: 'One word about me—'

'Let me guess. You'll shoot me?'

'You're a fast learner.'

I pressed the number to get Fitzgerald on speed-dial, heard it start to ring with a hammering heart and racing thoughts. *Stay calm*, I told myself, *show him nothing's wrong.*

'I'll be listening,' he said with one last jab of the gun in my back.

'Tell me something I don't know.'

On the fourth ring, Fitzgerald picked up.

'Saxon,' she said. (Technology ruins all surprises.)

'Hey,' I said, 'how are things going?'

'Terrific. I just finished talking to Tannar's wife. She's heading over as we speak to make an identification of her husband's body. What was left of it after the train had finished its work, that is.' She hesitated. 'Is everything all right? Healy said you were on your way to give a helping hand after the hostel, but you never showed.'

'Everything's fine. I just had to step back to my apartment for a while to pick something up. You know how forgetful I am.'

'I do?'

I almost laughed out loud at the puzzlement in her voice. Fitzgerald had accused me of many things down the years, but forgetfulness wasn't one of them.

If anything, I was a woman who remembered too much.

'So where are you now?' I said.

'Just leaving Tannar's house. I'll pick you up, if you like . . .'

I pressed the cellphone harder against my ear, hoping Leko hadn't heard.

'Good idea,' I said. 'Just tell me where you are and I'll be right there.'

'You don't have to meet me, I told you I'll pick—'

'That's OK, I understand, no need to apologize. In about ten minutes? No problem.'

A vague puzzlement had now turned to anxiety. She knew I was trying to tell her something. The question was: What?

'Saxon,' said Fitzgerald, 'is someone there with you?'

'Yeah, I'll be there. You take care now.'

I handed the cellphone back to Leko, hoping he'd be too distracted to notice that I hadn't ended the call and the line was still open, letting Fitzgerald hear every word.

'She's at Christ Church,' I told him, raising my voice.

He held my gaze a long time, trying in vain to read my thoughts. That didn't bother me. I'd hidden them from better men than him before. And at least I had my answer. He hadn't heard what had passed between Fitzgerald and me. The first obstacle was overcome.

'What's up with you?' I snapped. 'I found out what you wanted to know, didn't I?'

'I don't trust you,' he said.

'And you think I have one hundred per cent faith in you?'

Leko opened his mouth as if to answer, but couldn't think of any reply. So he struck me across the side of the head instead with the back of his hand, so hard that I saw those proverbial stars twinkling prettily in front of my eyes and tasted blood in my mouth.

'Ouch,' I said sarcastically.

'Just shut up, that's all,' said Leko, and he grabbed my arm, twisted me round and pushed me roughly down the stairs. Defiance made me keep my footing.

In a few moments, we'd reached the basement parking lot. There was no one around, not even the hobos who sometimes sneaked in here to escape the cold up above and who were tolerated as long as they didn't start setting fires.

'It's clear,' I told him.

'Find a car.'

'That shouldn't be too hard down here.'

Another smack on the side of the head was avoided only because Leko was too busy trying to find a car that would be easy to break into and start up. He must have been out of practice, though, because the first few he tried resisted his clumsy attempts at entry.

An alarm going off was his only reward, its shrill

call echoing round the basement and inducing in Leko an immediate sense of panic.

'Here, let me do it,' I said, and took his place, my misspent youth once more coming in useful as I gently forced the door to open and stepped back to let him climb in. 'See?'

'You drive,' he commanded.

He needed his hands free for the gun, after all.

I was glad to oblige.

Once in the driver's seat, it was a moment's work to reach down, pull out the wires, and hotwire the car into life. If I'd been quicker, I might have managed to get away before he climbed in. No such luck. As it was, I snapped on my seatbelt and put the car into reverse.

'You're good,' he conceded grudgingly.

'I know,' I said, and as I picked up speed and headed for the ramp, I saw Hugh the doorman stumble out from a side door, alerted by the car alarm going off, and then stand with astonishment as he saw me drive past in a stolen car. Hugh had always regarded me as a mystery, I think, but now he was going to figure that I'd really snapped my cap.

I was glad Hugh hadn't been quicker. The last thing I wanted was him getting heroic with Leko. My new travelling companion wasn't one to appreciate an old man's decency.

'You know what your problem is, Leko?' I said to him as we pulled into St Stephen's Green and Hugh diminished in the rear-view mirror. 'You've spent too long running things from the top and forgotten the basics. What do you think the boys back in Crumlin would say if they knew you couldn't even break into a locked car any more? You're losing your touch. And that's the way you lose everything in the end. You never worry that one of your loyal lieutenants might turn out not so loyal, after all?'

'They know what'll happen to them if they do.'

'Same as Allenka, huh?'

'Allenka had it easy. It's what happened to the guy she was screwing they should be worried about.'

'I heard it was nasty.'

'You heard right. Of course, I wasn't there. I was inside when he died.'

'The perfect alibi.'

'But I had them videotape it,' Leko said with relish, 'so that I could watch it when I got out. You can't know how long I've been looking forward to it . . .'

Though not nearly as much as he was looking forward to having his revenge on Fitzgerald. I could see it in his face. He was flushed, excited; his breathing had quickened; he couldn't stay still. He kept fidgeting in his seat like a small child. The killing mood was building inside him, preparing him like an athlete for the triumph ahead.

The grin vanished from his face, though, as he noticed, for the first time, the direction in which we were headed. Strange how he'd trusted me to take the right route.

Did he really think I was a kindred spirit because I could hotwire a stolen car?

'Where the fuck are you going?'

'Keep your hair on, Al Capone. It's not my fault there's a one-way system in this town. We'll be back on course before you know it. There, see?'

And now we were returning back along the other side of the Green, and he relaxed a little. He was right, though. There had been a quicker way, but I had a plan of my own in mind, that's why I'd made it Christ Church and I needed to approach the cathedral from this direction. Kevin Street now. Not far to go. Left into Patrick Street.

The nearer we came to the meeting point with Fitzgerald, the more I felt the tension building in the car, radiating from Leko like heat from an oven.

Now we could see Christ Church rising up over the crest of the road ahead as we drove towards the junction at the top of Patrick Street, the lights turning red as we approached.

I pressed my foot to the accelerator.

40kph ... 50kph ...

'Slow down!' demanded Leko, but I ignored him, and now I saw that he had finally noticed what I'd seen back in the car park under my building, and which I'd been relying on.

He hadn't put on his seatbelt.

'Shit!' he said as we went through the red light and headed straight towards the gates of the cathedral on the other side of the junction, and a car driving mercifully slowly in the other direction screeched to a halt. 'You're dead, bitch!'

He raised the gun, and I heard a shot as I pulled the wheel sharply to the right and the car spun round and the glass in the windscreen exploded into fragments. The left side of the car crunched into the metal railings with a sound that seemed to make my eardrums scream and there was a jolt that threw me forwards against the seatbelt.

Pain gripped my chest where the belt tightened against me.

Leko was not so fortunate. Any faster and he would have been thrown through the windscreen for sure. As it was, the impact of the crash crumpled him in his seat, and the gun was sent spinning from his fingers. The only sound as we came to rest in the middle of the road again was that of Leko groaning, talking to himself in what I presumed was his native language, or it may have been a senseless babble brought into being by his confusion.

'Move,' I told myself, and managed somehow to reach down and unclip my belt.

The right side of the car was undamaged, so the door opened normally, and I stepped out on to the road, astonished at being uninjured but not questioning my good fortune. What's the old proverb about never looking a gift horse in the mouth?

Though perhaps I wasn't quite so uninjured as I imagined. As I stood there in the unnatural stillness, it seemed to me that the buildings around me appeared to be swaying, as in an earthquake. And then a darkness was coming over them, or was it over me? A wave of shadow that brought a sensation of sickness to my stomach, and made my knees weak.

My knees stopped obeying my orders, and I fell into the black hole that had opened up underneath me until there was no difference between me and the black hole, we were one and the same, and I didn't even mind surrendering myself to it.

52

Tamsin was still awake when the doorbell rang. Ever since she'd got back from the Concert Hall after being questioned by the police, she'd been anxious, expectant, checking every few minutes that the phone was on the hook, that she hadn't received a message on her mobile.

After the first hour dragged by, she remembered about her laptop too. Maybe he'd emailed her. But no, when she plugged it in and switched on the screen, there was nothing waiting for her. There never was.

For one crazy second, she even considered putting on her coat and calling a taxi to take her to his house. But the police would be there and how would she explain her silence earlier? She'd told them she knew nothing of his private life, so how could she now turn around and admit that they were lovers? Casual lovers, in his eyes – she wasn't twenty any more; she knew when she was being toyed with by a man – but very far from the picture of the distant colleagues, bound together purely by music, that she'd portrayed to the police.

Her coat was on and she was pulling the door of

her apartment closed behind her, though, before she came to her senses and went back inside to wait some more.

Waiting was a woman's game. Men don't sit around waiting for their wives and girlfriends like this, Tamsin admonished herself. It was a female weakness.

Would Sean be worrying himself sick if she'd done what he did?

But what was she saying? *If* she'd done what he'd done earlier tonight at the Concert Hall? Knocking out a policeman, climbing out through the lavatory window and going on the run? The idea was preposterous. Tamsin felt like her life had become an alien entity, unknown and unknowable to her, and that the gap between what she thought was true yesterday and what she'd find to be true tomorrow was too great for her to bridge.

As for Sean, how could she ever make sense of him again?

She made coffee, though she knew it wouldn't help her sleep when she finally decided she was ready for it, and then she took a couple of the sleeping tablets the doctor had given her for her insomnia in order to counteract the effect of the coffee.

She surfed channels on the TV but she kept seeing Riordan's picture. Last night's events at the Concert Hall were never going to stay secret for long.

It was only a matter of time before reporters wheedled her phone number out of one of her so-called friends and then she'd have that intrusion to contend with too.

She wondered if that had been a reporter who called to the door a few hours earlier. He hadn't looked like a reporter, but then how could you tell? They didn't walk around any more in trench coats and pork-pie hats with a card saying PRESS poking out from the brim.

The way he'd looked at her had made her feel uncomfortable too.

Like he could see inside her head . . .

What was that? She must have nearly dropped off, because she came to her senses violently with a jerk, and realized that something had changed. Only when the doorbell rang again did she understand what it must have been. The reporters really had found her then? She ran down the corridor of her apartment to the front door and put her eye to the peephole.

'Sean?'

Just when she'd given up hope of seeing him again that night, here he was; but even in her delight, she was disgusted with herself for being so thrilled to see him.

Was she that needy?

Riordan almost knocked her over in his eagerness to get inside, then promptly ignored her. Soon as the door was shut, he put his own eye to the peephole to make sure there was no one there. Only then did he turn round and acknowledge her presence.

'Tamsin.'

She put her arms round his neck and pulled him close, finding his lips with her own and kissing him fiercely before realizing that he wasn't returning her kiss so much as letting her continue out of kindness. Or should that be indifference?

She let go. 'You shouldn't have come,' she said softly. 'They might be following you.'

'Do you think I haven't thought of that?'

He pushed past her to the tiny kitchenette that serviced her flat and tugged open the door of the fridge, the light illuminating the contours of his face almost eerily.

'I need a drink,' he said. 'Is this all you have?'

He held up a half-empty bottle of white wine, bought for dinner two nights ago, only he hadn't shown up and three glasses was her limit, though she'd felt like drinking more.

'I'm sorry,' she found herself saying.

'It'll have to do.'

He pulled out the cork and drank it straight from the bottle, slumping into the nearest armchair at the same time and glancing around the room like it was unfamiliar to him.

'Where have you been?' she said from the doorway.

'Here and there.'

'The police said—'

'Never mind what they said,' Riordan interrupted. 'What did you say to them?'

'Nothing,' said Tamsin. 'I told them nothing. I promise.'

'The others?'

'They don't know anything about us,' she pointed out. 'You said not to tell them, remember?' And of course she hadn't, though she'd never liked keeping secrets.

Riordan seemed to relax slightly at that, knowing there was no way the police could have guessed about him and Tamsin so were unlikely to be on their way. All the same . . .

'Has anyone else been here?' he asked.

'There was a man came earlier,' said Tamsin. 'I guessed he was a reporter of some kind. He said his name was Knox or Nott, I think it was. He told me he was a doctor.'

'So he was here,' Riordan said, half to himself.

'You know him then?'

'I know him all right,' said Riordan with a dry laugh. 'Though not as well as he thinks he knows me. I wonder how he found out about you when I've been so discreet?'

'Ashamed, you mean,' Tamsin said bitterly.

'Is that what you think? Well, I don't blame you for that. What would you say if I told you I'd been keeping you secret for your own benefit? To protect you?'

'From what?'

'From everything. Oh, I can't explain right now . . . it would take too long . . .'

'Sean, you're scaring me. Tell me what's wrong.'

'I can't.'

'At least tell me why you ran tonight when the police came to talk to you.'

'You wouldn't understand even if I did.'

Riordan drained the dregs of the wine, holding up the bottle to let the last few drips fall into his mouth, and placed it down on the table, disappointed that there wasn't more.

Tamsin slid into a chair, and reached out a hand to touch his fingers, and he let her. She enfolded his hand inside hers, and he let her do that too.

'I don't want to lose you,' she whispered, but something in her voice, its desperate neediness perhaps, made him pull his hand away.

'It's too late,' he said sharply. 'What's done is done. Now I have to finish it.'

'What about me?'

'You can always write to me in jail,' he answered flatly, 'and when I get out, you can tie a yellow ribbon round the old oak tree to let me know you still want me.'

'Are you making fun of me?' she said.

'Or you can bring flowers to my graveside instead. Those are the only two destinations I can see for myself right now.'

'Tell me you're joking.'

'I wish I was.' Unexpectedly, she watched him soften. 'Tamsin?'

'Yes?'

'I just want you to know that I'm sorry if ... if I wasn't the man you wanted me to be. You deserved better. I just needed to say that in case I don't get the chance later.'

'Please don't say that.'

'Come here.'

He held her tightly, like her touch meant something to him. The way she'd always wanted him to hold her. She didn't know if this was real or just his parting gift to her.

'There's something else I want you to do for me,' he whispered. 'It won't make any sense right now, but I want you to do it exactly as I tell you. Do you understand?'

'I'll do anything,' she said.

Because wasn't that what she'd always longed for – to be needed by him?

He whispered what it was, and the concern in her face transformed slowly into fear. Not fear of what was outside her door any more, but of what was in her own apartment.

'Sean,' she said, 'tell me it's not true. *What have you done?*'

53

A thousand years later, I heard a voice saying: 'She's coming round.'

'We'll still have to get her to the hospital,' said another, and I recognized that one.

'Fuck the hospital,' I said.

'Saxon.'

I opened my eyes to find Fitzgerald's face flying above me, and then it stopped flying and became just a face, though, as faces go, I don't think I'd ever been so relieved to see one before, or could ever be so glad to see another one again.

'Did you get him?' I managed to say.

She shook her head

'Don't even think about—' she added quickly, as I pulled myself up into a sitting position, though by that point the order was too late.

I'd already gone beyond thinking, and done it.

'You shouldn't move,' she tried again helplessly, to equally little effect.

'I'm perfectly OK,' I said.

'You might have concussion.'

'I don't have concussion,' I said. 'I didn't even hit my head.'

'Then what's that mark on your cheek?'

I lifted my fingers and touched the graze against my skin.

'That? That's just a memento of my meeting with your biggest fan. Speaking of which . . .'

This time my knees did as they were told, and allowed me to stand upright and see the world from the correct angle. There was an ambulance, blue light flashing, and a couple of squad cars. Fewer curious bystanders than normal, but then most of the people who might have been expected to stand about staring were home in bed and missing all this nocturnal fun.

Then there was the crashed car – Exhibit A, as it now was – with cops poking into its every nook and cranny. I wondered which of my neighbours in the apartment block it belonged to and what they'd think if they could see it now, getting all this attention.

I walked over to it, still a little gingerly, because it wasn't like I was Bionic Woman, able to shrug off car crashes the way lesser mortals did a slight head cold.

The door in the passenger side of the car was open. Somehow, Leko had managed to get out and make his getaway, though I couldn't believe he could have got far in his condition. Even without serious injury, he would've been disoriented.

I was walking evidence of that.

'At least he left his gun behind,' I said, for there it was lying under the seat. 'Either he was in too much of a hurry to escape before you got here, or he forgot all about it in the confusion. How long did it take for you to get here after the crash?'

'Only a couple of minutes,' said Fitzgerald. 'The guy you forced off the road at the lights told us what happened. He saw you get out and collapse in the road, then he saw Leko climb out of the passenger side and start making his way down towards Merchant's Quay. He tried shouting after him but he wouldn't listen.'

'I found him in my apartment,' I said, 'he was trying to find out where you were. He wanted me to lure you to my place so that he could ... well, you don't need me to tell you what he had in mind. I had to think of a way to warn you. Damn. So near and yet so far.'

'I don't care about Leko,' Fitzgerald said. 'We'll pick him up soon enough. It's you I was worried about. You could have been killed.'

'Occupational hazard.'

'Don't joke about it.'

'Joking about it's what I do,' I said. 'It's part of the treatment.'

Fitzgerald sighed. 'You really are incorrigible,' she said. 'At least let them take a look at you in the ambulance. I want to make sure you really are as indestructible as you look.'

So I let them take my pulse and ask me seemingly endless questions and get me to stick my tongue out and shine a light into my eyes, presumably to prove there was something between my eyes and the back of my skull apart from thin air, despite all rumours to the contrary. They found nothing to trouble them, so were predictably troubled. That's the problem with doctors: they hate to find people with nothing wrong with them.

They wanted to take me to the hospital for further tests, but I refused.

'It's your call, I can't force you,' conceded the senior ambulance officer. 'But you do know that just because you have no symptoms yet doesn't mean you don't have concussion?'

'I know.'

'So if you vomit, or start feeling drowsy or disoriented again, or you get a ringing in your ears, or your headache gets any worse – don't bother lying, I know you have one – then come straight to Casualty. And even if you don't have any of the signs, come in anyway. This type of injury doesn't always manifest itself straightaway. It can take a few days.'

'I will.'

'You should go home,' said Fitzgerald when they let me go.

'Any excuse to get someone else to finish the unpacking,' I said. 'Besides, isn't that what the Assistant Commissioner said to you when she heard Leko was on the loose?'

'*I* hadn't been injured in a car accident.'

'And nor have I. You heard the man. There's nothing wrong with me.'

'Apart from a headache—'

'I had that before the crash.'

'—and a tendency to lose consciousness in the middle of a main road.'

'Once isn't a tendency,' I said, 'and I'm telling you, I simply got up too quickly after the crash. I should have waited for help to come, but you know me. I got impatient. And now I want to stop talking about me and listen instead while you tell me what you've got.'

'What makes you think I've got anything?'

'Because I saw you talking to O'Neill over there whilst I was getting interfered with in the ambulance, and O'Neill wouldn't have come out of his way to ask after my health.'

'He didn't,' she admitted. 'Though he did mention how impressed he was with your idea about keeping the phone on so that you could tell us where you were.'

'You'll not distract me that easily. Forget the flattery. Out with it.'

'Lester Coyle's turned up,' she said with a sigh. 'You remember him, the guy who made the initial call about Daniel Erskine?'

'Sandals Man? I remember. The amnesia hasn't kicked in totally yet.'

'I was beginning to think he'd vanished off the face of the earth,' she said. 'I don't know if it'll lead to anything, but what else have we got to cling on to?'

'Then what are we waiting for?'

'Saxon,' she pleaded, 'I don't know if this is such a good idea.'

'Good ideas are overrated,' I interrupted. 'That's what makes bad ideas so much more fun.'

Fitzgerald wanted to object, but as she put it resignedly: 'How can I say no to a woman who just crashed into railings outside the cathedral to save my life?'

'I must remember that next time it's my turn to take out the trash. Remind me to thank you for introducing me to a whole new line in emotional blackmail.'

54

He ran the moment he saw us. One minute Coyle was standing outside his local church, holding a hymn book and singing along enthusiastically with his circle of like-minded battlers against satanic depravity, and the next he'd dropped the hymn book at his feet and made a run for it, sprinting in an almost comically clumsy fashion down the street whilst the rest of the choir looked astonished at the impromptu departure of one of their members.

'For fuck's sake,' muttered Fitzgerald. 'O'Neill, could you do the honours?'

'My pleasure.'

I was glad we'd brought O'Neill along with us. I wasn't going to be up to Olympic-standard suspect pursuit for a while yet, and having other people to do your running for you was one of the perks of the job for a Detective Chief Superintendent. Within a few seconds, O'Neill had raced after Lester Coyle and wrestled the guy to the ground.

He wasn't putting up much of a struggle.

'Now why would you do a stupid thing like that?' said Fitzgerald as we caught up with them.

'A stupid thing like what?' he gasped as O'Neill hauled him to his feet.

'A stupid thing like running away when you saw us,' Fitzgerald said. 'Some people might think that was a touch suspicious. Like you had a guilty conscience about something.'

'I didn't do it!' he insisted, his voice rising.

'No one said you did anything,' Fitzgerald said. 'We only wanted to talk to you. I told you earlier we'd be in touch again.'

'When I saw your faces,' he said, 'I knew you didn't just want to talk. I wasn't thinking – I thought you'd come to – I don't know what I thought—'

'That's what happens when you don't tell the police the truth, the whole truth and nothing but the truth. When you hold things back. Important things.'

'I don't want to go back inside,' he pleaded.

'There you go jumping to conclusions again,' she said. 'No one said anything about prison. Unfortunately for us, we can't just send witnesses who waste our time immediately to jail, without passing Go or collecting £200. What were you doing back there, anyway?'

He looked back at the church, where the singing had stopped temporarily and the other members of his church group were standing about awkwardly, waiting for an explanation.

'It's an all-night Halloween vigil,' Coyle said. 'I gave you a leaflet about it back at the house, don't you remember?'

'*Halloween: Beware The Occult! Dark Influences Can Ruin Your Life!*,' I recalled, feeling foolish. That's what comes of not keeping up to date with your reading. The answer to Coyle's apparent disappearance overnight had been in front of our eyes all along.

'That's what I was doing. I was delivering the leaflets inviting people down here to join in,' he said. 'Halloween's a dangerous time. People think it's harmless fun, but dabbling in the occult is never innocent. Things get stirred up unwittingly. Things that should be left undisturbed. That's what the vigil's all about. Prayer keeps the dark forces back.'

'It's not having much effect tonight,' I muttered grimly.

'And it still doesn't explain,' Fitzgerald added, 'why you were less than straight with us about your past – how shall I put this? – indiscretions. You could have avoided a lot of trouble if you'd been upfront about things. I thought you people were all for the truth?'

'I couldn't,' he said. 'I didn't want them finding out.'

Fitzgerald looked like she was about to point out that being manhandled to the ground by the police in front of them wasn't exactly going to look good either, but something made her pause. Pity, perhaps. 'You want to go somewhere to talk?' she said.

'My house is just around the corner.'

He pointed in the direction he was headed when caught.

'You were running to your own house?' said Fitzgerald with a shake of the head. 'Did it never occur to you that might be the first place we'd come looking?'

'I wasn't—'

'Thinking, yes, I spotted that. But if you want my advice, this would be a very wise time to start. Come on,' she said quietly, 'lead the way. O'Neill?'

'Yes, Chief.'

'You stay here and explain to Mr Coyle's friends at the church what this is about. No need to go into details. I just don't want them thinking he's been abducted by Halloween-loving Satanists trying to disrupt their vigil. Come by when you've finished.'

It was a very different Lester Coyle who took us to his front door than the one who'd been sitting in Erskine's house earlier that night. This was the meek and mild version. Soon as he was in, he switched on the lights, went straight to a chair in his front room and sat down heavily. The house was cold. He clearly didn't have the central heating on, waiting for his arrival. The air smelt of damp. The damp of an unheated house in fall, with winter coming on.

It sure was a long way from Erskine's world.

'Why didn't you tell us about Arbour Hill, Coyle?' Fitzgerald said.

'Do you think I tell everyone I meet that I'm a peeping Tom?' he said, scratching at that weird chinstrap-style beard of his like he'd suddenly decided he didn't like it.

'We're hardly *everyone*,' Fitzgerald shot right back. 'Did you honestly think you were going to get away with hiding it?'

'I was frightened,' he whispered. 'I thought if I told you what I saw in the house, then you'd think I was ... you know ... looking in ... spying ...'

'Were you?'

'No! You people are all the same. You think just because I have one black mark against my name, then I can't change. That I'm bad all through.'

'We have a witness says she saw you earlier tonight, looking in people's houses.'

'Shit!' he spat. 'Shit, that's all I need.' He got to his feet so suddenly I thought he was going to lash out, but it wasn't that. He had too much nervous energy in him to sit still, that was all. So he paced, paced, banging his forehead with the palm of his hand as if that would knock the right thoughts into him. 'Are you going to arrest me?' he said in the end.

'Not necessarily,' said Fitzgerald carefully. 'I could see the whole matter's quietly dropped, if that's what you'd prefer. As long as it doesn't happen again, that is.'

Hope flashed in Coyle's eyes.

'It won't, it won't, I promise,' he began, but she cut him off bluntly.

'It all depends,' she said, 'on how cooperative you're willing to be. So I'm only going to ask you one time. What were you doing at Daniel Erskine's house?'

'I was looking through windows,' he said, defeated. 'That's what I do. That's my life. I'm on the outside, looking in.'

'Spare us the self-dramatization,' said Fitzgerald. 'You do it because you get a thrill out of it, it isn't an exercise in existential loneliness. Is that why you volunteered to deliver leaflets for the church? So that you can spy on people in their own houses?'

'No, I swear ... my faith is genuine ... I've been trying to get my life in order ... the church has been helping me ... but sometimes, when I'm out, walking around – well, there's no point denying it. You seem to have all the answers. I do sometimes stray from the straight path and, yes, I look. I looked tonight. There was a light on, I was curious. I just went down the steps and looked in the basement. There's a window. You can see everything.'

'What do you mean by everything?'

'I saw ... I saw a man putting a body into the freezer,' he confessed.

'You *saw* the killer?' I gasped.

'Why didn't you tell us what you'd seen?' demanded Fitzgerald.

'I'm not stupid,' said Coyle, clearly oblivious to the irony of making such a claim whilst every word he spoke was proving the opposite. 'If I told the police I'd been looking in someone's window, it's like, well, signing a confession. I'd be incriminating myself.' He said this like he was explaining a particularly difficult legal point to a bunch of idiots.

'So you just told us that you'd been knocked down by the killer instead?'

'I didn't think it would matter. As long as I told the

police something, I knew they'd go to the house and find the body anyway.'

'So it was all a lie?' I said. 'The stranger at Erskine's house, the white van, everything?'

'I just thought I should add a few details to make it more believable. I didn't realize there were going to be so many questions ... I got trapped in the story ...'

It was a classic mistake. Instead of keeping things simple, liars added details to make their story seem more credible, whereas in fact it had the opposite effect and drew suspicion. Murderers often made that mistake too. But was Coyle telling the truth now, or was this another lie to add to the list of ones already told?

'You told us you saw a man putting a body in the freezer,' I pressed him.

'I did.'

'By that, do you mean you saw someone putting a body in a freezer, or that you actually did see him, the way you see me? Could you identify him again, I mean?'

'I saw his face all right,' said Coyle. 'And he saw me too. I must've made a noise at the window because he turned round and his eyes just burned into me. Do you know the bit in *The Devil Rides Out* where the demon appears in the smoke with the scary red eyes?' Coyle was evidently getting his religious education from unorthodox theological sources. 'It was like that. I knew he'd kill me too if he caught me. I just ran as fast as I could.'

'Then you can give us a description of him?' said Fitzgerald. 'A proper description this time, not the same crap you invented earlier about the man in the white van?'

'I suppose so,' he said reluctantly, 'but I'm not very good at describing things.'

'Don't worry about that. We have people there who can help you.'

'There?'

'Dublin Castle,' said Fitzgerald.

'Do I have to?' he groaned.

'Yes,' she said, 'you do. The only thing left to be decided is whether you make the journey in hand-cuffs or out of them. The choice is entirely up to you.'

Coyle didn't make the mistake of complaining a second time.

55

Coyle was on his way to Dublin Castle. O'Neill had accompanied him in the car. From the look on his face, you'd have thought he was being transported to an electric chair in San Quentin for summary execution rather than a heated interview room in DMP headquarters.

Soon as he'd helped put together a photofit picture of the man he claimed to have seen, Fitzgerald had told the junior officer, he was to send it to her on her cellphone.

'I don't get it,' I said as we watched them drive away. 'Why didn't Coyle just tell us from the start that he'd seen someone in Daniel Erskine's basement?'

'Our lives are not meant to be so simple. It's not part of God's plan.'

'You mean all this is planned?'

'Either that, or he's simply one of those people who make my life hell. You know, the ones who are physiologically incapable of telling the truth,' Fitzgerald said. 'They live a lie so long that they can't tell the difference any more.'

I knew the kind she meant well enough. Their version of events is up for constant negogiation, rather like Groucho Marx's principles. If you didn't like what they said, then they had another version ready to replace it. But if he was still lying, what was in it for him?

That was what I didn't get.

He couldn't possibly be connected to all this, could he?

'You heard what the man said,' Fitzgerald reasoned when I voiced my doubts. 'Maybe he really did just get trapped inside his own story, and it became easier to carry on regardless than row back? He didn't want to have to admit what he was really doing, so he comes up with some elaborate story that he thinks will solve all his problems but in fact it only makes his problems worse. We should be glad he called the police at all. Many another pervert in his position would have simply run home and pretended to forget what he saw.'

'So Coyle's a civic-minded citizen now, is he?'

'I wouldn't go that far. Who knows, he could even be one of those people who need to keep their involvement in a case going for as long as possible to make themselves feel important and so ration out the little snippets of information they have one piece at a time?'

'Seeing the main suspect putting a body in the freezer is more than a little snippet of information,' I pointed out, 'and I doubt Coyle wants to string out his involvement with this case either. I'd say if he never saw your face again, it would still be too soon.'

'The feeling's mutual.'

Coyle was well named either way. His reasoning was so twisted and coiled in on itself that disentangling his various neuroses would be a lifetime's work, and it was debatable if the true Coyle which was uncovered at the end of it would have been worth the digging.

'Let's hope he can redeem himself by coming up with the goods, at any rate.'

'I'll drink to that.'

Except where *was* there to drink at this time of day?

'Especially when we're supposed to be on duty,' Fitzgerald reminded me.

'Screw it,' I said. 'I knew there was a flaw in the plan somewhere. Come on then, Chief Superintendent, what have you got lined up as an alternative?'

'Walking back to town,' she replied.

'So that's why you let O'Neill steal our only ride?'

'It's not far, and I need some air. If you're up to it?' she added, concern for my well-being inevitably reasserting itself after a reassuring but brief lull.

'I'm as fit as the proverbial fiddle,' I said.

So we walked, first making our way past the vigil outside the church which Coyle had been so unceremoniously hauled away from a short while ago. Eyes glared at us resentfully as they recognized who we were. So much for Christian kindness.

One of them held up a poster with the words *Halloween Kills* painted on it.

If only he'd known how right he was.

'Happy Holidays,' Fitzgerald wished them mischievously as we neared.

They didn't offer a greeting back.

A few minutes later, we were strolling through empty, close-packed city streets, our echoing footsteps keeping us company, and enjoying the silence.

It was a peculiar hour, night starting to lose its grip but morning still seemingly distant, as if the light was unsure which way to go, even if it always made the same decision in the end. The air still held a trace of fire, the residue of the previous evening's fireworks. The blackened sticks of exhausted sky rockets could be seen in the gutters.

I barely took notice of which way we walked. We were tending in the general direction of town, I knew that. The rest was mere detail.

Fitzgerald had made the right decision, I soon realized. After all that had happened overnight, walking was a chance to clear the head, and to wonder where we were going next. All in all, it looked like we had been outwitted. Someone had set out to get rid of the Second Circle and had almost accomplished it. We'd done little more than inconvenience him.

It was on nights like this that you started to question the value of what you did.

Or you did, if you were any good. It was those who never doubted their own judgements and abilities who were the ones to cause concern.

At least there was a good chance that we didn't

have to worry about Leko any more. My guess was that he wouldn't be in any position for a while to finish what he'd escaped from prison to do, if ever. It wouldn't have surprised me if that particular rat had crawled away into a drain somewhere to die. And if he had, he wouldn't be missed.

We were determined to make the most of the respite, however long it lasted, especially since Fitzgerald had managed to temporarily shake off the tail which Serious Crime had put on her. All that confusion at the crash scene had come in useful.

Gradually, I noticed that our route back to town was taking us, as if our feet were answering some call that we hadn't even realized was being issued, in the direction of the hospital in whose grounds Erin Gilroy's body had been found all those years ago.

Or had Fitzgerald made her way here deliberately, with me merely trailing in her wake, a scrap of seaweed caught up in a stronger tide? I guessed that must be it.

It certainly seemed fortuitous that we should be here, because there was definitely an atmosphere in the air, as of too much activity and too many people about for that time.

Confirming that this was no ordinary occurrence, the first thing we saw when we reached the gate of the hospital was a uniformed police officer mumbling into a hand-held walkie-talkie. It looked like it was the end of his shift and this was the last thing he needed when he could have been back at his local station instead, keeping warm till the clock told him he was free to go. Wisps of grey hair peeped out from under his cap.

'What's going on?' said Fitzgerald, showing him her ID.

'We're looking for a body, Chief Superintendent. Some joker called 999 to say there was a dead woman somewhere in the car park here, but we haven't been able to find anything. Some members of the public have a very strange sense of humour, that's all I can say.'

I was gripped with the strangest sensation almost of having slipped back twenty years, finding myself standing in this parking lot on the very night that Erin Gilroy had died. What had really changed, after all? The buildings may have been a little taller, the cars shinier, but the heart of the city hadn't altered. The air it exuded was the same.

'Tell me more about this 999 call,' Fitzgerald said.

'It came in about half an hour ago. We were sent out to take a look, but the message had already gone out on police radio, so by the time we got here there were already two more squad cars on site with officers searching the grounds for any sign of a body.'

'Who made the call?'

'A woman,' he said. 'She claimed to work in the hospital. A doctor, I think.'

'Dr Nott?' I suggested.

'That's the one,' he said. 'You know her then?'

'I didn't even know she was a woman until I met you,' I replied, but even as I said the words, I still wasn't sure I knew that she was. Or that I knew anything. There was something nightmarish about this whole thing. Like our own subconscious was playing tricks on us, purely to see how we would react. And how *would* we?

In Fitzgerald's case, there was never any question but that she would rise to the occasion. She took charge. That she didn't know what the hell was going on wouldn't get in her way. She did what had to be done, and left the making sense of it for later.

The cops on the ground exhibited all the signs of being delighted to be ordered about. The alternative was thinking for themselves and, at their age, they wouldn't have still been in uniform and on night patrol if they'd ever shown that much initiative.

She broke the area to be searched down into segments for them. She made them check again the places they'd already covered, this time using the new system. She supervised their efforts to secure the scene from unwitting intruders. She reminded me of a kindergarten teacher pulling a bunch of wayward kids into shape whilst making them think that they are doing it all by themselves. The only thing missing here was a body to help the cops feel that all their efforts had not been in vain; but there *was* no body. The call had been a hoax.

But it had been no ordinary hoax.

This hospital of all hospitals on *this* night of all nights? We were meant to be here.

'Let's find out why,' Fitzgerald said.

56

In Reception, a senior nurse was explaining how they'd only finished dealing with the stream of traditional fireworks injuries in the Accident and Emergency unit in the last hour, and now there was this disruption to contend with as well. The way she spoke made it seem like it was our fault. And no, she answered sniffily when asked, they didn't have a Dr Nott working in the hospital. There hadn't been any member of staff with that name during her time at the hospital. How long had that been? Ten years. And what about doctors prior to her arrival? The concept of the hospital having both existed and managed to function before she walked through the door threw her for a moment, but she recovered quickly. We'd have to speak to someone in Personnel, she said. They didn't start work until 9 a.m.

Now if we'd excuse her . . .

'She was helpful,' I observed as the nurse returned to work.

'And then some,' Fitzgerald agreed. 'To misquote another movie, I think we lost her on "Hello". You want some coffee? I think I saw a machine somewhere.'

Hospitals were never really silent. Even in the

middle of the night there was always noise from somewhere. Doors swishing, distant telephones ringing, a murmur of voices. Footsteps most often of all, their echo impossible to place or follow.

We sat on plastic chairs in Reception and forced ourselves to drink what was labelled coffee on the machine but might, in truth, have been anything.

'To think so many coffee beans died for *this*,' I remarked.

The shot of caffeine into our bloodstreams should have made us more alert, but I felt I was coming to the limit of my endurance tonight. If I didn't get some sleep soon, they'd have to scrape me off the floor come morning. My thoughts drifted, unanchored, bumping into one another like ships in a fog. There must have been a reason why someone called 999 to report a dead body in the parking lot, but at that moment it was beyond my comprehension.

I found myself wondering about the mysterious Dr Nott. I'd assumed all along that we were looking for an academic doctor, not a medical one. I suppose I'd come to that conclusion because it was at Trinity College that the Second Circle had first met and at which the photograph in Ronan Blunt's study had been taken.

I'd assumed the untraceable doctor was a man for the same reason. There was something almost militantly masculine about these men's view of the world. Daniel Erskine's friends didn't seem like they would've been too welcoming to a woman entering their circle.

Unless she was a stripper, that is, and we knew what happened to those women.

So had we been wrong all along? Was Dr Nott really a woman? No, the emergency call had been about something else, I was sure of it. It wasn't really *for* the police at all.

Not only for the police, that is.

There was a message there for someone else.

Outside, the local cops were finishing their second search of the parking lot. Fitzgerald finally conceded defeat and binned her coffee before heading out the revolving doors to tell them they could go. There was no point in them hanging around any longer.

I'd call O'Neill, that's what I'd do; find out what he'd managed to tease out of Lester Coyle's infuriatingly muddled head. But when I checked my cellphone, I realized I was low on power. Typical. Whose head was muddled now? I rose to look for a payphone. There must be one nearby. This was a hospital. Giving up, I asked the girl behind Reception.

'Down the corridor on the left. You can't miss it.'

Why do people always say that? How do they know what I could miss? I'd missed plenty more obvious things in my time than a mere payphone.

But as it happened, she was right. Down the corridor on the left was all the direction I needed. I dug into my pockets for spare change, and remembered Leko had emptied my pockets. I was broke. I tried the rejected coins slot, hoping against hope.

Miracles do happen. I lifted the receiver, fed the found coin into the slot.

Somewhere in Dublin Castle across the city, I made a phone ring.

'O'Neill?'

'He's not here,' said a grumpy voice.

'Is that Dalton? I see you're in no better mood than last time we met.'

'What do you expect? I heard you crashed your car into a railing and walked away without a scratch. Of course I'm in a bad mood.'

'You heard wrong. It wasn't *my* car.'

'That makes it even worse. Means both you and your car are without a scratch. What do you want with O'Neill anyway? He's not your type. He's a man, for one thing.'

'Then you obviously have nothing in common with him,' I said, and added quickly, before he could insult me in return: 'I only want to know how he's getting on with Coyle.'

'They're still putting together a photofit,' said Dalton. 'Though why you believe a word that little faggot told you beats me. The only thing he saw in Erskine's window last night was his own reflection jerking off. Hello? You still there?'

Reflection.

Momentarily, as Dalton spoke, I focused on the laminated board in front of my eyes, listing various telephone codes and charges. The poster was black with white lettering, so the blackness formed a sort of mirror, illuminated dully by the strip lights overhead in the corridor. And in that rough mirror, I had seen someone pass silently.

And not just any someone.

I spun round sharply, but there was no one there. No one anywhere near. The corridor was deserted in both directions. It was as if the figure had been there previously, but it was only Dalton's words which had made it register in my mind's eye.

Either that or I was going crazy.

'I have to go,' I said to Dalton. 'Tell O'Neill I rang.'

'Sure, it's not as if I have anything better to do than run messages for you.'

'That's what I figured,' I said, and replaced the receiver.

I hastened back towards Reception. The girl who had been behind the desk a few moments earlier was not there any more, and the revolving doors at the front of the building were spinning slowly on their own, as if powered by ghosts.

What was going on?

I pushed through the doors and out into the open. Fitzgerald was climbing the steps back to the building. Behind her, the last of the squad cars was turning out of the car park into the main road. Her eyes widened as she saw my haste.

'Something's happened,' she said.

Had it?

'Did anyone pass you on the way out?' I said.

She shook her head.

'Then he must still be in here.'

If he'd ever been here in the first place.

'Saxon—?'

She followed me back into Reception, and there was the girl sitting on her chair again behind the desk.

'Where were you?' I demanded.

'What?'

'A moment ago, where were you? You weren't here.'

'I went to the toilet,' the girl said with exaggerated sarcasm. 'Is it a crime now?'

'What is it, Saxon?' said Fitzgerald, taking my arm and forcing me to stand still and take notice of what she was saying. 'You saw somebody. Who was it?'

'I saw Michael Erskine,' I said, 'down the corridor there whilst I was making a call. Or I saw his reflection, at least. I don't even know if I imagined it.'

Fitzgerald refused to let my imagination come into it.

If I'd seen Erskine, that was enough for her.

'Which way was he going?' she said.

'He wasn't exactly *going* anywhere,' I said. 'But he couldn't have gone out the front way . . .'

'Because he'd have had to pass me,' she finished. Then she pointed to the left and demanded of the girl behind the desk, 'What's down that way?'

'The emergency exit,' she said.

'No stairs?'

'No.'

'No lift.'

'No.'

'Not that way either then,' Fitzgerald said. 'He'd have tripped the alarm on his way out. That means he must still be down there.'

She headed down the corridor where I'd been standing a few minutes earlier, and now it was my turn to follow her. She tried each door as she came to it. Locked. Locked. Broom cupboard. Disabled toilet. Locked. Admin office. Locked. Locked. Locked.

Elevator. *Out Of Order.*

'If Erskine *is* here,' I said, still doubtful of what I'd seen, 'you'll need back-up.'

'By the time they turn up, it'll be too late,' she insisted, 'and I'm not sitting around waiting for another hour whilst he gets away. Back-up can wait. Fuck it!'

The last exclamation was for the door opening on to the stairwell. If Erskine had gone through here, then he could be anywhere in the whole hospital, or, more likely, out of it.

Where would we even start to look?

'We'll just have to pray he didn't see it,' I said hopelessly.

'The prayers can wait,' Fitzgerald answered wryly. 'There's still one last door.'

Which opened, when pushed, into a darkened,

empty ward. The mingled smell of paint and disinfectant hung heavy in the air, so strong that it practically made my head spin. This place was a junkie's dream. It was obviously a new ward, not yet opened, with beds still awaiting sheets lined up on either side of the wall with narrow, curtainless windows between each one. The polished floor glistened like water. Our shoes squeaked as we stepped on it.

'There's no way out of here,' she said, and then all doubt vanished as shouting erupted behind us, and I knew at once where it was coming from.

'The stairwell,' I said.

There was another cry from above. Of anger? Fear? The echo made it difficult to interpret, or even know how far away the sound was coming from. We ran back into the corridor and through the door leading to the stairs and almost ran into the nurse we'd seen earlier. She was rushing through the door to escape whatever was happening above our heads.

'Two men,' she managed to get out when we asked what was happening. 'Fighting. Third floor.' And she pushed past us and ran towards Reception.

'Call Dublin Castle!' Fitzgerald yelled after her. 'Tell them Michael Erskine's here! *Michael Erskine*, do you hear me?'

Without waiting to ensure that she'd got the message right, we clattered our way up the enclosed stairway, unable to make out what was happening up ahead but simply following the sound of the commotion, turning one corner and then another. What floor had the nurse said they'd been on? The third. Round another corner – and then we were forced to step back as a man's body tumbled down the stairs towards us, rolling over heavily and coming to a rest, face down, at our feet. We knelt at his side and turned him to face upwards.

It wasn't Michael Erskine.

'It's Riordan,' I said.

57

Sean Riordan was not dead, but he might easily have been so. Whoever he'd been fighting with had stabbed him a number of times in the stomach before kicking him down the stairs. Now he lay on a trolley in the corridor, being tended by a doctor who was doing his best to remain calm despite his bewilderment at what was happening in his hospital, and the same senior nurse who had been so unhelpful to us in Reception a short while earlier.

She kept glancing over her shoulder as if expecting another attack to come at any moment. I guess she wouldn't feel totally safe until the police arrived in strength. Till then, this place still felt exposed. Open. At least she didn't think we were wasting her time with pointless enquiries any more, I thought acidly. That was something.

Fitzgerald had read Riordan his rights and arrested him as soon as she was sure he was still alive, and now she was trying to ask him questions about what had happened, despite anxious objections from the doctor who couldn't stress enough how the patient shouldn't be disturbed until he'd received the proper treatment and his condition had been fully assessed. The stab wounds had been made with a syringe, and seemed superficial, but they couldn't rule out internal bleeding yet or that the needle had done damage to one of his organs.

The argument over asking questions of a patient who'd just been stabbed was academic anyway, as Riordan wasn't exactly being cooperative. Or rather he was engaging in a bizarre kind of advance and retreat manoeuvre in his responses which made it impossible to predict at any given moment whether he was going to answer each question.

'Who did this to you?' Fitzgerald kept asking him.

'I told you, I don't want to talk about it.'

'Someone just tried to kill you, Riordan. They could still be in the building, waiting to try a second time.' I saw the nurse flinch. 'Why hold out on us any longer?'

'I'm sorry, I can't.'

'Was it Michael?' I said, remembering the reflection I'd seen a short time earlier.

'*No*,' he said angrily.

'Did he attack you because he knows you killed his brother?'

A look of disgust came into his face. 'Is that really what you think?'

'Why should I think otherwise? You don't have an alibi for the time of Daniel's death,' said Fitzgerald. 'Or Oliver Niland's. You said you were rehearsing at the time, but we know that's not true. And when we tried to ask you some questions, you assaulted a detective and chose to go on the run rather than answer them.'

'I did not kill Niles!' Riordan said, quieter now.

'I note you didn't include Daniel in that statement.'

'Fuck Daniel,' he said, his voice rising again. 'I told you at the Concert Hall what I thought about him, but I didn't kill him. I wish I had, but I didn't. I haven't killed anyone.'

'Perhaps Michael doesn't believe you,' I said.

'You don't know how ridiculous you sound,' said Riordan, 'standing there pretending to know all about Michael. You don't know anything about him.'

'I know that Michael was seen in the hospital in the last half-hour.'

'Then why aren't you trying to find him instead of asking me stupid questions?'

'We'll find Michael soon enough, don't you worry,' I said, but we were getting nowhere with this and Riordan knew it. He was holding on so tightly to his secrets that it would take a crowbar to separate him from them. Fitzgerald tried a different tack.

'Tell us about Gilroy,' she said.

'Please, Chief Superintendent,' the doctor interjected desperately, 'I cannot allow this to continue. This man is my patient, I am trying to treat his injuries.'

But his own pleas on Riordan's behalf were in vain because the mention of Gilroy's name had clearly unsettled him.

'Oh yes,' said Fitzgerald, 'we know about Conn Gilroy. We know about Erin.'

'You don't know anything,' said Riordan, repeating his earlier words, though there was less conviction in them this time; and then he winced with pain as the nurse set about cleaning his wounds. 'If you did, you wouldn't still be fishing for information.'

'We know Gilroy found out what happened to his mother when she spent the evening with you,' she said. 'We know he was blackmailing you. We know plenty.'

Riordan tried to laugh, then thought better of it as another flash of pain fixed him to the trolley like nails to a wall.

'Chief Superintendent,' the doctor tried again, 'this is unacceptable. You are making this situation intolerable.' But King Canute would have had better luck holding back the waves than the doctor did in stopping Fitzgerald from questioning Riordan.

Especially now that Riordan's own interest had been piqued. He was as fascinated to find out what we knew as the other way round, I could see the hunger for it in his eyes.

Mutual dependency was the perfect situation in any interrogation. And having achieved it, the important thing was never to let your own desire for their answers show.

'Gilroy the great blackmailer,' Riordan said when the pangs that momentarily gripped him had passed, 'is that really the angle you're going on?'

'We found one of his letters at Michael Erskine's house.'

'That's convenient.'

'We also know that he was gathering information on all the members of the Second Circle, including you. We have it from Ronan Blunt's own testimony that he was being blackmailed. Why would Gilroy have left you out?'

'I'm not saying Gilroy didn't try it on,' Riordan said tentatively, selecting his words one at a time to see how comfortable he felt with them. 'We all got letters from him. But the man was an idiot. It was obvious he thought he'd discovered some magical ATM machine from which he could come and withdraw money whenever he felt like it. We threw him a little cash to begin with to keep him quiet, but he started to get greedy. That's when Blunt panicked and went to Daniel for help. Talk about out of the frying pan into the fire.'

'What makes you say that?'

'Because next to Daniel, Gilroy was an amateur.'

'You're saying Daniel was blackmailing you too?' I said.

'It wasn't what you'd call blackmail,' said Riordan. 'Not in the conventional sense. But he'd used what happened to Erin Gilroy that night against us for years. Right from the start when we went to him and told him about it, wanting his help in hushing it up, he'd recorded us all on a tape. Our confessions, you might say. After that, we were his. He never had to say anything explicitly, the very fact that he had us on tape meant that we couldn't escape him. He made our lives a misery. If he wanted to meet every Friday, then that's what we did. Didn't matter what other commitments we had, we had to be at his beck and call. We were the chess pieces and he was the grand-master, pushing us around the board.'

'But you weren't Daniel's chess piece,' said Fitzgerald. 'You were semi-detached from the group. If anything, you were more like an opposing player.'

'I was the only one he couldn't control,' he admitted, 'but I still knew I had to watch my step for the sake of the others. For Niles, most of all. They were terrified of standing up to him. Terrified of what he might do to them. Because of them, Daniel Erskine and I stayed at arm's length. I suppose you'd call it an uneasy truce.'

'Which you broke tonight by killing him,' I said.

I'd pushed him too far.

'Here we go again,' he said dismissively. 'No, it's all right,' he added when the doctor attempted to intercede for a third time on his behalf, 'I don't mind them being here.'

And that was the strange thing about him. He said he didn't want to talk, then talked. He expressed contempt for our lack of understanding of the night's events, but kept pressing to uncover exactly what we knew. Intermittently, it almost seemed like he wanted to say more, but still wasn't sure how far he should go. His mood was hard to read. He exuded the air of a man who knew he was beaten but who still didn't want to reveal too much about his losing strategy just in case the chance came again, however remote, to get back into the game.

'For the last time,' he said, 'I haven't killed anyone.'

'Then who did?' Fitzgerald said.

Again, the hesitation, the desire to talk, the holding back.

'I need to think,' he said.

'At least tell me one thing,' she said, because she knew as well as I did that making him feel like he had the power to withhold or impart information was often a much more effective way of learning the truth than making him feel it was being forced out of him.

'What is it?' he said, curiosity making him nibble at the bait.

'Who is Dr Nott?'

Riordan's reaction was unexpected. He laughed bitterly, and this time not even the pain from his wound could stop him.

'Have you not even figured that part out yet?' he said. 'There *is* no Dr Nott. There never was.'

'We saw the name on a photograph in Blunt's house,' Fitzgerald insisted.

'It was a joke,' he said. 'Don't you get it? Dr M. Nott was just an imaginary character we made up when we were students. A fiction. He was our excuse for getting out of doing things we didn't want to do.

If one of our parents wanted us to go to some terrible family gathering, we'd say we couldn't go because we had an essay to write for Dr Nott. If we were in some boring situation we couldn't get out of, we'd get one of the others to call and say that Dr Nott needed us urgently in his office.'

'Blunt's wife said Dr Nott was a colleague of her husband's at the Dead Zoo,' I said.

'And had she ever actually met him?' he asked, something like amusement sparkling fiercely in his eyes.

'No,' I said reluctantly, remembering what she'd told us when his name was mentioned: *My loving husband never introduces me to any of his colleagues. He's ashamed of me.* Seemed like Dr Nott had gone on being a useful excuse for the boys well into adulthood.

'Then who called 999 claiming to be Nott earlier?'

'I'm afraid you have me to thank for that,' he confessed.

'It wasn't you. It was a woman's voice.'

'I got my girlfriend to call the police. Tamsin. She's the cellist in the quartet. You met her at the Concert Hall. I went round to her apartment earlier. I was the one who told her to call and say there was a woman's body in the car park.'

'Why?'

Riordan looked faintly embarrassed, despite his pain.

'There was something I had to do here. I didn't want to be alone, I suppose. I was … afraid. I'm not ashamed to admit it. I thought if the police were here, I'd be safer, but I didn't want them to know *I* was here. Not me, or – well, it doesn't matter.'

'But a woman's body? Here, in the very place where Erin Gilroy's body was found. That was a pretty tasteless tactic.'

'I had my reasons.'

'Tell us,' said Fitzgerald. 'You want to. I can see it.'

Riordan was plainly struggling with indecision.

'I can't,' he said. 'If I tell you everything now, it's over.'

'Don't you want it to be over?'

'Not yet.'

Something was bothering me about what he'd said. *Dr Nott was just an imaginary character we made up.* There was a part of it which didn't feel right, and I couldn't put my finger on precisely which part it was. All of it, maybe.

The doctor took the opportunity of the baffled silence which had fallen on us to spirit Riordan away. An orderly arrived to wheel him down to prepare for surgery just as more police arrived through the revolving hospital doors.

'You,' Fitzgerald told the first to appear, 'go with that man. Yes, the one on the trolley. He's under arrest. Wherever they take him, make sure that he doesn't get away or anyone else gets near him. Whether you decide to talk or not is entirely up to you, Riordan, but I haven't finished with you yet either way.'

The doctor shot her a glance as he followed his patient down the corridor. It was the sort of look that other people might reserve for a concentration camp guard. Whatever else Riordan might have done, to his doctor he was primarily a patient in need of treatment.

I think that's called compassion.

There were times it seemed to me like a very overrated virtue.

58

'Out with it,' said Fitzgerald. 'You don't think he did it, do you?'

'I didn't say that.'

'You were thinking it, though.'

'I was thinking about thinking it, will that do? And I know you were too, so don't bother denying it. But that's not what's eating me.'

'Then what is?'

'When I figure it out, you'll be the first to know.'

She'd finished briefing the newly arrived cops on the situation at the hospital, but she wouldn't be one hundred per cent happy until she had her own officers on the scene. Until then, it was a matter of holding it together and hoping that Michael Erskine turned up.

That he had been the one who attacked Riordan, there could surely be no doubt. And yet doubt there was. I kept going over the conversation with Riordan on the trolley in my head, looking for the bit that didn't fit so that the jigsaw could be fixed outwards from that point. The problem was, there were so many parts of tonight's puzzle which were still inexplicable that isolating one in particular from the bundle seemed like an impossible task.

'I wish O'Neill would hurry up,' I said.

Fitzgerald raised an eyebrow.

'I thought you didn't approve of O'Neill and his weak stomach?' she said.

'He's growing on me,' I conceded.

'Do I hear the sound of wedding bells?'

'I'm not sure about marriage, but if he comes through with the goods from Lester Coyle, I'll possibly consider a dirty weekend in Martha's Vineyard as a reward.'

'Well, I've had no word from him yet,' she said, and then she frowned as she reached into her pocket and realized that her cellphone wasn't there. 'Did I drop it on the stairs?'

We retraced our steps up the stairwell to the second floor but there was no sign of it anywhere.

'Damn,' she said, and I appreciated her frustration. O'Neill might have been trying to reach her. He might have sent her a copy of the photofit that Coyle was helping put together.

'There's a payphone back down in the hall,' I said.

'You got any change? I'm broke.'

'No, but I know a charity tin I could steal from.'

'Then nothing can stop us now. Welcome to twenty-first-century policing, Dublin-style. You know, it's not too late to beg for your old job back at the FBI.'

'They wouldn't want me now that I've been corrupted.'

'They wouldn't want you, full stop.'

'Cruel, but true.'

She raised a hand as we came back through the doors into the corridor. 'Hear that?' she said.

There was a low rumbling like machinery behind the wall.

Correction: not *like* machinery. It *was* machinery. The elevator was descending from a higher floor. The lighted numbers on the wall counted down as it got closer.

'I thought it was out of order,' I said.

'Clearly someone forgot to tell the lift that.'

Two.

'Stand back,' she said. 'It could be anyone.'

One.

We retreated out of sight.

Zero.

With a loud ping, the ground-floor doors opened, and out stepped –

'O'Neill!'

It was the second time that night he'd startled us by appearing out of nowhere.

It was a habit he'd do well to break.

'Chief,' said O'Neill as he emerged from the elevator, a thin file tucked under his arm, and saw us standing there, tensed, alert. 'What is it? You look like you've seen a ghost.'

'Ghosts I can handle,' Fitzgerald said. 'This is something else entirely. What were you doing up there?'

'I was looking for you,' he said. 'They said you'd gone upstairs.'

'Didn't you see the sign?'

She pointed to the notice pinned to the door saying *Out Of Order.*

He obviously hadn't.

'That's all we needed, you getting stuck in the lift,' she said. 'And come to think of it, what are you doing here at all? I told you to send me the picture once you had it.'

'I did, Chief. Then, when I got no reply, I tried calling your cellphone, and there was still no answer, so I thought I'd better come over and make sure you'd got it. Detective Dalton gave me a lift.' Back towards Reception, I now noticed Dalton feeding a stick of gum into his mouth as he lorded it over the uniformed cops. He was in his element.

'My phone's gone AWOL,' Fitzgerald explained. 'You have a copy with you?'

He handed her the file and she almost snatched it from his hands.

She whistled when she opened it.

'Coyle's sure this is the man he saw in Daniel Erskine's basement?' she said.

'That's what he said, Chief.'

She slid the picture out and held it up for me to see. The computer printout had the almost creepy artificiality of all photofit pictures, but the likeness was unmistakable.

'Michael Erskine,' she said.

It was the mirror image of what had happened earlier on the stairs. Then we'd expected to see Michael Erskine, and had been confronted by Riordan instead. This time we had expected to see Riordan's face and had been presented with Michael Erskine's.

'So Daniel Erskine was killed by his own brother?' said O'Neill. Because he hadn't been at the mortuary, he didn't know what Michael even looked like. To him, it had been only a picture of an anonymous suspect. 'What was his motive?'

'Perhaps because Daniel had found out his secret,' said Fitzgerald. 'Daniel knew everything, remember? He was like God watching over the city. Who knows, maybe it was even Michael who murdered Beth Griffin and the others, and his brother found out.'

'And was blackmailing him?' I said, remembering Riordan's words about Daniel's tendencies in that regard. 'Our man upstairs did say he made Gilroy look like an amateur.'

'But what was the use of killing the rest of the Second Circle?'

'To confuse the police about the motive for Daniel's death? To make it look like a collective rather than an individual punishment?' I suggested helplessly.

'What kind of man would kill his lifelong friends just to provide cover?'

'The same kind of man who could torture and kill

three young women for kicks,' said Fitzgerald. 'Next to what he did to them, his activities tonight would look practically benign.'

I hesitated. It seemed a huge leap from one grimy photofit.

And yet it felt right somehow.

'What about Riordan? Where does he fit into this scenario?'

'Riordan went on the run because he wanted to get to Michael Erskine first. He wanted his revenge for what we told him Michael had done to his friends.'

'But Riordan hated Daniel. You heard him at the Concert Hall. He was glad that Daniel was dead.'

'But he wasn't happy about Niland.'

'So you're saying that's what the two of them were doing here in the hospital when we arrived? They were finishing what Erskine had started? The final confrontation.'

'No,' I said, 'we're missing something. We're missing *everything*.'

'Such as,' said O'Neill, 'why hasn't Riordan just come clean? It's over.'

'Maybe he doesn't accept that it is. Maybe he's still awaiting his chance.'

'Both of you come with me,' said Fitzgerald firmly.

'Where are we going?'

'Back to Riordan.'

'He's in surgery.'

'To hell with his surgery. I want some answers.

Besides, we don't know for sure that he's in theatre yet. If we hurry, we might still catch him.'

I tried not to imagine the doctor's reaction. If he'd thought Fitzgerald had crossed the line earlier, God knows what he'd think of her now for interrogating a patient as he was wheeled in for surgery. Still, we could worry about that later.

'Let's risk the elevator,' I said, 'it'll be quicker.'

As long as it didn't break.

A few moments later, the automatic doors opened on to another corridor, virtually identical to the one we'd come from. Here was where Riordan had been taken to prepare for surgery, but where was he? No nurses were about and there was no evidence of activity.

In fact, all was a deathly silence.

Deathly?

Now what had brought that word to mind?

'Riordan, are you here?' Fitzgerald called out, hoping at least to be admonished for disturbing the patients, because that would prove, if nothing else, that we weren't entirely alone. And yet maybe that's what we were. 'Riordan?'

'Chief!'

The cry came from O'Neill, who had gone on ahead.

We hurried to catch him up, and found him kneeling at the side of a fallen police officer, who was slumped like a sleeping cat outside the door of a room further down the corridor. The door behind him was shut. No sound emerged from within.

Approaching, I recognized the cop that Fitzgerald had sent to watch over Riordan.

'Is he dead?' I said, keeping my voice low.

O'Neill said not.

'Then go and get a doctor for him,' Fitzgerald said. 'I'm going in.'

'Shouldn't we wait for back-up?'

'We should, but I'm not going to.'

Too long with me had clearly given Fitzgerald some very bad habits.

With a nod to show I was with her, I reached for the handle of the door that the unconscious cop had been guarding and turned it quickly, pushing it open.

In the corner crouched the nurse who had been left to watch over Riordan before surgery. She was hugging her knees and shaking but seemed to be otherwise unhurt.

Riordan, for his part, was still lying on the trolley.

I spoke his name softly, but he didn't answer.

He couldn't.

He was dead. From the side of his head protruded the handle of a large syringe. The needle had been thrust inside his ear and into his brain. Had the syringe been taken out again, a slight trickle of blood would have been the only outward sign of how death had occurred.

'Saxon,' said Fitzgerald.

I turned to the sound of her voice and saw why she had wanted my attention.

In a chair in the corner of the room sat Michael Erskine. He wasn't agitated or the least bit threatening. He merely sat there serenely like a visitor who had brought grapes and flowers as a gift rather than death. He was ready to give himself up.

He took no notice of me. His gaze was fixed on Fitzgerald.

'Chief Superintendent,' he said, 'it's a pleasure to see you.'

He rose and held out his hand as if to shake hers, and she took a step back involuntarily, not wanting to show any weakness, but not wanting to be too close to him either. But he hadn't been trying to shake her hand. He was holding out a photograph.

'Meet victim number four,' he said.

59

Her name was Mary Nelligan. She was twenty-two, five foot six, with long dark hair, and the kind of perfect skin that you normally only see on commercials. Mary worked as a personal shopper in one of the large department stores in Dublin's Grafton Street. Yesterday had been her day off. She lived alone in a rented apartment in the same square as Daniel Erskine.

Mary Nelligan was also O'Neill's girlfriend.

I'd forgotten about Sean Healy telling us O'Neill had a girlfriend in the area of the original crime scene. It hadn't seemed relevant at the time. How could it have?

The young detective was alternating between rage and fear. Rage at Michael Erskine, who claimed to have taken the woman early that afternoon and held her since at a secret location, and fear of, first, what he might have done to her, and, more importantly, what would happen to her if we didn't find her in time. Assuming she was still alive.

The possibility that she might be dead already had not been mentioned in O'Neill's presence. Right now, he was being calmed down in a room somewhere in Dublin Castle whilst Fitzgerald, Healy,

Patrick Walsh and I gathered in the interview suite, going over the few details we had managed to collate about Mary Nelligan's disappearance. Through the glass window Erskine sat, implacably calm, waiting to be questioned.

There wasn't much to go on. Two nights ago, Mary Nelligan had slept over at O'Neill's apartment in a high-rise in the north of the city. She had left at 11 a.m. the following morning to walk back across town, telling him she intended to do some shopping and maybe catch a movie before going home. O'Neill's shift was due to begin late afternoon, so they had no plans to meet later that night. He received a couple of texts from her shortly after they parted, but then nothing. He wasn't unduly worried. She'd told him she might go out to spend Halloween with friends. He had intended to drop in on her that evening when he took a break from working the scene at Daniel's house, but had followed Fitzgerald to return her cellphone first. After that, the prospect of sneaking away to visit his girlfriend had quickly receded.

Fitzgerald had sent round a team of uniformed police officers to check out Mary's apartment. Nothing was disturbed. Wherever Erskine took her from, it didn't look like it was there. The TV was on in the corner and there were unwashed dishes in the sink. It seemed like she had slipped out for a moment and simply not returned. Her cat was crying for food.

'You know what gets me?' asked Walsh, staring

again at the photograph of the missing woman which Erskine had presented at the hospital. She looked scared in the picture. I could scarcely bear to look at it. Her mouth was sealed with tape, her body bound with ropes to a chair, one arranged round the neck in such a way, it appeared, as to tighten if she struggled too strongly. 'How did he know that she was the girlfriend of a cop?'

'What makes you think that he knew?' asked Healy.

'It can't be a coincidence, surely?' Walsh answered.

'She didn't need to be involved with a police officer,' Healy pointed out. 'If all he wanted was someone to bargain with, any woman would do.'

'He might not have wanted to take a chance with any woman,' I said. 'He might have decided that who she was would add a little urgency to the negotiations.'

'We still don't even know that his plan *is* to negotiate,' Fitzgerald said.

'Why else would he take her?'

'To play with us. To give himself a hard-on. Take your pick.'

'He's strategic,' I said firmly. 'He wants to bargain all right.'

Michael Erskine himself had said nothing since his arrest. He hadn't even asked for so much as a glass of water, let alone a lawyer. He had made the first move. The next one was up to us. Even now, it seemed hard to believe that the man for whom we'd been searching for nearly two years was only metres away in a chair awaiting interrogation.

'You still haven't said how he knew,' Walsh returned to his theme.

'You're forgetting Daniel. Daniel seems to have known everything that was going on in the city. He'd have made it his business to find out all he could about his neighbours. From what we know of his psychology, it would have given him a feeling of power over them.'

'Yeah, but Michael didn't have the entire population under surveillance, did he? It was his brother who did that.'

'Brothers talk. Brothers share information.'

'There wasn't much sign of brotherly love in the freezer,' said Walsh.

'Brothers also fall out.'

'Maybe they were in it together,' speculated Fitzgerald. 'The women, the murders, the obsessive voyeurism. Then it all begins to come apart. They come into conflict. They fight.'

'And then the surviving one starts killing off all their friends,' I finished wryly. 'As you do.'

Fitzgerald sighed deeply. 'Well, whatever Erskine is at, we're not going to find out by sitting here.'

'You want me to come in with you?' said Healy.

'Not exactly,' said Fitzgerald. 'In fact, I'm not going in at all.'

Healy's look of confusion was replaced after a moment with an appreciative smile.

'You want to see how he reacts to the organ grinder's monkey instead,' he said.

'I wouldn't have put it quite like that, but that's the idea. He's an arrogant man, this much we have learned; he thinks he can beat the system. He thinks, what's more, that he has the upper hand. He expects to be treated with due respect as a result.'

'I understand,' said Healy, and he rose to take his place behind the glass.

Shortly afterwards, the door of the small room which we were looking out on to opened and Healy stepped inside. He was still out of eyesight of Michael Erskine, and Erskine did not turn his head to look at the new arrival. He assumed he knew already who it was.

When Healy finally sat down in front of him, Erskine's mouth stiffened immediately with irritation, though he tried to conceal it with a sneer. He looked up at the glass, as if aware of Fitzgerald's watching eyes behind it and trying to search them out.

'So,' said Healy, 'where is she?'

'I was about to ask you the same question,' Michael Erskine replied curtly.

Healy feigned ignorance. 'What are you talking about?'

'You know exactly what I'm talking about. Grace Fitzgerald, where is she?'

'You mean, the Chief Superintendent?' Healy said. 'She's gone home.'

'Home?'

'Even Chief Superintendents need their sleep. Besides, she's going to have a lot of paperwork to catch up on in the next few days thanks to your handiwork tonight.'

'So they sent you along instead?'

'That's right. I drew the short straw.'

'She should be here.'

'The Chief Superintendent?' said Healy, as if he had forgotten her already. 'What's there for her to stay for? You're here. You're not going anywhere. Case closed.'

'It'll be case closed for Mary Nelligan if you don't start taking me seriously.'

'This Mary Nelligan?' said Healy.

He took the photograph and slid it across the table towards Michael.

Erskine scarcely glanced at it.

'I know what she looks like, remember?' he said.

'Why did you take her?'

'Do you want the simple answer or the existential one?'

'I'm just an ordinary policeman, Mr Erskine, why don't we just take the simple explanation and work our way slowly upwards?'

'In that case, consider her my Plan B.'

'You were anticipating getting caught?'

'It was a possibility. I didn't care what happened after they were dead, but, yes, I was concerned that I might be apprehended before the job was done. Mary was my back-up.'

'But you did finish. They're all gone. Daniel, Blunt, Niland, Tannar, Riordan. You don't need her any more. So tell us where she is. You've got what you wanted.'

'Plans change,' said Erskine. 'Initially, I didn't care about being caught. Then, as the night went on, I realized I didn't want that to happen. I started to see possibilities of escape, of being able to carry on as before, not in Dublin, of course, but elsewhere. I have money. You can do anything with money. But there were too many police at the hospital, Riordan had seen to that. So I thought, "I have one last weapon in my armoury, why not use it?"'

'And the other answer . . . what did you call it?'

'Existential.'

'That's the one. You want to tell me about that one?'

'I'm not sure I care to discuss my innermost thoughts with an underling. Let's just say I took Mary because it's what I do.'

'It wasn't always what you did. Beth Griffin was the first, according to you.'

'She was. I never tell a lie.'

'You'd never killed before.'

'Not a woman.'

'So what changed?'

A smile took hold of Michael Erskine's features and transformed them. There was something like religious ecstasy in his face. He couldn't hide it.

'It was a revelation,' he said. 'Through Beth, I

discovered my vocation. I hadn't expected it. That wasn't why I killed her. Afterwards, everything was different. It was as if all my life I had been blind, and now I could see.'

'Like Saul on the Road to Damascus?'

'The same.'

'Only Saul didn't torture and murder innocent women, did he?'

In an instant, the light went out in Michael's eyes. He had not intended to give so much away. He shut himself down brutally. He regarded Healy with contempt.

'I'm not looking for your understanding,' he said coldly.

'What do you want?'

'I want you to let me go.'

'In return for Mary Nelligan?'

'That's the idea.'

'It's impossible.'

'Everything is possible.'

'Not this.'

'Then she will die, far more horribly than I would have killed her.'

'Is letting young women starve to death part of your vocation too?'

'That's not my responsibility any more,' said Erskine. 'It's yours.'

'Deals come in all shapes and sizes, Michael,' said Healy. 'No one's letting you go. You must know that. You're an intelligent man. But there are other things we can do for you, if you're cooperative. If you don't get stubborn.'

'Get me a nice comfortable cell, you mean? Extra pillows on the bed, a subscription to cable TV and a silver-plated chamber pot for the corner?'

'Don't knock it. The alternative won't be much fun for a man like you. You're used to the good life.'

'I didn't come all this way to give up as soon as the endgame's underway.'

'This is no endgame,' said Healy. 'It's already over. Look around you. You're caught. You were beaten.'

'It's not me who needs to look at my surroundings,' said Erskine. He jabbed a finger at the photograph. 'It's you who should be looking at hers.'

'We can still find her without you.'

'If you're so confident of that, why are you in here bargaining with me?'

Healy didn't answer.

Erskine was right.

'I don't understand,' was all Healy said in reply. 'You say taking and killing these women is your vocation. Well, you could have continued doing it as long as you liked. Shall I be honest? We were no closer to catching you than we were the day Beth Griffin's body was found. Instead you threw it all away in order to kill five of your friends. Why?'

'I've already told that story once tonight,' said Michael Erskine enigmatically. 'I don't intend to do it again. Let me go or Mary Nelligan dies. It's as straightforward as that.'

He lifted his head and looked directly at the glass wall behind which we were sitting.

'You must be a good judge of character by now, Chief Superintendent,' he said. He hadn't been fooled by Healy for one moment. 'You know what I'm saying is true. So you have to ask yourself one question. Do you want her blood on your hands?'

60

'If he'd been killed,' I said, 'we'd never have known of her abduction until it was too late.'

'It may already be too late,' said Fitzgerald. 'We don't even know that Mary Nelligan is still alive. And what are the chances of finding her without Erskine's help?'

I didn't answer.

I didn't need to.

Behind Fitzgerald, the window of her office looked down on to a city over which darkness was starting to fade slightly as the night finally came to an end. But I didn't believe it. There are some nights when it seems it could never become light again.

We were alone. Healy was continuing his efforts to get through to Erskine. Fitzgerald had been in to see him too. She was admitting the weakness of her position by doing so, but what alternative did she have? She'd had no more luck than Healy in getting through to him.

'I can't make a deal with a serial killer,' she said bluntly. 'That's what it comes down to. How many other young women would die in return for Mary's life?'

That was the dilemma. It was one real woman

against who knows how many other hypothetical women in the future. Only the women in the future were not so hypothetical. If Erskine was free, he would go on killing. He had acknowledged as much himself.

It was his *vocation*, for Christ's sake.

And serial killers don't stop voluntarily.

'Have you talked to the Assistant Commissioner?' I said.

'Trust me, you don't want to know what she said.'

'No deal?'

'Her career would be finished if it got out that she'd let Erskine go.'

'What if it was her daughter?'

'Saxon, don't make this harder than it is.'

'We could track him,' I said.

'And if we lose him?'

'Don't lose him.'

'It's too risky.'

'Not if I was there.'

Fitzgerald stopped what she was doing and stared at me like I'd gone insane. 'You're not serious?'

'Turn your back for ten minutes, and I'll get him out. I'll go with him. He can take me to where he's keeping Mary Nelligan.'

'And once you have her?'

'He won't be going anywhere,' I said defiantly.

There was a long pause as she digested my words. 'You're saying that you'll kill Michael Erskine.'

'If I have to.'

'No, Saxon, I can't—'

'It might not come to that,' I interrupted. 'But if it does, I'd rather have his blood on my hands than that of the women he'll kill if I don't. I won't let him vanish.'

'You don't know what you're saying. You don't know what it means.'

'I do. I know you can't protect me from the consequences.'

'You could go to jail.'

'Mary Nelligan could *die*.'

Fitzgerald shook her head.

'I can't authorize this,' she said.

'You don't have to know anything about it,' I told her. I tried a self-mocking smile. 'I always was a loose cannon, after all. No one will blame you for what I've done.'

'Saxon—'

Again, I wouldn't let her finish. 'I'm not letting Erskine win,' I insisted.

She was silent for a long while, staring into my eyes.

I couldn't read her expression.

I guessed she was calculating the chances of finding the place where Mary Nelligan was being held without Erskine's assistance. How long did she have? Four, five days at most. How many locks-up and garages could be searched in that time? Not enough. She might be found by chance, yes, but Michael Erskine wouldn't have put himself in this situation if he wasn't confident that Mary would be safe from accidental detection.

What if she was underground? What if he'd managed to take her out of the city yesterday? She could be anywhere.

'I can't let you do this alone,' she said at last.

'There's no other way.'

'There is another way,' said Fitzgerald. 'I'm coming with you.'

Now it was my turn to stare. 'I thought I was supposed to be the crazy one,' I said quietly.

She had turned the tables on me expertly. There I was, making the grand sacrifice, showboating, dogmatic as always, simply expecting her to bite her tongue and go along with it. Instead she had presented me with the same conundrum that I had dropped into her lap. Now I too was having to face the possibility – in fact, more like the *inevitability*, if she took part in the release of Erskine – of her life and career crashing and burning as well.

'You need me,' Fitzgerald pointed out. 'They won't let you take him away without my permission, so either way I'm implicated. I might as well be there.'

'I don't want you to do it,' I said.

'I don't want you to do it either,' Fitzgerald shot right back. 'But I don't want another young woman to die because of Erskine. Something has to give. I don't know,' she said with what sounded like despair, 'maybe it's because I'm tired and not thinking straight. Maybe if I went home and slept on it, I wouldn't dream of doing what I'm suggesting that we do. But I've seen enough death tonight, and not just this night, but night after night, and never thinking that you can make a difference, you're only putting sticking plasters on a gaping wound, and mopping up the blood when it's all done. It's not enough. Never enough.'

'You make a difference,' I told her. 'You hold the line.'

'I can't feel good about that if Mary Nelligan dies as a result. I'll have done everything right, according to the rule book, but I'll know in my heart that I did the wrong thing.' She smiled. 'Besides, we're neither of us getting any younger. Everyone should get the chance to embrace craziness freely before senility sets in and leaves you with no choice.'

'Enough already with the getting-old speech. You speak for yourself, girl.'

I looked down at the photograph of Mary Nelligan on her desk.

Tried to imagine what she was going through.

And then I thought how much worse it could get if no one came, day after day, night after night. She wouldn't last long. But to Mary, it would feel like an eternity.

'What if she's dead already and Erskine is just fucking with our heads?'

'That's a risk we have to take.'

'For Mary's sake.'

'For Mary, yes, but also to show the Erskines of this world that they don't have it all figured out, they won't always get the last word. Besides, if I'm there, there's less chance of you going all Dirty Harry on me and doing something we'll both regret. We can still bring him back in unharmed when all this is done. The only casualty will be my career.'

'Dismissed with ignominy.'

'Fuck it, I didn't come into this job to climb the career ladder anyway. And you always said you wanted to travel more. We should think of it as an opportunity to spend more quality time together. Of course, we'll have to sell the house.'

'Shall I tell you something? I never liked that bloody house anyway.'

'Now you tell me . . .'

A few minutes later, we were ready.

'As ready as we'll ever be,' as Fitzgerald put it.

She called down to tell Healy to end the interrogation with Erskine for now and come back upstairs to her office. We could take the back staircase down and hope that he'd come up in the elevator, thereby missing each other. My hands were shaking. A terror I'd never known before was coursing through me, but it was Fitzgerald I was afraid for, not myself.

'It's not too late to change your mind,' I said.

'You first,' she retorted.

I was beginning to see what an infuriating person I must be to have around, if this is what I was like when my mind was made up.

'Enough talking then,' I said. 'Let's do this.'

The elevator was humming as we walked down the corridor towards the stairs. Healy on his way up, presumably. We quickened our steps till we were out of sight and hurried down two floors. Fortunately, the building was still relatively quiet at this hour. But as we approached the interview room, the stillness started to seem bizarre rather than merely useful.

The corridor leading down to the suite where Michael Erskine was being held was so deserted that it was almost eerie.

'Where is everyone?' muttered Fitzgerald.

And then we saw that the door to the interview room was standing open, and there was no guard outside, and we started to run. Fitzgerald reached it first and cursed.

Michael Erskine was gone.

61

We met Morgan coming the other way. Fitzgerald's knight in shining armour from the Serious Crime's armed unit. He was stumbling slightly. His eyes were unfocused. Blood trickled from a gash on his forehead. I thought he'd gone home. He probably wished he had.

'What happened?' I demanded.

'I fell,' he explained. 'I think I cut . . .' He raised his hand to his head and it came away red. 'Shit,' he said, wiping it on his pants. 'I was struggling with that young detective, I don't know his name, the one whose girlfriend was abducted.'

'O'Neill?'

'Is that him? He got my gun.'

'Inspector Fogarty's best man, huh?' I remarked sarcastically. 'I'd hate to see his worst one.'

'Hey, give me a break,' Morgan said. 'He took me by surprise. When I was told to provide protection, I didn't expect to be attacked by your own people. He was out of control.'

'Did he say anything?'

'Only that he wouldn't let anything happen to her.'

'Did you see which way he went?'

'Towards the interview room.'

'It must have been O'Neill who got Erskine out. Where's the guard?'

'Maybe he followed him.'

'You're sure no one passed you?' Fitzgerald asked Morgan.

'I don't think so. I may have passed out for a while, I'm not sure.'

'We'll take the other way,' she decided. 'And give me your phone. Mine's still back at the hospital somewhere.'

There was a back entrance out of Dublin Castle. Stairs led down from the other end of the corridor. That was the way we ran. Behind us, a commotion began to rise as news spread of what had happened. Confused voices echoed down through the stairwell.

'Chief Superintendent?'

'Where's Erskine?'

'Where's O'Neill?'

'Lock the doors!'

But the horse had already bolted.

Fitzgerald punched Healy's number into the borrowed cellphone as we ran. Breathlessly, she told him what had happened. 'Meet me downstairs,' she said.

'If I hadn't called him away,' she added helplessly to me.

She didn't need to finish the sentence.

'O'Neill had a gun,' I said. 'There's nothing Healy could've done. Except get hurt.'

She shook her head. 'It's all my fault,' she said.

'It's Erskine's fault,' I retorted. 'We just have to make sure he pays.'

At the foot of the stairwell, the bolts were pulled back on the exterior doors. There was no doubt now that this was the route O'Neill and Erskine had taken.

Out into the parking lot we went – just in time to see my Jeep go speeding past, pursued on foot by the missing guard. In the driver's seat, I saw Erskine, with O'Neill next to him. He showed a haunted stare. It was the look of a man who doesn't know what he's doing, and is afraid to find out. It was unnerving, watching him do what Fitzgerald and I had planned on doing only a few minutes earlier. Suddenly it didn't seem like such a great idea.

How close had we come to disaster?

I saw in Fitzgerald's eyes that she was harbouring the same thought, but thinking was a luxury right now that we couldn't indulge for too long.

My Jeep was already out of sight.

Of all the cars they had to take . . .

'Chief, I'm sorry,' said the cop who'd been put on guard duty outside the interview room as he gave up the chase on O'Neill and Erskine and ran back towards us. 'O'Neill had a gun . . . he threatened to shoot me if I didn't let him in . . .'

'It's OK,' said Fitzgerald. 'Go get back-up. Bring them down here.'

He rushed back inside the building.

'You,' she said to Morgan, 'get over here. Try to remember. What did O'Neill say?'

'It was all over so fast. He said he wanted to find Mary.'

'That's all?'

'He said he was sorry too.'

'For that, I presume?' she indicated his wound.

'Or maybe just for what he was going to do.'

'And you don't remember anything else?'

'No. Nothing, except . . . well . . .'

'What?'

'He said he wanted my mobile phone.'

'He wanted your mobile?'

'That's what he said.'

'Did you give it to him?'

'Did I do wrong?'

'The man had a gun, Morgan, you said so yourself.'

'Why a phone?' I wondered aloud.

Suddenly, as if in answer, in the car park, there came the sound of ringing. Disconnected, like electronic birdsong and hard to place, the harsh call filled the early-morning air. I spun around, trying to locate it, willing it not to stop.

'Back that way,' said Fitzgerald. 'There!'

There was a gap where my Jeep had been parked until a couple of minutes earlier. On the car which would have been parked adjacent to the passenger side, a cellphone sat, ringing.

'Is that yours?' I said.

Morgan confirmed that it wasn't.

'It must be O'Neill's,' I said, and then it all became clear. 'Don't you see? It's like what happened to me earlier. You said yourself how impressed he was when I kept the phone line open to let you hear my conversation with Leko. O'Neill's doing the same thing.'

'Answer it,' said Fitzgerald.

'Not a sound from anyone,' I warned.

I picked up the phone and pressed the answer button. From the other end of the line there came the low hum of an engine, and then voices, murmuring.

'It's them,' I mouthed, and covered the mouthpiece with my hand. I didn't know where O'Neill was keeping the other phone. I couldn't take the risk of Erskine hearing anything unusual and getting suspicious. He would be wary enough as it was.

'Have you any idea where they are?' whispered Fitzgerald.

'Not yet.'

'We'll take a car,' she said. 'You, Morgan, tell them where we've gone. Tell them to follow and await further instructions. I'll call Healy once we know where we're headed.'

She pointed at the nearest unmarked police car, and I followed her, climbing into the passenger seat whilst she took her place behind the wheel. The keys were in the ignition. This wasn't a place where the average car thief would risk his luck. Fitzgerald turned on the engine and reversed out, turning so that we faced the same direction that Erskine had taken.

In a moment, we were out of the gates.

'Which way are we going then?' I said.

'Until we know for sure Erskine's destination, one direction is as good as another.'

I found a length of oil-stained cloth in the glove compartment and wound it round the mouthpiece of O'Neill's phone so that we could talk without being overheard.

'Put it on speakerphone,' Fitzgerald said.

Once the phone was set up, the two men's voices appeared as clearly as if they were in the car with us. They were somewhere out there in the maze of streets. We drove in pursuit of a shadow, waiting impatiently for clearer directions.

'You know I'm not taking you anywhere until you get rid of that gun,' said Erskine.

He sounded unperturbed by the events of the past half-hour. The timbre of his voice didn't alter a fraction. If he was nervous or excited, he wasn't letting it show.

'I won't tell you again. Take me to Mary or I'll shoot you,' O'Neill replied.

'Shoot away,' said Erskine.

'You think I'm joking.'

'On the contrary. The only problem for you is that I'm not afraid of death. Is Mary?'

'Fuck you,' spat O'Neill.

'Stop trying to play the hero, officer. You know

the deal. You get your Mary and I get my freedom. There's no need to bring guns into it.'

'Without the gun, how do I know you'll do what you say?'

'That's a risk you'll have to take, because with the gun I definitely won't.'

'If you've hurt her—' O'Neill was getting angry.

'Lose the gun.'

'If you've *touched* her—'

'Wind down the window and toss out the gun,' continued Erskine calmly. '*I* won't tell you again either. This is your last chance.'

There was a long silence, so long that I thought for a moment the connection was lost.

Then O'Neill spoke.

'Do you know where we are?' he said.

'I'm familiar with the layout of the city.'

'This is Summerhill,' said O'Neill, his voice rising slightly.

'Fitzgerald,' I said.

'I heard.'

She slowed as we approached the next corner and turned to follow his cue.

'Call Healy . . .'

'My cellphone's out of power.'

'Then take my mobile from my pocket and get word back to him where they are.'

'I don't care where we are,' said Erskine, answering O'Neill's earlier enquiry. 'Get rid of the gun or the deal's off.'

'Some of the city's worst drug dealers live round here,' said O'Neill. 'I can't just leave a gun lying around. I'm a police officer.'

'It's a bit late to be worrying about that now.'

'There are children . . .'

'The gun. Now.'

There was the sound of wind rushing as O'Neill wound down the window and presumably threw out the gun. Anxiety tightened knots inside me. I didn't know whether Erskine intended to keep his end of the bargain now that he'd got what he wanted.

He could escape at any time.

'I only want Mary,' O'Neill said, and he sounded pitiful.

We were cruising through Summerhill now, but I could see no sign of my Jeep. It was past 7 a.m. and a dirty light was starting to show between the cracks of darkness.

The city was stirring.

'Come on, O'Neill,' I muttered, 'where are you now?'

It was as if he heard.

'Why are we going back to town?' he said.

'Fuck me,' said Fitzgerald, 'I'll get dizzy if I have to turn around once more.'

'I wanted to make sure you were serious,' said Erskine.

'You'll take me to her now?'

'I said I would, didn't I?'

'Just let me have her, I don't care what you do or where you go afterwards.'

'You're welcome to her. She wasn't my type anyway.'

'You're a sick fucker.'

'You set me free. What does that make you?'

'I did it for Mary, not for you. Mary doesn't deserve this.'

'Stop panicking.'

'I'm not panicking,' said O'Neill. 'I can see the river.'

'What *are* you talking about?' said Erskine.

'The Fr Mathew Bridge,' the young policeman answered. 'I walked across that on my first date with Mary. Up Bridge Street and into Cornmarket.'

'Good boy,' said Fitzgerald.

'Very romantic,' said Erskine.

'Down Francis Street, yes, then on towards St Stephen's Green.'

'Then consider this a stroll down Memory Lane.'

'Why's Erskine heading back into town?' I said. 'It's dangerous for him.'

'Maybe he intends to keep his promise and give him Mary,' said Fitzgerald, but I didn't believe it. He was up to something. He hadn't finished playing with us yet.

'Can't you go any faster?' I hissed.

'Not without killing us both.'

We were approaching the centre of town from

the opposite direction to Erskine and O'Neill. I kept expecting to find them coming the other way, straight towards us, headlights charging like the eyes of some furious wild animal.

And then we had it. O'Neill spoke the words that revealed their destination, and I recognized at once where they were. It was a row of houses at the back of my apartment building. Mackie's Lane. There must have been half a dozen of them, with garages on the ground floor. Did he really have Mary there? I had a bad feeling about this.

'I'm sure the place in the photograph was bigger,' I said.

'You don't think she's there?'

'What is Erskine up to?'

I got back on the line to tell Healy where to find us. By this time, we were driving down Pembroke Street West and turning right into Quinn's Lane. Fitzgerald parked untidily and we both climbed out, grabbing the cellphone so that we could hear what was happening.

We glanced round the corner of Mackie's Lane.

My Jeep was parked up ahead at the far end of the road.

'Is this the place?' crackled O'Neill's voice nervously.

'This is the place. It's not locked. All you have to do is open the garage door.'

'How do I know she's really in there?'

'How will you find out unless you try?'

'But if I get out, you could drive away.'

'If you don't, what was the point of the journey?'

Still O'Neill hesitated.

What reason did he have to trust Michael Erskine, after all?

'Shall we move in?' I said.

'Not yet. We have to know if she's in there.'

'I'll do it,' O'Neill said at last, 'but if she's not here, I swear I'll kill you. I don't care how long it takes or what I have to do to make it happen, but I'll kill you.'

'You're wasting valuable time.'

Up ahead, we saw the passenger-side door open and O'Neill get out. He walked gingerly towards the garage that Erskine had pointed out to him, stopping once to glance back as if for confirmation that this was not some trick. He stopped in front of the garage door.

Raised his fingers to the handle.

At that moment, Erskine put his foot to the accelerator. O'Neill reacted too late. He turned and stretched out his hands as if he could stop the car that way, but it crashed into him and he was forced back into the metal of the door behind him. The door buckled under the impact, taking his shape. O'Neill didn't make a sound.

In the cellphone, Erskine was laughing.

He reversed the Jeep. Free now, O'Neill's body slumped to the floor and lay still. Erskine didn't stop. He kept reversing fast down Mackie's Lane. We only just stepped out of the way before he pulled out into

Quinn's Lane, straightened the car, showing blood on the silver grille, and turned left down past the old hospital dispensary and out of sight.

I wasn't sure he had even seen us.

'Back to the car!' screamed Fitzgerald.

This time she wasn't going to lose him. I didn't need to tell her to pick up the pace. The buildings on either side of us shot by in a blur. The city had ceased to exist.

There was only Erskine and us.

He wouldn't get away this time.

62

It was as we were in pursuit of my Jeep that it came to me. The thing which had been bothering me ever since we left the hospital swam clear like a moon breaking through clouds. It struck me with such a force that I didn't know why it had taken me so long to see it

'It's not Michael,' I said.

'What are you saying?'

'It's Daniel,' I said.

'It's not possible.'

'It's more than possible, it was easy. Think. The only reason we decided the body in the freezer was definitely that of Daniel Erskine was A, because it was in his house, and B, because his brother identified him at the morgue. It was as simple as that. We never had independent verification. There weren't even any photographs of Daniel to disprove it. He was the secretive type, remember what Healy told us? Kept his picture out of the papers. All he had to do was pose as his own brother and say the body was him.'

Fitzgerald struggled to dispel her doubts. I couldn't blame her. It sounded incredible to me too. 'How can you be sure?' she said.

'Riordan was telling us, in a roundabout way, only we didn't see it. He said Dr M Nott was an imaginary character. But where did they get the name? It's like that piece of music he was playing tonight at the Concert Hall. What was it called?'

'The *Lyric Suite*, by Alban Berg.'

'Berg encoded the initials of his secret lover into the musical notes of his piece. That's what the Second Circle did too. They took the name of their imaginary friend from the letters of their own first names. D for Daniel, R for Ronan, M for Michael, and so on – Nat, Oliver, Toby and Sean Riordan. His real name was Tybalt, remember? T for Tybalt.'

'So they made an anagram out of their names? So what?'

'Because,' I said, 'they were standing in order in the photograph. Daniel first, then Ronan, and all the way through to Riordan. We just assumed it was Michael first because that was the man we'd met at the morgue. But Riordan saw it at once at the Concert Hall. When we showed him the photograph, he realized immediately that we'd got it wrong. He knew that Daniel had killed his own brother and was now pretending to be him, and that he'd killed Oliver Niland and was probably going to go after the others. That was what made him run. He didn't want to tell us. He wanted to track down Daniel by himself and stop him for good. He practically told us at the hospital. *You don't know anything about Daniel*, he said.'

Her resistance was crumbling fast.

'It would certainly explain how he knew about Mary Nelligan,' she said.

'Daniel knows about everyone, right? It all fits with what we know about his psychology. *He* was the dominant one. The superego. The manipulator.'

'But he'd never have got away with it,' said Fitzgerald. 'Someone was bound to realize that he wasn't Michael eventually.'

'Not until the morning.'

'So he did all that just to take out the Second Circle? *Why?*'

'That,' I said, 'is the part of the equation that still doesn't make sense.'

'Then I guess we'd better catch him and find out.'

But he was driving as if possessed. Reckless to the danger, it took all Fitzgerald's skill behind the wheel to keep up with him. Once or twice, I thought we'd lost him, but then she would accelerate again and the back of the Jeep would come into view.

'He can't get away in the car,' I said. 'He'll be too easy to follow.'

'You think he'll run?'

'He'll have to. On foot, he has a chance.'

'I think he's headed for the docks.'

Fitzgerald's cellphone rang.

'Healy.'

'Saxon, are you OK?'

'We're fine. Have you got a trace on Erskine?'

'There are three cars behind you.'

'What about O'Neill?'

465

'The ambulance is on its way for him,' said Healy, 'but it doesn't look good.'

I caught Fitzgerald's eye.

That could so easily have been us.

'What about the garage? Was Mary there?'

'No,' he said, and I could hear the astonishment in his voice as he spoke the next words. 'It was Nick Elliott. He was tied up inside. He seems to be unhurt. Apart from being in deep shock, that is. I haven't been able to get much sense out of him yet.'

'Nothing new there then,' I said, unable to resist.

'There's just one peculiar thing,' said Healy.

'Is it about Daniel?'

'How did you—?'

'Never mind that now. I'll explain later. What did Elliott say?'

'Elliott?' repeated Fitzgerald perplexedly.

'He says we have to find Daniel. Just keeps repeating it.'

Warehouses rose around us, brick mausoleums pulsing darkness like radiation. There were glimpses of ships, a gleam of metal between the edges of buildings, and water too.

Empty roads.

Or not so empty.

My Jeep was pulled up to the kerb. We screeched to a halt beside it.

No one inside.

'Healy, we have to go. Erskine's made a break for it on foot.'

As quickly as I could, I gave him the address. By the time I got out, Fitzgerald had already given the Jeep the once over, just to be sure. She shook her head.

I raised a finger to my lips.

The silence sent back an echo of running steps.

'This way,' I said.

An alleyway opened up ahead as we ran. Three doorways.

And in one the door was closing.

'Careful,' she whispered as we reached it. 'We don't know if he has a weapon.'

Was this one of the Erskine brothers' properties? Was this where he'd been keeping Mary Nelligan the whole time? If so, then we would surely have found her without Erskine's help, assuming that the building was listed in his records. But we weren't to know that.

Nor was O'Neill.

I saw him again, being crushed against the metal door of the garage and slumping to the floor. I saw the blood on the grille. '*It doesn't look good,*' Healy had said.

We had to do this now for O'Neill as well as Mary.

If he was going to die, he wouldn't die in vain.

'You ready?' I said.

The door was caked with rust. I pushed it open.

Listened a moment before stepping inside.

I had half-expected a murmur of machinery, but there was nothing. The warehouse was deserted.

Abandoned. Of course it was. Daniel Erskine needed his privacy.

Daniel. It sounded so right, I was astonished I hadn't realized it earlier.

There were metal pillars, a concrete floor, heavy chains coiled. The light was too murky to make out details. Balconies of criss-crossed iron encircled the space.

More doors.

Above our heads the roof soared like a cathedral.

'We need a flashlight,' I whispered.

Fitzgerald raised her voice. 'Daniel!' she called. 'Daniel, we know you're here.'

But did we really? We hadn't actually seen him enter the building. In truth, we were only guessing. And if we were wrong, Erskine might have already made his escape.

We *had* to believe he was here.

'What is he doing?' she said to me.

'It must be Mary Nelligan,' I said. 'The only reason he'd still be hanging around is because he hasn't finished with her.'

'He'd risk being caught for that?'

'Who knows what he'd do? The man's a psychopath. If I was after Fisher's job, I might even say he can't stand the thought of her getting away from him. No one else has before. He doesn't like failure. Hell, I don't know. I'm as much in the dark as you.'

But I could see her warming to the idea.

'Or maybe he realizes there are too many eyes

looking for him to escape and he figures he might as well have his final fling? Either way, we have to find her first.'

'Erskine!' I called.

The only reply was a rushing overhead as a length of metal chain unravelled through the air like a giant cobra dropping from a tree. 'Watch out!' I shouted, and I pulled her back desperately as the chain landed with an explosion of noise only yards away.

We had our answer.

Erskine was here.

And he wasn't messing around.

In one corner lay a heap of steel rods, each about three feet long. I lifted one for myself and another for Fitzgerald. She didn't need to ask what it was for when I handed it to her. The weight of it was good in my hands. It made me feel less vulnerable.

'There he is,' I said.

'Where?'

A shadow on a higher balcony had detached itself from the rest and disappeared through one of the doors. I pulled Fitzgerald's arm to follow me, running across the floor whilst it was safe from any more projectiles hurled from above. The warehouse still reverberated faintly with the clank of the falling chain, like a warning.

A metal ladder rose into the silver maze of walkways higher up. It swayed as I put my weight on it but I didn't hesitate. If I delayed too long, I might lose my nerve.

Fitzgerald waited until I was at the next level before stepping on to the ladder herself. It wouldn't bear the weight of two simultaneously. She climbed up nimbly like a spider.

'Where now?' she whispered.

'He went this way. I think. You see that door?'

Beyond it lay another part of the building, where the offices for the warehouse must once have been situated. There were numerous small glass-enclosed cubicles. The glass in most was smashed and lay sprinkled across the floor like solidified confetti. Numerous scurryings in the dark betrayed the presence of rodents. I hoped it was only mice.

I tried the light switch on the wall. It was probably as well that there was no power or I might have been electrocuted, the wiring in the building was so old. I saw exposed bundles of wires peeking from cracks in the brickwork. Water dripped from uncovered light bulbs.

Perhaps it was raining again outside.

Was there an outside world any more? For now, it had ceased to exist. There was simply this hostile universe of concrete, steel and glass.

Fitzgerald had gone ahead. For a moment, I lost sight of her, and felt a wave of panic engulf me. I didn't want her to find Erskine without me. Seeing what he had done to O'Neill scared me almost more than knowing what he had done to those three young women.

They could be explained with all manner of psychiatric and behavioural labels. The impulses inside him, if you were so minded, could even be excused away as not his fault, as a dysfunction of the wiring in the brain analagous to the faulty electrics in this building.

But there had been an effortless sadism in driving at O'Neill that made me realize he was capable of anything. There had been no irresistible urge overtaking him at that moment. He had done it for no other reason than that he wanted to. And then he had laughed.

He would kill Fitzgerald without a qualm.

Me too.

I hurried after Fitzgerald, making her jump and raise the steel rod in defence as I turned the corner and found her edging cautiously down the side of the narrow corridor.

'For Christ's sake, Saxon, I thought—'

She stopped.

It was better not to talk, not even to whisper. Our own voices could give Erskine too much cover to approach unawares. Noise is as good a camouflage as darkness. To avoid speech allowed us to adjust better to the sound of the warehouse instead.

To listen to its heartbeat.

Something drew us to the next door, although perhaps that was only how it seemed in retrospect. But certainly, out of all the routes we could have taken, this was the one that seemed most promising. Perhaps Erskine's aura lingered imperceptibly in the air.

The scent of evil.

As soon as we opened the door, we knew what it was. Mary Nelligan sat in the centre of a large familiar room, tied to a chair, her mouth gagged tight, a rope around her neck.

She gave a terrified moan when she saw the door begin to open. She expected to see Daniel Erskine. Instead her eyes widened at the sight of two women creeping in, carrying steel rods. Instantly, she tried to speak, mumbling fiercely behind the gag.

'No,' whispered Fitzgerald.

She put her hand across her lips to tell Mary to stay quiet.

I ran across the room towards her. More than anything, I wanted to take the gag from her mouth and let her breathe freely, if such a thing was possible in this fetid place. But I couldn't risk her crying out, or merely crying. Erskine might not know yet she was discovered and I wanted to keep it that way. We couldn't untie her bonds for the same reason.

I touched her hair, a gesture of intended comfort, though it was crazy to believe that anything could reach her in the bad state she was in.

It was like releasing a balloon and hoping that it made it to the moon.

Before we could figure out a plan of action, however, the worst possible thing happened. Or the second worst, barring Daniel Erskine arriving on the scene.

Fitzgerald's cellphone rang.

'Shit,' and she fumbled for it clumsily, before remembering that I still had in in my pocket. Now it was my turn to curse as I dug it out and pressed answer, though even when it was silent again the ghost of her ringtone still remained like a beacon to be traced.

'Healy,' I said. 'Is that you?'

'Saxon, are you both there?'

'Yes, and we've found Mary Nelligan.'

'Erskine?'

'He's still in the building.'

'We're coming in.'

'Thank Christ for that.'

'Sit tight.'

'We're upstairs,' I told him, and I mouthed to Fitzgerald: *They're here.*

Saw the relief in her face.

'But Saxon,' Healy said.

'What is it?'

'I have to tell you something. I'm not really sure what to make of it. The first officer who came on the scene says he saw someone climbing out of the boot of your Jeep.'

'That can't be right.'

'That's what I thought, but I checked. There was blood in the boot.'

Could Erskine have taken another victim? No, that couldn't be right. Why would the victim be in the trunk of my car? There must have been someone else in there already when they took it from the parking lot at Dublin Castle.

'He says it was a man.'

Someone who wanted to get to me.

I looked up at Fitzgerald and saw at once his reflection in her eyes. A figure rising behind my shoulder. Fitzgerald saw him at the same moment and shouted my name.

I turned, and felt his weight slam into me. The steel rod in my hand spun out of my grasp and clattered under Mary Nelligan's chair, and I collapsed to the floor and rolled over, him on top of me, looking up, expecting Erskine but seeing –

'Leko!'

Of course. Leko knew the car I drove. After what happened at Christ Church, he must have made his way, injured, to Dublin Castle, looking for a second opportunity to finish what he'd started. He saw my car in the parking lot. What better way to have me unknowingly take him to Fitzgerald? Come morning, we'd have driven back together to our new house.

All he had to do was wait for his moment.

It must have been a shock when Erskine took the car instead and proceeded to hurtle round the city, pursued by the police, with Leko getting more angry by the minute.

He didn't know what he'd blundered into here. It made no difference anyway. All he wanted was blood. Ours. He probably hadn't even noticed the young woman tied to a chair.

I held tight to his wrist. His fingers were folded round a wheel brace, which he must have lifted from the trunk of my car. If I loosened it a fraction, he would bring it down on my skull. I felt my grasp weaken – and then Fitzgerald's shoe swung into view, and she kicked Leko in the face, making him cry out in fury and pain, but mostly fury, because he was beyond normal sensations, and consumed only by his desire for revenge.

I rolled out of his way, and clambered unsteadily to my feet.

Leko was standing up too, but he was disoriented, and he stared at the two of us, Fitzgerald with the metal club in her hands, practically defying him to attack her. The wheel brace didn't look so menacing any more. And then he noticed Mary.

'Put it down,' he said. 'Put it down or I'll kill her.'

He advanced behind her chair, pulling back her head by the hair, and raised his hand, readying to strike. She struggled to escape his touch, and the rope pulled harder at her neck.

'Don't make me do it,' Leko said.

Fitzgerald tossed the steel rod aside. She had no choice. She hadn't been through all this to watch Mary Nelligan die. And Leko smiled.

It was the last thing he did.

Mary was Daniel Erskine's possession. He wasn't going to share her death with anyone. He must have been watching the whole time, biding his time.

Leko had gone too far.

Out of the shadows he came, and, before Leko was even aware of his presence, Erskine had pulled down a length of cable from a pulley overhead and wound it round Leko's neck, once, twice – twice was enough – before stepping back and hauling him up as if he was no heavier than a dog. His feet kicked wildly as they lost contact with the ground, and he dropped the wheel brace and lifted his hands to his neck where the cable was starting to bite.

The sound of his choking was horrible, but it didn't last long.

Leko shuddered one final time on the end of the cable, then hung still, turning slowly like a caterpillar in a wind, until Erskine let go and the hanged man crumpled to the concrete.

'It's over, Daniel, let her go.'

Daniel Erskine almost looked as if he was considering it, before eventually shaking his head half-regretfully. The tide couldn't help coming in twice a day.

The sun couldn't help rising.

He was what he was.

He put his hands around Mary Nelligan's neck.

I ran to gather up the steel rod that Fitzgerald had thrown down on Leko's demand, not knowing if I could reach it and afterwards him before Mary died. But I had to try.

As I bent to lift the crude weapon, I saw the side of Erskine's head explode in a burst of colour and a look of surprise enter his eyes as he was thrown backwards, opening himself for the next shot, which hit him in the chest, and the next one in the same place.

He was dead before he hit the ground.

'Healy,' I said, as the detective ran in, accompanied by Morgan, who seemed to have found himself a new gun and finally had the chance to prove himself as gifted with it as his boss in Serious Crime always claimed that he was, 'could you not cut it so fine next time?'

'Next time?' he said. 'Haven't you caused enough trouble as it is?'

63

Nick Elliott hadn't known if anyone would ever find him alive. His gain was journalism's loss, I guess. He quickly reverted to type, however, quarrelling with the officers who took away his tape recorder as evidence. That was his passport back to the big time. I think he was more terrified of never seeing it again than he had been of Daniel Erskine.

'I've told that story once tonight,' Daniel had said.

We hadn't known at the time that Elliott was his unlikely father confessor.

Fitzgerald and I had now listened to the tape three times, and it sounded weirder each time. It was the matter-of-factness in Erskine's voice which was so unnerving. He spoke of murder as if it was no bigger deal than heading down to the store to pick up milk.

It made the fine hairs on my arms stand up as with the cold.

Lawrence Fisher said it was to be expected in such a controlling individual. Erskine, he observed, had the classic dissociative tendencies of the psychopath. Those around him could have had no idea how remote from them he really was. He could carry on a relatively normal life; some psychopaths maintained the semblance of being the same as everyone else for their entire lives. For others, the wrong trigger could tip them into violence.

'*They had to die,*' Erskine's disembodied voice drifted from the speaker as we listened again the following afternoon in Fitzgerald's office. '*They betrayed me. I did everything for them. I paid their bills, I settled their debts, I put them in contact with all the right people. And when they came to me to say they were being blackmailed by Conn Gilroy, and what could I do to help, I knew what they wanted from me. I did what had to be done. I didn't hesitate. They were my friends. I made sure he wouldn't bother them again.*'

'You . . . killed him?' Elliott asked him nervously.

'*I killed him, yes. What of it? He wouldn't be missed. You want to know where he is? He's right here under your feet.*' And again, there it was, the same no-nonsense tone, like there was nothing remarkable about burying people under the concrete in your garage.

'*But were they grateful?*' he said, the first trace of discomposure creeping into his voice. '*Did they thank me? They did not. They came to me and said they knew what I'd done, they knew about this place. They said they'd turn me in if I didn't give them the tape.*'

'The tape?' echoed Elliott.

'*I owned a tape of them talking about what happened to Erin Gilroy,*' he said disingenuously, like it had happened purely by accident. '*I'd never played it to anyone else, never told another soul of its existence, but for some reason they thought I shouldn't have it. They wanted it in*

479

return for their silence. My own brother! After all I'd done for him. I knew they wouldn't go to the police because, if they did, then their secret would be out too. But I played along. I told them I'd think about it. Michael was to come round tonight, on Halloween, to pick up the tape. Instead I killed him. And then I killed the others too.'

'I don't understand.' Poor Elliott. He never knew when to keep his mouth shut. 'Why didn't you just give them the tape and then you could all have carried on as before?'

'Haven't you been listening?' said Erskine. 'Haven't you heard a single word I've been saying? You know, I'm beginning to think I should put you down there with Gilroy and get Bill McMahon in here instead. Oh, don't start whimpering like a girl. I haven't got time to go looking for another reporter anyhow. You'll have to do. Just listen, OK? I couldn't do what they demanded because that wasn't the way things worked, do you understand? It wasn't their place to walk away from me. I hadn't let Toby walk away when he said he was going to America; I told him he couldn't break the circle. Why should they be any different?'

That was textbook stuff too, according to Fisher. The urge to control others was closely tied to anxiety. The fear of losing your hold on someone. Of letting go.

In some, they'd rather other people were dead than out from under their influence.

Pretending to be Michael had provided Erskine with the perfect cover for getting close to Niland, Blunt and the rest. They were waiting to hear from

Michael how his meeting with Daniel had gone. When Michael texted them and asked to meet somewhere quiet, they went without question or fear. It was Daniel they were afraid of, not Michael.

'*All I had to do after I killed him was plant my ID on his body and hope for the best. As it happened, the police were dumber even than I expected. They didn't question that it was me in the freezer, but then they thought they had all the time in the world to fill in the detail and all I needed was the night. I was at Michael's house when they turned up to tell me my dear brother had died and would I kindly come to the mortuary to identify his body. It couldn't have gone more smoothly. No one questions a grieving brother's identity.*'

The deception couldn't last, but it didn't need to. Once they were dead, he'd go back to being Daniel Erskine. The police could arrest him, shoot him, he didn't care.

The only one Erskine couldn't be sure about was Sean Riordan. He knew Riordan wouldn't be so easy to fool and that, when he realized what had happened, he'd come after him. That was why, he told Elliott, he'd tried to kill him first that afternoon. Then, when that failed, they made an appointment to meet at the hospital. The two kings, the last two pieces on the board, were to face each other. One way or another, one player would force victory.

What he hadn't expected was that Riordan would get his girlfriend to call 999, claiming to be Dr M Nott, and say there was a body in the car park of the hospital where Erin Gilroy had died. Riordan must have figured that Daniel would be monitoring the police radio broadcasts in his car. He'd know it was a message for him, telling him they wouldn't be alone. It would put him on his guard. Give Riordan the edge. Plus, I guessed that Riordan wanted to ensure there was back-up there if he needed it, if it all went wrong.

As it had. Daniel Erskine was the best player to the last. But Riordan's sacrifice had proved in vain. A hospital full of cops had been no protection at all.

Once we had the diagnosis for Erskine's disorder, the rest fell into place. It was chilling, as he described coolly how he'd even torn a large clump of hair from Oliver Niland's head and smashed the tooth from his mouth, knowing that the fire would destroy the evidence, just so that he could stage the scene of a struggle at his brother's house and convince us he'd been attacked too – but not surprising. The one surprise was his admission that it was he who'd tracked down Conn Gilroy and told him the story of what happened to his mother.

Daniel relished the pleasure in seeing his friends suffer.

In needing *him* to put things right.

The mistake they had made was trying to turn what he'd done against him. They didn't know who they were dealing with. He wasn't the Daniel Erskine they had always known any more. He was the killer of Beth Griffin and Shirley Heuston and Joss Finch.

He had found his vocation. Next to what he'd done to them, wiping out the Second Circle was merely business. And yet there was more to it than that, wasn't there? Erskine wanted to be understood, that's why he went out of his way to lead the police to the garage where Elliott was tied up. He needed the tape to explain what he'd done.

He wanted a final testimony to the rightness of his actions.

'Of course,' I said to Fitzgerald when the tape was over, 'if we were better read, we would have known from the start that it was the brother who killed the body in the freezer.'

'We would?'

'It's all in Dante,' I explained, tapping Fisher's copy of the *Inferno* which lay on the desk between us. 'I was reading it again on the way over here. Everyone thinks Hell is all about fire and flame and burning flesh, but being eternally frozen in ice was the punishment meted out by Dante to people who betrayed their own family.'

'I'm not sure poetry would stand up in court as evidence,' Fitzgerald said, but I could tell that she wasn't really listening. I couldn't blame her for being distracted. Word had come through in the last hour that O'Neill had died in hospital. Aidan, his name was, apparently.

How strange that I hadn't known it before now.

'At least they were able to tell him that Mary was safe before he died,' I said.

Fitzgerald didn't answer. I soon saw why. It had been a long night.

I draped my coat around her shoulders and left her to sleep.

December Again

64

For another Christmas, it was snowing in Dublin. I should have been at home, packing for our journey. Fitzgerald had finally succumbed to my nagging. We were going to New York for the holidays, and from there up into the Catskill Mountains for the skiing, because Fitzgerald didn't think it was a real vacation unless there was a chance of breaking a limb somewhere along the way. But that was the compromise. Christmas in the city for me, then New Year in the mountains for her. I hadn't even started my packing yet, though.

Dublin looked so pretty under a blanket of white that I'd decided to do some last-minute shopping instead, then thought *to hell with that* as well and gone for a drink.

Irish coffee: strong black coffee with whiskey, a teaspoon of brown sugar, poured over with double cream. The cold of the cream gives way to the warmth of the coffee and the kick of the whiskey. The perfect combination. They served it all over the world now, under different names. Sometimes they added Bourbon or Rum instead, or left out the sugar. But I say, why mess with what's already perfect? Like Guinness, it never tasted as good as it did here in

Dublin. The effect was probably all in the mind, but none the worse for it.

It was so damned good that I had another, and then forced myself to rise to my feet and leave the bar, otherwise I'd have been there all day. Not that there's anything wrong with whiling away the afternoon in a bar, but I had a plane to catch in the morning and I didn't intend to miss it. The prospect of Christmas in New York was too blissful to pass up.

Fitzgerald would have joined me, but she'd been called away at the last minute. A guy out walking his dog had found the body of a down and out in Stoneybatter.

What, I often wondered, would the police do without dogwalkers? Half the dead bodies in the world seem to be found by people out walking their dogs. It was only a pity people didn't walk their cats too, or they'd find the rest of them.

'My aunt used to walk her cat,' Fitzgerald answered brightly when I shared that little sparkling gem of wisdom with her. 'She was worried about it getting run over, so she bought this little harness and leash, and used to take it with her to the shops.'

'Are you sure you've not started making up your ancedotes as well?'

'It's true. It was quite a sight.'

'I'd love to have seen her when it started chasing up a tree after a bird,' I said.

She promised that she wouldn't be long. It was Sean Healy's case. He was in charge of the Murder

Squad till her return. She was simply taking a look because . . .

'You're a control freak and you can't let go?'

'I don't care if it's Jack the Ripper,' she insisted. 'I've made it clear to everyone. Control freak or not, nothing's keeping me from my holiday. We deserve it after all that's happened.' And she would get no quarrel from me on that score.

Life had been frenetic since Halloween. Just because a case has been closed doesn't mean it's finished. It's not over till every loose thread has been neatly tied up.

Daniel Erskine's garage had been taken apart and every inch combed and raked for evidence. Conn Gilroy's body was there, as Erskine had said, and Toby Fraser's too. The concrete had kept it well preserved so that, even given the long gap since he died, it hadn't taken the City Pathologist too long to identify strangulation as the most likely cause of death.

Nick Elliott had been dining out on his ordeal within days, and he hadn't stopped since. There wasn't a TV or radio station which hadn't interviewed him. He'd written extensively in the press about his meeting with Daniel Erskine. He'd signed a lucrative book deal. There was even talk of auctioning the film rights. Things were looking up for him. His paper had also made a big splash with Elliott's exclusive about the corruption links between government minister Fergus Costigan and the now infamous Erskine.

Costigan may have had nothing to do with the deaths on Halloween, but he was ruined all the same. A serial murderer was the very worst person in whose pocket to be found.

The one disappointment was that no one would stand trial for the murder of Beth Griffin and the two other young women, or for the abduction of Mary Nelligan.

Beth's parents had actually flown back into town without fanfare from Lake Taho earlier in the week. Fitzgerald had called earlier and told them that she wanted to speak to them, to update them on what we now knew of their daughter's murder. Not that there was much to tell. An appointment had been made for that evening.

I wasn't looking forward to it, but I tried to stay positive.

Tomorrow we'd be in New York.

This would be behind us.

Fitzgerald picked me up on the street a little after six, when the dark was well settled and the chill in my blood made the the Irish coffee seem like a distant memory.

She was quiet. Crime scenes often had that effect. Words became superfluous afterwards, even frivolous. But she was determined too. Healy was in charge. She was done.

'Looks like he was beaten to death,' she said. 'Another wino, maybe, or worse.'

I knew what worse meant. Groups of young

men sometimes set upon the homeless and filmed themselves on cellphones kicking them till they lost consciousness. Unashamed, they then posted the videos of the act on the internet. At least the winos knew no better. Some of these young men were educated, well off. They went to the best schools.

What was their excuse?

'You know,' she said, 'sometimes I think it wouldn't be such a bad idea if we didn't bother coming back from New York.'

'They have murders there too. More, statistically.'

'But we wouldn't have to investigate them, would we?'

The Griffins' Dublin house was in the section of the city known as the embassy belt. Here was where foreign governments housed their diplomatic missions. Give or take the odd billionaire, they were practically the only buyers who could afford the property prices.

As we turned into the snow-covered driveway, the gates closed silently behind us.

No one came out of the house to meet us. The huge Victorian facade was exactly as it had been when the Griffins weren't in residence. Ours were the only tyre tracks.

'Are you sure your information was right about them flying in?' I said.

'I spoke to his secretary. She told me they'd be here till after Christmas.'

We rang the doorbell, but no one answered. We

peered through the letter box into darkness, and tried to squint through the gaps in the drapes. No one. Nothing.

Fitzgerald frowned.

'Can you hear that?' she said.

I listened – and sure enough, there was singing, if it could be called that. A woman's voice was rising and falling, as if calling the scales, doh ray me, but there were words in it, incomprehensible words but words all the same. And then she appeared.

Beth Griffin's mother came walking out from the side of the house, dressed only in a flimsy nightgown, barefoot, her hair awry. Her skin was visible through the thin material that covered her, but she appeared unaware of the cold. Her feet didn't flinch at the touch of snow. It was she who was singing. She didn't know we were there.

'Mrs Griffin?' said Fitzgerald.

The singing stopped abruptly.

The woman's head twisted sharply in our direction.

'You,' she said when she saw us, and there was hate in her eyes. There was no other word for it. She despised our very existence. 'Why did you have to come here?'

'What are you talking about?'

'Why did you have to ruin everything?'

Fitzgerald tried to take a step towards her, but she looked like she might flee.

'Mrs Griffin, I think you should go inside—'

'Don't tell me what to do!'

'Where is your husband?'

'He's gone,' she said, and her face dissolved into an awful mask of misery. Tears ran grey against the foundation on her skin. It was a wonder they didn't freeze.

'Where has he gone?'

'He wouldn't say. He only said that you were coming and he had to get away. Why did you have to come?' she repeated, and she sank to her knees in the snow. The strap of the nightgown slipped from her shoulder, exposing her breast, but she made no move to fix it.

What had happened since the last time we'd seen her? Had the stress of Beth's murder driven her mad? Was she drunk? She needed help desperately, that much couldn't be denied, but there was something not right about the situation as well that no madness or grief could explain. It wasn't that she'd lost contact with reality. It was reality that pained her.

'We tried to keep it secret, our coming back. We told no one. I didn't want to come back at all, but Gordon said we had to. It was only for a few days. He needed to see some people on business. I begged him, but he wouldn't listen. Then you called and said you were coming, and he knew he had to get away. He wouldn't take me with him.'

'Why?' said Fitzgerald. 'Why did he have to get away?'

'Because he realized that you *knew*. All that talk about wanting to update him on Beth's death –

do you think he was fooled? He saw through you.'

'And what did he see on the other side?'

'That you finally understood what happened to her.'

I phrased the question as cautiously as I could, still not quite believing it.

'Are you saying your husband knew all along who killed Beth?'

'He had no choice,' she said, and her eyes bore the conviction of the religious fundamentalist, the cult follower, the brainwashed acolyte. 'It was *her* fault, the little slut.'

'Beth?'

'Gordon and Beth were ... intimate.' She formed the word with distaste, but it was evidently distaste at the act itself rather than the fact it was Griffin's own daughter he'd been screwing. 'I knew it was going on, but I didn't say anything. My husband and I stopped all that when Beth was still young. It was dirty. It revolted me. She took my place.'

'How do you know this?'

'Because he told me. He told me everything, how she led him on, and the filthy things she made him do, how she forced him to come to her bed at night. And then she said she was going to go to the police and tell them what he'd done. She blamed *him*.'

She made it sound unreasonable that a child should blame a father for abusing her.

'Mrs Griffin,' said Fitzgerald, 'Beth was only a child.'

494

'She was a whore,' her mother shot back, and I had to resist the urge to slap her, to stop the stream of craziness that was coming from her mouth, the things her husband had twisted her mind into accepting against all her natural instincts as a mother.

'She was his child,' Fitzgerald repeated stonily. 'Your husband should have protected her, not abused her. You should have protected her too.'

'Tell us what happened,' I said.

'When she threatened to tell everyone, Gordon went to Daniel Erskine for help,' she said. 'They were old friends. He thought Daniel would put him in touch with lawyers. He thought Daniel could talk to Beth and make her see sense.'

'Instead he killed her . . .'

It was the same as it would subsequently be with Conn Gilroy. If his friends had a problem, Daniel sorted it out. He made it go away. And in so doing, this time he found his vocation. That's why Shirley Heuston and Joss Finch had died. Because Beth Griffin's father had unwittingly unleashed Daniel Erskine's true self, the one he hadn't even known was inside him, waiting to emerge like an alligator from its fragile shell.

'He didn't expect Daniel to kill her, but what could he do? If he told the police, then it would all have come out, he would have been ruined.'

'What about Beth? Didn't she deserve justice?'

'It was her own fault. She got what she deserved. It would have been fine if you'd let it go. If you'd

495

only forgotten about her, the way we did. And now I've lost him. Lost him.'

And she suddenly began to dance around the garden in the snow, whirling, whirling, her dress floating out like the sheets of a ghost's costume, her nakedness strangely sinister beneath it, until she fell, crumpled, in a heap, cocooned in her madness like a quilt.

Griffin had a head start of hours on us. He was probably out of the country already. If he wanted, he could stay lost for ever, his path as hidden as footprints after heavy snow.

Suddenly I envied him his invisibility. To disappear from your own life, cast it off like a shell and don another. What could be more enticing than that?

Winter was the season for transformation, after all.

And if he could do it, why not us?

'Let's go,' I said to Fitzgerald. 'We still have some packing to do.'

'What about *her*?'

'Leave her. We can call Healy on the way. Someone else can deal with it.'

We left her, witless and wild, in the white garden.

We didn't look back.

INGRID BLACK

THE JUDAS HEART

Marsha Reed was just another aspiring young actress trying to make it in Dublin. But now she's found fame for all the wrong reasons – as victim of a brutal murder, her body left tied to her bed.

With former FBI agent Saxon now living in Dublin, the murder squad have the perfect expert to call on - particularly when it turns out Saxon once knew the victim.

However Saxon is already in the middle of another, more personal, mission – to track down her ex-colleague, Agent Leon Kaminski, who bizarrely seems to be hiding out in the streets of Dublin. It's not the first time he's gone missing – but it's the first time since his wife was murdered…

Soon enough, though, it's clear that Saxon's hunt for Marsha's killer and her search for her old friend are disturbingly heading in the same direction …

'Ingrid Black kept me guessing until the very end' *Daily Telegraph*

CHRIS MOONEY

THE SECRET FRIEND

Two dead girls in the river
Two tiny statues of the Virgin Mary concealed in their clothing
One CSI on the hunt for their killer

When Judith Chen is found floating in Boston's harbour, links are made with the murder of Emma Hale, a student who vanished without trace, only for her body to wash up months later.

CSI Darby McCormick is assigned to the case and uncovers a piece of overlooked evidence from the Hale investigation – which brings her into contact with Malcolm Fletcher, a former FBI agent now on the Most Wanted list after a string of bloody murders. And when a third student goes missing, Darby is led into a dangerous game of cat-and-mouse with deadly links to the past – and a man who speaks to the Blessed Virgin. A man who wants to be a secret friend to the girls he abducts …

'Masterful … dark and disturbing' Linda Fairstein

'Chris Mooney is a wonderful writer' Michael Connelly

MICHAEL MORLEY

SPIDER

> *'For a second she thinks she is dead,*
> *then she opens her eyes and wishes she was.'*

The press call him the Black River Killer and his stats are shocking: 16 murders; not captured in 20 years; the FBI's best profiler – Jack King – burned out and beaten, his career shattered.

Jack and his wife now run a hotel in Tuscany. And though he still gets nightmares, rural Italy is a whole world away from BRK's brutal crime scenes in South Carolina. Or so Jack thought …

As Italian cops discover the body of a young woman – her remains mutilated like BRK's victims – a gruesome package arrives at the FBI, twin events that conspire to lure the profiler back into the hunt.

But this time, who is the spider and who is the fly?

'A terrifying read that will keep you hooked' Simon Kernick

'*Spider* chillingly captures the harsh realities of a deteriorated mind' Lynda La Plante

'A chillingly vivid thriller. Don't read it alone in the middle of the night' Steven Bochco

NICK STONE

KING OF SWORDS

From the author of the award-winning *Mr Clarinet*

Miami, 1980.

The cop: Det. Max Mingus, barely keeping his head above the filth

The corpse: decomposed, with a tarot card in his bloated belly

The bloody trail: six more bodies at the victim's house

The suspect: fork-tongued crimelord Solomon Boukman, king of the streets

In a city rife with drugs, voodoo and corruption, finding the truth and protecting the good from the bad guys is almost impossible.

The closer Max gets to Solomon Boukman, the more he finds himself in his power. And once Boukman has a hold of you, he never, ever lets go …

'An adrenaline-fuelled masterpiece' *Metro*

'A delicious undercurrent of darkness . . . rivals some of the greats of the thriller genre' *Daily Express*

'A cracking opening … with many turns and twists. A powerful and original story' *Independent*

NICCI FRENCH

LOSING YOU

Nina Landry has given up city life for the isolated community of Sandling Island, lying off the bleak east coast of England. At night the wind howls. Sometimes they are cut off by the incoming tide. For Nina though it is home. It is safe.

But when Nina's teenage daughter Charlie fails to return from a sleepover on the day they're due to go on holiday, the island becomes a different place altogether. A place of secrets and suspicions. Where no one – friends, neighbours or the police – believes Nina's instinctive fear that her daughter is in terrible danger. Alone, she undergoes a frantic search for Charlie. And as day turns to night, she begins to doubt not just whether they'll leave the island for their holiday – but whether they will ever leave it again.

'You live through every nail-biting minute' *Guardian*

CARO RAMSAY

ABSOLUTION

The Crucifixion Killer is stalking Glasgow, leaving victims' mutilated bodies in a Christ-like pose. DCI Alan McAlpine – a renowned and successful police officer – is drafted in to lead the hunt, supported by local officers DI Anderson and DS Costello.

But the past holds horrific memories for McAlpine. He last worked this beat some twenty years earlier, when he was assigned to guard a woman – nameless and faceless after a sadistic acid attack – at a Glasgow hospital. An obsession was born in that hospital room that has never quite left McAlpine and now it seems to be resurfacing. For a reason.

As the chase to halt the gruesome murders intensifies, so Anderson and Costello find chilling cause for concern uncomfortably close to home ...

'The dialogue crackles...A most auspicious debut' *Observer*

'A cracker...many shivers in store' *The Times*

DAN WADDELL

THE BLOOD DETECTIVE

**From the author of the bestselling *Who Do You Think You Are?*
comes a haunting crime novel of blood-stained family histories and
gruesome secrets …**

*'The past isn't like that; you can't just bury it, mark it down as history.
It's taken more than 125 years, but the events of 1879 have finally
washed up …'*

As dawn breaks over London, the body of a young man is discovered in
a windswept Notting Hill churchyard. The killer has left Detective Chief
Inspector Grant Foster and his team a grisly, cryptic clue …

However it's not until the clue is handed to Nigel Barnes, a specialist in
compiling family trees, that the full message becomes spine-chillingly
clear. For it leads Barnes back more than one hundred years - to the
victim of a demented Victorian serial killer …

When a second body is discovered Foster needs Barnes's skills more
than ever. Because the murderer's clues appear to run along the tangled
bloodlines that lie between 1879 and now. And if Barnes is right about
his blood-history, the killing spree has only just begun …

'There's panache a-plenty in this intriguing tale…Sharp plotting,
elegant writing, engaging characters, a cracking climax. A series is
promised. Bring it on!' Reginald Hill

'A fascinating and original investigation into the dark roots of our
family trees' Val McDermid

He just wanted a decent book to read ...

Not too much to ask, is it? It was in 1935 when Allen Lane, Managing Director of Bodley Head Publishers, stood on a platform at Exeter railway station looking for something good to read on his journey back to London. His choice was limited to popular magazines and poor-quality paperbacks – the same choice faced every day by the vast majority of readers, few of whom could afford hardbacks. Lane's disappointment and subsequent anger at the range of books generally available led him to found a company – and change the world.

'We believed in the existence in this country of a vast reading public for intelligent books at a low price, and staked everything on it'
Sir Allen Lane, 1902–1970, founder of Penguin Books

The quality paperback had arrived – and not just in bookshops. Lane was adamant that his Penguins should appear in chain stores and tobacconists, and should cost no more than a packet of cigarettes.

Reading habits (and cigarette prices) have changed since 1935, but Penguin still believes in publishing the best books for everybody to enjoy. We still believe that good design costs no more than bad design, and we still believe that quality books published passionately and responsibly make the world a better place.

So wherever you see the little bird – whether it's on a piece of prize-winning literary fiction or a celebrity autobiography, political tour de force or historical masterpiece, a serial-killer thriller, reference book, world classic or a piece of pure escapism – you can bet that it represents the very best that the genre has to offer.

Whatever you like to read – trust Penguin.